# ALASKA
# BECKONS

*The Called, Book 2*

# PATRICIA FRIEND

WESTBOW
PRESS®
A DIVISION OF THOMAS NELSON
& ZONDERVAN

This is a work of fiction. All of the characters, names, incidents, organizations, and dialogue in this novel are either the products of the author's imagination or are used fictitiously.

Scripture quotations marked NKJV are taken from the New King James Version. Copyright 1982 by Thomas Nelson, Inc. Used by permission. All rights reserved.

WestBow Press books may be ordered through booksellers or by contacting:

WestBow Press
A Division of Thomas Nelson & Zondervan
1663 Liberty Drive
Bloomington, IN 47403
www.westbowpress.com
1 (866) 928-1240

Because of the dynamic nature of the Internet, any web addresses or links contained in this book may have changed since publication and may no longer be valid. The views expressed in this work are solely those of the author and do not necessarily reflect the views of the publisher, and the publisher hereby disclaims any responsibility for them.

Any people depicted in stock imagery provided by Thinkstock are models, and such images are being used for illustrative purposes only. Certain stock imagery © Thinkstock.

ISBN: 978-1-5127-9507-3 (sc)
ISBN: 978-1-5127-9509-7 (hc)
ISBN: 978-1-5127-9508-0 (e)

Library of Congress Control Number: 2017910930

Print information available on the last page.

WestBow Press rev. date: 7/25/2017

## DEDICATION

To Kathy Alden, a fellow music teacher, who encouraged love for God, enthusiasm for life, and praise for our Savior. Your words of blessing kept me forging ahead as a beginning author. I miss you. See you again at Heaven's gate.

# ACKNOWLEDGEMENTS

MANY THANKS TO FAMILY AND FRIENDS who supported me even while I wrote all hours of the day and night. Thank you to Dee Prickett, former Executive Director of the Palmer Visitor's Center in Palmer, Alaska for your friendship during the research for this book. Special heartfelt thanks to my wonderful friend, Julie Gray, who helped prepare the manuscript for publishing. You made it so much better than it would have been without your diligence to detail. Sincere thanks to Pastor Jerry Prevo of the Anchorage Baptist Temple for teaching the importance of building the Christian life on the Bible, the Word of God.

# INTRODUCTION

ONE DECADE AFTER THE 1986 CHERNOBYL nuclear disaster, national newscasters remembered the incident reporting a higher rate of cancer among the European population. Alaska, the northernmost state outside the contiguous United States and the closest to Russia, noted the media report with marked interest. Greater measures were taken to test and study air and soil quality in the 49<sup>th</sup> State following the Soviet disaster.

In addition to co-owning a business as a guide for hunting and fishing excursions for locals and tourists, Thad Tucker also worked with the U. S. Department of Agriculture gathering crop and livestock statistics for South Central Alaska. Another growing season in the Matanuska Farm Valley had passed and Thad was finishing the statistics for 1996. The quality of farm produce had been excellent. It had been a good year for Alaskan farmers with near record highs in farm commodities. Thad had another reason to be optimistic about the future and her name was Leah Grant. Although engaged to be married, an association of his fiancée's family with Chernobyl would bring Thad face-to-face with one of the survivors in a chase across the Alaskan wilderness. God's call of saving faith would prove irresistible in the desperate heart of a fugitive.

# CONTENTS

# 1

## THE HURRICANE EXPRESS

DENISE COX WAS ON A MISSION to rescue her best friend, Leah Grant, from a disastrous marriage to an Alaskan bachelor and she was determined to recruit help from at least one of the Grants. It was Leah's mother who heard the request for troop deployment to Alaska, the arctic north.

"Sarah would be the only one who could go with you. She could probably get away for a few days, but the rest of us couldn't. I don't know why you're so concerned. Leah called us last evening and said she was doing fine." Mrs. Grant's lips pinched in annoyance. "If you take Sarah off to Alaska, I'll have to arrange babysitting for Angie, too. Are you sure you really need to go up there? As far as I'm concerned, Leah left so she could be on her own. She's made her choice like Sarah did a few years ago. I expect it will turn out the same," she predicted with a passive sigh. Joyless wrinkle lines creased the corners of her brown eyes. Strands of gray hair were interwoven with brown at her temples. Her once-trim figure had long since expanded a few dress sizes. Quick witted and winsome by design, the demands of life and ministry had affected her personality over the years. Authoritarian and practical, she was a force to be reckoned with.

Denise refused to accept either guilt or rebuke for the decisions of others from a woman who seemed unwilling to forgive or forget human error. She kept to her purpose and respectfully stood her ground. Soft ebony shoulders were squared while dark-brown eyes were level and sincere.

"I'm sorry to inconvenience your family, Mrs. Grant, but I'm very concerned for Leah, and I *am* going to Alaska to see if she needs help. If Sarah is able to come, I'd be glad to have her company and support."

"Where are we going, Denise?" Sarah Grant had just walked through the front door of the church parsonage when she caught Denise's last few words. Just above average height, Sarah was toothpick thin. Her oval face was framed with long brown hair to her elbows. Hazel eyes softly reflected the color of the gray T-shirt that hung loosely about her bony figure. Charcoal-colored sweatpants with a navy stripe running down the pocket side of the leg was the only color splash to the dull combination. Bulky well-worn sliders with thick rubber soles made a speed-bump rumble when she walked across the worn linoleum floor.

"We're going to Alaska to rescue Leah!" Denise said emphatically.

"When do we leave?" Sarah asked. Her voice was calm and steady, though she quaked with both irritation and excitement at this new development.

"We leave just as soon as you're packed. I'll call the airline and see if another seat is available."

"See if there are two seats. I'm taking Angie too. She'll enjoy the trip to see Aunt Leah."

Mrs. Grant's mouth flew open in protest, but Sarah was determined. "She's coming with me, Mom. She's my responsibility." Sarah barely managed to breathe for the courage it took to stand steady in her decision. Most of the time, she quietly acquiesced to matriarchal dictates while enduring the constant reminders of past mistakes. Denise's supportive presence was a godsend.

When Leah left, Sarah lost the one person who showed unconditional love, acceptance, and understanding. Leah treated Sarah as a person of worth instead of as an inconvenience. Even then, Sarah had longed to pack Angie up and go off to dreamy Alaska with Leah. Now, with Denise's invitation, she had an opportunity to leave the tension-filled home and make a new life with little Angie. Sarah wasn't going to miss this second chance. If Leah married Thad, Sarah would find work and stay in Alaska near them. If Leah didn't marry him, they'd all stay in Alaska anyway. Resolved, Sarah moved forward making a mental list of preparations for the trip to the far north.

Denise made the final ticket arrangements over the phone then helped Sarah pack, just as she had helped Leah only a few days ago. One hour later, Sarah and Angie stood in the living room with two suitcases, a duffel bag, and the only winter coats and hats they owned.

Pastor Grant came to say good-bye to his daughter and granddaughter. His heart was breaking even though he knew it was best for Sarah. His future son-in-law, Thad, had called earlier that morning to request Leah's hand in marriage. A blessing had been spoken over the phone to the happy couple. He'd told none of this to anyone yet. Later, he would tell his wife- after Sarah had a chance to leave this hamlet for a fresh start. There was nothing here for her to build a dream of happiness.

"God's best and His good care to you, Sarah and little Angie." He hugged them both, and when Angie faltered as tears welled in her eyes, he said, "Now, none of that, Sugar and Spice." He often addressed the two of them in this affectionate manner. "You're going to be just fine with Thad and Leah. Maybe your gramma and I will come visit all of you in Alaska. So it's not 'good-bye'—"

"It's 'see ya later,' Grandpa!" five-year-old Angie piped up with a smile of delight.

"Right!" he said, matching her enthusiasm while patting her curly black hair. Her brilliant violet eyes twinkled up at him, making Pastor Grant's heart constrict at losing even more joy in his life.

"Okay, girls, let's go!" Denise bustled. "We have three hours before the plane leaves, and it takes one hour just to get to the airport in Pittsburgh. We'll let you know as soon as we get to the cabin, Pastor Grant. On second thought, I may have to confront Mr. Tucker first!" she said tersely.

"I'm sure you'll find Leah to be just fine, Denise. Don't be too hard on Thad." Pastor Grant cautioned.

"Are you on his side too?" Denise asked with raised eyebrows.

"I'm on the Lord's side and so are you, Denise. So make sure you react in the Spirit of Christ by being courteous," he admonished kindly.

"You sure know how to take the wind out of a girl's sails, Pastor Grant." Denise fumed in retreat. "I seem to be having bad experiences with men lately."

"Oh? You've broken off the engagement with Mr. Diamond?" he asked carefully.

"I call him 'Mr. Two-Timing Diamond,' and we're through!" Denise announced with a great sweep of her ring-less hand.

Pastor Grant extended his hand to shake hers. "I congratulate you on a wise and sensible decision, Denise. I pray that God will send you to a good Christian man in His time." Denise blinked, surprised that he congratulated her breakup without any condolences whatsoever.

"Let's hope God's time isn't equivalent to His day of a thousand years, or I'm destined to be a hopeless old maid," Denise glanced skyward, hoping heaven's ear was attentive and actively moving destiny in her direction or she moving in *his* direction.

"All things work together in God's time for the called," Pastor Grant said. His heart felt the loss God's will was exacting at his last remaining daughter's departure from home. He and Mrs. Grant would be without children in their home to add fun and frenzy to their daily activities. Strangers they would be until finding common ground as a couple again.

The front door clicked shut after the echo of good-byes faded into silence. Hasty footfalls across the wooden floorboards of the porch ended their patter and started dull thumping sounds along the cement sidewalk to the waiting vehicle. Car doors slammed, an engine revved, and then the rescuers were gone, headed to Alaska. Dad Grant watched the white rental car until it was out of sight. In his mid-fifties and shorter than his middle daughter, Dad Grant was stocky but fit. Though his hair was more gray than brown, it was thick, neatly combed, and parted on his left side. His wife was cloudy with a chance of thunderstorms while he was mostly sunny with periods of fog. Hazel eyes shone with merriment or compassion as a person needed. His pulpit style was stoic and earnest in sermon delivery though at times a humorous illustration wiggled its way into the sacred message to the relief and delight of parishioners. Dad Grant was a reasonable man who understood that Sarah's decision to go with Denise was her chance for a new beginning.

Thad turned hazel eyes, reflecting light-blue from the blue-and-white striped dress shirt he wore under a brown leather jacket to search the arrival side of flight listings for the Seattle flight number 1095. His six-foot, three-inch sturdy frame towered confidently over Leah's feminine vessel. Thick dark-brown hair was cut short with a side part and trimmed neatly over the ears and the back of the neck. His clean-shaven face was oval shaped with a square jaw. Thin lips with a curve toward the corners suggested a pleasant disposition and a willingness to be helpful. The international airport terminal in Anchorage, Alaska, was busy at 7:43 p.m. Denise had called the Tucker residence from the Seattle airport at around 1:55 p.m. to let Leah know of their impending arrival. Leah could hardly believe Denise was on her way to Palmer.

When Thad, Leah, and Tyrone left for the Anchorage airport at six thirty that evening, Alma and Taima were taking a break and sipping coffee. Alaska Natives and siblings, they ranged in age from her early forties to his late fifties. Alma was hearing and speech impaired though she could read lips. Members of their household, including the newest member, Thad's fiancée, communicated either in sign language or by facing Alma when speaking. Alma had been in the process of preparing for Denise's arrival before a second call alerting them that two more guests were to be added to their merry bunch. Taima brusquely remarked that they were fast becoming a bed-and-breakfast instead of a hunting lodge. Alma waved it off with a delighted smile at her guest-wary brother. Taima faked a sweaty brow salute, chuckled, and headed into the laundry room to get extra bedding from the linen cabinet.

Nine and a half hours after taking off from Pittsburgh a weary Denise and Sarah disembarked from the 747 with stiff legs and subdued spirits. There had been only thirty-minutes in Seattle for the two ladies, one with a piggybacked Angie, to sprint from the arrival gate to a departure gate for yet another far-north flight. Angie slept soundly in Sarah's arms—her dark curly head resting on her mom's cramping shoulder. Thankfully, the well-behaved little girl who had journeyed into wonderland, enjoyed the adventure with Alice-like curiosity and charming good manners until confinement in the seat and the drone of the airplane's engines had lulled her to sleep.

Neither woman had any idea of what awaited them in this great land. They were both completely out of their element. It took only a glance out the terminal windows at the jagged heights of the Chugach mountain range for Denise to realize she was far, far away from the home fires she commanded so well. This was Alaska, and the rocky giants loomed ominously before her. Once out on the concourse, Sarah checked the posted signs for directions to any place familiar. "BAGGAGE CLAIM" caught her attention about the same time Denise pointed to it. Wordlessly, they trudged forward. The pilot's weather report upon landing in Anchorage fixed the temperature at a chilly forty-one degrees. It was a drastic change from the sunny, humid ninety-two degrees in Pittsburgh. Both Denise and Sarah each had worn only cotton summer dresses with thin sweaters. Tan sandals, though comfortable, assured that they would have to endure cold feet until warmer footwear could be procured sooner rather than later. Unprepared as they were for Alaska, first impressions of the forty-ninth state only provoked Denise's dislike for the cold land, so opposite of Leah's first impressions. Following Denise, Sarah shifted Angie to her other shoulder. Her legs were jumpy and her body ached all over, making her wish for a bed on which to stretch out full length. Though she had been relieved to leave her familiar lifestyle for a frontier one, reality pressed her sense of anxiety making her feel breathless and panicky.

"Denise," she called. "I need to stop for a minute and catch my breath."

"Are you all right?"

"Not at the moment, but I will be. I need some water and my purse."

Denise saw the exhaustion on Sarah's face and took Angie into her arms as Sarah reached for a half-empty bottle of tepid water, which she opened and handed to a bewildered Denise to hold for her while she rummaged through the bulging pack for her purse. Pulling a prescription bottle from her purse, she quickly opened the cap and poured a tiny white pill onto her shaking palm. A quick toss to her mouth with swallows of water, and Sarah began to relax.

"What was that, Sarah?" Denise asked frowning.

"It's medicine for panic attacks, Denise. I was feeling overwhelmed. That's all." Sarah reached for Angie, but Denise stopped her.

"I've got her," Denise said gently. "You carry the other stuff for a while." It began to dawn on Denise that she'd spent too much time thinking about her own problems and missed the needs of others who had far greater struggles than she could imagine. "God forgive me for being so self-absorbed when I could have helped make life easier for a sister in Christ," she confessed silently and moved ahead at a slower pace so that Sarah could walk beside her instead of being dragged along behind.

"I hope we're almost to the baggage claim area. We can find a seat there and wait for our luggage to come onto the carousel. I'll call Leah and see if they're on their way yet."

Sarah merely nodded and walked on silently. Would she ever be strong again?

Though expectations differed, both Leah and Tyrone waited and watched arriving passengers trek toward the conveyor belt in the baggage claim area. Thad quietly observed the two with amusement. His sweet Leah had long curly black hair that cascaded past her shoulders. Her large, chocolate-brown eyes held his heart in love's sweet captivity. She was much shorter than he was, but in virtue, she stood taller than many a saint in his eyes even if she had a knack for mishaps and mayhem. Of medium build, Leah had a shapely feminine figure Thad found attractive, though Leah bemoaned the size of her hips and her short stature. The fact that she didn't walk, talk, or act like a man was very important to him. Her favorite color was maroon, like the color of his pullover sweater. She liked Orange Zinger herb tea with a spoonful of honey. He loved to hear her laugh. It reminded him of a rippling wilderness stream and helped him not to take life too seriously. The touch of her hand in his meant there was more to him than work. Where once there had been skepticism and doubt, now there was optimism and faith.

Thad turned his attention to his best friend from college days, who was also his business partner in their Alaskan hunting and fishing adventures. At the moment, Tyrone was feeling like a decoy instead of a hopeful suitor for one Denise Cox who was Thad's fiancée's best friend. Though Tyrone had two sisters and was familiar with their "excitable motion," women in general made him nervous. Perhaps the nine-hour flight from Pittsburgh had sweetened her disposition. Just in case it hadn't, he hoped a bouquet of autumn colored blooms and a box of local handmade chocolates might curry a peace accord. For some strange reason, Tyrone kept thinking he might need a bullfighter's red cape! His grandparents were from Kingston, Jamaica, and when his family made annual visits from Anchorage to the island country to see relatives each February, his grandpa would take his dad, brother, and him to watch bronco riding. The rodeo clowns always did a hilarious act posing as brave bullfighters until the beast came romping out of the gate. Then their bright red capes flapped behind them as they ran away from a playful young calf! He remembered them all laughing heartily. Their laughter together spanned age barriers. Unfortunately, he'd forgotten his red cape.

"You seem a little nervous," Thad grinned knowingly. Tyrone swallowed with difficulty. His Adam's apple rose up and down like a wave under his dark-brown skin. At six feet, four inches, he was taller than Thad and thinner. High school basketball had been his bent throughout adolescence, and there was an MVP trophy to show for it still displayed in his mother's china cabinet in her Anchorage home. Tyrone's thick black hair was clipped short in the popular temp fade style the barber had suggested for what he hoped would make a positive first impression on the lucky lady. Clean-shaven and carefully groomed, Tyrone had made a muscle pose in his bathroom mirror, satisfied that this was the best it was going to get.

"I'm not nervous. Just terrified. It's like walking behind a bull moose and hollering 'Boo!' Somebody's gonna' get kicked and stomped."

"You're a smart man, Tyrone," Thad praised before adding, "just know where your exits are located."

"Huh!" he grumbled, "You owe me BIG for taking the heat off you, my friend. I can't remember the last time I bought candy and flowers for anyone but my mom!"

"You're a good man, Tyrone." Thad smiled broadly. Joy radiated from Thad's face where once rugged determination and self-reliance had marked his disposition and faithless heart.

When Denise walked into the baggage claim area, Tyrone swallowed and willed his legs to move forward. It was Leah, however, who reacted first when she saw Denise carrying Angie as Sarah walked beside, shouldering both backpacks.

"Denise! Sarah? Angie?" she exclaimed, puzzled, while hurrying toward them with outstretched arms. Denise's smile brightened as she walked toward Leah. Not wanting to disturb Angie's sleep, she realized any confrontation with Thad would have to wait. Besides, the hasty trip into unfamiliar surroundings had taken a lot of steam out of her charge northward.

After a hug between sisters, Sarah reached for a stirring Angie so Denise could receive a welcoming hug. Thad could see that Leah's sister struggled with the little girl whose head raised long enough to know her mom was near. Her curly head slowly drifted to Sarah's shoulder as her eyelids fluttered when he stepped forward to take Angie. Sarah sighed in relief and thanked him genuinely. Angie felt the change to strong-armed support and a broader chest. The new smell of leather mixed with the familiar scent of her Grandpa Grant's aftershave lotion both confused and comforted her back to sleep. Home and heaven were the same place at Angie's age.

"You must be Sarah, and this angel must be Angie." The child was transferred into his arms as if she were merely feather weight. Thad saw the facial resemblance of the two sisters but noticed that Sarah's hair was lighter and perfectly straight, falling well below her shoulders. Though somewhat taller than Leah, Sarah was much thinner to the point of appearing gaunt and frail.

"I'm Thad Tucker, and we're happy you're here, Sarah. I hope you'll let us make you comfortable for as long as you wish to stay with us." Sarah blinked at the sincere welcome, nodded, and smiled humbly.

"Thank you, Thad." Sarah began to relax while Thad remembered seeing the same reaction in Leah just after she'd arrived. It always amazed him how uptight outside people were until genuine Alaskan hospitality did its work to mellow frazzled lifestyles. His welcome encouraged an explanation from Sarah. "Denise asked if one of Leah's family members could come with her, and I was volunteered to come along as backup. I can see that my sister is in no real danger," Sarah offered with a smile of conspiracy. "I'm so glad Angie and I jumped at the offer to rescue Leah from certain and impending happiness." Thad smiled broadly, taking a liking to his future sister-in-law. He sensed she was wiser for her trials and understood diplomacy in the moment. "I hope we haven't inconvenienced you'uns." The word *inconvenience* seemed to follow her.

"Not at all. We've got plenty of room for everyone," he affirmed, inviting friendship. "As I'm beginning to understand, we're all part of God's family as believers in Christ."

"Yes, that's right. Thank you, Thad," she replied as Thad's profession of faith registered. Could it be possible that Thad's love for Leah and his faith in Christ were both genuine? She hoped it was true. There had been a man who claimed his love for her was God-based and then he'd disappeared completely from society.

Leah turned and walked over to Sarah just as Tyrone approached Denise with gifts.

"I'm amazed that you're here too. How did this happen?"

"Quickly," Sarah stated firmly. They exchanged a meaningful look conveying the truth that both had taken the opportunity to decamp from home fires when opportunity had presented itself. Pushing resentment aside, Sarah added sincerely, "Angie and I missed you and decided to come see you." Leah understood, nodded with a smile of welcome, and engulfed Sarah in a hug. Tears of relief gathered in Sarah's eyes.

"I'm so glad you and Angie are with us. Come on, Sarah, let's go *home*," Leah said simply. Sarah pushed tears away from her eyes as a smile spread across her face. Her strength was being renewed.

"Thanks, Little Sis."

Leah laughed with joy and shrugged. "I'm delighted you came all this way to make sure Thad's a gentleman."

"Actually, I came all this way to see the engagement ring." Sarah was beginning to join into the lighthearted banter surrounding their welcome to Alaska. Immediately, Leah flashed the gemstone setting into the spotlight. She hadn't had the opportunity to show it to Denise during all the lively greetings.

"Ah-h-h-h. It's beautiful, Leah." Sarah beamed with happiness for her sister. "I can tell you're very happy. Thad's a good man too. I can already tell."

"He is." Leah nodded, her eyes moving to admire her fiancé who was watching the drama unfolding between Tyrone and Denise with interest. Angie still slept peacefully, cradled in his arms.

When Leah and Sarah started walking to a seating area to wait for luggage to arrive, Thad followed until Leah motioned their change of direction to the ladies' room. He found a seat nearby and sat down to watch Tyrone in action. Thad was no coward, but he was glad he held a sleeping child, and that Tyrone was diverting attention away from him for the moment. Best girlfriend or not, her effect on Leah following the phone call and her subsequent trip to *confront* him encouraged caution where the peace of his home was concerned. Angie suddenly jerked in her sleep, and he quickly looked down to check her well-being. She took a few deep breaths, sighed and relaxed once again. *Another dreamer like your Aunt Leah*, Thad thought to himself, reflecting on the idea of a house full of little girls like Angie, or little boys. Startled that he could be a dad someday, Thad experienced a quantum-leap moment when bachelorhood parted company for a higher stratum of matrimonial duty. This was a new idea for a man who, only a year ago, thought horses would be the only ones to have babies romping around on *his* property.

When Leah and Sarah returned, they sat next to Thad and continued chatting. He couldn't help listening as they talked quietly back and forth. Thad soon realized Sarah was the anchor of the two. Practical and sensible, there was no drama in her movements or her speech, just even tones speaking words of encouragement or inquiry. Even though Sarah was only a year older than the fun-loving Leah, she seemed almost matronly. It was as though something had suppressed the joy of her soul for so long that happiness seemed unnatural and awkward. She possessed a meek and quiet spirit, but youthful beauty had faded, replaced by shadows of intense hardship. It was as if she accepted life as it was without prospects of anything better. And yet Sarah Grant sat here, four time zones away from all she had ever known, just to be near her sister. There was no effort on her part to be attractive or to attract attention of any kind to her person either. Thad wondered about her story. Leah hadn't said much about Sarah's past, but he knew everyone had a story. At the moment, he sensed the need to pray for Sarah and little Angie. Remembering how his mother started her prayers, Thad, who had never known an earthly father, addressed his Heavenly Father without hesitation.

*Father, I don't know Sarah's story, but now I realize You do, and You've brought her and little Angie to us because they need us somehow. I think You want us to help them. I'll feed them and shelter them. You'll do Your part. Please let me know what more I can do. Oh, I think Tyrone needs some help. Thanks. Amen.*

Thad's study of the scene unfolding just a short distance away signaled an alert in his mind. Tyrone had approached Denise when Leah had turned to greet Sarah. However, luggage had started rolling off the long car wash-style conveyor belt. It drew Denise's attention away from the man coming toward her with candy and flowers, and she whisked past him to check for their luggage. On second thought, he wondered if she had *dodged* Tyrone's advance. Not one to be put off, Tyrone retraced his steps and walked directly to Denise, blocking her view of the slow-moving luggage this time.

"Who *are* you?" Denise asked with tired annoyance. Tyrone stood speechless in front of her trying to swallow without gulping and feeling like he was in junior high all over again. Rarely at a loss for words, suddenly every phrase of introduction running through his mind seemed like addled nonsense. His mouth somehow came open, but Denise spoke before he found his voice.

"I'm assuming you're with Thad and Leah?" She was not amused in the least.

"Yes," he managed in a deep baritone voice. He saw Denise's eyes rise a little with what he hoped was interest. The resonance in the tone of his one-word answer echoed to her very soul.

Though Tyrone had brought flowers and candy, he now felt foolish as he stood gazing at her beautiful face while she tried to stifle a sudden yawn. He couldn't seem to move. Denise tried again.

"I'm Denise Cox, Leah's best friend. Who are *you*?" she asked pointedly, amused by this handsome man's awkward presence. Tyrone nervously cleared his throat. This seemed to reset his response mechanism.

"I'm Tyrone Johnson. I'm Thad's best friend and business partner." He was tempted to say "best friend and bodyguard" but figured that wouldn't encourage a peace accord.

"Who are the flowers and candy for? Arriving business clientele?" The sarcasm was unmistakable. Tyrone's eyes narrowed at the sour demeanor of this society princess who could spark his anger in an instant. He had the strongest urge to excuse himself and disappear into the wilderness until she left Alaska! However, he swallowed the anger away with a courteous reply that reminded him of lines from Shakespeare's *Taming of the Shrew*.

"These are for you, Miss Cox, because Miss Leah speaks so highly of you." *Mr. Grace* presented them as if Denise was visiting royalty. His polite response to her bad manners unnerved Denise somewhat.

"Call me Denise," she informed him stiffly while accepting the gifts. "Thank you."

"Call me Tyrone," he managed a smile of friendship, and Denise found herself smiling back. Admittedly, he was good-looking, and his voice was smooth and resonant enough to lullaby a grizzly bear to sleep. Sensing his nervousness, Denise toyed with the idea of keeping him on edge for as long as possible. However, Pastor Grant's admonition to act in a Christ-like manner commanded kinder regard, especially since the fragrant flowers she held like a wedding bouquet signaled a peace treaty in the making. She tried conversation to set the *bear whisperer* at ease; but what Denise said didn't curry endearment in the least. Tyrone reckoned Denise was beautiful until she opened her mouth.

"Just twenty-four hours ago, I was ready to take Mr. Thad Tucker apart piece by piece," Denise declared, "but Leah's dad reminded me to be careful about doing anything so hasty or drastic to him." She glanced over her shoulder to scrutinize the man holding a sleeping child. "He seems like a real gentleman after all, or else I'm just too dog-tired to notice any difference." She frowned. "A girl never knows these days. He's not the two-timing type, is he? I know all about that kind." She looked directly at Tyrone and exclaimed, "Men!"

Tyrone regarded her coolly, noting the prejudice she displayed not only toward his best friend, but himself.

"Thad is a gentleman." Tyrone's tone was straightforward. "And Leah brings out the best in him. You're her best friend. You ought to know she'd be a good judge of character, and you should have given her some credit for her choice. You're mistaken."

Not one to be censured, Denise's head cocked to the side in annoyance as Tyrone continued before she could interject another barb.

"You didn't need to rush up here to save her. She's perfectly fine as you can very well see, and even more so since she arrived in Alaska. She can finally breathe without people trying to manipulate her or put her in a box of stifling expectations. What did you expect to find?" Tyrone was amazing himself. Words kept coming. Somewhere along the line, he would need to stop or be stopped. Denise obliged.

"And just what makes you privy to her recent decisions?" Denise shot back, encouraging a quarrel with Tyrone just because she wanted one. He saw the challenge in her sparking dark-brown eyes and wondered if this foray would reveal any common sense or just plain obstinacy.

"I've known the man she's going to marry since college, and he's the closest thing to a brother I've known," he shot back, determined that one Denise Cox wasn't going to run all over him like she had run all over Leah a few days ago. "I heard you over the phone with Leah. She hardly got a word in before you were charging up here to her rescue." A smile broke across his face suddenly, "The Hurricane Express!" he bellowed, then laughed out loud and saw her eyes bulge with indignation. His last remark was made before giving consideration to the effect it would have on a Denise and, shortly, on him.

"Well, aren't you rude," she retorted. "No one has ever spoken to me like that."

"Maybe if someone had years ago, you wouldn't be so impetuous," Tyrone shot back. Seeing new fire rise in her countenance, he realized they would get nowhere barking insults back and forth, so he raised his right hand in a sign of truce. "I'm sorry, Miss Cox," he addressed her formally, "I'm just trying to take some heat off Thad in hopes you'll give him and the rest of us a chance for friendship," he ventured, trying to return some civility in a first meeting gone woefully awry. It didn't work.

"Well, you took the heat off Thad all right!" Denise spat back in irritation. "And as for your offered friendship, you can bury it with these flowers and this box of candy in China!" Denise finished, shoving the peace offerings into his chest. He juggled the unwanted tokens of esteem as she stormed off to retrieve baggage.

Thad had witnessed the tangle and sauntered over to the dismayed Tyrone. He still cradled his sleeping charge.

"That went well," he commented dryly. Tyrone sighed in disgust.

"I haven't been that irked in years. And I walked right into it, too." He shook his head and watched her thoughtfully as she lifted an oversized suitcase easily and swung it into place beside an identical one. She was not a weakling where luggage was concerned, and no man would stand in her way if something needed doing or defending. He liked this trait, though he figured it needed some tweaking. He wondered if *three little words* might change her disposition.

"What happens now?" Thad asked as Leah and Sarah walked up to them with mystified looks following Denise's display of annoyance.

"I'm going over there to help her with the luggage," Tyrone said calmly as he handed the sagging flowers and candy box to Leah then walked over to where Denise was yanking more luggage from the carousel with polar bear paw swipes. He approached and reached for the suitcase Denise was hefting. His large hand covered her long fingers causing her to look up in surprise.

"I'm sorry, Denise." His *three little words* were sincere. "Please let me redeem myself and help you with this luggage." Denise felt the pressure of his hand on hers while his proximity initiated some positive second impressions. The genuine tone of his voice thwarted a good share of her anger and encouraged retreat and compliance. She let go, yielding the strap to his strong grip, noting the touch of his hand as hers slipped away.

"I can take the beauty case," she offered, subdued. Tyrone's peacemaking efforts were of some interest. The irritation she'd felt toward him still remained, but the fact that he called her bluff when he confronted her motives for coming to Alaska encouraged further study of this wilderness man. For once, she realized her beauty would only go so far with him. Depth of character moved Tyrone's affections, and Denise wondered if her buried character would ever shine in his heart. She'd been so used to drawing her man's attentions with outward affectations and drama that her inner woman, where purpose and service should thrive, seemed mechanical, not genuine. She would have to be more grace and truth than glitter where Tyrone Johnson was concerned.

"Good. That will help me handle the rest of the stuff." He encouraged the team effort with a smile but didn't see one returned. Only a nod of acknowledgement, and she turned away with the beauty case. Tyrone sighed at what appeared to be stubbornness and knew they would have a few more battles before…well, he wasn't sure what would result; but he hoped for more than mere friendship. He liked her spirit. The drama queen was alive and well. Surely there was more than skin-deep beauty. Right from the moment he'd seen her picture, the word *marriage* had popped into his mind. Things could be awfully unpleasant for a while, but as the little group left the airport and the city of Anchorage for Palmer, Mr. Tyrone Johnson was smiling. Even though he'd apologize, he'd had the last word. Tyrone glanced over at Denise as they entered the Glenn Highway. He smiled broadly at her; she frowned back at him. Later, as they unloaded luggage from the SUV, she managed a few catch glances in his direction and even offered to carry both the beauty case and a duffle bag—something she would never have thought of doing in another land and time for a guy she was mad at.

## 2

## Easy Does It

Over the next two days, the hunting lodge swarmed with hosts and guests. Sarah and Angie stayed in a guestroom across the hall from Leah, while Denise was comfortably settled in a guestroom across from Alma. A rollaway bed was set up for a delighted Angie who had danced around the spacious room like a princess. By now, the little girl had formed an attachment to both Thad and Taima and was with one or the other most of the time. Taima, especially, showered his attentions on the little girl whenever he could. Alma invited Michelle Dorance over on the second day after their arrival, and both Angie and Michelle took to each other like kindred spirits. Joe Dorance stopped by a few hours later to pick up Michelle and was invited to stay for lunch. He accepted and joined in the good-natured banter. It reminded the quiet man of a noisy church supper. Stories flowed in ridiculous frenzy among Sarah, Leah, and Denise. Thad, Taima, Joe, and Alma could only laugh as they learned more about the three lively guests who were entertaining them.

Alma rose to clear the table before serving warm brownies topped with ice cream. As she did, Denise immediately got up and gathered the plates and silverware to be loaded into the dishwasher. About this time, Tyrone walked in the front door and hollered a jovial, "Hello, anybody!" which was returned with a, "We're in the kitchen, Tyrone!" Entering the crowded kitchen, Tyrone took the first seat available, not knowing it had been Denise's.

"I came at the right time," he commented before greeting everyone. Denise didn't turn to acknowledge him. Not because she was still mad at him—that was done and over with. Denise was not one to hold grudges for a long period of time. Every time Tyrone looked into her eyes, it seemed he could discern her inner character. She liked to keep a guy guessing in order to stay in control of the relationship. At first it was fun; now it had become a defensive act to protect against making a commitment. Then, too, she was strangely attracted to Tyrone because he was neither intimidated nor manipulated by her. He'd been the first guy ever to stand up to her tirades and not falter or give up and walk away, so she didn't turn to greet him as the others had, but kept busy piling the plates and corralling silverware for the dishwasher.

Tyrone sensed her distance but decided to ignore her for a while. With sisters at home, he well understood the silent treatment. It would pass, eventually.

Alma began dishing the brownies and ice cream to be served to everyone. As Denise picked them up, she was mystified to find that her hands shook with nervousness.

*Oh, great,* she thought, *now, I'll spill something for sure.* Turning, she steadied herself and handed a dessert plate to Taima, who didn't notice the waver of her wrist, thank goodness. In the end, Denise managed to deliver the chocolate treats without any catastrophe—not that Tyrone noticed. In one sense, Denise was relieved, but in another sense, she wanted his notice, and this peeved her too.

"Coffee anyone?" Taima asked before noticing that Alma was already pulling cups from the cupboard. Denise almost panicked when Alma pushed the hot pot of coffee toward her. It would be absurd to refuse to pour coffee because Tyrone's presence made her too nervous. She steadied her nerves and turned to fill the cups already on the table. Again, Tyrone ignored her until he reached for the last cup.

He had been telling about a client who had caught a small five-pound salmon.

"How big is a five-pound salmon?" Angie innocently asked.

Tyrone spread his arms out to show her just as Denise tilted the coffee pot to fill his cup. Leah saw the inevitable collision and put out her hand to stop both Tyrone and Denise. Alas, she was too late. Tyrone's hand hit the glass pot with a whack, knocking it out of Denise's hands. Fortunately, the pot spilled only a few scalding drops on Denise's hand before crashing to the floor.

"Oh!" she cried out, shaking her hand and rubbing the coffee splatters off in haste.

Instantly, Tyrone was on his feet in front of her, apologizing and gently pulling her over to the sink to run cold water over her hand. It had happened so fast that Denise was stunned.

"I'm so sorry, Denise. I didn't realize you were right there," Tyrone offered sincerely, hoping she would accept his apology and not be angry.

"Obviously." Denise muttered the rebuke.

He turned his head to regard her with mild surprise. Denise both wouldn't and couldn't look up at him.

"Are you all right, Denise?" Leah spoke for all who were sitting around the table.

Denise turned and smiled. "Yes. I just caught a few drops. It's okay. This cold water is helping just fine," she assured, returning her attention to the cold running water while rubbing her hand gingerly.

"No thanks to me," Tyrone mumbled very close to her, further unnerving her so that she turned the water off abruptly and turned away from him to pat dry her hands carefully on a dish towel. Tyrone exhaled and shook his head, turning from the sink to sit down again.

Leah and Thad saw the little drama going on between Denise and Tyrone. They shared a knowing glance. *Their best friends were navigating uncharted waters.*

"Let's take them for a drive up to the old cabin and see if they can sort their differences out calmly," Thad suggested.

"Knowing Denise, it won't be too calm around here for a while." Leah said this in a lowered voice. "I'm not sure the old cabin will foster any friendship between them, but the walk up the side of the mountain and across the meadow might expend some of Denise's pent-up feelings and change her perspective."

"Of course, she'll need Tyrone's help to manage the climb and maybe that will help them get to know each other better," offered Thad helpfully.

"Thank goodness for letters and phone calls," Leah remarked.

"It worked for us, but I'm not so sure it would have worked for them," Thad offered, giving consideration to Tyrone and Denise who were moving to opposite corners of the kitchen. "It looks like a boxing match." Their eyes met as they smiled in agreement.

Angie's bubbly giggle broke the magic. Leah turned and noticed that Sarah had been watching her and Thad. Sarah dropped her eyes to check her daughter's reason for laughter. Taima was making faces at the little girl and smiling more than he had smiled in years.

Taima regarded the whole clan gathered in his home and noted two things: Joe Dorance was watching Alma's every move, and the lonely Sarah Grant was needing help. To Sarah, he made an invitation, "Sarah, how would you like to spend some time down at the Trading Post this afternoon? I understand you are a bookkeeper for a construction company back in Pennsylvania. I could use some help with my books. Bring Angie too. I can tell she'll bring me good business with her curly hair and pretty face." He wrinkled his nose at Angie and smiled when she giggled. Sarah and Leah both knew that Taima's kindly attention to Angie reminded the little girl of her Grandpa Grant whom she loved and missed.

So, that afternoon, Alma had the quiet lodge all to herself to think over the changes taking place in the lives of those sheltered under this roof. She'd seen a log haven rise out of dirt and stone only a few years ago. For some time, she read the Bible, enjoying Matthew, the first book of the New Testament. Later, she prayed, giving thanks to her newfound Savior. Finally, she brought before the Lord the man who had been in her thoughts for some time—Joe Dorance. Michelle came to mind, and Alma wondered if she might ever be given a chance to be a good mother to the little girl when her own body, by her own will, had expelled a child by abortion. Guilt rose up inside her; then the remembrance of Christ's forgiveness and her choice to be forgiven rushed over her in peace. Everything was committed to the Lord Jesus Christ. Peace filled her soul as she finished the quiet time. With a heart of joy, Alma signed thankfulness to God for the lodge that Thad had built.

# 3

## Puzzle Pieces Lost

The request to join Thad and Leah on an afternoon excursion was met with doubtful looks by both Tyrone and Denise, but not refused. Neither one wanted to disappoint the happy couple by turning down the invitation. After a brief discussion it was decided to skip the old cabin and instead visit some of the historic places in the Palmer area. It was hoped this would put conversation on neutral ground.

"Palmer is said to be Alaska's gateway to Denali Park," Thad quoted as they continued past highway markers which indicated that Denali National Park was 205 miles up the George Park's Highway. "We'd love to show you ladies the vastness of this national park, however, there is a great deal to show you right here in town with regards to the history of the farm colony. Also, Palmer is host to the Alaska State Fair. The city's population will increase significantly with visitors from all over Alaska and the lower forty-eight states. It's really a great fair. If you're still here, Denise, we'll all go," Thad encouraged as they made their first stop at the Visitor's Center and Colony Museum on South Valley Way. The visitor center and the museum were both located inside a cabin constructed of notched logs. Leah couldn't tell if her friend was impressed or mortified by her rugged surroundings. Denise was a city girl after all. Camels at the North Pole could not have received more astonishment than Denise was directing toward this rustic shelter of history and welcome.

"Hello, Dee," Thad greeted introducing Leah and Denise to the executive director of the visitor's center. A ready smile from Dee welcomed the newcomers to Palmer as she encouraged them to browse around the displays of all things Alaskan. Her eyebrows rose in interest as she glanced from Leah and Denise to Thad and Tyrone. It was the first time she had ever seen Thad or Tyrone with dates in all the years she'd known them.

Leah pulled Denise over to a display of wooden carvings of caribou, wolves, bear, and salmon. The detailed etching made the carvings look lifelike in miniature form. After some study and comments, both moved on to the jewelry counter to see the handcrafted native art. Denise loved the colors and designs of the earrings and necklaces.

"Those lovely ladies look like very special clients," Dee commented kindly.

"Are there many visitors in for the fair yet?" Tyrone asked, steering Dee to another subject. Dee smiled and accepted the detour with grace and deference.

"They're beginning to trickle in steadily. It's going to be a good turnout this year, I think." She gave Tyrone a questioning glance then smiled and shook her head. "I hope your lady friends enjoy their stay in Alaska."

"If you need to use the van for transportation again this year, let Tyrone or me know. We'll get it over to you," Thad volunteered easily and moved toward Leah. Dee nodded and moved to assist other visitors arriving by tour bus. Denise found the seemingly ever-present Tyrone beside her. Instead of being annoyed, she chose to be amiable, comparing Tyrone to Jack and finding that Tyrone had some very positive qualities. Whereas Jack would invariably disappear with his mobile phone or saunter off to another department to check out things that held his interest, Tyrone was right beside her, helping and offering information— interested in what she was looking at, regardless of her disposition.

She felt valued not because she was someone's ornamental property, but because she was a person. It dawned on Denise that both Tyrone and Thad served people. They weren't just a business exploiting the beauty of Alaska for profit. They knew people and they knew how to make the Alaskan experience genuine and memorable for guests and friends. Maybe Tyrone could read her like a book because he was an honest man himself. This thought pricked her conscience and challenged her motives. Tyrone was a unique man. Her estimation of him was growing while her own elevated importance seemed to be dwindling. "God resists the proud, but gives grace to the humble." This verse she'd memorized as a child raced through her mind with renewed meaning. With Jack, she was proud and loud. With Tyrone she was--different.

In the Colony Museum, there were pictures of the valley showing the people who settled here and the construction of their homes and town over the ensuing months and years. Items of memorabilia marked the passage of time and broadened the understanding of pioneering, so often capturing the present in quiet reflection of the past. Dee rejoined the foursome and began to recite a short history of the Matanuska Valley aloud as she pointed to some of the black-and-white photos and farm artifacts.

"The Matanuska Valley's modern history of homesteading began as early as 1916 when there were some four hundred homesteads in the area. During World War I, tremendous transportation difficulties all but prohibited the marketing of farm products to Anchorage and other populated areas of Alaska. Only forty or fifty homesteaders remained in the valley by 1935.

"In 1929, the stock market plummeted, taking with it the wealth of the American businessman and the savings and dreams of Americans everywhere. Though this catastrophe marked the beginning of a ten-year depression both financial and physical, nowhere was it felt more than in the drought lands of the north central United States. Dust storms blasted the dry, cracked earth and left a dead land that would necessitate many years of inactivity to rebuild the once fertile soils and souls of its people.

"Those who had farmed the area for generations struggled to survive off the meager yields of parched gardens until finally, they were forced to enter the Federal Emergency Relief program in order to keep their families alive. Others lost factory jobs and businesses as a result of the stock market crash. Masses of Americans entered bread lines for relief. Truly, the dignity of hardworking Americans was tested by the necessity of government intervention for a Band Aid existence. The situation was desperate. People needed hope and opportunity.

"In March of 1935, previous plans to develop the Matanuska Valley into a productive farm community finally were underway as part of Roosevelt's New Deal took effect. Representatives of the State Emergency Relief Administration from Minnesota, Wisconsin, and Michigan met with the Federal Emergency Relief Administration's staff in Washington, DC to discuss the formation of a farm colony in the Matanuska Valley of Alaska. Two hundred two families were to be selected from these particular states for this new venture. Americans from other states across the country got wind of this program and thousands of letters flooded the FERA's Department of Interior in Washington, DC with requests to be part of the move to Alaska. It was a desperate time in our nation's history.

"Those families who were selected for colonization in Alaska gladly accepted the opportunity to make a new start in the Matanuska Valley. After fond farewells were exchanged amidst tears, after the parades, speeches, and bands played, these forward-sighted colonists sailed north to Alaska to meet the challenges of a new homeland. Many were the challenges that greeted the colonists in the early years. During the first months, the colonists endured the frustration of inadequate supplies and odd shipments of mismatched equipment from Seattle until competent dock supervision was procured to organize materials. Acclimation to the new homeland came with adjustments to the Alaska Rural Rehabilitation Corporation (ARRC), which directed the Washington, DC government's policies and procedures for the colony. Conformity to these policies was often difficult and impractical for Alaska's frontier farmer. Differences between some colonists and the ARRC often tested the American spirit of individualism under the government-sponsored project. While some of the colonists eventually left due to ill health and other reasons, many remained and worked with the Matanuska Farm Program.

"On May 23, 1935, two hundred eight slips of paper designating 208 tracts of land were pulled from an available cardboard box. Colonists each received a tract of land, and construction of their homes was begun by some six hundred transient workers who accompanied the colonists to Alaska. These workers had been sent to help complete the Matanuska building program. They arrived in Palmer before the colonists in order to set up the tent city which was needed until the tracts of land were issued. These transient workers continued to assist in the construction of the colony throughout the first year. Colonists who labored diligently and patiently at their farms and in their community of Palmer not only embraced the dream of a new homeland in a frontier territory that had not yet achieved statehood, they proved that colonization in Alaska's Matanuska Valley could succeed beyond differences in people and politics.

"There were notable men like Don Irwin, Colonel Leroy P. Hunt, and many others who offered a listening ear and wisdom in action as this rich farm valley developed. Evangeline Atwood quotes in her book, *We Shall Be Remembered,* the statement made by Colonist Ores Powell, 'We'll make Palmer a model American city.' And they did. Palmer was chosen as an all-American city finalist in 1989." Dee finished with a smile of pride, then asked if anyone had questions or comments before inviting the visitors to view the exhibits of the area's gold mining history.

Both Leah and Denise listened with interest, beginning to understand the significance of the Matanuska Valley and its history. Palmer wasn't just another pindot on a road map, it was the continuing story of the American pioneering spirit in their lifetime, their century. The old west was still alive and well.

After leaving the Palmer Visitor Center, they walked to the Felton Store and post office constructed in 1934 as the section house for the Alaska Railroad. The Felton house was located beside the store and post office and had been used as a boarding house by Mr. Jim Felton. It was also the home of a trader by the name of George Palmer, for whom the town was named. He was the first white man to remain in the Matanuska Valley, operating several stores over the years as well as serving as postmaster of the first United States Post Office in the Matanuska Valley. At the turn of the century (1900), George Palmer and another gentleman by the name of Mitchell began experimenting with vegetables in the southwestern part of the Matanuska Valley near Knik. Giant cabbages, turnips, carrots, and other vegetables resulted from their efforts, proving that the area could provide a sustainable food base for people. George Palmer encouraged the commercial development of the area through most of the successes of his business endeavors in the early era of the valley's history.

Thad and Tyrone recited history to Leah and Denise until their meanderings returned the foursome to the colony monument beside the visitor center. This monument listed the original families along with their home states. Thad knew some of the families and had worked on their farms doing research for university studies. Some descendants of the original colonists still operated the tracts of farmland issued on the slips of paper pulled from the cardboard box in 1935. The Alaska Rural Rehabilitation Corporation still assisted farmers in the Matanuska Valley with agricultural programs.

After a while, Thad and Leah drifted off to sit down and talk about their own wedding plans. Tyrone and Denise stood by the monument until the silence between them became awkward.

"Would you like to walk over by the flower gardens?" Tyrone offered, wondering if Denise had a favorite flower while giving her the opportunity to let him know if she'd like to continue in his company or on her own.

"Sure," she said easily, putting her hands in the pockets of the bulky navy sweater Alma had lent for the cool excursion. "I bet you have a favorite flower, right?" Denise encouraged or teased or both. Tyrone smiled, leading the way with his hands in his own pockets.

"Bachelor Buttons," he said casually, and Denise burst out laughing. It broke the tension between them and invited friendship.

"You're all right, Tyrone Johnson. I'm starting to warm up to you."

"Good, because I was feeling like breakup would never come."

"Breakup? I don't get it. We're not dating." She frowned.

"Up here, breakup occurs when the rivers start to thaw, and the ice cracks and breaks up into large chunks, melting as it flows downriver. Its evidence that springtime has arrived in Alaska."

"Oh. I guess we've just experienced our first breakup," Denise said brightly and heard Tyrone's groan, then chuckled. They could understand and accept each other's sense of humor.

"So tell me about your family, Tyrone." Denise had walked over to look at some tall magenta-colored flowers that looked more like wild weeds than domestic blooms. She loved magenta and that's why these drew her study. "What are these? They don't quite fit my idea of a flower garden, but they're pretty."

"Those are called fireweed, and they are a wildflower that grows all over Alaska. The flower part blooms from the bottom in early summer then moves to the top by the beginning of autumn," Tyrone answered, always helpful and kind but wondering why she was asking about his family.

"It means that summer is almost over?" Denise asked, leaning closer to admire the gentle magenta petals opened like helicopter blades to the harvest blue sky.

"Yes. I like to think of them as God's timekeepers reminding us of the change of the warm season to winter. Most Alaskans think the petals creep to the top too soon. We love our summers with the extra daylight."

Denise was surprised by Tyrone's reference to God. Questions instantly came to mind.

"Are you a Christian?"

"Yes, I am and have been since I was a boy going to church every Sunday with my family."

They walked along dirt paths between raised flower beds. Here and there, kidney-bean sized bees buzzed and bumbled from bloom to bloom like bumper cars at a carnival ride. Denise felt like a miniature character in the story of *The Borrowers*. At present, she was feeling very little in this unfamiliar world. She had been pretty big in her own world. Standing by this man in this place and beginning to perceive the value he placed on life and faith made her consider that God might have more to do with her being here in Alaska than her hasty flight to attempt a Joan of Arc performance to save Leah from Thad. Maybe Denise was the one who needed saving. From herself.

"I like the fireweed. It just might become my new favorite." She smiled genuinely up at Tyrone. He swallowed hard to quell the rising admiration he felt for her that was squeezing the air out of his lungs and making him light-headed. The last time he'd felt this way, a moose had charged out of the woods and crossed the two-lane southbound Glenn Highway between his 1970 Corvette and another vehicle. He remembered it as a blur in his rearview mirror.

Clearing his throat, Tyrone began his family story.

"I'm the oldest of four siblings. I have a younger brother, Jeremy, who is married to a nice girl named Sandra. They have a three-year-old son, named Kipling. We call him the Kipster because he loves monster truck shows. Jeremy is a career man in the United States Air Force. He and his family are presently stationed in Germany. Then I have two younger sisters. Terry is twenty-two and Gina, the youngest, is seventeen and spoiled." He grinned. "My dad is an Air Force veteran of the Vietnam war. He worked for the Alaska Railroad until he retired a year ago. My mom teaches second grade at the Elmendorf Air Force Base school. Dad is several years older than Mom, but they are devoted to each other and to the church." He finished and looked at Denise.

"How about your family?"

"I'm the youngest of six: three boys and three girls. Your sister, Gina, and I have something in common where being spoiled is concerned, though I wouldn't call it that. I've watched and learned enough from older siblings to know what works and what doesn't work with parents. Being the youngest does have its advantages as long as older siblings don't mess up too bad," Denise said dryly.

"What are their names?" Tyrone asked, wondering if her older siblings might be criminals or something.

"We all have names that start with the letter *D*: Darrell, Donna, Danielle, Donald, Daniel, and Denise," she gestured with a sweep of her right hand. "Darrell is a federal prosecutor working between Chicago and Washington, DC. Donna is a stay-at-home mom with two middle-school kids, Arthur and Chezney. Her husband, Carter, works for a pharmaceutical company out of Akron, Ohio. Danielle and her husband, Marcus, own a restaurant in Springfield, Illinois. He's the chef and she's the bookkeeper. Donald hasn't found his calling in life yet. He's still at home and works at odd jobs. He's a good guy, just doesn't have focus. He regularly attends the jail ministry…if you get my drift." Denise gave a long sigh. Tyrone nodded, understanding. "Then there's sweet, wonderful Daniel. After graduating from Moody Bible Institute, he moved to Houston, Texas, to teach Math and coach football and basketball in a Christian school. Dan is our family's athlete and sports enthusiast. He's single too. A spinal injury while playing high school football has left him paralyzed from the waist down. He's a wheelchair athlete, though, and plays basketball on a team with all wheelchair guys. Chicago winters were too hard on him, or so he says." Denise chuckled. "He's a Dallas Cowboys fan through and through and loves living in Texas.

"I'm the last Cox kid in our family. Until a week ago, I was gainfully employed as a department store clerk on the south side of Chicago. This past spring, I accepted a teaching position at the academy where Leah has taught for the last six years…until she decided to become a mail-order bride." Denise stopped beside a raised bed of large cabbages. Looking up at Tyrone with a frown, she confessed, "I was looking so forward to teaching with Leah this year and getting away from the daily grind. When she told me about her trip to meet Thad in Alaska, it was the greatest disappointment to me. Honestly, it made me mad, but not at Leah. I know how tedious life was for her and Sarah. It just messed up my plans for fun."

"Well here you are, now, and having fun in Alaska too," Tyrone tried cheerfulness but saw one eyebrow arch in annoyance on Denise's lovely face. It matched his growing annoyance at her self-centeredness. "That probably wasn't the right thing to say, was it?" he scrambled. "I can understand why you're not happy to be here now, but I hope you'll keep an open mind about Alaska while you're visiting." All of a sudden, Tyrone found himself sounding like a tour guide. He was shutting the door to any friendship with Denise Cox because he wasn't going to compete with her plans.

Denise blinked at his "turnoff" statement while searching his face. The warmth and kindness his face had displayed earlier was now cool, business-like, and distant. She'd always been the one to play cat and mouse with a guy's heartstrings. This incredibly fine man was about to walk away and let her have her own fun by herself. It was a defining moment in Denise's life, when she could either swallow her pride and recognize the value of this good man or choose to be offended and let her pride drive her back to men like Jack, who liked the distinction pretty women brought to a guy without having to make any commitment to love, honor, and cherish one woman forever.

She dropped her eyes for a moment then raised them to look directly at Tyrone.

"I'm sorry, Tyrone. I've had my own way for so long that I've been blind to the needs of others and their feelings. I've manipulated guys for so long I don't even begin to know how to act in a Christ-like way around them. I had no business bringing my bad self up here and dragging Sarah along just so I could be self-important and show everybody how righteous I am. That was wrong." Denise stopped. It was too much to confess all at once!

"Come on." Tyrone led her over to a park bench across from reindeer nibbling on hay behind wire fences. Their quiet unassuming munching gave a peaceful ambiance to the flower garden around the visitor's center. "Let's sit for a while. You can keep talking," he encouraged with a humorous smile. "Confession's good for the soul—"

"But bad for the reputation," Denise finished with a chuckle, glad to sense that friendship could be regained. Leah and Thad sat at a distance off to their left. Denise saw that they were engrossed in wedding plans. When she groaned mournfully, Tyrone laughed at her obvious misery.

"Why so blue?" he asked. Denise looked at him and wondered how he could be so easygoing. For some reason, she felt compelled to talk to him as if he was an older brother. However, that didn't last long when he extended both arms out along the back of the park bench. He was careful not to touch her, but Denise knew his right arm was close. It prompted her to start talking fast in order to quell butterflies flutters in her stomach.

"Well," she started, "I recently broke up with a fellow I've been engaged to on and off for the last five years. When Leah called me on Monday, she didn't realize it, but she gave me a way to leave the area for a while." She paused to reflect. "I knew from the letters Thad wrote to Leah that he was a fine man. I also knew that Leah was searching for authentic Christianity too. It's so amazing that both she and Thad have trusted Christ as savior. Even if her coming to Alaska was so that she could place her faith in Christ, it was worth it." Denise assured. "You mentioned that you're a Christian. What's your story?"

"Yes. I made a profession of faith as a ten-year-old boy at a Billy Graham Crusade in Anchorage some years ago, but I lost touch with the people who counseled me after I went to college. My folks continued to attend church."

*Was there some guilt detected?*

"It's hard to get back into church," she offered. "I know that much too."

"How so?" Tyrone asked, noticing an amicable change as her defenses waned.

"After college, I left the area to teach at a Christian school near Springfield, Illinois. I taught special education there for five years until the school consolidated with another Christian academy for financial reasons. Another teacher had seniority, so I returned home to North Chicago to see if I could get a teaching position near my family. I still had one college loan to pay off, and I figured I could help my parents out by paying room and board while getting that student loan paid off. I'd have had to pay rent somewhere anyway. But I couldn't seem to find a teaching position. Most Christian schools are too small for special education programs even though many of them would like to make such a program available.

"Public schools, on the other hand, often have waiting lists of teachers looking for these positions. I ended up taking a job at a local department store. It was open seven days a week, twenty-four hours a day. I worked all kinds of weird hours both day and night, including Sundays. When I did get a Sunday off, it was just too easy to sleep in or make other plans." Denise shrugged her shoulders. "I could have looked for another job with weekends free, but I didn't. By last January, I'd become manager of the women's fashion department and was working on the side for a catalogue company, choosing fashions for their spring clothing line. The money was good, and I loved working in the fashion industry. I got to the place where Sunday was just another day of the week until Leah called for a friendly chat and asked me if I'd invited any clients to church lately." Denise rolled her eyes, and Tyrone laughed. "For fighting salvation as long as Leah did, she did the pious pilgrim act really well. The Holy Spirit convicted me to the point that I resigned my manager's position and dropped to a lower-pay grade in another department so I could have Sundays off to go to church. It stunned the department heads and store supervisor, but it became my testimony in honoring the Lord's Day. And, yes, a few clients were brave enough to come to church with me." She laughed, and Tyrone enjoyed the delightful sound. "Now you know about my lapse in church attendance." Denise still smiled at him.

"The church would fall in if I returned." Tyrone quipped with a deep-sounding chuckle.

"I thought that very same thing too." Denise nodded in agreement. "But it didn't. What fell in was my pride when I fell on my knees and asked God to forgive me for neglecting fellowship with other believers in His church." Denise saw Tyrone's troubled expression. "I didn't mean that to become a rebuke, Tyrone. I only know it was how God dealt with me. The experience helped me to understand God's grace and patience toward me in a greater way." Denise finished, a bit sheepish at talking of such a thing openly with Tyrone. This was unusual for her, especially with a guy. Not many people knew Denise beyond the picturesque face and outward activity of her motion or commotion as the case may be. She realized also that she had told Tyrone more about her honest self than she'd ever disclosed to Jack Diamond in the six years she had known him. She'd never discussed her faith with Jack, either. Five of those years, she had been engaged to him and almost married to him. This fact startled her and caused her more than a little inward disquiet.

"Why the frown?" he asked.

"Why all the questions?" she returned, unable to disclose any further information about herself, especially now that her heart was finding a new avenue of friendship and feeling for Tyrone. These possibilities tested her defense system again. Tyrone waited until Denise spoke.

"I was just reflecting on a few things and seeing that God works things in peculiar ways at times." Denise stood as if to end the conversation. Tyrone sensed that their conversation was finished and stood also. He ventured a question to see if Denise was shutting him out once again and hoped she wasn't.

"I'm not sure what your plans are, Denise, but would you mind if I keep in contact with you by e-mail or phone?" he asked nonchalantly. Denise hesitated before she spoke with sincerity.

"Tyrone, I wouldn't mind if we e-mailed or called to talk occasionally, but you would have to answer one question just as I would have to answer the same one myself."

"What's your question?" he encouraged.

"If we should become more than friends, would you leave Alaska for me?" Tyrone was a little stunned by her directness. Before he could venture an answer, Denise spoke.

"Right now, if you asked me to leave my teaching position to come here and live with you in Alaska, my answer would be, 'no'."

"That might change, Denise," he stated quietly, already knowing where this line of conversation was headed.

"For whom?" Denise persisted. Tyrone could see it was a no-win situation. Instead, he urged her soberly.

"Keep all the options open, Denise. I promise you, I will," he said as he took her elbow and they began to walk silently toward Thad and Leah, who were laughing about something only they fancied. Tyrone noticed that Thad laughed a lot more these days while he was laughing less.

Later, as they drove back to the lodge, Denise thought about her question to Tyrone. She felt a little guilty for asking him such a selfish question. Actually, she wondered if she had asked it because she was frightened by the whole idea of Alaska in general, and marriage in particular. More than ever, she realized the disastrous mistake it would have been to marry Jack Diamond! Especially sobering was this thought when she compared Jack to one unique Tyrone Johnson.

By her own words, "If we should become more than friends..." Denise glanced over at the handsome Tyrone who was talking to Thad about a fishing trip for everyone at Kepler-Bradley Lakes. She made a dubious face as she turned away to watch the landscape pass in a blur of thoughts. *If we should become more than friends...if we should become... if...*, then like a flash through her subconscious, WHEN *we became more than friends...* broke upon her restive muse. That was really the truth of it. How could she ask him to give up the life he had chosen? It would be like taking the Christmas puppy and chaining it to a makeshift doghouse in the backyard just because it had grown up and wasn't cute anymore. She had seen these dogs yanking on their chains, making trenches with their paw treads around the circumference of their leaky shacks. It repulsed her.

She wouldn't do it to Tyrone. But, could she live here the way Leah was planning to do as Thad's wife? Denise couldn't even imagine it. She didn't dare. She was used to well-defined neighborhoods and city life.

This was open land with great distances. Not all neighborhoods were neat and well-kept. Indeed, she hadn't seen any manicured yards yet. It all bewildered Denise and made her feel out of her element and out of control—like a picture puzzle coming together one section at a time. She wondered. *Would the puzzle pieces ever come together for them?*

# 4

## PUZZLE PIECES FOUND

MEANWHILE, TAIMA ALREADY HAD SARAH WORKING in his "office" in the small closet-like room at the rear of the rustic trading post. When Sarah first walked into the office, she couldn't believe her eyes. There was a small path to the desk that was covered in clutter as high as the desk was tall. A variety of papers, order slips, magazines, receipts, and a barrage of newspapers and sales slips met Sarah's astonished eyes. Sample items from salesmen lay in random piles all over the office. The walls were covered with pictures of sportsmen and their hunting and fishing trophies as well as numerous calendars which had dates from before Sarah's birth.

Taima had only one two-drawer file, which he opened to show Sarah where he kept his bills, billings, and record books. These were just laid in the bottom of the first drawer as if in a shoebox. There were no file folders that Sarah could see anywhere.

"What's in the bottom drawer, Taima?" she asked with a curious frown. He bent to open the drawer she designated, and Sarah gasped, but not with horror. She tried to contain the laughter that threatened to erupt. Every kind, color, and shape of coffee mug imaginable was stacked to the top of the file drawer. All of them were brand-new and unused.

"This is my collection of mugs," Taima explained. "The salespeople bring them to me all the time, and I just put them in here. When it gets full, I box them up and put them in the storage shed."

"About how many mugs do you have?" Sarah inquired, unable to guess how many he might have stored in the shed over the years.

"Oh…my best guess would be about five hundred or so," he estimated with a shrug of indifference. "I hope to make a wall display of them someday. Maybe sell them to a collector." He joked at his own irony then pushed the drawer shut with his foot. "Well, you can see this room could use a little cleaning up," Taima acknowledged. Sarah considered the challenge calmly, already organizing a list of priorities for the cleanup. Taima watched her scan the entire office space with an air of confidence. She reminded him of Sonya in that brief moment.

"In Western Pennsylvania, we would say this room needed to be *read up*." Sarah offered lightheartedly, happy to have something useful to do. The colloquialism eluded Taima while her reference to Western Pennsylvania registered. She didn't refer to her roots as being *back home*. It was a topographical location. Leah had made the same distinction.

"Why don't you refer to Pennsylvania as *back home?*" he emphasized.

Sarah smiled and nodded. "We've lived in so many places that we really don't have any one place that we call home," Sarah replied with a shrug. "My dad has pastored seven churches in the last thirty-one years. So we've moved several times. I guess we never stayed long enough in any one place to consider it to be home." This seemed odd to a man who had lived in the Mat-Su Valley all his life.

"You don't like to stay in one place very long?" He frowned.

Sarah laughed but saw he was serious and quickly explained. "In every place we lived, we hoped we would stay for good. But you have to know that our dad is a deliverance-type preacher." Taima was clearly puzzled, so Sarah went on. "The Bible speaks of God delivering the people of Israel out of Egypt to the Promised Land of Canaan. He called Moses to be their leader. After leading the Israelites out of Egypt into the wilderness, God gave Moses the Ten Commandments to teach the Israelites how to live as free men after living in slavery for generations. It established law and order by teaching people how to do what was right in the sight of God so that when they got to the Promised Land, they would enjoy peace and the blessings of a Holy God.

"But sometimes, people don't want deliverance if they have to give up a lifestyle they're used to. Many of the Israelites never got over their homesickness for Egypt. They rebelled at these new commandments. Often we don't like to be told what the Bible says because it makes us feel bad about ourselves or condemns some of the activities we enjoy. It makes us accountable for our actions before others and before God. My dad preaches what God's Word, the Bible, says. Sometimes it makes people mad, especially church people who get stuck in the old ways of their church ancestors." Sarah stopped to see if Taima was following.

"Go on. I'm listening," Taima urged though he'd crossed his arms over his chest. She swallowed and continued. Unknown to Sarah, her reference to *ancestors* perked his curiosity as an Alaskan native.

"Moses didn't make it to the Promised Land with the Israelites. Sometimes preachers don't stay long in churches where the Bible is in conflict with the interests of the church body. Then, too, sometimes the preacher's fellowship with God and people is compromised because of personal problems. When Jesus was preaching the Kingdom of God, it was the Pharisees or pious religious leaders of that time who delivered Him up to be crucified. He moved around from place to place as well. Some places received Him, and other places rejected Him. Deliverance preaching is not popular. Are you familiar with the Gospel of Jesus Christ?"

"Yes, we've had any number of witnesses come to our door and try to get us to sign up with their church and its beliefs. But I tell them I believe in all of them already. There are many ways the spirits will lead a person to faith in the Great Spirit. I've covered all the bases, I think." He was content with his answer.

"It's true, there are many gospels proclaimed everywhere and many different Jesuses. There is only one Jesus who is the Son of God. Dad was good at stirring things up in churches where people enjoyed comfortable sins, even though he didn't purposely try to offend them. We moved a lot when I was younger. Dad always told us girls that our real home was in heaven. We were just passing through this world to a permanent place." Her voice cracked with emotion at the longing for a permanent home of her own, anyway. Taima silently regarded her for a few moments.

Religion was confusing. How could one really know what was true and what was fantasy?

"Well, I'll go put Angie to work too." He dismissed further conversation on the topic because of his good nature. "Before you two leave for your home back in Pennsylvania, I'm thinking this trading post will be in pretty good shape."

Sarah looked at Taima, a troubled expression on her thin face. He needed to know the truth. "We're not going back, Taima," she said simply. "I can't. I called my boss before I left and told him I was going out of town indefinitely. That's why I brought Angie with me. My dad knows and understands." Sarah paused, noting Taima's eyebrows arched up in interest. "I stopped at the bank and closed my accounts before Denise and I left town. I've managed to save a little over $5,000 over the last five years since Angie's birth. It's in the form of a cashier's check in my purse. I'm staying here close to Leah. I need a fresh start where people won't look at me with pity or condescension or whisper behind my back about my daughter." Sarah spilled it all out. "I know that I'll always have to explain about Angie and myself, but I can decide what people hear about me firsthand, and I can work to prove myself worthy of some little bit of acceptance," she finished quietly.

"You don't have to prove anything to me, Sarah," Taima stated frankly; then lightheartedly, "just clean up this office, and we'll talk about some plans after that. I'll take you to the bank first thing tomorrow morning to open an account and deposit your funds. You and Angie are welcome to stay with us until you find your own place." He offered a tight-lipped smile as assurance of his help. Turning, he saw Angie studying a picture of a grizzly bear by a shelf of ammo. The picture was twice her size in height, and she was obviously considering the fierce-looking bear's fangs and claws. A memory of Sonya came to mind with the wonder of a son he'd never had opportunity to raise to manhood. He determined to help Sarah and Angie as he wished he could have helped his own family. It could be a second chance when he considered all that was transpiring around Thad's effort to find a wife. The word *deliverance* entered his thoughts briefly then exited.

"That bear looks pretty mean, Angie." He tried to figure how it must look to an impressionable little girl. She turned to see him smiling at her.

"Yes, I think so too, Taima," her little girl's voice agreed. "Did you ever shoot a bear?" she asked with wonder in her large violet eyes.

"Yup! I've got the skin and head over there on the wall." He pointed, and Angie walked over to get a closer look at the lifeless beast.

"Wow! It's ugly," she commented with childlike truthfulness.

"Yup!" Taima agreed with a chuckle.

"Were you a little scared?" Her eyes were large.

"Nope!" he answered. Angie regarded him with hero-like wonder. "I was *a lot* scared. But I was determined to get the bear before the bear got me."

"And you got the bear anyway." Angie smiled, pleased with Taima's bravery and his honesty as well.

"That's right. Can you count, Angie?" he asked.

"Sure. I can count up to fifty," Angie said proudly. "This summer, I went to kindergarten camp for two weeks. It gets little kids like me ready for school, so we're not afraid of anything," she informed most precisely. "I already knew how to count to fifty even before I went. I also know how to write my numbers to fifty too. My grandma showed me. She's real good at drawing numbers for me to trace over. I guess I'm going to miss her." Angie's voice fell.

"I'm sure your grandma misses you too, Angie. She gave you the gift of numbers so you can feel closer to her between phone calls and visits," he kindly encouraged and saw her countenance brighten.

"I never thought of calling Grandma because we're so far away."

"Well, we even have phones up here too, Angie. In the meantime, I was wondering if you might like to count the stock on the shelves and write how many items there are on this paper." Taima drew a picture of each item and a line beside it so that Angie could write the number on the line. With some colored markers Taima supplied to her, Angie colored each item as Taima instructed. There were five items for her to count. Brown camouflage hats, green wool gloves, white wool socks, black leather gloves, and tan rawhide mittens. Angie listened intently and set to work with careful diligence just like her mother. Taima offered some help here and there until he could see she was doing very well at her job.

He glanced in on Sarah as she pulled papers together in a pile to sort.

He mumbled contentedly, "That ought to keep her busy for a couple of months." Snickering happily, he moved to the counter to unlock the cash register and welcome customers.

After a while, Sarah came to ask Taima about purchasing some filing supplies, and he followed her to the little office just as Lance Kroft showed up in front of the trading post. Charlie wasn't with him, which was a little unusual, so Lance Kroft's haggard, predatory appearance and his stealth-like entrance went unnoticed. He entered the store noting that Taima wasn't around to offer either assistance or resistance. Emboldened, he proceeded past the counter toward the gun display.

Angie was so engrossed in counting green wool gloves she didn't realize a stranger was near until an ominous shadow fell over her pint-sized person. Of course, Lance Kroft was bearded, wore a black fur parka and was about the same size as Taima's trophy bear—the likes of which promised the little girl future nightmares!

Kroft's focus on the gun display ahead blocked any thought that another human being might share some space in time with him. Neither was aware of the other until Kroft bumped into Angie. Her head shot up in surprise, then her mouth dropped open in sheer horror as shock registered in her uplifted eyes. The clipboard she was holding fell from her hands to the floor with a clatter. Her high-pitched scream startled Kroft. He uttered a blasphemous oath, and Angie promptly kicked him in the ankle as hard as she could. He yelped with pain and uttered yet another curse to which Angie delivered a second swift kick. This time, her hard-soled shoe found its target with a punishing blow to the ankle bone. Kroft cried out in pain. When he bent down to rub the throbbing pain, he was amazed to meet a pair of angry violet eyes that matched his own. Stunned, all reason left him as if he was frozen in time. His own history passed like a time line before his mind's eye. Angie's heated rebuke broke his mental fog.

"Shame on you for saying bad words about God...and scaring me to death!" she hollered like a Puritan preacher. "You look like that ugly grizzly bear on Taima's wall over there"—she wrinkled her nose in disgust—"and you need a bath too!" Kroft's watery eyes blinked in unbelief at the child's audacity. Overcome at the resemblance to her mother and himself, he straightened before hobbling quickly toward the door, nearly knocking Taima and Sarah against a rack of fishing waders. Sarah recovered and reached for Angie, fear and panic evident in her shallow breaths. She felt like she was suffocating.

"Shame on you!" Angie shouted after him boldly. She looked like a pint sized superhero standing there with her hands on her hips and eyes shooting rays of courage and light. Taima looked from the maiden champion to the fleeing foe limping quickly down the steps. He recognized Lance Kroft and would file a police report on him, again. Sarah looked beyond her daughter in confusion trying earnestly to get a clear view of the stranger but saw only his dark retreating form.

"What did he do to you, Angie?" Taima quizzed.

"He scared me, and I scared him back," she stated triumphantly.

"Did he touch you?" Taima asked, checking for marks of any kind.

"Nope. But I kicked him as hard as I could because he said God's name in vain," she justified with a nod, feeling her mom's arms came around her shoulders protectively.

"Are you all right?" Sarah asked calmly though her hands shook, and she willed herself to take deeper breaths.

"I'm okay, Mommy," she said matter-of-factly. "But he's not," she assured. "Grandpa says when people make God's name common and use it to curse others, it's the devil doing the talking, and we should give that old devil a good swift kick. So that's what I did. I kicked that ugly old devil in the ankles two times!"

"Well, good for you, Angie." Taima commended heartily, making a mental note to censor his own language with more diligence. "I don't need guard dogs with you around."

Angie's butterfly giggles restored a sense of utopia. Sun poured through the windows casting shafts of golden light across the aisles of trade goods. The alarm had passed, and life resumed as each went back to work.

"You know, Mommy? That man had eyes just like mine."

"Did he, Angie?" Sarah commented without much thought. It was becoming easier to breathe.

"He says bad words in a funny way, too." She giggled.

"Angelina Joy!" Sarah corrected. "That's a strange thing to say."

"He has a Russian accent, Sarah," Taima interceded mildly. He saw the startled look on her face before her eyes darted to the window in search of the departed stranger. In that brief moment, it dawned on Taima that there was much more to Sarah's story than any of them knew.

"We have many people in Alaska who are of Russian descent. The United States purchased the territory of Alaska from Russia in 1867. So, Angie, you'll probably see many people around here with eyes like yours. They may even have accents like Kroft too," he finished easily. Sarah seemed to relax with this logic. After all, it wasn't possible that she would know anyone by the name of Lance Kroft.

# 5

## A LOOK IN THE MIRROR

LANCE KROFT HOBBLED AS FAST AS he could until he came to the old Ford pickup he and Charlie sometimes used for getting supplies. He breathed heavily, not so much from the exertion of his getaway, but because he was shaken by the encounter with the little girl.

Charlie had gone to the post office to pick up mail while Lance had decided to try his luck and see if he could pick up a new rifle and ammo at the trading post. After his first meeting with Leah at the store last Saturday, he instantly had felt the need to leave the area. He knew whose sister she was because Leah reminded him of Sarah. There was something in remembering Sarah that both comforted him and condemned him. But what had shaken him to his soul was the resemblance of himself he saw in the little girl. As the recipient of her rebuke, he also realized for the first time that he was a father and that Sarah must be here in Alaska. But how could this be? The knowledge filled him with hopelessness.

Jumping up into the truck, he caught his reflection in the side view mirror as he closed the door. The childish words regarding his haggard appearance grieved him deeply because he had not always been crude and unrefined. As for his language, he had allowed it to become much worse around Charlie. Until he'd met Sarah at the rescue mission and heard the Gospel, he'd blasphemed God with no thought about breaking one of His Ten Commandments. While he'd known her for a short time, he tried to act religious to please her, win her affection and admiration. The little girl's sharp rebuke batter-rammed the walls of his unbelieving heart. He pounded the steering wheel in silent frustration, unable to utter any oath lest she should hear him even at this distance.

Guilt, or divine conviction, or both matched his pulse's throb, breaking down his walls of resistance and rebellion. These two earmarks of his will were the motivation for survival. He felt trapped. If Sarah was here with their daughter, they would be put in danger because of his past associations with criminals. He made a decision to flee again. The battering-ram stopped its death thump as adrenalin raced in to supply energy for the escape from unseen enemies. Deep within the hidden caverns of his heart stirred the agonizing longing for a home with Sarah and the little girl whose name he didn't even know.

Looking quickly from side to side, he opened the door enough to slide quietly from the truck. Kroft left the key in the ignition and started walking out of town. Charlie would wander this way and take the truck at his leisure. It would be better if he just disappeared, and so he did. Only Taima noted his direction from the window of the trading post.

It was almost dark as Kroft ascended the rocky path toward the only secluded cabin he knew to be vacant—Thad's old place. He reasoned that he would stay there to watch and see if anyone followed him. When he reached the cabin, the door was ajar, and he entered cautiously. All remained quiet and serene as far as he could see. Exhausted from the hike and the emotional spin, Kroft found the cot and dropped onto it, sleeping fitfully. Above him, tiny specks of stars appeared as cotton ball clouds moved silently east. The mid-August night was cool and mild on his side of the mountain while in the valley house lights faded as Palmer's neighborhoods slept peacefully.

At about five o'clock the following morning, Kroft busied himself with finding and eating a breakfast of stale crackers and a small box of hardened raisins. Taima, on the other hand, left the crowded bed-and-breakfast to search for the vanished man. Charlie had hazarded an inquiry about Kroft at the trading post, but Taima gave up no information to the surly partner-in-crime.

Thad watched Taima leave in the pickup taking a route away from Palmer and the trading post. It piqued his curiosity, but he figured maybe Taima just needed some space. His old friend had told him about Kroft's second appearance at the trading post within a week's time. It was indeed uncharacteristic for those two scoundrels.

Thad sipped hot coffee and returned to the kitchen table to read from the book of Acts. During a phone conversation in which Thad let Leah's dad know that Sarah and Denise had arrived safely with Angie, Pastor Grant had encouraged Thad to read the Bible book of John first, then the book of Acts. He'd read all twenty-one chapters of John before going to bed last evening and was amazed at how much of it made sense now that he knew Jesus Christ as Savior. Rebellion had blinded him to spiritual truth. Surrender had opened his heart to the wisdom of God. Acts awaited his attention. He began in chapter one and read through to chapter ten before he picked up the coffee cup and sipped cold coffee. He popped his black-roasted brew into the microwave and waited until it beeped the end of the reheating time. The steam warmed his nose as Thad pondered what he'd read.

Jesus had met with the disciples after He rose from the dead. Forty days later, He ascended to heaven leaving them with the Father's promise of a Comforter who would empower them to preach the gospel of Jesus Christ to the world. The day of Pentecost had come and gone in a global outreach of powerful proportions. Every nation under heaven heard the Gospel that day through the gathering of peoples in Jerusalem. Like migratory birds moving north and south as seasons change, so God gathered the multitudes from every nation to witness the change from the season of God's law to the age of God's grace. It reminded Thad of God gathering the animals and bringing them into Noah's Ark on the appointed day prior to the great deluge.

The power of God brought men to their knees when Peter preached about the Holy Spirit. Ananias and Saphira conspired to deceive the church leaders about the sale of some land and the monies gathered for their offering unto God. Their mutual lie offended the Holy Spirit, and God administered the first church discipline resulting in instant death for both husband and wife. Thad read about Peter's and John's arrest for preaching that Jesus rose from the dead and that He was the true Messiah. He read that Stephen's defense of the Gospel resulted in martyrdom. The conversion of Saul to Paul began the Gospel's journey to the Gentile nations of the known world of that time. So much happened in these chapters in Acts that Thad was surprised at the action adventure recorded of the early church. He was struck by the rapid spread of the gospel to all nations of the Roman Empire and beyond.

It was a wonder to him that he had been so stubborn and closed to God and His Word. He picked up the Bible and held it open in both hands as if it suddenly had become a treasure of priceless jewels. There was so much to learn, and he wanted to know and read it all. He bowed his head in prayer, humbling himself before his Heavenly Father.

"Show me and teach me Your Word and Your way, Father." The Holy Spirit would answer this oft repeated prayer over and over again through the days and years ahead. The formation of a student and servant of the Lord had commenced.

By the time Taima reached the rough ground near Thad's old cabin, the sun had risen enough for him to start hiking up the side of the mountain with a sack of food and a thermos of hot coffee. When he approached the cabin, it was with extreme caution and a deliberate attempt to let the churlish Kroft know he had company.

Sure enough, Kroft met him at the door with a snarl of displeasure, but Taima wasn't to be put off.

"What do you want?" Kroft muttered in annoyance.

"I brought you breakfast, Kroft. I want to talk to you." Taima wasn't asking.

"About what?" Kroft growled, though he wouldn't turn down the offer of warm pancakes and sausage after the earlier fare of meager findings.

"Sarah Grant and her little daughter." Taima snapped back in irritation, tired with the "twenty questions" routine and Kroft's sullen attitude. "You know who I mean." He waited and wondered if Kroft would let him past the front step.

At the mention of Sarah's name, Kroft's face turned pensive. His eyes shot side to side to check the wilderness beyond Taima, then he stepped aside and beckoned Taima quickly inside.

"Did anyone follow you up here?" he demanded in a whisper. Taima wondered if Kroft was in his right mind or delusional. Taima brushed Kroft's hand from its grip on his parka sleeve.

"No. Why would anyone follow me? What's the matter with you, Kroft?"

Kroft sighed and ran his hand through thick knotted hair and turned away. When no answer was forthcoming, Taima opened the sack of food and handed it to Kroft. He then poured two cups of coffee. Kroft took the food and sat down at the makeshift table using a fork and knife with practiced good manners. A napkin was used to carefully blot away any crumbs from his mouth and beard. He ate like a meticulously trained gentleman. Lance Kroft was not a bum; he only gave the appearance of being one. After folding and replacing the napkin neatly on the table, he regarded Taima calmly.

"What about Sarah Grant and her daughter?" He sipped the coffee as though indifferent and unconcerned.

"Why don't you tell me?" Taima paused, "that little girl made you run like a scared rabbit!"

"How did you know I was here?" Kroft suddenly asked.

"It wasn't too hard to figure out once I put a few things together. The little girl resembles you for one thing, and then Sarah's reaction when I mentioned you spoke with a Russian accent. It made me wonder what the connection was. I also figured if you did know them, you'd want to stay close. This cabin is vacant at the moment. Everything else around here is occupied due to the State Fair next week."

"I won't be here long," Kroft stated flatly.

"Why not?" Taima asked. "Did you mistreat Sarah Grant—"

"No!" he shouted, turning to face Taima. Checking his irritation, he exhaled and spoke in a lower tone. Agony and fear were reflected when he started to answer.

"I love Sarah," he acknowledged, "but I can't let her know I'm alive. She and—"

"Angie," Taima filled in. "Angelina Joy," he corrected.

"Angelina Joy," Kroft repeated reverently as he took her name into his heart forever. "They would be in danger because of me."

"Who are you?" Taima said in a guarded tone. Kroft shook his head from side to side.

"It's better if you don't know."

"Stop stalling, Kroft, and tell the truth. You make me sick." Taima stood, screwed the cap back on the thermos, and made ready to leave the cabin, but Kroft stopped him.

"Wait!" he pleaded. "I will tell you who I am and what happened."

Taima gave him a long look of tolerance before sitting down again. Kroft paced the rough wood-planked floor for a few minutes pulling his hand through his bushy, wild hair again and again. He acted as if he didn't know where to start or what to say first. Suddenly, he stopped, and taking a seat in the old stuffed chair, he leaned forward and talked directly to Taima. It was as if he had been caged up on the inside for a long time. Once memories broke through trust barriers, all at once they wrestled for verbal freedom.

"My name is Andrei Garankof," he began. "I was sixteen years old when my father, a professor of nuclear science at Moscow State University, and my family were moved to Pripyat (Pree-yawt) in northern Ukraine. The Russian government was building a modern city powered by the latest nuclear technology of the time. Nuclear power was derived from what was viewed as being the *peaceful atom*. Though Chernobyl was already an outdated nuclear facility built in 1970, the government had plans to modernize the plant. Some 49,000 people lived in Pripyat by the time my family was relocated there in 1984. Many, like my father, were top scientists and engineers.

"A labor force of experienced tradesman numbered in the thousands. Teachers, including my mother who taught what you would know as high school physics and chemistry, as well as doctors and nurses filled positions in state-of-the-art facilities. High-rise apartment complexes housed many families in convenience and comfort. Everything about Pripyat was designed to show the world a model nuclear-powered city. The urban layout was triangular allowing for wide spaces between buildings. The streets were designed for easy navigation to prevent traffic jams. There were modern playgrounds and grassy parks for mothers and children to socialize and play. There was even an amusement park complete with a roller coaster, carousel, and a newly constructed Ferris wheel. For Russia, Pripyat was a developing utopia, the toast of a scientific society of enlightenment energized by nuclear power. But it all went terribly wrong," Kroft said matter-of-factly.

"On the evening of April 25th, 1986, my father got a call from the plant's main control station. The heat levels in Reactor 4 were dangerously elevated. They needed his expertise to get the cooling system working again. Plant workers had performed tests on the system without using the emergency safety and cooling systems. They had ignored safety regulations and turned these protective systems off. By the time my father got to the area where Reactor 4 was controlled, gases had built up to a point that the cooling system could not handle the overheating reactor. Both heat and pressure were at crisis levels. It was just a matter of time before the reactor would blow.

"Just after midnight, my mother received a phone call from my father telling her to get me out of bed and get out of Pripyat immediately. He instructed her to drive south to her sister's home in Kiev, which was about ninety-five miles away. He would meet us there when he could. If he didn't contact my mother and me within twenty-four hours, we were to wait at my aunt's home until it was safe to go on to Moscow and stay with a professor-friend and his family at university." Kroft stopped and stared out the window for several minutes. Memories came flooding back. Taima waited quietly, thinking the present time seemed to drag when a man's mind reflected on the images of horror that raced across the screen of his youthful memory.

"My mother pulled me out of a warm bed, wrapped a blanket around me, and told me to put my shoes on. I could tell by the tone of her voice that she wasn't going to take any attitude from me this time. I was cocky and rebellious in those days," he confessed with a nod while Taima wondered that Kroft would think he had changed at all. "My mother and I left our apartment at about 12:30 in the morning. She drove our compact car to the city checkpoint, showed her ID, and when asked the purpose for the late-night drive out of Pripyat, told the guard she was driving to her sister's place in Kiev to take care of a family emergency. She told him that my father was working at the reactor and couldn't accompany her at this time. The guard called the plant office to check if my father was there, and it was verified. The guard let us pass."

Taima reached for the thermos and refilled Kroft's cup when it seemed he might be unable to continue. The movement jolted his wandering mind. He cleared his throat. "I remember my mother starting to cry after we left the checkpoint. I didn't realize we might never see my father alive again, but she knew." He sighed. "At 1:23 a.m. on April 26th, 1986, the Chernobyl nightmare began with a reactor explosion," he recited as if the time and date had flashed across the pathways of his brain over and over and over again since that night. "It was unthinkable, inconceivable that such a thing should happen. Mother had driven almost sixty miles when she noticed the orange-colored horizon in the rearview mirror." Kroft's eyes moistened as tears gathered. He blinked them away and cleared his throat to control the tremor in his voice.

"My mother cried out, and I turned to look out the back window. She yelled, 'Don't look back, Andrei! Don't look back!' But I couldn't help looking back. It looked like the destruction of Sodom and Gomorrah from the ancient texts. The explosion blew the one-thousand-ton steel top off Reactor 4. A ball of fire shot one thousand feet into the air sending torrents of radioactive debris raining down on the sleeping city of Pripyat and the surrounding villages. The disaster loomed like a fast-emerging thundercloud of death above the entire region surrounding Chernobyl. I remember my mother choking back sobs as she pushed the accelerator to the floor. I watched the speedometer reach top speed at ninety on the open road. The only other traffic was trucks with freight headed in the direction from which we were fleeing. Mother flashed her headlights to warn them, but they drove on toward the disaster like bugs into a neon trap." Kroft's fist hit the table beside him, jolting the coffee cup. The dark liquid shot up and fell in splatters on the rough pine table. Helpless, hopeless anger filled him again. He looked at Taima with wild eyes.

"Take it easy there, Kroft," Taima said evenly. "Did you get to your aunt's safely?" He saw Kroft blink away the anger and regain his senses.

"Yes, though what is safe when the air is contaminated?" He rose from the chair, picked up the coffee cup, and set it down gently on the makeshift countertop. Retrieving a napkin from the food sack, he cleaned up the spilled coffee from the table. Taima was amazed that this scruffy man took such meticulous care at keeping things in order. "My mother and I made it to Aunt Irina's. We stayed inside her home waiting for news from my father, which never came. We watched TV for news reports about Chernobyl, but not much information was forthcoming except to encourage people to stay inside their homes until further evaluations could be made by government officials. After a few days of waiting, my mother thought it necessary to drive the nearly six hundred miles north to Moscow to contact father's professor friend. Mother took what precautions she could to keep us safe, and we, along with my Aunt Irina, left Kiev and drove north to Moscow in a day's time, stopping only for fuel."

Kroft's brow wrinkled in thought. "Pripyat was a modern city, but in less than forty-eight hours, it became a ghost town. Contaminated by radioactive fallout, Pripyat's comforts and treasures were *all* left behind in the hasty evacuation some thirty-six hours after the initial explosion showered unsuspecting inhabitants with radiation, yet my mother and I escaped because my father warned us ahead of time. When we reached Professor Yuri's home near the university, he was relieved to see my mother and me. In the few moments before the blast and subsequent meltdown, my father had called the professor and told him of the critical state of Reactor 4. He and other engineers were still trying to shut it down, but to no avail. He had called at one o'clock, just twenty-three minutes before the explosion had occurred. The professor had told him to start evacuation procedures immediately."

A solemn silence permeated the rustic cabin in Alaska where Kroft and Taima sat, so far removed from the crisis now over a decade in the past. Kroft remembered, *Tell Inna and Andrei I love them still, I love them always.* The professor had related his father's last phone message to his devastated mother and son. Kroft did not mention this to Taima. His father's last words belonged to him alone.

"While we gathered what information we could about the meltdown at Chernobyl, a huge cloud of radioisotopes floated across the landscapes of Russia, Finland, Sweden, and the European continent. The monster would threaten millions of people. The dream of a nuclear utopia at

Pripyat was no more. Even the name of this city has been removed from most present-day maps. It is in an area called the *Exclusion Zone.*

"Now we are here in the year of 1997. It's been ten years since Chernobyl. I am no longer Andrei Garankof. My visa has expired. I am now Lance Kroft."

"Who does Sarah know you to be?" Taima asked.

"She knew me as Andrei Garankof," he pledged truthfully.

"So what happened next? Did you find your father?" Taima kept him on task for the whole story. The question about his father charged old resentments.

"Yes and no," he grumped. "My father came back. He and a few engineers were able to escape in the few remaining minutes before the reactor blew. Because they escaped, it was figured that they had planned the meltdown and caused the reactor to explode by not following the safety regulations. The government needed someone to blame. My father had nothing to do with the irresponsible, foolish actions of those conducting the tests. The plant operators only called him in to help when they couldn't keep the reactors from exploding and causing a complete meltdown of the nuclear plant. My father accepted the blame. After all, he couldn't fix it! The truth of it was that nobody could have. Much of it was experimental science mixed with human carelessness. My father was never the same. He made a full report of everything that transpired in those last hours before the explosion and subsequent meltdown took place.

"It was his desire to put his effort into seeking answers so that something like this would never happen again—anywhere else in the world. He submitted the report then disappeared. My mother and I tried to find him, but he was simply gone from the face of the earth. My mother was heartbroken. She went to live with her sister, my Aunt Irina, who, by this time had returned to Kiev. I was too much trouble for my grieving mother to handle, so I stayed with Professor Yuri and his family until I was eighteen. Military service is mandatory at age eighteen, so I joined the Russian army. I had a keen mind for solving problems, so I was assigned to the intelligence unit. It was perfect. All of a sudden I had access to information. I worked my way up through the security levels until I had clearance for government documents. I wanted to find my father. I wanted to know why he had disappeared and where he was, if he was still alive.

"In the process of finding the Chernobyl report my father had submitted, I noticed an attached memo for orders to fly someone named Simon Kroft to Berlin, West Germany. It was dated June 7th, 1986. You may guess that I searched for him in Berlin. Indeed, my father had been in Berlin, but only for a short time. He had checked into a hospital there to do research on cancer treatments for radiation poisoning, but he had been encouraged to continue his research at the Mayo Clinic in the United States. I traced him to a hostel where he'd stayed while doing research at the hospital in Berlin. The landlady said he'd talked about visiting a cousin in Chicago, America. I had only a few weeks left of military service to complete, so I returned to Russia and finished my duties.

"I visited my mother only to find that she had thyroid cancer and was dying. By then, reports had started circulating out of Sweden about higher rates of cancer in European regions. The report cited the disaster at Chernobyl as a probable cause for the increased rate of cancer diagnoses and deaths. My homeland denied it, of course, stating evidence to the contrary. All I knew was that my mother was dying, my father was off chasing down cures for radiation poisoning under a different name, and I was..."—Kroft shook his head from side to side—"...lost in the middle of a horrible nightmare." He stood and walked over by the door to look out at the sunny highland meadow. He looked for movement of any kind. A moose nibbled the bark off a birch tree some twenty feet away. Late summer forget-me-nots dotted the trampled grasses. All appeared tranquil and pristine.

"I stayed with my mother until she died in June 1991. She was only forty-four years old." Turning from the window, Kroft sat down again. The hardy alpine flowers reminded him of his brave mother. "I put off the search for my father and remained with my mother and aunt for three years. During that time, I enrolled at university and studied finance and economics. There was no way I was going to study anything that could blow up or cause cancer," he snickered. Taima managed an appreciative grin. "I finished my degree early then applied for a work visa to go abroad for Global Financial Investors. They had corporate offices in St. Petersburg, Hong Kong, Sydney, and Chicago. I chose to go to Chicago, America, since I hoped my father might still be living in this city.

"In mid-July, after my mother's death, I left Russia and flew to London, then on to New York, and finally to Chicago. I had an address of one of my father's uncles who lived on Canal Street in Chicago and went there first. What I found was not my uncle's home but a rescue mission called Pacific Garden Mission. It was very disappointing to find this religious organization instead. There was a big lighted cross on the side of the building that read, JESUS SAVES. I didn't even bother to go into the building because anything to do with religion was disgusting. I just hailed another taxi that took me directly to GFI in the Chicago Loop and settled into the job for about a week, but something kept nagging at me to inquire about my uncle at that rescue mission. So that weekend, I took a taxi back to the mission and walked inside. I got there just in time for a religious meeting. There was nothing else to do but sit and wait for the meeting to conclude."

"Was that where you met Sarah?" Taima was guessing. Kroft's head came up and he looked directly at Taima.

"I didn't meet Sarah. I saw her first," he corrected. "She was part of a singing group of college kids from the rescue mission. She sang a solo then played the piano for the group. I couldn't take my eyes off her. She was beautiful," he recalled. The sight of her had erased all the grief in his life and made his dead heart beat again. "I didn't hear a word of the message—mostly because religion was not viewed as being scientific or enlightening. It was for the soft, ignorant mind. I just wanted to look at something beautiful. After Chernobyl, my perspective on life changed. All my interests as an adolescent seemed childish and meaningless. Both my parents found refuge and contentment in work, so that's what moved me forward. There was no time for frivolous affairs of the heart until I saw Sarah that Saturday afternoon. There was a meal after the meeting, and I decided to stay and see if I could find out anything about my uncle"—he smiled—"and about the *music girl*, as I called her." A chuckle bubbled up, and for the first time, Taima saw Kroft smile broadly. He looked human.

"She was serving asparagus. It is not my favorite vegetable, but for the sake of being near her, I accepted the awful asparagus and even smiled as I said *thank you* with my Russian accent," he chuckled lightheartedly. Taima had seen the same lightheartedness rise in Thad upon getting to know Leah. These two sisters had positive effects on those who were smart enough to recognize quality and brave enough to pursue their love.

"When our eyes met for the first time, I determined to move heaven and earth to make her mine." Kroft sighed and continued, "However, getting to know her was a problem. The mission had strict rules for single people who served there, especially the single women. I met with the director of the mission to inquire about my uncle, Viktor Garankof, first of all. I had to stick to my purpose. Director Samuels checked mission records for the name and found that my uncle had stayed at the mission for about a month, then left after sobering up from an alcohol drinking binge. There was an address given on Cicero in North Chicago that could be checked out, but there were no guarantees that it was valid. I didn't have to ask who the *music girl* was because she knocked at the director's door and was invited in to submit a purchase order for groceries and supplies needed for the mission's kitchen. He called her *Sarah* then introduced us quickly as he signed the purchase orders.

"We exchanged greetings, and I had an idea. I asked her if she could tell me where Cicero was and how to get to the address the director had given me. She said she could take me there when she ran some errands for the mission." Kroft snorted at the humor. "I was thinking about the great luck I was having until the director said that some guy named Moe could ride along and help carry boxes of printer paper for her too. Moe turned out to be as big as a football field. He also squeezed his way into the front seat of the little car ahead of me! Sarah drove, and I rode the backseat feeling like a mob boss." He laughed out loud, and Taima joined in, realizing he was beginning to like this rough-cut Russian a little more than he thought possible. The humor subsided with a sweet sigh before Kroft turned somber once again.

"We drove to the address first. It was one of those horrible old apartment buildings. My family had always lived in college housing for university staff that was well-managed and comfortable. Anyway," he waved away the memory, "Sarah and Moe stayed in the car while I made my inquiry. The place smelled like urine and rotted garbage. The floors were filthy, and I didn't even want to touch the call buttons on the mail boxes for fear of disease." He looked at Taima. "You can see how far I have fallen, and I am ashamed of myself."

"Go on. I'm listening." Taima encouraged the confessor.

"I pressed the button, and a man's voice answered. I told him who I was and asked if I could come up. He hesitated but pressed the buzzer to unlock the lobby door. I grabbed the knob and opened the door leading to a stairwell. Rancid cooking smells assaulted my nose as I moved up the flights of steps to the third floor apartment. Trash left from drug users cluttered the landings. It made me sick to my stomach to think I had a family member living in this kind of squalor. How could this be?" he reasoned aloud.

"Uncle Viktor answered the door and let me in. I prepared myself for more disgusting sights inside his apartment, but was surprised to see that it was spotlessly clean and nicely furnished. It was such a contrast that it took a minute for me to adjust to the change. He knew I was looking for my father. We sat down, and he told me that my father had been there until his death a month before. He'd died of thyroid cancer, like my mother. I asked about his stay at the Pacific Garden Mission, and at this, he stood and walked over to a bookcase. Pulling a book from the top shelf, he brought it to me telling me that it was my father's Bible, and it had a letter in it for me to read." Kroft paused, thinking that he had never known his father to have any interest in reading a Bible. "Uncle Viktor explained that he had become a Christian during his own stay at the mission. My father found him there the same way I did. Somewhere in the process of finding my uncle and struggling with cancer, my father had also become a Christian. Uncle Viktor told me where my father was buried. I left shortly afterward with the letter from my father and his Bible. The letter I would read at his grave the next day when I could be alone. The Bible I would leave at the mission when I returned with Sarah and Moe."

"Did you see Sarah again?" Taima asked. He was surrounded by Christians all of a sudden.

"Yes, I saw Sarah again—Moe too," he said tongue-in-cheek. "The three of us saw the sights of Chicago every chance we got away from my job and her mission service. I heard the Gospel every time I went to the mission to pick Sarah and Moe up for a date." He paused to chuckle. "Every time I tried to leave my father's Bible at the mission, it came back to me or found me. It was actually stolen and returned to me a short time later. I couldn't get rid of it!" Kroft tossed his head to the left over his shoulder. There on a plank of wood nailed to the wall was a makeshift bookshelf, and on it was a black-bound leather book. It was worn around the edges but still gold-leafed from gentle use.

"You should read it, Kroft. It might be a sign," Taima offered.

"I have been, but just a little at a time," he assured, raising his eyebrows at Taima.

"Back to you and Sarah and Moe," Taima prompted with a grin for Moe's sake.

"Sarah and I eventually found some time to talk without Moe around. Actually, we stayed at the mission and sat in the chapel and talked. When I asked her to leave the mission and move in with me until we got married, she adamantly refused to be anything other than my wife and told me she wouldn't see me again! So two days later, we stood before a justice of the peace and got married."

"Can you prove it?" Taima jumped in. Kroft promptly pulled his wallet out and retrieved the well-worn marriage license. He unfolded it carefully and presented it to Taima who stared at it in astonishment.

"I also have our wedding bands." He pulled a long, neck chain out over his shirt, and Taima saw at once the golden circles symbolizing eternal commitment. "We had taken them to a jeweler to engrave our marriage date and names on them. I never was able to give Sarah her ring." There was despair in his voice as he continued, "Global Financial Investors was under investigation for corruption in stock investments. I was just the new guy, but I suspected things weren't right when I started noticing bank and stock records with offices in the other countries. Russia has been wracked with corruption this past decade. Because of my intelligence training in the Russian army, I found out things about political leaders that would have cataclysmic effects on their positions and on the economies in countries around the world.

"It was like Chernobyl happening all over again, this time as an economic blast instead of a nuclear one. I made up my mind that I would get out as fast as I could. There was only one problem. GFI knew about my findings as, of course, they would. I downloaded what information I could onto disks, put them in a small steel box, and buried them near my father's grave. It's been seven years ago already. When I headed for our apartment, FBI agents were at the door. I knew Sarah was at the mission, working. I hated myself for leaving her with no explanation or contact, but I feared for our lives. She didn't know any of this anyway," Kroft stressed. "I've been running ever since."

"Man! Kroft, you've got problems bigger than Mount McKinley, I'd say," Taima declared. "You can't keep running, especially since you have a family now. Why don't you go to the FBI? Get this thing figured out and put behind you."

"I've thought about that since I saw my little girl--Angelina," he said softheartedly. "It's such a nightmare, Taima."

"We all have nightmares, Kroft. Sooner or later, we have to face them and separate what we imagine will happen with what is, in fact, reality. The facts are, Kroft, that you have a wife and daughter who need you. If you're hiding, this is the wrong place to hide. Alaska won't hide you. It may be a big land, but it's not a sea of faces to fade into and lose your identity. You'd better go back to Chicago. A man's form on this landscape is very obvious! It's just a matter of time." Taima nodded with assurance. "You have a decision to make, Kroft or Garankof...is it? Now, do you want to see Sarah and Angie?" Taima ventured frankly.

Kroft looked over at him with an expression of misery etched on his rugged face. "I can't," he said simply, swallowing with difficulty.

"You can't or you won't, Kroft. You've become a coward!" Taima stood and started gathering the food sack and thermos. "I'm only going to ask you one last time. Do you want to see Sarah and Angie?"

"Yes! Of course I want to see them," Kroft said with some agitation. He rubbed his hands over his bearded face and looked down at his dirty clothes.

Taima suddenly laughed out loud. "Hah! Ha-ha! Now I'm the fairy godmother! I guess you know that you need a bath and a good cleaning up."

Kroft managed a smile in agreement.

"I'll bring you some clothes and cleaning stuff after lunch," Taima replied and glanced around the desolate cabin. "I'll bring some other things too. Thad and Tyrone are taking everybody out to the Kepler-Bradley Lakes for a fishing excursion today. So, I can take care of this without anybody being the wiser of it for a while. I'll plan to bring Sarah and Angie here tomorrow afternoon for a picnic. You can decide whether you want to speak to them or not. At least you will be able to see them," he finished lamely as he thought about his own sad choices in life and headed for the cabin door.

"I thank you for…" Kroft stumbled, "for hearing me out and for your help," he finished sincerely.

Taima turned and grinned. "Well, Kroft, you're not the bum I thought you were. Glad to know you. Now don't go anywhere," he commanded and gave an easy salute before stepping outside.

Kroft looked around the cabin and, seeing an old bucket, he left the cabin and went up to a gurgling mountain stream for water. For the rest of the morning, he worked on the cabin first then began heating water to prepare a bath of sorts. He'd found the stovepipe behind the cabin and reconnected it to the stove and hole in the log wall for ventilation. It was a comfort to have heat in the cold, damp cabin. It was freeing to know that smoke could drift out above the cabin, and it was okay to rest in this lowly place without feeling like a squatter or criminal.

Even though Kroft was both of these at the moment, just knowing that another human being knew his story and seemed willing to allow him some value as a husband and father stirred the first hope he'd experienced in years. His eyes flew to his father's Bible. He'd been reading the Psalms and recognized Psalm 23 from a picture of a shepherd watching sheep hanging on the wall at his Aunt Irina's. He reached for the holy book and reread the Psalm aloud.

The Lord is my shepherd; I shall not want.
He maketh me to lie down in green pastures;
He leadeth me beside the still waters.
He restoreth my soul; he leadeth me in the paths of righteousness
For his name's sake.

Yea, though I walk through the valley of the shadow of death,
I will fear no evil; for Thou art with me;
Thy rod and thy staff they comfort me.
Thou preparest a table before me
In the presence of mine enemies;
Thou anointest my head with oil;
My cup runneth over.
Surely goodness and mercy
Shall follow me all the days of my life;
And I will dwell in the house of the LORD forever.

Around noon, Taima returned and saw at once the progress of the man he knew as Kroft. "You don't look like Lance Kroft anymore," Taima commented favorably.

Kroft looked at Taima for a moment as if giving some consideration to the statement. "If you saw the name on the marriage license as Andrei Garankof, you know that is my real name."

"Too bad you can't take Sarah's last name, or can you?" Taima proposed, but Kroft shook his head back and forth.

"So Lance Kroft it will remain," Taima said aloud then added, "at least for now."

"Yes," he spoke flatly. "Andrei Garankof is still in hiding."

They regarded one another for a brief moment. Taima turned to leave saying over his shoulder, "Tomorrow at two o'clock, rain or shine, they'll be here."

"Rain or shine," Kroft repeated thoughtfully then went back to work on his cleaning crusade but not without some trepidation. He wondered if Sarah would be angry with him. He wouldn't blame her if she was. He would wait and see. If she was angry with him, what would he do? What if she made demands or threatened to have him arrested for abandonment. Beginning to feel the panic rising inside him, the urge to flee grew strong. However, he remembered the words of Psalm 23 and the comfort they gave of a Shepherd who cared for him no matter where he seemed to wander and no matter what danger surrounded him.

Then too, the animated face of Angelina peering into his matching violet eyes pierced his soul as a father. Oh, for the chance to see Sarah, beautiful Sarah, whom he loved. To have both of them close without putting them in danger was his entire hope. He wondered how he could keep from talking to Sarah and telling her that he was near after all these years. But then he'd have to tell them he couldn't be with them. Kroft shook his head to clear these conflicting thoughts. Frustration rose like mercury on a thermometer. A picture came to mind of the illuminated cross on the side of the rescue mission, JESUS SAVES.

"Jesus saves," Kroft repeated aloud. "How can Jesus save me from this?"

# 6

## Gone Fishin'

Thad was dog-tired. It was one o'clock in the afternoon, and it felt as if it had been the longest day of his life. Never had he expected seven women and a little girl to exert such a drain on his strength and tenacity. He glanced over at Tyrone. His business partner was soaked to the bone, and his waders were mud-caked up to the knees. Tyrone wore a sour expression as he squish-squashed past Thad. His teeth chattered from an unexpected dip in frigid water. At least Thad was still dry and relatively warm. There had been several mishaps to keep both men hopping between Leah's bunch and business clients. He rubbed his forehead with the back of his hand to wipe the sweat away. Next, he rubbed the side of his face with the palm of his hand, then massaged the back of his neck to soothe the rising ache caused by muscle tension.

Three of the seven ladies were clients. In their mid-sixties, these spinster schoolteachers had scheduled this fishing trip at the recommendation of Ishioti, who was a frequent client of Thad and Tyrone. They were also more interested in male bashing than fishing, in a good-natured way, of course. Leah, Sarah, and Denise joined right in with them. Even the mild Alma signed a few stories of her early dates that brought hoots of laughter from all the ladies when Leah interpreted for her. The only one not laughing was little Angie, who had been Thad's constant companion because Taima wasn't around. She was as accident prone as his sweet Leah. There had been snagged hooks and lines aplenty as well as one fishing pole lost to the current. A whole bucket of bait sank beneath the murky waters as the result of two blood-curdling screams from Angie. It had nearly shattered his nerves. Granted, the fish were almost half her size in length and in weight, so he could understand a little anxiety when one flopped onto her lap! He remembered her sleeping repose as he carried her through the airport and wondered how peace and calamity could be interchangeable at a moment's notice.

Watching all seven ladies standing next to the lake and quietly concentrating on fishing, Thad realized it had taken four hours of sheer chaos to get them to this tranquil moment. What usually only required one man's expertise could have used a third man's help today. Leah, Sarah, and Denise reminded him of the *Three Stooges*. One thought up a scheme, the second added to it, and the third one rallied the gang to try it. That's when Tyrone had taken a dip in the cold lake. Thad had watched it all happen. It had seemed so innocent, yet afterward he began to realize the three of them had most likely done it many times in order to execute it so well now.

The comic routine had started with the somber-faced Sarah pointing to something in the water. She started to get excited as she moved over by Leah. Leah started to look where Sarah was pointing, and they both started talking, chattering like noisy chipmunks. They moved over to Denise who was, as usual, giving Tyrone the dickens over something. Leah and Sarah both pointed toward the water together. Thad had frowned at their odd actions, but the day had already been so unpredictable, he figured unless he heard screams from this bunch, all was well. Then Denise had seen it, whatever *it* was. She began to describe how ugly it was. Tyrone had ventured an innocent gander at the mysterious monster in the lake. In fact, he was glad something else was catching Denise's flak instead of him, for a change. All of a sudden, the ordinarily quiet Sarah shouted.

"There it is!"

It seemed that they all moved closer to the water's edge, except when Thad shot a look in Sarah's direction, he saw Tyrone falling forward with arms spread like an eagle. In he went with a huge splash while all three ladies pointed at him.

"It's a monster!" they yelled at the top of their voices, then they laughed out loud. Denise had been laughing so hard that she sat down at the water's edge and slapped the ground while pointing at Tyrone. At that moment, Tyrone really did look like a monster as he came up out of the water, spitting and sputtering. Intense irritation registered on his face as water dripped off his nose and chin. When the three friends stopped laughing long enough to check the monster's stumbling progress to shore, Tyrone's angry countenance was hard evidence that they'd outdone themselves. Great effort was made to squelch their laughter and appear sober-faced, but that only lasted until the angry beast lost his footing on the muddy bank and skidded backward, flapping his arms like a landing seagull.

Two long trenches made by the heels of his camouflage waders marked his descent into the murky abyss, yet again. Thad stifled the urge to laugh and moved to aid his friend, who was trying to gain back his equilibrium and his dignity with measured success. Tyrone's waders were full of frigid water, and the extra weight and cold were sapping his energy quickly. On his knees, and thankful he was only in two inches of water, he pulled the shoulder straps down over his arms and crawled out of the waders. Thad reached Tyrone and gave him a strong arm, pulling him up the bank to safety. From the seagulls' perspective, the only noises to be heard along the stony bank were their own, mocking the suddenly quiet *fish ticklers* and the *giant mud slider*. A thoughtful grin remained on Thad's face. Mischief and mayhem now had names.

"What are you smiling about?" Tyrone's deep voice echoed his dour feelings.

"Those three"—Thad nodded his head toward the serious lady anglers—"fed you to the fish," A chuckle erupted as Thad took off his jacket and handed it to Tyrone who pulled the warm jacket on and started for the Suburban where an extra set of dry clothes and some heat would take the chill off.

"I know who had the idea." Tyrone's eyes found the back of Denise's form and noted that her shoulders shook with laughter every so often.

"Leah and Sarah may have started this little skit, but Denise instigated the whole thing."

"Either Denise can't stand you, Tyrone…or else…" Thad shrugged and watched Tyrone slog toward Denise. Thad wondered if she would even acknowledge Tyrone with a passing glance then saw her give him a triumphant smile. His good nature recovered, Tyrone bent at the waist and bowed like a maestro after an encore performance. Applause sounded from all seven maiden ladies. Thad laughed heartily. Tyrone had trumped Denise again.

Denise watched Tyrone trudge stiff-legged toward the Suburban. He was visibly shaking from the cold dip he'd taken as a result of her practical joke. *If he got sick*, guilt washed over her.

"Tyrone, wait!" She hurried to catch up with him. "I'm sorry, Tyrone." Remorse was genuine. "You're going to be sick now because of my foolishness."

"*Achoo!*" He sneezed with gusto and then groaned in misery. His nose was already running, and he ached all over from the icy dip.

"We have to get you to Thad and Leah's place," she asserted as she reached for the car door, but Tyrone put a hand on her arm to stop her. Looking at her in earnest, he asked, "I just gotta know something, first, Denise. Did I fall in the lake for nothing?"

Denise's mouth opened to retort, but she saw he was absolutely miserable. A thought came to mind: *Love is like a flower, it blossoms with kindness.* It was her mother's oft-repeated saying to Denise.

"The question is, who fell first?" She smiled, and Tyrone was warmed, heart and soul. "I'll go get the others. I think Thad has had enough fishing for one day anyway," Denise guessed correctly with a chuckle as she winked at Tyrone and headed toward the weary anglers.

The ride home was noisy with conversation about recent fishing escapades and trips taken to faraway places around the globe. Two vehicles had transported the happy group to the fishing destination. Thad and Tyrone had been the drivers, but Tyrone was feeling sick, so Alma drove, and Thad followed. Sarah and Angie rode with Alma and the three schoolteachers. They turned their attention from travels to quizzing Angie on her numbers and letters, praising her aptitude for learning.

Later, Alma delivered the teachers to their bed-and-breakfast accommodations in Palmer before heading back to the lodge. Thad and the others were already unloading gear when Alma drove onto the cement driveway in front of the garage. They saw Denise fussing over Tyrone and helping him into the large garage, which led into a large ground level den. The huge area had a wall of windows opposite the entrance from the garage. Beyond the windows was a stone patio. On the left in the spacious den was a fireplace built two feet off the floor with a hearth to provide seating the entire length of that wall. Various comfortable chairs and couches were placed for conversational settings and TV viewing.

A pool table stood ready for a contest of angles. Bookshelves with a myriad of titles formed a backdrop for the prestigious game table. Across the room was a small kitchenette complete with a stove, sink, dishwasher, and refrigerator. Pictures of wildlife hung on the walls in a tasteful manner with potted plants of all sizes and phyla, bringing green life into the space. Scenic pictures of the Alaska Railroad brightened the neutral wall color; their engines and passenger cars painted in dark blue with a yellow stripe running the length of the shiny train. Mounted busts of moose, Dall sheep, and caribou dotted the walls in a tasteful manner befitting a modern hunting lodge. It was a room for encouraging all things related to the Alaskan outdoor experience.

Sometime later after Tyrone was made comfortable on the couch with pillows and blankets, Denise brought a tray of food down to her patient. Steam rose from the bowl of salmon and chive chowder, which was served with toasted cheese sandwiches. Gingerbread cake with a dollop of whipped cream crowned the repast with spicy flare.

"Here's something to make you feel better, Tyrone." Denise set the tempting tray of food down on the large solid oak coffee table.

"I know something that would make me feel a lot better," he ventured as she looked up from stirring a cup of tea and honey. "But then you'd be sick too." Disappointment rang in his nasal voice.

Denise's eyebrows rose incredulously. "I see the frog prince has high hopes for a kiss?" she teased as she handed hot tea to Tyrone.

"Hope springs eternal," he rebounded, accepting the prepared sweet tea.

"You may be hoping that long."

"Why is that?" He frowned.

"I've got to get back and get ready to teach in two weeks, which means you won't be over your cold by the time I leave. So, the frog prince you will remain."

"Then I'll just show up on your doorstep sometime and claim it," he promised.

"Right," she was doubtful. "You'd come some five thousand miles for a chance to turn into a handsome prince?" Denise shook her head. "I signed a teaching contract, and I'm sticking to it. Besides, it would give us some time to get to know each other's backgrounds. I just broke off an engagement with a guy. It would have been a terrible mistake to marry him. I don't want you to be a rebound for a missed basket."

Tyrone had wondered why it seemed she was stalling. He also knew she was right about honoring her teaching contract for the next school year. It would take planning to court her from a distance, and he was willing to do so if it meant she had peace about it.

"I don't want to be a rebound either, Denise. But I will come visit you anywhere you are, whenever we can see each other. We'll start as friends. No more pressure from this frog prince, okay?" Tyrone saw instant relief in Denise's countenance. It meant sacrificing his dreams of a double wedding for her sake.

"Thanks, Tyrone." Denise was amazed by his willingness to set aside his own desires in order to give her time to know her heart. While dating Jack, she'd had to sidestep his advances for intimacy until finding out that several others had endured his rude behavior even during the years of his engagements to her. It had hurt, angered, and humiliated her profoundly. Now there was Tyrone Johnson from Alaska. He was easygoing, frank, and honest in his dealings with people and with her. She welcomed his transparency, wholeheartedly enjoying the fact that she didn't have to second guess his motives or endure his contrary comments which made her feel ignorant and incapable of valuable input. They talked for a while until laughter pulled their attention from one another to the kitchenette. Thad and Leah were opening cans of pop for those who wanted something to drink. They worked well and were happy together. Tyrone stirred out from under the blankets and stood.

"Let's go see what all the commotion is about over there." He extended a hand to pull Denise up, and she took it, grateful for her new friend's thoughtfulness.

"What's so funny?" he asked, entering the circle of mirth.

"When Denise and I were in college, we were both part of a work scholarship program that helped defray tuition costs. We worked in the Snack Shop for ten hours a week as soda jerks. Once, we got goofing around with the pop machines and the snow cone syrups trying all the flavors in various combinations to see what they would taste like. We discovered that mixing syrups and pop made us burp long and loud when we gulped the concoctions down quickly."

Denise cleared her throat and took over as Leah politely excused a burp. "We had contests to see who could burp the longest and loudest. Of course, we laughed and goofed off more than we worked." Denise confessed. "We called one particular mix of coke, orange pop, and cherry syrup, *The Cure,* and highly recommended it to first-time dating couples who seemed nervous and somewhat inhibited."

"We figured if they made it past this first hurdle, they were meant for each other. The odd thing about it is that now they're all married, and we're still single," Leah said tongue-in-cheek.

"Not for long, Leah." Thad winked and moved closer to his mail-order bride. Tyrone pursed his lips to keep from wrecking a friendship, though he'd love to say the same for Denise.

"Well, we didn't last long in the Snack Shop." Denise admitted. "Student Resources put us down in the basement making one thousand boxed lunches two times a week. We called ourselves *the Chain Gang* because it felt like a prison down there." Denise snorted. "There were actually bars on the windows in the bakery."

"How long were you in solitary confinement?" Thad tried with a chuckle.

"Not too long. We lasted just short of two months down there," Denise answered with a shrug.

"Yah. About two months," Leah agreed with a nod.

"I'm almost afraid to ask what happened." Tyrone saw the merriment rise in Denise's eyes at his inquiry.

"Our job was to mix up a huge steel vat of peanut butter and jelly and spread the mixture between two slices of whole wheat bread. We made about a thousand PB&J sandwiches and about the same amount of bologna and cheese sandwiches. We were part of a kitchen team that put the boxed lunches together and filled them with food for Saturdays and Sundays. The college kitchen served a hot supper only on Saturday evening. No meals were served in the Dining Hall on Sundays," Denise explained. "After making the sandwiches, we had to individually wrap each one in Saran Wrap. Baggies were too expensive, so the kitchen supplied huge rolls of plastic wrap for sandwiches or pieces of chicken or whatever was supposed to go into the boxes. The boxes were the same size as the Kentucky Fried Chicken ones, but they were yellow. It took four hours, two times a week to make these boxed lunches. When you stand in one spot for that length of time and spread that awful stuff on endless slices of wheat bread, it doesn't take long before a person is repulsed by the smell and sight of PB&Js. We smelled like PB&J sandwiches." Both Denise and Leah wrinkled their noses.

"Always the same thing. We would empty large, heavy buckets of peanut butter into the man-sized mixing bowl, dump large, ten-pound cans of grape jelly on top of the peanut butter then turn the fan-shaped beater on," Leah drawled on with a voice of pure drudgery. "It sounded like a cement truck with a big, fat belly ache." Thad and Tyrone laughed at Leah's description of the kitchen beast master.

"One Friday afternoon, the two of us were left behind to finish making up the last one hundred PB&J sandwiches. A couple of the other girls in *the Chain Gang* had to leave early to be part of a soul-winning team going to the Pacific Garden Mission in Chicago, so we got stuck doing some of their work too. It wasn't a problem. We girls covered for each other on occasion especially when there were dating events or game nights at the college. Anyhow, Leah and I were dragging with boredom by the time the last one hundred sandwiches needed to be made. The bakery supervisor had already gone home after the pans were washed and put away. All that was left to wash were the trays to stack the PB&Js after wrapping. That's when Leah noticed a large one-gallon jar of dill pickle slices already opened. She loves crackers with peanut butter, strawberry jelly, and dill pickle slices on them."

Thad looked at Leah with a puzzled expression. Leah licked her lips.

"Best snack in the world!" she declared. "I just never liked whole wheat bread."

"Leah suggested we add dill pickle slices to the PB&Js. We called them our secret ingredient, and we filled the last one hundred PB&J sandwiches with dill pickle slices."

Tyrone and Thad couldn't help laughing in astonishment at their antics.

"But that's not the weird part," Leah hastened to say. "Only *one* person ever complained about our pickled PB&Js." She held up an index finger for emphasis.

"Mr. Dinger, the chief chef and manager of College Food Services happened onto one of our creations. We honestly didn't think he ate the same food we college students ate." Denise pointed out. The two best friends groaned in remembrance of the consequences.

"That was yet another trip to the dean's office--"

"--and more dish duty," Denise added holding up her dish-pan hands.

"The next work scholarship job they put us on was scrubbing floors and buffing them. We did buffer duty for the last few weeks of the semester. Once we got the hang of it, it was fun! I learned how to waterski on a buffer," Leah offered jokingly.

"We literally had to scrape off all the old floor polish on hands and knees all over that entire campus facility." Denise wailed. "We called ourselves 'Cinderellas with no fellas'."

"And there was no fairy godmother to rescue us either, just the Dean of Women to remind us that the law of sewing and reaping would have a harvest in our lives," Leah piped up then, "We put in for window washing but got denied."

"Those buffers had a wild side of their own too," Denise added.

"Afternoon classes had just been dismissed the first time Denise buffed the hallway. The guy who was showing her how to run the buffer was in a hurry to meet his girlfriend, so he just breezed through the operation of the buffer real fast. There are several buttons on the handle of those buffers. One button in particular locks the buffer in the ON position so that the operator doesn't have to squeeze the grips constantly. But that's not all. There's miles of electrical cord that gets tangled around everything and everyone.

"The first time anyone uses a buffer, they usually don't realize those buffers have a tendency to take off in all directions. The first time I used one, the crazy thing took me for a wild ride and just about yanked my arms off my shoulders. Anyhow, Denise got a little mixed up and pushed the Lock button. That buffer cleared a path right down the middle of the hallway during a class change. Bodies flew in all directions, trying to dodge the runaway buffer and the whip-slithering cord. Denise caught up with it and tackled that crazy serpent, but it got loose again and started down a flight of steps. A security guard tackled it and finally turned it off. That was a memorable day, which included another trip to the dean's office. We worked extra hours to pay for the damages. And that was why there was no time for dating the rest of the semester." Leah gave a long sigh.

"I was so embarrassed," Denise recalled. "After that fateful day, they had the guys on work scholarship buff the floors so girls wouldn't have to wrestle those buffers anymore."

"What other jobs did you two have in the course of your college career?" Thad was curious.

"Well, when we came back the next semester, they separated us and gave us jobs in different areas. Denise worked in the library, and I became a secretary to a meticulously organized professor. It was the hardest job I ever loved," Leah acknowledged. "I learned a lot about organization though I know he must have learned a lot of patience. We kind of balanced each other out eventually."

"It solved a few problems and kept us out of the dean's office for the most part, but we were still roommates," Denise testified, "so the mishaps still occurred every once and a while."

"Both of you attended a Christian college, right?" Tyrone asked.

"Yes, we did," Leah answered. "It was not a choice in my family after high school graduation. My sisters and I knew from early childhood that we would be expected to attend a Christian college for at least one year before we could pursue a career of our choice. Honestly, I didn't want to attend any Christian college, period. I just figured I'd put in my time that first year then transfer to Cal Poly in San Luis Obispo, California, to study Architecture. I wanted three things"—she held up counting fingers—"to be an architect, to live as far away from home as possible, and I wanted to live in a warm, sunny climate for the rest of my life. No more long, cold Pennsylvania winters for this gal." The irony of her present situation triggered laughter around the group.

"So much for those dreams, my friend," blurted Denise.

"I was so filled with resentment and rebellion that I determined to make the *least* of that year in college by doing just what was necessary to get to the month of May. No chapel speaker was going to persuade me to dedicate my life to Christian service, and no dean of women was going to mold me into an assembly line model of feminine godliness for the Master's use. And *I* wasn't going to allow some preacher boy to dominate me either. I acted at being cooperative outwardly, but inwardly I resisted everything associated with spiritual things," Leah confessed, shaking her head. "I was wrong. I was so mad at God for so many things." She looked at Thad and continued, "My grades were so bad that I couldn't have gotten into Cal Poly without starting as a freshman all over again. And to think I'd been the valedictorian of my high school class no less. The finances weren't there to follow my dream. So I stayed put, tried harder, and graduated with a teaching degree." It had been the only option for Leah.

"Then Denise and I went to that TV show. It didn't occur to me to contact a dating service until Valentine's Day. I'd looked out the classroom windows to the snow-covered countryside and knew if I didn't do something soon, I'd be looking out that same window every February 14th for the rest of my old-maid life. That morning, the students' Bible lesson was taken from excerpts of *Pilgrim's Progress*. I'd never read *Pilgrim's Progress* up to that time, but the new Bible curriculum we were using suggested it for a classroom reading challenge. So, my teacher's aide, Amanda, read the story aloud, and I interpreted for my deaf students.

"We were reading chapter 3, where Christian looks up at the cross and his heavy backpack just rolls off his back and into the opening of the cave. Christian was lighthearted and free of the burden of his sins. He also has been given a new robe, a mark on his forehead, and a book of instructions with a passport ID for entrance into the Celestial City. He was rejoicing when two other characters jumped over the wall of salvation and caught up to him. Their names were Formality and Hypocrisy. They were false Christians because they did not come through the narrow gate. They believed they would be permitted entrance into the city of the Lord on their own merits because they had followed the law and the ordinances for thousands of years. However, Christian was told these characters were following their own fanciful ideas while he was following the Master's.

He said to them, 'You came in by yourselves without His direction, and you shall go out by yourselves without His mercy.' That particular statement made by Christian kept running over and over again in my mind all afternoon. As I looked beyond the windows where the students had taped their red hearts for Valentine's Day, I realized I was not the genuine Christian teacher my students thought I was. I carried the burden of hypocrisy on my back along with a host of other sins. I wondered what it would be like to have my burdens rolled away and to experience the power of freedom like Christian. My heart began to open up to God. It was also the day I decided to drive to Pittsburgh and find myself an Alaskan bachelor."

"So you're a pilgrim from Pittsburgh?" Tyrone quipped.

"Now I am," she smiled at each member of the circle. Leah's testimony was genuine.

# 7

## OUT OF DARKNESS

THE EVENING CLIMAXED WITH WELL-WISHING WHEN Thad and Leah made an announcement. Thad had read a portion of scripture from the book of Acts about Paul's conversion experience, now a favorite passage. Alma had prayed in sign, which Thad interpreted aloud to the cozy group. Quiet reflection had settled over them like a benediction when Thad drew attention to Leah and himself.

"Leah and I want to tell you about an event we are looking forward to with much happiness." He smiled at Leah who winked encouragement back. "Pastor Paytor has agreed to marry us Saturday at two o'clock in the afternoon." There were cheers of delight around the room. Congratulations came next with hugs and happy wishes for the couple's wedded bliss.

Taima had remained silent and a little aloof all evening. He had much to think about, including the reading in Acts about Saint Paul's conversion. He enjoyed watching those around him laugh and enjoy a good time together. He had missed that kind of family and basked in the sounds of lighthearted laughter and togetherness. Now he approached Thad and Leah giving his condolences to Leah and his congratulations to Thad.

Sarah, Alma, and Denise were already making wedding plans, and soon Leah was drawn into their frenzy. Tyrone couldn't stop smiling, knowing Denise would be staying a whole week longer than planned. This was good news indeed, and he congratulated Thad wholeheartedly.

"Who'd have thought such connections could have worked out so well." Tyrone beamed.

"Maybe certain connections will work out for you too, Tyrone," Thad offered.

"Eventually," he hoped with a not toward Denise.

"Can you imagine what it would be like having all three ladies up here?" Thad observed, noticing Alma's blend into the frantic wedding planning. Sarah was starting to perk up too. In fact, in just two days, her countenance had brightened. It was good to see others flourish while staying in this hunting lodge.

"They all come alive when there's a wedding to be planned, don't they?" Tyrone pointed Alma's direction, watching her hands fly and her lips move, giving decorating ideas to Leah for a small wedding reception for friends and family in the large den.

"Yep," Thad talked above all the chatter, "the only thing I want to do is to be the groom. Leah and the ladies can plan to their hearts' content." He was beginning to realize that frenzy is part of wedding planning. "Wow!" He exhaled.

"It will definitely make life more interesting for you, won't it?" Tyrone took the opportunity to encourage Thad as a best-man should. He whistled in awe. "Are you ready for this?"

Thad looked from Leah to Tyrone, smiling. "I guess I'm as ready as Adam was in the Garden of Eden."

"How's that?" Tyrone frowned.

"The same day God presented Eve to Adam, they were married. At least, I've had a few months of letter writing and phone calls to get used to the idea of a wedding day." Thad chuckled. "Can you imagine marrying Denise the minute you two met?"

"Hah," Tyrone exclaimed loudly and saw Denise look over at him with a frown. "It's too staggering to contemplate right now," he assured in a hushed voice. "My wedding day is a long, long way off."

"I thought mine was too, until Leah set the date for Saturday." Thad grinned as he saw the surprise register on Tyrone's face. "I told her she could take as much time as she wanted for planning the wedding." He shrugged with a smile he couldn't hide because he was glad they weren't waiting.

"Maybe Leah will inspire Denise somehow." Tyrone hoped. Thad cocked his head to the side to regard Tyrone.

"You've already asked Denise to marry you?" Thad was incredulous.

"Just about." Tyrone acknowledged.

"How did she react?" Thad was amazed at his friend.

"She smiled, but her eyes made me think she was going to clobber me!"

"At least she didn't say, 'No'." Thad tried optimism.

"At least I can go visit her wherever she calls home."

"You'd leave Alaska for her?" Thad wasn't prepared to lose his best friend and business partner for the sake of love. He was fortunate Leah was willing to make her home here in Alaska with him. They would make family visits to Pennsylvania for her sake if she wanted to, but their permanent residence would always be Palmer, Alaska.

"I'd *visit* and see what happens, Thad. That's all I can do. I love it here, but lately, I've been considering the changes I've seen in your life since you became a believer in Jesus. It's brought back memories of summer Bible camps I attended in junior high. I've wandered away from the commitments I made to the Lord while giving a testimony at the bonfires. At one time, I felt like God wanted me to be a youth leader in a local church somewhere, but I got interested in sports, and the games took me out of church and away from spiritual things. I've totally forgotten about those campfire commitments I made over the years. Listening to you read about Paul's conversion in Acts a little while ago pricked my conscience. I look at Denise and hear about her struggles with spiritual things, and I find that we are much alike. We understand the struggle even though it seems we are at odds with each other most of the time. She makes me own up to my flaws like true north on a compass." Tyrone shook his head. "It pains me to admit that, but it's true." He chuckled. "I like her spunk."

Thad regarded Tyrone in thoughtful silence. A month ago, he would never have thought of Tyrone working as a youth leader in a church, but his own heart had been so closed to God that such a talk as they were having now would not have been conceivable. Tyrone was a good, moral man who always did the right thing and lived a principled life. Thad trusted him without question and relied on his good sense and wisdom when dealing with people. Thad had the hunting skills while Tyrone could discern motives and situations for the benefit of their business. Now Thad understood that Tyrone's childhood had been influenced by church attendance and the guidance of Christian parents. Neither he nor Tyrone ever participated in drinking parties, smoked cigarettes, used drugs, or dated promiscuous girls. Their aim in college was to obtain degrees in their chosen career field that would move them toward an area of community service and training that would promote a successful lifestyle in Alaska. To this end they were devoted. It seemed as if they were entering a time of transition as friends and business partners.

"It sounds like there may be more changes coming than just a wedding," Thad suggested. "The more I read the Bible, the more I'm beginning to understand that God is working things out in my life in ways I could never arrange with my own effort. I used to think I could control almost everything except the taxes, weather, and people. But I'm realizing that giving up control of everything actually allows God to make something I may have started on my own of greater worth. Look at all the good things that are happening. A year ago, I was in my own little world doing my own thing and thinking it all was okay. God has given me so much more now." They stood side by side in reflective silence watching the flurry of happy feminine drama playing out in front of their eyes. "I don't want you to go, Tyrone. That's a hard one," Thad groaned, "but if God is moving you to obey a promise you made years ago at a campfire, you've got to check it out, my friend."

"Well, let's not rush anything just yet. I sure would like it if we could pray together about this, though."

"Sure. We normally get together to talk about the business each morning when we're here at the lodge. It would be a good time to pray."

"Sounds good, Thad." Tyrone studied his friend. "You're changing, Thad, and it's all good."

Thad nodded. He saw Leah and Sarah laughing together and wondered how two sisters could be so different and yet share the same humorous gestures when talking. Both covered their mouth when they laughed. Both pushed hair behind their ears. Both were perpetual fidgets moving constantly at fast speed. The difference was in the eyes. Leah's eyes sparkled with hope while Sarah's eyes shone with resolve.

"Sarah is staying in Alaska?" Tyrone hadn't known until Thad mentioned it on the way back to the lodge.

"Yes," Thad confirmed. "She wants to make a new start for herself and Angie."

"Ah. I see Taima's kind of taken her and Angie under his wing. That little Angie has warmed her way into his heart." Tyrone observed Taima as the older man brought a picture book over to Angie, and sat down with her to look at it together. "These ladies seem to have a way of taking up a lot of space in the heart, don't they?" Tyrone remarked soberly as Denise's lively voice held his attention.

"Their company is better than snagging lines, trudging through cold streams, and freezing in a blind waiting and hoping for a trophy catch—except when they admire the guy who brings home meat for the table." Thad agreed thinking about Taima's recent visit to the old cabin and their talk about Kroft's situation. Tyrone had been called in on their conversation about Kroft as well, and the three men had discussed options. Sarah, as yet, knew nothing about her husband's close proximity.

"Did we catch any fish today?" Tyrone asked. "I can't remember."

"Angie caught a salmon with Taima's help, but it escaped. She screamed and scared a year off my life when it flopped out of Taima's hands and landed in her lap. Other than that one catch, the fish stayed away from our bunch."

"We weren't a successful Alaskan fishing advertisement today, were we?"

"Nope. You'd have won *America's Funniest Videos* for best practical jokes, though." Thad laughed wholeheartedly.

Up in a lonely cabin nestled in a meadow on the side of a mountain, Lance Kroft was thinking about the one who still filled his heart with love. He had cleaned the cabin and made it as comfortable as he could with what Taima had provided. Why? Maybe because he thought it necessary to keep mind and body busy to quell the trepidation in his hopeful heart.

By means of a brief dip in a mountain stream and a good scrubbing with soap and hot water in the warm cabin, it felt good to get the grime and stench washed away. If only his soul could be clean and free of guilt and condemnation. The bath restored the meticulous man he had been as Andrei Garankof. He may not be able to speak or use his own name again, but he could retain the characteristics and qualities he had all but lost fleeing from criminal darkness.

He looked in the small, round mirror Taima had brought and saw an older man. Would Sarah receive him should he have the courage to speak with her? This terrified him, causing him to consider a path leading away from confrontation. Yet his desire to see Sarah again was stronger than the fear nagging for escape. Even if she rejected him, he wanted to see her and fill his memory bank with her lovely face and the face of his child, Angelina, that he might have proof of some happiness to carry away. Taima had called him a coward, and it caused a rise of fortitude strong enough to hold him in this place long enough to keep this divine appointment.

Darkness settled around the alpine shack. A strong wind bent the tops of aspen and spruce with sustained wind gusts that rattled the door and windows of Kroft's abode. The roof beams creaked against the tugs of powerful air currents swirling in all directions. Nocturnal creatures huddled closer to tree trunks and gave up the will to fly in pursuit of prey. A keening wind whistled and howled in unrelenting woe, halting any intruder from disturbing Kroft's contemplation of Psalm 91 he had read from his father's Bible.

He that dwelleth in the secret place of the most High
Shall abide under the shadow of the Almighty.
I will say of the LORD, He is my refuge and
My fortress; my God; in Him will I trust.
Surely He shall deliver thee from the snare of the fowler,
And from the noisome pestilence.

He shall cover thee with His feathers, and under His wings
Shalt thou trust; His truth shall be thy
Shield and buckler.
Thou shalt not be afaid for the terror by night;
Nor for the arrow that flieth by day;
Nor for the pestilence that walketh in darkness;
Nor for the destruction that wasteth at noonday.
A thousand shall fall at thy side, and ten thousand
At thy right hand; but it shall not come nigh thee.
Only with thine eyes shalt thou behold and
see the reward of the wicked.
Because thou hast made the Lord, which is my refuge,
Even the most High, thy habitation;
There shall no evil befall thee, neither shall any
Plague come nigh thy dwelling.
For He shall give His angels charge over thee,
To keep thee in all thy ways.
They shall bear thee up in their hands,
Lest thou dash thy foot against a stone.
Thou shalt tread upon the lion and adder;
The young lion and the dragon shalt thou trample under feet.
Because he hath set his love upon me, therefore will I deliver him;
I will set him on high, because he hath known My Name.
He shall call upon Me,
And I will answer him; I will be with him in
trouble; I will deliver him, and honor him.
With long life will I satisfy him, and shew him My salvation.

His father had marked these two psalms with red ink and placed the Bible's gold ribbon in the center crease. Though the windstorm outside raged against the four corners of the old shack, inside, the lantern light revealed God's ability to protect those who hide in the secret places of the Almighty because they languish in the shadows of this life. Lance Kroft needed a dwelling place, and he was beginning to find it as he read his father's Bible. He reread Psalm 91 then read the previous Psalm 90.

LORD, Thou hast been our dwelling place in all generations.
Before the mountains were brought forth; or ever Thou hadst
Formed the earth and the world, even from everlasting to everlasting,
Thou art God.
Thou turnest man to destruction; and sayest,
Return, ye children of men.
For a thousand years in Thy sight are but as yesterday
When it is past, and as a watch in the night.
Thou carriest them away as with a flood;
They are as sleep; in the morning they are like grass
Which groweth up.
In the morning it flourisheth, and groweth up;
In the evening it is cut down, and withereth.
For we are consumed by Thine anger; and
by Thy wrath are we troubled.
Thou hast set our iniquities before Thee, our secret
Sins in the light of Thy countenance.
For all our days are passed away in Thy wrath;
We spend our years as a tale that is told.
The days of our years are threescore years and ten;
And if by reason of strength they be fourscore years,
Yet is their strength labor and sorrow;
For it is soon cut off, and we fly away.
Who knoweth the power of Thine anger?
Even according to Thy fear, so is Thy wrath.
So teach us to number our days,
That we might apply our hearts to wisdom.
Return, O LORD, how long?
And let it repent Thee concerning Thy servants.
O satisfy us early with Thy mercy;
That we might rejoice and be glad all our days.

Make us glad according to the days wherein Thou hast afflicted us,
And the years wherein we have seen evil.
Let Thy work appear unto Thy servants,
And Thy glory unto their children.
And let the beauty of the LORD our God be upon us;
And establish Thou the work of our hands upon us;
Yea, the work of our hands establish Thou it.

Could it be possible that God would restore all the years of pain and loss caused to him and his family as a result of tragedy? It seemed illogical and fanciful, yet the words of these two psalms replayed the scenario of his life since Chernobyl. These ancient words cut deep into his heart and stung like salt in a cut. Then they promised God's sheltering for the wounded when overwhelmed by evil's bombardment.

He thought about what it might mean to dwell in the secret place of the Most High. Suddenly there was an ear-splitting crack of a tree trunk as it broke and yielded to hurricane force winds surging above and around the creaking walls of his retreat. He heard branches snap like the sharp report of a high-powered rifle as the tree fell against other timber. Kroft's eyes shot upward, scanning the rafters of the shack, knowing the tree might come crashing through the roof and crush this place of solitude with him in it. Frozen in fear, he couldn't move. A cry for divine help exploded from his lips amid the noise of impending disaster.

The floor beneath the table shook violently at the same time the tree made impact with the ground only a few feet from the shack. Supplies flew off the shelf as if pinched in a game of Tiddlywinks. Kroft crossed his hands in front of his face to block the projectiles falling around him. Then there was silence. Muffled sounds of the retreating windstorm gave way to a downpour of rain. Kroft was still alive. He wept not because he was relieved, but because once again, death seemed to tease him. And yet the words of Psalm 91 arrested his attention,

*I will say of the LORD, He is my refuge and my fortress...Thou shalt not be afraid for the terror by night...A thousand shall fall at thy side,*

*and ten thousand at thy right hand; but it shall not come nigh thee…*
*Because thou hast made the* LORD, *which is my refuge, even the most*
*High, thy habitation: there shall no evil befall thee…For He shall give*
*His angels charge over thee, to keep thee in all Thy ways…He shall*
*call upon Me and I will answer him: I will be with him in trouble…I*
*will deliver him, and honor him…with long life will I satisfy him…*

Kroft blinked the moisture from his blurred eyes as he read the verses over again and again until the anxiety subsided and emotional exhaustion caused his head and shoulders to fall slowly forward. His head rested on the open Bible on the table, and he slept soundly. The last cognitive thought, planted deep in his subconscious mind, was of his father's confession of faith in Jesus Christ written in the front of the Bible. How could it be that his father had forsaken the philosophies of socialism for faith in an unseen God? Yet, obviously, he had. His father's faith was his last will and testament to his son. The mission sign JESUS SAVES had immediately registered in Kroft's mind and heart at the same time. He believed that Jesus forgives and saves. In that moment of faith, God became his dwelling place, his refuge, and his Redeemer.

The wilderness outside the cabin door, though lately bruised and battered by a mighty force of warrior winds, now rested, quiet and still. Darkness slithered away in serpent's defeat. The North Star emerged like the star over Bethlehem marking the Savior's birth place in the heart of Andrei Garankof. A heavenly aurora formed a ribbon of wavy white across the starry sky while night creatures began their praise to Him Who keeps them in all their ways. Wolves resumed music lessons for young pups eager to imitate ancient anthems first sung within Eden's Gate. Peace was restored after victory's charge to rescue holy ground. Another one of Adam's seed chose fellowship with Almighty God over the knowledge of good and evil.

Taima parked the pickup at the base of the mountain path. He frowned at the wild sight of fallen trees and debris beyond the windshield. It looked as if a tornado had ripped up the side of the mountain, but he couldn't figure how this could be when there hadn't been any storms in the Mat-Su Valley since this past weekend when Thad and Leah hiked up to the old cabin after eating his roadkill stew.

Caution made him hesitate when Sarah asked where the picnic spot was. She halted Angie's eager attempts to exit the truck by holding out a hand to stop her progress.

"I don't think we can get to the picnic spot today." Taima tried cheerfulness as fear gripped him for Kroft's sake. The path was completely impassable. A mental picture of Kroft being trapped in the cabin, or worse, flashed across Taima's mind, and he started the truck engine as he told Sarah and Angie to buckle up again.

"We'll head back to the lodge. I think we'll need to take a rain check on the picnic, Sarah and Angie. I'm sorry. I'll have to let Thad and Tyrone know about the downed trees, and we'll have to come back and check for damages to the cabin. If it's not too bad, we can reschedule our picnic for tomorrow or as soon as a path is cleared. I'm sorry," he repeated as he turned the truck around and headed back to the lodge at a faster speed.

Sarah wondered at the change in his demeanor from easygoing to serious. *Why would some old cabin need to be checked for damages, just rebuild it for heaven's sakes.*

Once back at the lodge, Taima left Sarah and Angie at the garage door with the picnic basket and headed to Homestead Chapel, where Thad was meeting with Pastor Paytor about wedding arrangements. Tyrone was returning from a trip to Anchorage for supplies from Costco when Taima hailed him on the cell phone and told him what he'd seen. Within fifteen minutes, Thad, Pastor Paytor, Tyrone, and Taima were headed to the site of the storm's destructive path.

"Whoa! What happened here?" Tyrone commented when they gathered at the base of the mountain. Up-rooted birch trees with tangled branches of yellow leaves littered the muddy path where they stood. Farther up the incline, a mass of downed trees converged like a barbed barrier some sixty-feet wide. It looked like a giant had stomped through the wilderness crushing and grinding all living vegetation that impeded its charge of destruction. "Did we miss a storm last night?"

"Not that I know of," Thad assured as the others agreed.

"I hope Kroft is okay." Tyrone pulled a chain saw from the back of his jeep and began checking the gas level and the oil plug. The others pulled equipment from their vehicles and started working to clear a path up toward the cabin.

An hour later, sweat-soaked and muddy, the four men were relieved to see the cabin still standing, though a huge black spruce had fallen near the shack taking with it several tall aspen in its timber to the ground. They crossed the meadow grasses now flattened and dampened by downpours of rain. Here and there, ground squirrels skittered atop the landscape looking for holes or familiar landmarks to show them home, but they were now displaced critters and would have to engineer new underground passages for habitation against cold and enemies.

Andrei saw the men coming and opened the wooden door to greet them. His smiling, clean-shaven form took all four huntsmen by surprise. Pastor Paytor stepped ahead of the group and greeted the notorious drifter. They had met before when Bachman and Kroft broke into the church to find shelter one bitter, cold night last February. The duo raided the food pantry and used the quilts made by the Ladies' Missionary Circle to make warm beds for themselves. Nothing was stolen or damaged except for the locks on the rear exit door; and the kitchen was left a mess. Pastor Paytor found them sleeping soundly early the next morning when he came to the church to turn the heat up for Sunday services taking place later that morning. They deserved to be thrown in jail, but the pastor opted for their help in cleaning up after themselves and asked for their attendance at the morning service in return for freedom. Bachman had flatly refused, cursing his way out the back door as he was escorted to the waiting police cruiser. Kroft, however, chose to remain and clean up the evidence of their overnight slumber party, even making a cursory apology on his way out the door after the church service, addressing Pastor Paytor as *Father Paytor*. It had been a humorous moment for the Baptist pastor who blinked in surprise at the misdirected title.

"Hello, Kroft," he greeted cheerfully, wondering if a friendly approach would curry a favorable response of any kind from the often sullen man. "I see you weathered the storm."

"It was a wild one, yes, Father Paytor." Kroft addressed the church leader with the only title familiar to his Russian knowledge of religion. That there should be numerous clergy titles with respect to every denomination under the sun was lost to Kroft. "I thought I was going to die when I heard the spruce fall." Andrei paused, noticing the surprised look on the men's faces. He smiled broadly and motioned them inside as a light rain began to blanket the area again. "Come inside. It's warm and dry. I fixed the hole in the roof with some of the warped particle board that was over by the wood pile. No more leaks." Arms opened wide to show the dryness of the living space. His voice was no longer snarly and irritated like that of an embittered man.

One by one, they entered the one-room dwelling wondering about the change in Kroft. Thad looked up out of habit to check the hole in the ceiling and saw it was neatly and efficiently patched. The stovepipe was properly connected to the pot-bellied stove and to the fitting in the wall for proper ventilation of smoke. It was warm and cozy as if someone cared about making it a home again.

"You've made some repairs on the place. It looks good." Thad was impressed.

"It's all cleaned up," Tyrone commented, pulling a stool out from under the makeshift table. The other men peeled off coats and gloves before finding a place to sit. Andrei poured hot coffee into clean mugs from the cabin's supply of mismatched dishes. The contents of Taima's box of supplies lined the shelves by size from shortest to tallest. A plate of Ritz Crackers stacked precisely in tens around a centered jar of peanut butter encouraged a peace accord between Kroft and his guests.

"I'm grateful for a place to stay for the time being. I'd like to see Sarah and my daughter before I leave," Andrei stated.

"You can stay as long as you like, especially if you are willing to fix up this place and clear the land around it," Thad offered. "Taima and I can bring supplies to the base of the mountain."

"I have a four-wheeler with a small cart on the back for hauling materials if you want to use it," Pastor Paytor put in. "It might need a little work to keep it running. I'll make sure it has gas and some tools."

Andrei's eyes blurred with emotion that these men should offer any kindness. He had hoped only for their tolerance until he moved on.

"I, uh, told these men your story, Kroft," Taima confessed. "They will keep it in confidence until after you've had a chance to decide about Sarah and Angie. We came to make sure you were okay. I didn't want to bring Sarah and Angie up here if something had happened to you. It's a mess down by the road. I did bring the girls for the picnic, but when I saw the destruction up the side of this mountain, I turned around and took them back to Thad's place. I asked these guys to come with me in case help was needed."

"I came along, too," Pastor Paytor explained, "when I heard you were up here. We weren't sure what we would find, and by the mayhem outside, some kind of major battle was fought on this side of the mountain last night because our side didn't get any storm at all."

"What happened?" Tyrone asked, noticing an open Bible on the smoothly made cot in the corner. The window above was spotlessly clean. The man's past and present seemed out of sync for some reason he couldn't quite comprehend. Why was all this happening now?

"It was calm outside until I came in to fix something to eat. I'd finished mending the hole in the roof, and it was starting to get dark as the clouds began to close in for rain. It was the lightning that startled me the most just as I was heating up some soup. It seemed too cold outside for a thunderstorm, which didn't make any sense to me." Andrei shrugged. "The wind started to gust, so I checked the windows and door to make sure they were closed tightly. I decided to read my father's Bible to get my mind off the storm outside. It was so loud I could hardly concentrate on what I was reading. I read from Psalms." Andrei paused, trying to recall the chapter number. He reached to his right side past Tyrone and lifted the open Bible off the cot. "Psalms 90 and 91 were what I was reading."

"Those are two great psalms to read when there is a sense of danger," Pastor Paytor acknowledged with a nod. "I prayed Psalm 91 over my son, David, every morning while he was in Kuwait during Desert Storm. God mercifully brought him home to us for a while. Now he's in Hungary working with a missionary group. Anyway, you were saying, Kroft?"

"I was in Desert Storm too," Kroft put in dryly, "but I was involved in a different way…" he drifted for a moment then snapped back into the present, "which has no bearing on present things." He waved those memories away with the sweep of a hand. Looking at Pastor Paytor, he said with sincerity, "I'm glad your son came home safely, Father Paytor."

Paytor smiled, nodded, and said, "Please, just call me Frank. You can call me pastor in front of the women and children." He chuckled good-naturedly and saw Tyrone stifle laughter in understanding. Thad and Taima liked the common ground and friendship offered on a first name basis. Paytor, a sincere, humble man, just wanted to be included in this group of men who seemed to be seeking heaven's answers at this point in time. He had been seeking and finding the same answers for many years. Ever since Thad had come to him and shared his salvation testimony, Paytor had taken him under his wing as a spiritual brother in Christ. He prayed for this influential man and his future wife and friends.

"Okay, Frank," Kroft amended with some reserve. "Many times in my life, I've been in great danger, and somehow I've survived when thousands of others have died. This psalm is one that fits my life. I couldn't figure out why I should still be alive. It made me miserable. My father and mother never gave any thought to religion or God. They were scientific people trained to reject religious dogma because it was considered irrational thinking. But at the end of their lives when science had failed them, they both turned to God. My aunt was involved with the underground Christian church. I ignored her talk of faith in Christ as simply fanatical hysterics, yet, as I read the verses of this psalm over and over again, I began to understand something. God isn't a religion. God is God!" Andrei's voice rose in excitement.

He had made a life-changing discovery. "Science limits man to what surrounds him on earth and in the known universe. Science has boundaries and consequences man cannot completely control, especially life and death." His eyes sparkled with excitement. "God is limitless, and that's when the wind blew so hard I heard the trunk of a tree crack and snap. I heard other trees snap as it fell into them." Andrei's eyes were wide with the recounting of danger. "I thought the whole mountain would fall on this cabin, and I cried out to God to save me. In my soul I cried, 'My God, in You I trust!' Everything was chaos around me. The trees hit the ground so close to this cabin it shook the dishes and cans off the shelves. These four walls should have collapsed, I know it. But they

didn't. I knew in my heart and soul that God spared me, yet again..."
Andrei wept openly, realizing afresh that the grace of God had reached out and saved him. The illuminated JESUS SAVES cross on the building of the Chicago mission flashed across his memory. Now he understood. Though he didn't deserve God's mercy and forgiveness, he had it all the same, and it astonished him profoundly.

The other men remained silent as each contemplated Andrei's harrowing experience and his confession of faith. Pastor Paytor stood and moved to Andrei's side. He put a hand on Andrei's shoulder as a father would do to comfort a distressed child.

"Thank you, Father God, for Your redeeming work in this man's life. I ask you to restore him to a normal life with his wife and daughter for Your glory. In Jesus saving name we pray, amen."

Tyrone sat with bowed head thinking about how coldhearted he'd become to God over the years. God had been merciful to him though he had forgotten the commitment to faith that he had made as a young boy. He renewed his commitment to Christ and made a promise to confess his Savior to those who had no idea he was a follower of Jesus Christ.

Thad marveled at the growing evidence of God's moving in the hearts of the people encompassing his life. A desire to read aloud Psalms 90 and 91 in this significant moment moved him to reach for Kroft's Bible and begin reading. The sound of his voice resonating the Word of God's protection filled the mountain cabin with peace.

Afternoon sunshine poured through the window panes, turning the interior decor golden with light. Birds called to other birds in lyrics humans could only imagine to be divine. And yet, God gave to man His Word in David's psalms to show how much He cares for us beyond the sparrow's song.

Taima observed the sacred scene with a skeptical eye. The supernatural had occurred in the storm and in this place. What others called myths and fantasy from spirit realms, he'd believed to be real from childhood stories heard while sitting at the feet of tribal matriarchs. His native background could explain away what had happened last evening. However, they couldn't explain away the soul's transformation by a loving God. Taima had never known a loving deity. As Thad read, Taima observed the younger man's altered demeanor. Thad was genuine, steady, dependable, unwavering in principle, and not given to fanatical activity.

Taima had been his mentor in the early years of the lodge's operation. Both Thad and Tyrone had worked tirelessly to build a solid clientele who returned annually to experience the Alaskan outdoors through fishing and trophy hunting. No parts of the downed animals were wasted, because the meat was donated to feed families through the Alaska Native programs in the Anchorage and Mat-Su Valley. Taima was a member of one of the Alaska Native Corporations and helped arrange for such donations. Lately, Thad was taking more leadership in both the business and his personal life. Leadership for some men meant entitlement to do as they pleased at the expense of others' well-being, but not Thad. Though he was making more decisions and taking on more responsibility, Thad led by serving, by making life better for others, and by wisely protecting those who were dependent upon him. Taima had watched Thad move into manhood. Now he saw an active faith calling him to follow a new leader. Taima would have to make a decision.

# 8

## INTO LIGHT

SARAH WAS ALONE. FOR ONCE IN a long time, *alone* felt good. Taima and Angie had walked back to the Chevy Suburban for more picnic supplies, including blankets. It was cloudy with breaks of sunshine casting long thin timberline shadows across the pre-winter landscape. A picnic in the Alaskan Autumn seemed impractical to Sarah as she rubbed gloved hands together after setting an Igloo cooler on the tumbledown porch of the old cabin. Even with gloves, her hands were freezing.

Checking the tranquility of the wilderness for any sign of wildlife, Sarah wrapped the heavy parka more securely around her thin frame and tucked her gloved hands into the sleeves. A wind stirred the leafless aspens making their lofty branches sway like the ruffling of waves on a small pond. Looking up, she saw the first flakes of snow descend lazily and disappear upon reaching the alpine crest. Sarah blinked when they gently landed on her lashes as if to coax her lids closed in order to enjoy the wonder of winter's first touch. *God sends the snow to lighten the darkest nights.* This thought came to her as the last six years flashed snapshots of memories across her mind's eye.

Sarah had depended on the Light of the world to help her navigate the dark places where emotional trauma had tempted her to succumb to despair. The taunts of rejection had caused her to withdraw from socializing with anyone but her immediate family. Though people were polite, they did not engage her in meaningful conversation nor did she attempt to form close friendships with any of them. She simply did her work in a business-like manner, cordially greeted fellow Christians on Sunday then retired within the safe walls she had made for herself and Angie. The only problem was that Angie was a totally social being, uninhibited, inquisitive, and almost fearless, except for the fact that she didn't like bears anymore—stuffed or otherwise.

It was Angie who always pulled her from the shadows to join life again. As she stood, face lifted toward the heavens, Psalm 91 verse 1 came to mind, "He that dwelleth in the secret place of the most High shall abide under the shadow of the Almighty." A sense of God's presence filled her soul with peace. It was marvelous to experience well-being in lonely places. Sarah braced herself against the panic that so often stalked the edges of her psyche, but there was no sense of impending doom. Amazingly, she hadn't taken any anxiety pills since arriving at the lodge mainly because there had been no need for such medication. The heaviness and paranoia were gone.

Sarah thought about this remarkable fact and realized how different the atmosphere was in Thad's home. She felt completely welcomed and accepted. There was no tension among family members who tried to keep the peace because one person couldn't find it in herself to be agreeable about anything. Everyone got along, showing deference and being considerate of others in speech and actions. Nobody threw temper tantrums when they didn't have their demands and expectations met. And there was no judging via the endless negative remarks made against others, their ideas, way of life, mannerisms, nor were there disparaging remarks about ministry's low income. In Thad's huge lodge, there was genuine hospitality. RELIEF! That's what Sarah called it: blessed, glorious RELIEF! She began to laugh with the pure joy of such relief. "Thank you, God, for giving me courage to break free." It was as if the Holy Spirit could breathe new life and power into her soul. She hadn't known His fullness since working at the mission in Chicago.

Though faith welcomed God's presence always, His power had diminished to a point where Sarah's Christian service seemed hard and fruitless. The constant barrage of resentment from a nurturer had sapped her resilience. God had seen her battle weariness and heard her prayers, not for deliverance, but for some demonstration of grace toward Angie and herself. After a few moments of solitude, Sarah stood and began moving things around for the picnic on the little porch outside the rustic old cabin. The trio of hikers had climbed the mountain path only lately cleared from fallen trees. Taima's brief mention of the storm didn't mean much to Sarah and Angie. It just looked like a tangled wilderness in a place they'd never been before. A little girl's voice from some distance away asked questions, and the answers came from a deep familiar tone Sarah recognized, smiling. Their words were muffled in the distance, but she knew Angie and Taima were near, though unseen.

Kroft had watched Taima leave with Angie. He considered the opportunity given to him to speak with Sarah without frightening her. When she stood up, he moved toward the door. As he did, he bumped the lamp table which scraped the rough wood floor. The sound halted his progress, and he stood perfectly still, wondering if she'd heard anything. Worse yet, he could not even see her to know if she had been alerted. He sighed, thinking how ridiculous all of this was. With resolve, he pulled the door open just as Sarah pushed it. She all but flew through the door into his arms.

"Sarah," he spoke reverently.

The familiar sound of her husband's voice instantly brought her eyes up to his face. A gasp escaped her lips, not of fear, but of recognition that he was flesh and blood and standing before her.

"Andrei." Her lips formed his name in a whisper, and he smiled. She reached up and wrapped her arms around his neck. She was already crying, and he held her tightly to himself as he felt tears of joy slide down his own face at being received with loving kindness. They stood there, holding each other for fear of being separated again. He stroked her hair as he always had. Her head rested against his shoulder contentedly.

"I love you, Sarianna." He breathed these words, and they were like honey to her heart; soul-soothing, healing, and restorative. Leaning back to look into her husband's eyes, she uttered her love and devotion without question.

"I love you, Andrei." There was none of the anger or accusation in her voice that he rightly deserved. Only love, relief, and welcome. He bent and kissed his wife for the first time in over six years. Sarah's memories awakened of their short wedded life of happiness. It had been worth her insistence that they marry even though it could have meant loosing Andrei. Her adamant persistence secured his proposal and the subsequent visit to the court house on West Randolph Street, where they recited their wedding vows to each other. Her memory of that day became a comfort over the years when bewilderment and heartbreak fanned the smoky haze of depression.

When Andrei had disappeared, Sarah had looked for him until she was forced to return home after discovering she was pregnant. First a wife and then a mother, this personal knowledge was her anchor regardless of how others judged her situation. Only Leah and her dad had believed her claim of marriage even though she had nothing to prove the ceremony ever took place. Sarah had tried in vain to get a copy of their marriage license from the Cook County Court records, but when she entered Andrei's name along with hers, it came up as being invalid. Phone calls to the courthouse got the same results. Andrei Garankof didn't exist. Her mother had accused her of making up a name and a husband. Angie had been her only proof. That she had married an unbeliever had been torture over the years because if Andrei was dead, there was no hope of ever seeing him again on earth or in heaven. This had been her greatest fear and one given in prayer for God's intervention many times.

"Do you have our marriage license?" she wondered. Andrei smiled, reaching for his wallet and pulling a faded paper from a leather fold. The imprinted great seal of Illinois was almost flat against the deeply creased document; however, the ink signatures of the officiating judge and witnesses were clearly seen along with their own. He handed it to her, and they spent some time talking quietly about their memories of October 23rd, 1990. Next, Andrei pulled a chain necklace from under his shirt with two wedding bands dangling together. Breaking the chain, he loosed the rings then took Sarah's hand and slipped the engraved ring over her finger. Sarah could not stop the tears that rolled down her cheeks as she placed Andrei's ring over his finger and held his hand firmly in her own. They enjoyed their reunion until Andrei gently pulled Sarah over to the old stuffed chair where they sat down. Sarah still held the marriage license as she sat on his lap and snuggled. Happiness enveloped them both in this moment of reunion.

"Sarianna," he began, "you have not asked me what happened or why I disappeared without getting in contact with you. You deserve answers and so much more." He sighed. "I had no idea we had a little girl." He swallowed hard. "I can only imagine what these past six years have been for you and Angelina." Sarah frowned in puzzlement. "Yes, I know her name. Taima found me up here after the incident at the trading post. He asked me if I wanted to see you and our daughter." Tears gathered in his eyes, and his voice faltered. "I…want…so badly for us to be a family."

"Why can't we be a family? Have you been here all the time?" The questions were starting to come. "What happened?" Sarah wanted to understand, to forgive, and to live happily ever after. Andrei nodded, knowing he had a lot of explaining to do.

"I will tell you everything, even starting before we met. You know about my parents and how I grew up living near universities in Moscow and St. Petersburg, but I never told you about the Chernobyl disaster or why I came to Chicago. It wasn't exactly because of a job offer here in the United States. Six years ago, I couldn't tell you anything without the possibility of endangering your life." He saw concern rise in Sarah's countenance and spoke quickly to curb any anxiety.

"Chernobyl?" Sarah frowned. An inkling of foreboding tickled the edges of reason.

"Yes, my parents and I lived in Pripyat near the nuclear plant until the meltdown of the reactor. My mother and I escaped right before the explosion just after my father called to warn us to leave immediately." He related the events of his life until he came to their marriage at the court house in Chicago and paused to allow Sarah some time to register it all. Her quiet contemplation lengthened to the point that he wondered what she might be thinking.

"Sarah, I'm sorry for what happened to you and our Angelina."

Sarah considered his sincere apology. She was conflicted between the safe, comfortable life she had known a world away from his and the abnormal, tragic life he had known. His had been anything but a normal past. Was his present situation any less dangerous? She wanted to know.

"What will our future be, Andrei? I heard Thad and Taima call you Kroft. Who is Kroft?"

"Kroft is the name I am called now."

"But that's not your real name. Your real name is Andrei Garankof. Why can't you use your real name?"

"The company I worked for was not honest in its business dealings with other countries around the world. I stumbled on to this as I worked on their computer files. They must have known I would figure things out eventually and use what I found out against me. I would be the scapegoat, but I downloaded the evidence onto floppy discs and hid them before I disappeared that day. There was no time to contact you or see you. Hartman was a powerful man with lots of connections. I only had a temporary work visa. I was an officer in the Russian military with a background in intelligence, and my missing father was connected with the Chernobyl disaster. It would have made for spectacular international news." Andrei shrugged then looked directly into Sarah's eyes. "I had no choice if I wanted to protect you. I've changed my name several times over the last six years—at least until coming to Alaska about two years ago. At one time, I thought about catching a ride with a trucker across the frozen land bridge back into Russia, but every time I attempted it, one thing and another hindered me from making a deal with a driver for transportation."

Never, in all her life, had Sarah thought she would be part of such an alliance with any person. Naïve and ignorant of anything other than a wholesome Christian upbringing in a country as free and great as America, Sarah realized that, as Andrei's wife, she was part of his past associations and his present circumstances as a fugitive. He would always be on the run until he returned to Russia--without her and Angie. She and Angie would be left on their own again. It was as if a thousand screams of protest sounded in her soul. Panic gripped her ability to cope while twisting reason into unrealistic monsters. Mortified to think that she was married to a man with such troubling connections to criminal activity, Sarah saw any chance for happiness as hopeless. There would only be more pain.

"No!" She pushed away from Andrei in agony. Startled by her sudden declaration as she struggled to move from his lap, his eyes filled with deep hurt as he reached to calm her, but she stepped away, reaching for the door. She felt suffocated and in need of fresh air.

"Sarianna," he pleaded. "Please, don't leave."

Sarah fled from the cabin. Her rejection tore his heart in half and killed any hopes of a future with a family. His head bowed in quiet resignation. No words came to him that could form a prayer other than to repeat what he already knew by faith: Jesus saves! He hadn't even had the chance to tell Sarah he truly believed in her God. Andrei listened as her retreating footsteps moved further away. He could not call her back. Once again, their love story passed from reality to make-believe.

# 9

## The Trail of Tears

Sarah had been too distraught by the time Taima and Angie saw her walking briskly down the trail toward them to offer any explanation other than that they were leaving right away. Grabbing the picnic basket and blanket from the porch, she headed away from Kroft's hiding place. A multitude of emotions collided with thoughts, both accusing and excusing her behavior toward the husband she had longed for and prayed for with such hope and dreams. Reality was nothing like she had figured it would be. Though the Spirit of God urged her to return to the cabin and face this new reality, her fear refused to accept any challenge that threatened her sense of the familiar.

Taima was heartsick and feeling guilty for causing these people more pain. Angie looked at her mother with a puzzled expression and sighed then reached for her hand to pat it soothingly. It appeared to Taima that as young as Angie was, she understood emotional pain enough to offer her mother comfort. Sarah regarded her daughter for a few moments then silently bent to pick up a corner of the blanket that dragged on the ground.

"I love you, Mommy," Angie said simply. Sarah's eyes moved back to her daughter's where the resemblance of Angie's father was so vividly copied. She managed a tight-lipped smile but did not return the loving sentiment. Angie was troubled by her mother's uncharacteristic distance.

Usually, her mommy reached to hug her and reassure her that all was okay. Sarah could only stand motionless.

"Mommy?" Angie faltered, "Why are you looking at me like Grandma does." Angie's voice was choked with dejection.

At once, Sarah realized what she was doing and reached for her daughter. "I love you, Angie, so very much. I'm just...just remembering some things that happened. They made me sad, but I'm okay now... because you're here." Sarah's throat felt tight. She thought of Andrei. Turning her gaze to the rustic cabin across the wilderness grasses, courage began to replace fear. *Lord, please remove this curse of rejection from my family by the powerful blood of Jesus Christ, I pray. Amen.* A sense of purpose filled her with resolve that turned her feet and moved them in the direction she had just left in fear. In that instant, Sarah knew what God's vision for her family could be with His power to overcome evil with good.

"Wait here, Angie. I'll be back. Everything will be okay." It was faith that moved her past a life of defeat, and faith would restore Andrei to the light of day.

Andrei pulled himself up from the chair and walked slowly to the window to catch one last glimpse of Sarah. Instead, he saw her quick progress back to the cabin. Alarm or surprise registered when her footsteps sounded confidently on the wood planks of the porch. He couldn't resist a humorous smile when she knocked before entering. *She always uses good manners.* This random thought seemed so out of sync, considering the torture inflicted only moments ago. Still, he braced himself for anything while pulling the door open.

"Andrei." Her eyes sparked resolve, and there was no nonsense in her voice. "No more running from life no matter what issues arise. Whatever has to be faced, we will face together, and God will help us." He remembered this look on her face when marriage had been an issue, and it stirred the love and respect for her now as then. Even if he wanted to, and six years ago he had wanted his own way in their relationship, he couldn't say "no" to Sarah. There was a sense of authority when she spoke with conviction about anything that made argument ridiculous. Yes, he had seen the fear in her eyes that had driven her from him only moments earlier, but there was more to Sarah than flesh-and-blood fear.

She had spirit, but not just her own spirit to act in defiance or bravery in a situation. He understood more now than ever before that her faith in Jesus Christ was the power that moved through her quiet faith with gracious endurance. He recognized this because Jesus Christ's saving power was at work in him too.

"I agree. God will help us," he answered, folding her in his arms. They held each other for a few moments until Andrei gently pushed Sarah back to look into her eyes. "I know what I must do. I must go back to Russia. I need to make things right, and it may take some time. If you need to get a message to me, contact Professor Yuri Marianov at the university's finance college in St. Petersburg. He'll get your message to me." Andrei ripped a corner off a newspaper and wrote down a phone number with a name. Folding the dog-ear-shaped paper once, he placed it in Sarah's hand and gently pressed her fingers around it. "Use this number only in case of emergency. If you don't hear from me in two weeks, call the professor." He saw her eyes blink in contemplation of his request as if she was fighting fear. "Sarianna, you are a brave woman in whom God has placed a warrior heart by His Spirit. Rely on Him. I also know Him as Savior, Sarianna. He will fight for us and for our family. I've been reading about this in the Bible my own father left for me after he died. Tell Angelina about me..." He stopped abruptly, fighting emotions that awakened duty in fatherhood.

"Tell me about who?" a child's soprano voice interrupted, but before either parent could answer, a *why* question came. "Hey, Mommy! Why are you talking to a stranger?" Angie's eyes squinted as her bottom lip jutted out like a bulldog. "He's the smelly one who was at Taima's store." Boldness was *not* one of Angie's weak points. Andrei saw this and smiled broadly at his daughter. Her bravery inspired him and made him stand taller as her protector and provider. He answered for himself.

"You are right, Angelina. I am a stranger to you, but not to your mother. I have known your mother for many years, and she is the finest lady I know." Andrei saw Angie's eyes move to Sarah's and back to him. Sarah smiled and nodded encouragement. "Your mother and I met a long time ago and became friends, then we grew to love each other so much that we got married." Eyebrows rose on the face of the inquiring little girl as she tried to put clues together in her childish mind.

"He's your husband, Mommy?"

"Yes, Angie. His name is Andrei Garankof, and he is my husband."

Angie's eyes opened wide, and her mouth dropped open. "Wow! My mommy has a husband just like my friends, Katie's and James's moms. Their mom's each have a husband too. I'm like them! Now they won't make fun of me anymore and say mean things about you, Mommy."

Tears gathered in Sarah's eyes while the weight of a hundred anvils dropped on Andrei's heart.

*God forgive me!* Andrei cried out from his heart as he knelt down in front of Angelina. The eyes of father and daughter met. "You are a brave little girl like your mother. God has given you a brave heart too, just like he gave young Joseph in the Bible. Do you know that story, Angelina?" She nodded slowly, remembering the color of his eyes from her first encounter with this strange man at Taima's Trading Post. They were familiar, as though she'd seen the likeness in a mirror recently. "I just started reading the Bible in the book of Genesis. Joseph was away from his father for many years, but God brought his father back to him." He smiled and winked.

Sarah wiped at tears that rolled over her cheeks and off her chin. Swallowing hard, she remained quiet and willed the sobs that rose in her throat to halt so that time could catch up with father and daughter. Angie stepped back, folded her arms over her chest, cocked her head off to the side, and studied the stranger with interest. Slowly, her head bobbed up and down. A grin started and moved across her face.

"You're my dad!"

Taima and Sarah told the men about the picnic meeting at the old cabin upon returning with one very excited Angie. When Sarah told them of her husband's determination to put his past behind him by coming out of hiding and going to the authorities, both Thad and Tyrone had exchanged looks of concern. If Kroft wanted his past resolved, he was going to need help from those who shared faith in Christ with him.

Leah came in search of Sarah after hearing Angie's claim of seeing her *old but new* dad.

"Sarah, what's this Angie tells me?" She pulled Sarah away from the group of men to the couch in front of a roaring fire in the fireplace. The two sisters bent toward each other questioning and relaying information nonstop. A wedding band was revealed, and a marriage license unfolded with wonder and pride. Thad leaned over the couch as Leah looked up and smiled at her fiancé.

"Tyrone and I are going out for a little while. We'll be back in an hour or call you if we're going to be longer."

"All right, Thad. Thanks." Leah leaned toward Thad for his kiss that touched her lips lightly. His closeness and the power of his attention thrilled her heart and soul.

When Thad and Tyrone reached the old cabin, it was plain to see Lance Kroft, aka Andrei Garankof, was gone. Tyrone lit the lantern as Thad began to search for any clues as to where Kroft might have gone. The one thing they both checked was to see if Kroft took any supplies because it would indicate the length of his trip over a short or long distance. Not a scrap of food remained in the cabin except a small can of hot dogs and beans and a half stack of saltines in case some other weary traveler should need shelter in this place. A paper with a list of camping items written on it lay on the table with three letters "IOU Taima" written at the bottom. Thad and Tyrone both smiled.

"Who would ever have thought a local bum would end up being your future brother-in-law?" Tyrone laughed, though the situation begged serious consideration.

"Knowing Leah, I'm not surprised by much anymore," Thad replied jovially. "I'm enjoying all the family stuff. Some guys like the life of solitude, but I always wanted to be part of a big family. Mom and I spent most holidays by ourselves with no place to go to visit relatives. Many times, Mom worked the holiday shifts at the hospital for the extra income. I spent many a Christmas day just watching TV and eating a microwaved dinner by myself. So I say, the more the merrier."

"I wish Kroft hadn't taken off. He seems like a smart man and one who was brought up with good manners and training. He's also a brother in Christ. We can help him get through this," Tyrone vouched.

The fact remained, Kroft was gone. If he had left shortly after Taima,

Sarah, and Angie had left, they figured by now he had a head start of two hours. But what was his direction?

They exited the cabin after extinguishing the lantern and began a search outside to find traces of footprints in the lengthening shadows of daylight. Thad glanced up at the sky and frowned. It looked like another storm front was proceeding directly toward them.

"Thad!" Tyrone called. When Thad approached, Tyrone pointed to a man's recent boot tracks leading due north. "I think he's headed to Charlie Bachman's place; maybe to pick up some belongings before heading out for other parts. At least, I'm assuming so. It's about a thirty-mile trek inland from our present location. The Hatcher Pass trailhead would cut the hike almost in half. We'll start from there."

"We're going to have to move fast." He exhaled as he unzipped a thermal vest pocket and pulled a cell phone out then flipped it open. Pushing a green button, a small pencil-thin screen lighted showing several bars wavering up and down before going to roaming mode. He held it up and turned until the roaming blinked to all green bars again. He hoped the signal would hold until he made the call.

"Taima," he spoke loudly, wishing for clear reception on both ends.

"Yes. Go ahead, Thad," Taima yelled back, plugging the other ear wondering if it would ever be possible to talk normally over a cell phone.

"Kroft is headed inland, and we're going after him. Can you pull the Trail-Pax together and have it ready for pick up at the Hatcher Pass trailhead?"

"Sure. I'm on it." So saying, Taima closed his cell and headed for Alma.

"T-Pax." He signed, and Alma flew into motion as though every second counted. Denise saw the signal pass between the two and the resulting actions. Her dad's police experiences flashed through her mind, and she followed Taima out the front door and down the steps.

"Taima, what can I do to help? I know about these things. Tell me what to do."

Without slowing, Taima reached the bottom of the steps, turned and tossed a set of keys at Denise. "Get the Ford truck and back it up to the garage," he ordered. Denise's eyes instantly darted around the parking area for the Ford. Questions came to mind, but she didn't ask them.

There was no time for them, and Taima wouldn't answer them anyway. Her eyes found the Ford, and she sprinted to the vehicle. Checking the area around her for any of the others, she opened the driver's door and hopped in. She found the shape of the key that was similar to her Ford Mustang and pushed it into the starter. A thumbs-up turn, and the engine fired smoothly. Glancing up at the rearview mirror and side mirrors, she beeped the horn to alert anyone behind her and reached for the shifter. To her surprise, the shifter was on the floor, not behind the steering wheel.

"Aw, gees!" she exclaimed aloud. "It's a stick shift!" Muttering under her breath, she looked at the shifting knob and saw the diagram of the shifting order on the top. Her eyes dropped to the floor beneath her feet where three pedals stood out. Two of them she understood to be the brake pedal and the gas pedal. The third pedal had something to do with the shifter, but only heaven knew what that could be. "Lord, give me some knowledge here, please," she prayed, and then she remembered the riding lawn mower she'd used when mowing the family yard as an adolescent. It had more than two pedals and a shifter too. Could it be the same?

"One way or the other, this truck is backing up to that garage," Denise said aloud with determination. Right foot pressed the brake. Left foot pressed the clutch. Right hand pushed the shifting knob forward. Right foot released the brake and pressed the gas. Tires spun gravel forward under the wheels as the Ford truck shot backward. Denise cranked the steering wheel so that the truck arched ever backward in the general direction of the rising garage door. Two boots appeared, then two knees as the garage door rose. If Taima had been able to see what was coming directly at him, there is no doubt he would have flinched, or maybe even scrambled to get out of the way. However, his sight was blocked by the rising panels in front of his face. Denise saw the garage door approaching fast and stomped the brake pedal hard. The Ford skidded to a tire-screeching stop just three inches from Taima's boots. And still, the garage door rose up past Taima's parka without him ever knowing how close he'd come to seeing his life flash before his eyes. Instead, his eyebrows arched in admiration as Denise hopped out of the truck flustered. Her legs felt like Jell-o because of the close call to Taima.

"Good job, Denise. Thanks." He called after her and started loading the bed of the truck with the T-Pax backpacks and other supplies, which consisted in part of subzero clothing/camping gear, rifles, ammunition, food supplies, first aid equipment, maps, and signaling devices.

"Sure," she said to him, but looking heavenward, uttered, "Thank you, Jesus, that I didn't kill Taima or anyone else." Out loud she sang, "Angels watchin' over me, my Lord, all night all day, angels watchin' over me," as she pulled her wobbly self up the steps to the front door. Taima frowned and shook his head, puzzled by her strange ways.

Alma tapped Taima on the shoulder as he closed the tailgate of the truck. He turned and read her lips as her fingers formed the words, "Remind Thad he's getting married in three days." She saw Taima's brows arch at this important communication.

"I'll remind him," Taima promised. "I'll be back." Less than a minute later the truck rumbled down the drive, turned right at the end of the driveway, and moved out of sight. Alma looked up at the windows of the lodge, knowing the next few days were going to be challenging for the bride-to-be. A silent prayer formed on her lips for God's grace to work everything out. Then Alma gave thanks. Faith wasn't just asking; it was giving thanks for what God was already at work doing on the behalf of His saints. She entered the garage, pressed the button on the security pad, and the door slid down smoothly. Leah would need to know what was transpiring. Alma would stick close to her and the others. There was the possibility that wedding plans might be postponed. Alma knew situations like these could take days before they were resolved.

The trailhead near Hatcher Pass came into view as Tyrone and Thad approached the parking area in the Chevy Suburban. Taima was about ten minutes away, so Thad took the opportunity to call the lodge and speak with Leah. The screen displayed the phone number, and he heard a gurgled buzz that half-sounded like a ring. To Thad's relief Leah answered, but her words were broken and scratchy. He walked away from the vehicle hoping to get a clearer signal and was rewarded when he heard her finish saying, "Trying to find Sarah's husband?"

"Yes. As soon as Taima comes, we're headed toward Charlie Bachman's place. I think that's where Kroft is headed. Hopefully, we'll pick up his trail sooner rather than later. There are cabins along the trail for hikers to duck into overnight. Tyrone is thinking we may need to use one of them." Thad paused, thinking about his next statement.

"Leah, this could take some time, maybe even a few days. Our wedding…" he stopped midsentence.

It was quiet on Leah's end for several moments before she answered. "Thad, I love you and I love my sister too. I've lived with her through the heartbreak, and I couldn't be perfectly happy knowing she and Andrei were still apart. We need to help them. If we have to delay our wedding day, then I'm okay with it. I want you all home safely, Thad. Do what you need to do. We'll all be praying and waiting."

"Thanks, Leah, for understanding. I love you."

"Love you too."

Thad smiled his good-bye and pressed the red button. Next he called Pastor Paytor and relayed their situation.

"What can I do besides pray for you guys?" the pastor asked.

"I have Leah's dad's phone number. Do you have something to write with? I'll give it to you."

"Yes." His fingers scrambled around the top of a desk for paper and pen. "Go ahead with the number." Thad called the numbers off.

"Would you call her dad, please? His name is Cole Grant. Tell him all that is going on with us and Sarah's husband. Have him contact Denise's dad. They know each other through their daughters, and Denise's dad is a police detective in Chicago. I need him to see what he can find out about Global Financial Investors dating back to 1990. Whatever information there is, have Pastor Grant or Denise's dad send it to the Alaska State Troopers. I'll contact you when I can get a signal. Thanks, Pastor. Hopefully, this can be resolved soon. I have a wedding date with you on Saturday that I'd like very much to keep," Thad said dubiously.

"I'm sure you would, Thad." He chuckled good-naturedly. "I'll get right on this. Godspeed to you and Tyrone. I've been praying for Andrei throughout the day."

"Thanks. Good-bye."

"Bye."

Thad looked at the cell screen and noticed the low battery warning. Some day he hoped somebody would make a cell phone that kept a charge longer than three calls. He flipped it shut with annoyance and tossed it on the seat. Then again, he should be thankful that he was able to get through to three people clearly. The first call placed right after leaving the old cabin where Kroft had been was to a friend at the Alaska State Trooper station near Wasilla who knew someone in the Anchorage FBI office. The proverbial ball was rolling, but time was short. They needed to find Kroft before it appeared he was running--again. With all his heart, Thad prayed Kroft wasn't running.

Taima rolled to a stop with the pickup. Thad greeted him, and they started pulling the Trail-Pax from the truck bed. Tyrone noted the late-afternoon sunlight as he slipped into warmer gear and prepared for their hike into the mountains.

"Does your cell have a full charge?" Thad asked.

"Yes," Tyrone answered. "We have maybe two hours of daylight left. We should be able to make it to the forest service cabin by nightfall."

"Right. Taima, does your cell have a full charge?"

"Almost a full charge. Take it." He handed the cell to Thad, and it was quickly stowed and zippered inside a chest pocket.

"My cell is on the seat. Take it with you and charge it at home. I'll call you on it when we have any news. I'm not using the landline for any more calls until we know where Kroft is."

"Got it. You guys be careful and don't go getting yourselves lost out there," Taima teased. Both men grinned and headed toward the trailhead. He watched them disappear into the dense arboreal wilderness before grabbing Thad's cell phone from the seat and locking the Suburban. A few steps and he was back inside the truck for the return trip to the lodge.

# 10

## Dad Can Fix It

Frank Paytor heard the dial tone before he replaced the cordless phone in its cradle. He had just finished a call to Cole Grant concerning Sarah's estranged husband. Sitting back into his black study chair, he tapped fingertips together as he contemplated all that was confronting the new believers who were looking to him for spiritual guidance.

For years, he had prayed for this Alaskan community and its diverse cultures. He and his wife, Betty, had come to Alaska over thirty years ago as missionaries endeavoring to reach people with the good news of the Savior, Jesus Christ. From a home Bible study, a group of believers had grown to the point that a church building had been constructed. In the years after the building program, the addition of new members had slowed to a point that there were no new faces in the congregation. It was as if the building of a physical church had been the only goal, and once that was completed, the membership became comfortable in their designated pews and ceased to reach out to the unchurched and unbelieving in their community.

*The soul-winning effort was the missionary pastor's responsibility.* Pastor Paytor reflected on this troubling thought wondering how he had failed to convey the missionary vision to the believers God had called him to recruit into service. Yes, there were one or two faithful deacons who accompanied him on visits to hospitals and on neighborhood door-to-door visits, but it had become a dutiful task as routine as washing one's hands before and after eating. On Sunday, they came; he preached, they ate the spiritual food. He prayed a blessing over them, they left for a week and returned the next Sunday to do the same thing over again like the never-ending song on the Barney show his grandchildren used to watch. It made him crazy. They would march around the living room singing it over and over until Grandma Betty would come to the rescue with chocolate chip cookies. A chuckle rumbled at the happy thoughts of his grandchildren.

His thoughts turned in the direction of a passage of scripture from Revelation about the seven churches. Reaching for his Bible, Pastor Paytor opened to the first chapter of Revelation and read through to chapter 4. The Holy Spirit directed his focus word by word, thought by thought through the familiar chronicles of the seven churches until he read of the church body known as the Laodiceans. Paul the Apostle had written letters to the churches in Asia Minor, encouraging them to walk worthy of their salvation in Christ Jesus. The churches in Galatia, Ephesus, Philippi, and Colossae had received letters from Paul, which were included in the canon of scripture the pastor often read. He wondered why Paul's letter to the church at Laodicea was not included in scripture though Paul mentioned sending an epistle to the Christians in Laodicea.

Thumbing several pages back to Paul's letter to the Colossians, he read through the four-chapter missive noting Paul's specific reference to the Laodecian Christians, not one, but five, times. In the closing remarks to the Colossian church members, Paul urges, "Now when this epistle is read among you, see that it is read also in the church of the Laodiceans, and that you likewise read the epistle from Laodicea" (Colossians 4:16). Creases formed above the pastor's brow as he contemplated Paul's instructions to the Colossian Christians. What happened to the letter written to the Laodiceans? Were these letters to the churches at Colossae and Laodicea ever exchanged and read aloud to their congregations? Could it be that though Paul had sent a letter to Laodicea, there had been no response from this church, and for this reason, he encouraged the exchange of letters between churches hoping to hear some news from the Laodicean Christians? Had the lethargy already permeated the Laodicean congregation to the point that Paul's letter was ignored or deemed unimportant and subsequently lost? It was a mystery.

In any case, Pastor Paytor considered Revelation's reference to this seventh church and its divine rebuke for being neither hot nor cold. These Christians had fallen under the examining eye of the Almighty. Lethargy had rendered them lukewarm, like stagnant pond water on a warm summer's day. The pastor knew lethargy was the enemy of vibrant Christianity. It drained love for lost souls from the Christian's heart and removed fervor for service. It also robbed the church of God's abundance ever available to meet the needs of His people as a testimony to the world. Like the church of Philadelphia, the Laodiceans had lost their fervent love for God. Pastor Paytor looked up from the holy writ and gazed out the large window beyond his study chair. Pioneer Peak framed the glass view like a picture rising from the bottom of the pane to the top of the header before coaxing eye movement across the majestic horizon. Creation displayed the handiwork of an ever energetic Creator.

*God,* he prayed earnestly, *forgive me for my own heart of indifference and please stir within me a fire for souls. I need more sensitivity and strength to serve these people, Lord. I pray that Your Holy Spirit might have the preeminence in every sermon I preach to move your people out of lethargy into victory for the sake of the cross and cause of Jesus Christ. God, increase my capacity to love You above all this world offers.* Pastor Paytor believed that God had heard his confession and request for the Spirit's promptings. He realized God's Spirit was moving in the lives of faces new to the area. He rejoiced for Alma, Thad, Leah, and the curious Andrei Garankof, who had become children in God's family of believers. He rejoiced for the evidence of God's work rekindled on this mission field. It was a blessing to see positive things happening again in a place where tragedy often comes knocking on the parsonage door.

The study chair squeaked as Pastor Paytor pushed out of it. Walking over to the sofa, his knees bent until they pressed the carpeted floor. With head bowed, he made supplication for Andrei's safe return, reciting the promise of Romans 8:28, "And we know that all things work together for good to those who love God, to those who are the called according to His purpose."

"We are the called, Lord," he prayed aloud, "who have placed our complete faith and trust in You. You are able to sanctify us and keep us from stumbling, and to present us faultless before the presence of Your glory with exceeding joy." An often repeated benediction followed. "To God our Savior, Who alone is wise, be glory and majesty, dominion and power, both now and forever. Amen" He pushed back from the sofa and stood. Refreshed and encouraged from soul fellowship in prayer with the One he'd known for years, Pastor Paytor left the study and headed to the kitchen to check on his wife's meal preparations. His cheerful inquiry was greeted with a smile.

"You're in a good mood," she said lightheartedly and looked up to see the shining face of her preacher husband. Nodding with a knowing smile, she guessed, "You've got a sermon brewing in your heart."

He laughed. "You know me well, my dear."

"The fear of the Lord is the beginning of knowledge, Proverbs 1, verse 7," she quoted with a smile, waiting for his verse recitation to follow.

"Thy Word is a lamp to my feet and a light to my path, Psalm 119 verse 105," he returned, enjoying the volley of scripture verses that was their custom since they had dated in bible college.

Pastor Cole Grant laid the cordless down on his study desk after talking with a new pastor friend from Alaska. Not only had Pastor Paytor relayed Thad's request for information on Sarah's husband, but wedding plans were discussed as well. A quick glance at the wall clock, minus one hour meant it was about five-fifteen in Chicago. He opened a desk drawer and pulled out a phone directory, running an index finger down the tabs to C where Denise's home phone number was listed along with the names of her dad and mom, Edward and Junia Cox. The number sequence was ready for finger depressions on the key pad, but Cole paused to reflect on Sarah's phone call just prior to Pastor Paytor's.

She had told him about Andrei's Russian background, including the disastrous Chernobyl crisis involving his family and their flight to safety. It seemed worlds away from this quiet little hamlet in Northwestern Pennsylvania. Then there was Andrei's arcane associations with international corporations that reeked of corruption, and it triggered a huge protective instinct in Cole Grant toward his daughter and granddaughter. Once this call was made, even as discreet as he hoped it would be, there was no telling what the results would be, or how the outcome would affect the lives of those he loved, whether in pain or triumph. He'd lived her heartache with her and defended her honor when others, even fellow pastors, had urged him to send her packing. Now she was far enough away that he couldn't shelter her anymore.

Doris Grant tapped three times on the study door and entered without waiting to be acknowledged. Seeing the troubled look on her husband's face, she straightened her shoulders, set her chin level, and walked to the chair in front of her husband's study desk. Her gray eyes met his dark-brown ones as she sat and crossed her legs as if anticipating a lengthy pow-wow. She was cool under fire and could make a saint squirm with a mother's frown of disapproval. She was respected in the church, though not usually befriended except by those who were willing to do her bidding simply because they were willing to serve, no matter the disposition of their Mrs. Pastor. Those who described her to newcomers said their pastor's wife was a tough lady who could organize any project and carry it through with success no matter what difficulty arose. Did she have a soft side? Yes, but nobody knew what it might be—except Cole Grant.

"I overheard the phone call from our Sarah," she confessed without any remorse for eavesdropping. "It sounds like her long-lost husband needs help," she understated dully.

"Yes. I was just about to call Ed Cox, but had to stop and think about it first." He was contemplative. The clock ticked in the silent space between the couple. Dust flecks danced slowly on long shafts of late-afternoon sunshine that poured through diamond-cut window panes on either side of the old fireplace.

"Let's pray together." Cole Grant bent forward with bowed head and began praying. Doris instantly bowed her head and followed his words until memories distracted her thoughts from the prayer. She was a young schoolgirl full of laughter and fun when it came to recess time on the playground at Unionville Elementary. She had friends and could make friends easily even if she couldn't spell most of the words on any given list of spelling words. Those awful addition and subtraction flashcards were all guesswork as far as she was concerned. And when the eight-year-old Doris Schleigle was asked to read from Dick and Jane's primer, she'd stutter through the words until the teacher was either distracted or dazed, then she would make up her own story by looking at the pictures and pretend to read faster than any student in the classroom. Of course, the boys would crow out loud that she was cheating while her girlfriends giggled their support as they crouched down behind their own primers. She had two favorite things in school. Art class and library were favorites because of a love to draw and a love to listen to Mrs. Perry reading stories about *Mr. Popper's Penguins* and about *The Boxcar Children.* Her other favorite thing about school was recess when she and her friends ran from the swings to the merry-go-round to the teeter-totter to the monkey bars, laughing and calling to each other like squirrels and chipmunks chasing one another, jumping from branch to branch.

Then a new boy from another country had entered her second grade class. He was blond with light-blue eyes that always seemed to gaze at her and make her want to look away in annoyance. This new boy was chubby, and when he spoke, his English wasn't clear like all the rest of her classmates. Unfortunately, his name was Wolfgang Brandt, and don't you know, the boys howled like wild wolves when they thought a teacher wasn't nearby to provide extra practice with subtraction tables for taunting the new student. For these two differences, he was mercilessly teased even though he tried to reach out in friendship to new classmates. Doris knew he was smart, too. When the teacher did the addition and subtraction flashcard drills, Wolfgang always got every answer correct. She was lucky if she got one correct answer out of the fifty cards flashed before her very eyes. And, he could spell, too!

Everyone wanted Wolfgang on their team because the winning line got a treat. When it came to recess, though, Wolfgang was a loner like no other. Well, not quite. He followed Doris around like a lovesick puppy dog--when he could catch up to her. When her classmates perceived Wolfgang had a crush on Doris Schleigle, she became their second target for teasing. In fact, the snooty Jenny-girl in third grade ended up on the ground with pea gravel in her mouth after Doris pushed her down for calling her Mrs. Wolfgang Brandt. She had yelled back that she would never like a fat boy like Wolfgang *ever*. It had been a defining moment in her early life. She saw the unmistakable hurt she had caused fill Wolfgang's eyes with tears of humiliation. Years later, those blue eyes shone so clearly in her memories.

The principal called her dad at work, and the next thing she knew, he was taking her hand, and they were walking out the front doors of the school to the toilet-blue Chevy Impala, which really was the twilight-blue Chevy Impala—but she couldn't say *twilight*. Dad Schleigle had gone right to the black couch where all the talks took place when she had been bad. The talking came first, then the spanking with the paddle, then the praying and the hug. Doris had been through this routine many, many times. But dad just talked this time. He told her a story about a disciple of Jesus named Peter, who walked with Jesus but denied even knowing Him when terrible things happened to Jesus. The Son of God stood alone as those who knew him turned their backs on him.

Dad wanted to know if Wolfgang had ever been unkind to Doris in any way. She had answered defensively that he always followed her and wanted to talk to her, but that he had never been unkind, just 'a-no-yin'. Dad had told her that maybe she should try to be just a friend to Wolfgang and see what happened. "That he has chosen to befriend you, Doris, shows that he sees something valuable in you. Have you ever called him names or teased him like the other students?" Doris answered that she had called Wolfgang a fat boy. Dad said it was unkind to call people names or make fun of them. God wanted her to be kind to everybody, even the ones who were mean—like Jenny-girl. At the mention of Jenny-girl, Doris realized she'd rather be friends with Wolfgang than with mean old Jenny-girl any day of the week. Besides, she didn't want to be mean to anybody *ever* again; she just wanted to play with her friends at recess and have fun out there.

To her great surprise, Wolfgang Brandt came to her church with his parents that Sunday after his first week at school. He wouldn't talk to her or even look at her. Now she felt the hurt and wanted to make it go away. After shaking the preacher's hand at the door, Doris dashed outside to check for Wolfgang. He stood quietly beside his parents, his back toward her. He always wore bulky sweaters with all the colors of her crayons. Walking up to him, Doris tapped him on the shoulder, hoping he would turn around, and then scared that he would turn around. Only Wolfgang's head turned slightly as the pupils of his blue eyes slid to the side to check the peripheral object off to his left side. Doris jumped on this tiny opportunity to tell him she was sorry for saying mean things to him and asked if they could be friends—not girlfriend or boyfriend kind of friends—just friends.

Wolfgang had turned to face Doris, regarding her with squinted eyes. He was working on trusting her. One side of his mouth turned up in a grin; nodding, he extended a hand as if making a contract with Doris. She shook his hand, pumping it as she had seen her dad shake hands with people at his auto, home, and life insurance business. After that, they were inseparable until Wolfgang's missionary parents had returned to Germany eight months later. When she asked him why he had always followed her that first week of school, his reply was that he had seen her coming out of church the Sunday before and figured she was a Christian too. Wolfgang's dad had preached that all believers around the world were brothers and sisters in Christ. He had felt lonely and out of place until seeing Doris in his class at the new school. Her rejection had caused him such confusion that he'd closed up to everything and everyone until her tap on the shoulder and subsequent apology had set his faith to right again.

"Lord, give us wisdom to help Sarah's husband, Andrei, find his way back to an honest life of fellowship with his family and with You." Pastor Grant's words of supplication brought Doris Grant's thoughts back to the present. "Help him find Your Way in his new faith. Give him courage to face whatever will be the means of bringing victory in Jesus to his family as a result of this situation. Now we give you thanksgiving and praise for how You will work all things together for those who love You and are the called according to Your purposes. We pray in Jesus wonderful name, amen."

"Amen," Doris Grant echoed mildly.

In those brief moments of childhood reflection, the Holy Spirit of God had worked on her heart: softening years of ministry service where she had become driven by relentless goals to see her husband's ministry grow. She had lost the tenderness for people by becoming a judge and jury instead of assisting people in their service for Christ. God knew Doris Grant's capacity to befriend people. He had created within her an ability to rally support and to see a challenge-through to its accomplishment with rejoicing instead of dismal relief. Wolfgang Brandt's influence during those eight months of friendship had broadened her view and helped her to understand that it was okay if people were different from what she was used to. He opened her heart to Germany and, as she'd grown into young adulthood, to the world. Amazing her at this moment was the fact that two of her three daughters had reached beyond the confines of their hometown to live in a place that was a mere pinpoint on the Belham floor globe over in the school's learning center. Doris had headed a fund-raiser to purchase that expensive world globe for the students' perusal in geography studies.

Sarah's husband was now another son-in-law to add to their growing family. Leah's fiancé, Thad, would be joining their clan this Saturday if all went as planned. Rachel's husband, Clive, had been welcomed with open arms because he was already a pastor of a church in Michigan. The common connection helped bridge differences in background and made it easier to get along. But Thad was a hunting guide in Alaska—a new Christian and one she hoped, for Leah's sake, was genuine. The elusive Andrei was Russian and on the run from two countries—not a good start for warm parent-in-law relations. Sarah said he was recently saved too. Had the world changed so much that single Christian men were in the minority? Or did God have bigger plans and a broader vision that only His grace could orchestrate no matter the circumstances of her daughters' choices? God had called these men to salvation through the love of her daughters. Doris could easily reject them for good reason and treat them with contempt, or she could accept them and offer friendship as she had to Wolfgang Brandt many years ago. It had been a life-changing friendship savored in youth. Doris had a choice to make.

"Cole," she started, looking him in the eye, "I think we need a vacation."

Grant's eyes blinked wider, and a smile spread across his face. "Those were my thoughts exactly, my dear. You call the airlines for a flight to Alaska with a layover in Chicago. I'll call Ed and arrange to meet him and Junia somewhere. We'll need overnight accommodations near O'Hare. I want to go with Ed to check this out. 'For though we walk in the flesh, we do not war according to the flesh; For the weapons of our warfare are not carnal but mighty in God for the pulling down of strongholds,'" he quoted out loud to Doris as he reached for the phone. Silently, he thanked the Lord his wife was in agreement. The hesitation was replaced with anticipation.

"Sounds like you're working on a sermon," she surmised knowingly then stood and left the study to find a phone book with listings of travel agencies. Four hours later, the travel agent called back to confirm their travel itinerary to Anchorage, Alaska, with a twenty-two-hour layover in Chicago that included overnight hotel reservations near O'Hare Airport. They would leave within the hour for Pittsburgh. After calling Ed Cox, Pastor Grant had called his deacons notifying them of their hasty travel plans for the next week. All five church services would be covered by a retired pastor from the area. Doris had them both packed and ready to go when Deacon Tom Couchman and his wife, Mary, drove up to the parsonage.

Quickly, the men loaded the minivan for the trip to the airport, and they were off for parts to the west and far north. The ladies chatted back and forth in the second seat about alterations in the church schedule of activities the next week before settling into conversation about family matters. In the front seat, Pastor Grant and his head deacon discussed the circumstances surrounding their trip to Alaska for a wedding. Grant had waited until they were on their way to the airport to mention anything about Sarah's estranged husband. Tom Couchman was a trustworthy man, a long-time Christian and a seasoned Pennsylvania State Trooper. Grant had relied on him many times for advice concerning safety matters at the church and the Christian academy. Upon hearing his pastor's account of Andrei's situation and their efforts to gain some knowledge of Global Financial Investors, Couchman lowered his voice.

"That's the investor company that was indicted on corruption charges some four years ago or so. I remember this well, because a local police auxiliary we both know as the Fraternal Order of Police had invested in GFI for the purpose of growing funds to assist disabled policeman and their families. GFI's corrupt financial dealings were discovered by an FBI plant in the company. As a result, a lot of charitable organizations lost hundreds of thousands of dollars. I can tell you for a fact that if this guy knows anything about GFI's business dealings, he better turn himself in to the FBI ASAP. A couple of the executive officers are in prison at present, but not all of them. The top exec wasn't indicted because his lawyer found a loophole."

"Great," Pastor Grant said without any enthusiasm. "Truth is fallen to the streets," he mumbled to himself. The Pennsylvania countryside passed like a blur when he glanced out the side window. *God,* he prayed silently, *this is so much bigger than I am. Do through us what we can't do.*

"Do you have help with this when you get to Chicago, Pastor?" Couchman asked.

"Yes. I've contacted a police detective who is a family friend."

"Good. If you need anything, call me. I have a few friends in Chicago too." He glanced over at his pastor and grinned.

"Thanks, Tom. I'll keep in touch."

"We'll be praying all the while you're gone, Pastor. Don't forget to enjoy your daughter's wedding. But not too much. We want you back with us." He reached into his jacket pocket with one hand and pulled out an envelope and handed it to Pastor Grant. "The deacons and I thought this would come in handy for your trip to Alaska."

Grant frowned as he accepted the envelope and carefully pulled the lip open. His eyes bulged then watered at the stack of travelers checks enclosed.

"You might need a rental car. Then too, Leah might need some wedding stuff. Or you might want to go sightseeing or buy souvenirs. Just take some time to have fun, Pastor. It's the chance of a lifetime."

Grant shot a side glance to the seat where Doris and Mary were engrossed in conversation about the fall mission's project. He looked at Tom with sincere gratitude in his voice. "Tell the men, 'thanks'."

"Got it." Tom smiled and glanced in the rearview mirror at his Mary. The gift had been her thoughtful idea on a moment's notice.

Ed and Junia Cox met Cole and Doris Grant in the lobby of the hotel connected to the O'Hare airport terminals in Chicago. They greeted one another and proceeded to a restaurant where a friendship could be rekindled over a meal. After a beef brisket dinner, Doris invited the Cox's up to their modest but comfortable room for coffee. Dessert was ordered via the room service menu, and the ladies found a comfortable couch on which to sit and discuss their daughters' recent adventures to the far north.

Cole and Ed each took a seat at a small bistro table next to a large window with a view of the Chicago skyline. The vertical lights of skyscrapers against the navy background of nightfall made the country pastor gaze in awe. *The fields are white for harvest, John 4 verse 35,* Grant thought to himself. It dawned on him that the lights of the city before him were mostly *white.* Although he knew the color white mentioned in the book of John had to do with grain fields ready for harvesting, the significance of the neat vertical rows of lights encased in modern towers of Babel reminded one of plump ears of sweet white corn. Could it be that this query on behalf of Andrei was really a mission to harvest souls for Christ? It was a divine reminder that the Gospel would be his first defense.

"It's a beautiful sight, isn't it, Brother?" Ed commented, pulling Cole's attention from the Tetris grid to the single cube they occupied.

"Yes." Cole leaned forward, fingers interlocked and resting on the shiny black tabletop. Time was limited, prompting him to focus on the telling of Andrei's story and his association with GFI along with the concerns this father had for his daughter, Sarah, and granddaughter, Angie. Ed listened intently as Cole related the information Tom had offered about GFI's corruption indictment. When Cole finished he sat back, waiting for Ed to comment. The room was quiet. Both ladies had turned to listen.

"Not a problem, Cole. Let's go downtown and check out a few things." So saying, Ed stood and waited for Cole to scramble out of his chair, surprised that there seemed to be an easy solution to this problem. Maybe in his ignorance, he had overreacted. Then again, Tom's comments had seemed weighty. Nevertheless, time would tell.

"We'll be back in a few hours, Doris, Junia. I'll give you a call if we're going to be longer." Ed winked at Junia while Cole gave Doris an uncertain frown. Quickly pulling on a jacket, he followed Ed out the door.

They took the elevator down to the lobby and walked out under the covered entrance. Ed handed a parking coupon to a uniformed valet who dashed away into the crowded airport. Shortly, a candy-apple-red Ford Mustang rumbled to a screeching stop in front of the two men.

"I need to have Denise's brake shoes replaced." Ed's head tilted off to the side as he grinned. "She goes through more brakes than a fleet of city buses." Cole laughed, enjoying the lighthearted Ed Cox. Both of them bent and twisted, ducked and hunched until at last their middle-aged bodies conformed to the classic bucket seats of the speedy red racer. Glad Ed knew his way around the city, Cole enjoyed the sights all around him as Ed pointed out various landmarks, giving facts like a tour guide. Only a few months ago, Denise had showed Leah similar places before landing them on the George Endicott Show to sit on Alaskan bachelors' laps.

When they stopped in front of a high-rise office building, Ed's right arm pointed off to Cole's right. "That's Global Financial Investors, Cole."

"It doesn't say that on the header." Cole observed, puzzled. The building header read Trans World E-Conomists.

"Similar outfit, new name, and a new game." The stoplight turned green, and Ed turned the Mustang right around the corner and right again onto a parking ramp.

"We're going to make a friendly visit up to the CEO's office."

Cole turned to look at Ed with something akin to alarm on his face. Ed smiled. "Not to worry, my friend. I wouldn't take you into the lion's den if I thought the lions weren't caged. I think you'll be pleasantly surprised by what you find."

"I'm totally mystified, Brother. Help me out here, please." This was just plain strange.

"I'll explain everything when we meet the CEO. I promise. Let's go see the boss," Ed said cheerfully, untangling himself from the compact Ford. Cole exited likewise, hoping with all his heart he wasn't going to be a lamb led to the slaughter. He didn't know Ed all that well—just a few phone calls back and forth to discuss their daughters' visits to the college dean in order to compare copies of the girls' lists of infractions and resulting demerits. Ed Cox was a dedicated Christian, and he seemed trustworthy—until now.

Putting his reservations aside, Cole straightened, hearing his crooked spine pop in several places after being contorted in the small car. He felt like an old man. They walked to an open elevator, took it up to the thirty-first floor, and entered a large polished lobby with groupings of modern furniture tastefully placed around plants and circular fountains. The sound of cascading water was soothing, suggesting evidence of the good life. *Do you see a man who excels in his work? He will stand before kings; He will not stand before unknown men. Proverbs 22 verse 29.* This verse entered Cole's thoughts. It seemed like a promise.

An older woman in professional attire looked up from the receptionist's cubicle to acknowledge their presence. Both men stepped up, but Ed initiated the greeting.

"Miss Irina, I see you're working late this evening." He smiled kindly.

"Yes, the boss had some sort of paperwork for me to finish before leaving for the evening. I'll let him know you're here to see him, Detective Cox," she said primly and waved a graceful hand in the direction of the comfortable waiting area. "Please be seated, gentlemen." A genuine smile directed at them made Cole relax somewhat. So far, it didn't feel like a lion's den.

"Nice place, isn't it?" Ed was smiling like the Cheshire cat in *Alice in Wonderland*. At the moment, Cole felt very much as if he were in Alice's Wonderland.

"Detective Cox," Miss Irina summoned, "the boss will see you and Pastor Grant now." Cole frowned, wondering how she knew his name and title. He hadn't been introduced. Moving from her giant desk, Miss Irina floated gracefully to the large double doors of the executive's suite and opened them into the boss's lair. She nodded as each man passed, like a sentinel acknowledging royalty. Ed entered first, then Cole. Cole had the feeling he was entering a throne room until Ed moved to the side allowing him to see the elderly man sitting behind the desk with a welcoming smile.

"Dr. Garankof, I would like to introduce you to Pastor Cole Grant."

# 11

## Trails in the Sunset

Snow in the higher elevations slowed Thad's and Tyrone's hike over the mountainous terrain of the Talkeetna Mountains near Willow. In the five miles and three hours since they had entered the trailhead below Hatcher Pass, seasons had changed from fall to winter making it necessary to strap on snowshoes. They needed to cover two more miles to a public shelter. It marked a halfway point to Charlie Bachman's remote shack from their starting point at the trailhead. Just before dark, Thad and Tyrone reached the unoccupied public shelter. They were able to rest during the brief hours of darkness before getting back on the trail at first light. Both men voiced the hope that Kroft would still be at Charlie's old mining shack.

A storm front was visible over the mountains to the northeast. Tyrone considered the darkening sky above and realized they might be engulfed in a snowstorm before reaching Charlie's remote shack. He tapped Thad's shoulder in front of him. "Let's trade. I'll break trail for a while." Thad nodded and fell back behind Tyrone who trudged through the eight inches of recently fallen snow, forging a path ahead so Thad could regain his stamina. Tyrone moved a rifle across the front of his chest, barrel up and left while Thad pushed the strap of his rifle over his left shoulder. Tyrone picked up the pace while looking down the trackless, white trail as Thad periodically checked peripherals for any kind of movement on the white arctic landscape.

"We're going to get more snow," Thad called to Tyrone, whose head bobbed up and down in agreement.

"I hope it holds off until we can find shelter or hike down to a lower elevation, at least," Tyrone answered. Both men silently prayed as the snow crunched beneath their snowshoes. Two miles later, they removed their snowshoes at the base of Sparrow Mountain, a lower elevation where there was no snow. They continued steadily down over rocky terrain until their path opened to a grassland valley with a glacial stream running between the mountains. In summer, such a scenic place would be perfect for a cabin beside the crystalline stream; however, the same picturesque location in winter would put the cabin right in the path of avalanches. God had made this otherworldly setting to be viewed with awe, though not to be practical for human habitation.

The experienced hunting guides followed the rushing stream until the grassland gave way to stony ground and turned back into the dense stand of aspen, spruce, and birch. Emerging from the scratchy limbs of stubby evergreen trees, the ground became stony again with boulders dotting the area. Past the boulders, they came to a steep incline covered with shifting slate. As Thad and Tyrone looked over the lay of the harsh land, they discussed the ascent up the loose slate ahead of them, knowing a slip and fall would be painful and costly. Step-by-step, they carefully navigated the slate encouraging one another until their boots were on muddy, but solid ground, again.

Thad noted the position of the setting sun and called to Tyrone that they should make it to Charlie's mining shack before nightfall. Suddenly, Tyrone stopped and motioned Thad up to his side. Tyrone pointed to two sets of tracks in the mud leading away from their present position.

"It looks like boot prints headed the same direction we're going." Thad bent down to examine the size of the first prints. They looked fairly fresh because the mud was still soft. The second set of prints make both men groan.

"Oh boy," Tyrone said dryly, "I hope the black bear's prints were here *before* the boot prints were. I hope we don't have a stalking situation here."

"Well, Charlie's shack should be pretty close. Maybe another mile... or so." Thad studied the rugged landscape then moved higher to a ledge, hoping the vista would afford a sight of the old mining shack. Opera-sized binoculars were pulled from a chest pocket and raised to his brown eyes.

"I don't like the 'or so' part of that statement, Thad," Tyrone grumbled as he pushed up from a knee bend after studying the tracks, noting that both sets led off in the same direction. His backpack had slipped sideways as a result of a loosened clasp which he quickly adjusted and cinched with practiced ease. "Stalking bears always make me nervous."

"Yeah, I don't like this either." Thad commented searching the magnified horizon for a man-made shelter, a man, or a beast. "I don't see what we are looking for, yet. Let's move on before that weather front catches up to us."

"I just hope Charlie's sober. I'd hate to dodge bullets, too." Tyrone intoned as they moved on, ever alert to their surroundings. Checking around for any trace of rising chimney smoke that would point a direction to the lonely mining shack, both men hoped the boot tracks they followed were indeed Kroft's. No traces of smoke were detected. Tyrone continued to follow the same tracks with growing concern as he pointed out small traces of blood in each left claw print. At this point, they both carried their rifles loaded keeping them at the ready, listening for sounds of danger as they descended through dense brush to the narrow valley Thad had just scouted with the binoculars. Just fifty yards later, they climbed to a summit where he halted, pointing to a small structure about a half mile away. It sat near a small clearing at the base of a mountain. A thin stream ran past the run-down shack.

Above the shack they saw another wood framed structure that looked to be barely clinging to the side of the mountain. Its precarious perch was supported by wooden posts that had been constructed on the narrow clefts of rock by gold seekers over a century ago. The mine's entrance was perhaps sixty-five to seventy feet off the ground. A pulley system would have been used to haul a man and his mining supplies from ground level up to the mine and back down. Only the long arm or boom of the pulley system remained. A junkyard of antique mining equipment lay scattered around the area. The rusty parts were half hidden in tall grasses and blueberry bushes. Over to the right was a rectangular collection of rocks marking the site of a forgotten grave. Wild daisies dotted the landscape having long since spread past the resting place of the unknown gold miner.

A makeshift bridge was constructed across the narrow stream connecting our hiking team to the lower shelter. This humble dwelling was to be their lodging for the evening. Thad looked skyward, noticing dark clouds overshadowing what daylight was left. They moved on, gingerly walking across the wood planks over the icy stream and up a slight grade toward the tumbledown shack. "Looks like we might get snowed-in here," he forecasted, praying silently for the weather front to pass over this area. The boot tracks reappeared some thirty feet from the shack. The bear tracks had disappeared in the low brush behind them. Thad ran ungloved fingers through his hair as he considered the solitude of the place. There was no smoke or evidence of anyone around the place at present—only boot tracks that approached the door of the shack, before turning and leading away again. "Why didn't he go inside?" Thad wondered out loud as Tyrone walked up beside him.

"Did you find any more tracks, Tyrone?" He rubbed the back of his neck. It was suddenly itchy. The feel of the place was all wrong. Again he searched the area, noting that the wind had started to whip tattered pieces of plastic covering the broken windows of the shack. Thad took comfort in the thought that God was with them here in this desolate place.

"The black bear's tracks seem to disappear..." He stopped, spotting more tracks behind the cabin. "Look at all the tracks over here. It looks like there was a scuffle of some kind." He hesitated as they drew closer. "And it was with a bear too. The bear's tracks come up from a point farther down the stream." Quickly glancing around their position, Tyrone protested, "I don't like this!"

Thad didn't reply though their feelings were mutual. The door of the shack creaked open and banged shut with a gust of wind.

"Let's take a look," Thad directed, walking around to the door. Snowflakes as tiny as ladybugs began falling and blowing sideways as the weather front slowed to a crawl over their location. Thad pushed the wood-carved handle into the opening of the shack until there was room to get his boot inside the door. Exerting more pressure with his body, the door started to give way until whatever had blocked its progress fell off to the side in a heap. They entered the tiny, dark shack and grimaced; the acrid smell causing both men to gag and dash outside to fresh air.

"Whew!" Tyrone sucked in fresh air while waving a hand in front of his nose as if to drive the foul odor away. "I think I'd rather take my chances sleeping outside with a black bear nearby than inside that shack." Tyrone coughed with disgust.

"Let's leave the door open until we can clean out the place and build a fire. At least the wood smoke will help cover some of the stench, I hope," Thad said as he covered his nose and mouth with a gloved hand and braced to reenter the shack with a flashlight in his free hand. The beam of the light probed the small cubicle until it fell on Charlie Bachman's quiet form sprawled lengthwise on a cot of sorts.

"Tyrone!" he shouted. Tyrone entered immediately, eyes wide as Thad pointed and said soberly, "It's Charlie." Squinting to adjust to the gray shadows beyond the beam of light, Thad crept slowly over to the man. "I'm not sure he's alive." The circle of light rested on Charlie's face. Thad held his breath and reached a hand down near something that protruded like a nose from a fur-rimmed parka. Even then, Charlie's shallow breath was so pungent that Thad had to hold his breath.

"Bring me a lamp," he croaked. Tyrone swiftly retrieved a Coleman lantern from a hook on his backpack.

"Here." Tyrone assisted by holding the stronger light over Thad's shoulder. The room filled with an amber glow only to reveal a wound made by bear claws across Charlie's right shoulder. "He's still alive. We'll do what we can with what first aid supplies we have and see if he can be coaxed back. We'll try a radio signal and see if we can get through to the State Troopers or Talkeetna Rescue even through this storm." By now, the wind whistled around the corners of the shack and the temperature was dropping quickly.

Tyrone pulled the first aid kit from their supplies so that Thad could start working on Charlie. After Tyrone hauled water from the stream for cleaning Charlie's wounds, he worked to make a blazing fire in an ancient potbellied stove for warmth and for heating food. The radio transmitter buzzed with static, indicating that no signal had as yet been found. Thad gently cleaned and medicating the wounds. Bandages were carefully applied. A plaid flannel shirt was spread over Charlie along with a sleeping bag in efforts to keep him warm. Thankfully, the wounds had been smaller than they had seemed at first glance. Thad wondered when the attack had occurred and if the boot prints they had been tracking were Charlie's. This curious thought drew his eyes to Charlie's mud-covered boots hanging over the cot beyond the sleeping bag.

"Hey, Tyrone? I wonder if Charlie's boots match the tracks we've been following."

"I'm way ahead of you, my friend. They don't match, but there are tracks all over the place."

Both men looked at each other, wondering if they had been lead on a wild-goose chase. Where was Kroft? If he hadn't come this way to Charlie's place, then where had he headed? And why was Charlie here?

"We need help," Thad acknowledged. He bowed his head, praying, "God, we need your help here in this place. Charlie is badly hurt. Kroft is somewhere only known to You while Tyrone and I are in the middle of a blizzard without radio communication or help of any kind, except Yours. I know You know where we are and what we need to do. Show us and give us Your power to see this through. Thank you, Father God. Amen."

"Amen," Tyrone echoed.

"Ooh-h-h." A moan erupted from Charlie. Thad saw Charlie's eyes blink open then close again as his breathing seemed steadier.

"He lives." Tyrone remarked with raised eyebrows.

"Let's see if he can take a few teaspoons of beef bouillon." Thad set to work preparing a camp cup of the hot broth from the beef-flavored cubes. Charlie's eyes popped open when Tyrone gently lifted his uninjured shoulder in order to place a small rolled-up tarp under his neck to prop up his head for some nourishment. Confused and dazed, the wily wilderness man tried to move, but Tyrone put a hand out to stop the attempt. Jagged pain in his shoulder ended his efforts.

"Easy there, Charlie. It's Tyrone Johnson. We found you here inside the shack. Thad Tucker and I are here to help any way we can. Just lie back and rest. Thad's got some broth to help you get your strength back. We're trying to contact the troopers, but we haven't been able to get through yet." Charlie seemed to calm down and nodded. His eyes darted around the dimly lit shack in wonderment.

"You found me in here?" His voice sounded gravelly and rough with weakness. "The last thing I saw was Kroft…" He drifted and shuddered as the terror of the bear's attack made his head swim in a faint.

"Easy, Charlie. You're safe now. We're here to keep watch." Tyrone patted the man's hand and saw the hardened man's eyes moisten as tears rolled from the sides of his eyes. He wept like a wounded child for several minutes as though crying cleansed the anxiety in both mind and body. Thad walked over with the cup of steaming broth and sat on an upturned log next to Charlie.

"Do you think you can take some broth now, Charlie?" Thad saw the nod and moved the cup to his lips carefully to allow little sips. Charlie received the nourishment, relishing the salty beef taste and the kindness of two men he had often annoyed and frustrated by stealing their hunting and fishing gear when they took clients into the wilderness to hunt and fish. While they slept, he'd often snuck into the campsite and foraged.

Charlie began to feel strength return in greater measure. His body was stiff and sore from the struggle with the powerful bear. He was glad to be alive, and very glad for the mercy shown by two better men than he.

"Why are you guys here?" He suddenly wanted to know.

"We're looking for your friend, Kroft," Thad answered, tipping the cup to allow Charlie as much of the warm liquid as he wanted. Charlie took a couple of gulps and moved his head slightly to let Thad know he was done. Standing, Thad took the remaining broth and set it on a ledge above the stove to catch some of the heat. "We need to find him and help him with a personal matter. You mentioned seeing him?"

"Yah," Charlie acknowledged, frowning in confusion. "Kroft came to my rescue."

Charlie felt woozy all of a sudden. "I can't explain it. I also can't explain why I'm inside this cabin because the last thing I remember was…Lance bending over me and talking, but I couldn't make any sense of what he was saying. I must have passed out then."

"Kroft was here, and he must have carried you inside at some point. But why didn't he stay with you?" Tyrone wondered.

"Maybe he went to get help." Thad offered willing positive thoughts on Kroft's behalf.

"It's too miserable outside for any kind of rescue attempt." Tyrone confirmed as all three men listened to the howl of early winter descending on the Alaskan backcountry. "I wish Kroft would just come back here and walk through that door," he said. Both Thad and Charlie chuckled at the ridiculous idea. "It sure would make life a whole lot easier for all of us."

"Easier rarely is a possibility in a blinding storm," Thad quipped, "but we can pray for the impossible."

"Now wouldn't that be something..." Tyrone was thoughtful. "I remember a Bible story from when I was a young boy in Sunday school. Jesus and the disciples had gotten into a boat to cross a lake. Jesus had found a dry spot in the boat to lie down and sleep. While he slept, a big storm came down the mountainside and blew over the lake tossing the boat in the wild waves. The disciples thought they were going to perish because the boat was filling with water. In panic they called to Jesus, waking him and alerting him to the crisis. Jesus stood up and rebuked the wind and the raging sea. Suddenly all was calm. The disciples were relieved, but that's not the end of the story." Tyrone was thoughtful. "I remember my Sunday school teacher, Mrs. Romarez, telling us that Jesus had asked his disciples what had happened to their faith. The disciples had seen Jesus heal people and cast out demons, but it never occurred to them that He could tell the wind and water to settle down and be quiet. It astonished them that Jesus could tell nature what to do, and nature would obey. They didn't yet understand that Jesus was Savior and Creator God standing right in front of them. It still boggles my mind, but I believe it. I remember thinking of Jesus as being the superhero of the world at that point in my life."

A keening wind continued to press against the ramshackle sanctuary in the heights of Alaska's frontier. The sound of the angry storm grew louder, making talking almost impossible. The possibilities of a long stay loomed in Thad's and Tyrone's thoughts. Both prayed for Lance Kroft to just show up. A glance over at Charlie's sleeping form encouraged rest. Thad added more wood to the hot belly of the stove before making a place to sit on the floor. Tyrone stuffed whatever rags were lying around into cracks in the log walls and under the door to keep the frigid blasts from seeping into the place. Both were thankful for what shelter was available.

"Where in the world is Kroft?" Thad mumbled with concern at the dismal prospects of finding his future brother-in-law with the blizzard wiping all tracks and traces away. "Lord, help us," he prayed, thinking of Tyrone's Bible story. "I believe You can tell this storm to stop at any time, perhaps when it has served Your higher purposes. Father, God, I don't want to miss my wedding day. I love Leah so much. Please help us out, here. Thanks." He spoke sincerely, though the howling of the wind muffled his words heavenward. Yet the One who calmed the wind and the waves on the Sea of Galilee for the fearful disciples two millennia ago, heard the prayer and rejoiced at the blossoming faith of a new son of redemption.

Pulling an envelope out of his jacket pocket, Thad's space was filled with the welcome scent of Leah's perfume. He smiled and opened the fragrant missive, recognizing her familiar handwriting—sensing her presence through her writing style.

*Dear Thad, my love,*

*I miss your kisses and the smell of your aftershave when you are close. The way your eyes find mine and hold them captive fills my heart with longing to be one with you in life and in purpose. I am amazed that you love me for me. I'm so different from what the world says is beautiful, yet you proudly introduce me to your friends and business acquaintances as if I am of greatest value. You let everyone know you love me, only and always.*

*Even when I make mistakes that cause you embarrassment, or I unwittingly hurt your man feelings, you blow those hurts away with sweet deeds of kindness and selfless acts of loving grace toward me.*

*Thad, you are my Prince. You melt my heart when you walk into the room and speak my name. Tall, dark, and handsome, your hair is wavy and black. Your dark eyes shine like jewels turned in firelight and stir awaiting ardor from this virgin's sleep. Your shoulders are widely set, ever ready to lead, guide, and protect all those who lodge secure with you.*

*I am yours, the one you desire, the one who waits for you, longs for you, watches breathlessly for your return. Come quickly, my love! Come quickly that our tender feelings may awaken love's sacred consummation.*

*I love you,*

*Leah*
*From the Song of Solomon*

Thad leaned back against the log wall of the shack closing his eyes, envisioning his beloved Leah's smiles of love. The warmth of her love quelled the chill of the storm-rammed shack and filled Thad Tucker with inner strength and determination to get back to his bride-to-be—the sooner, the better.

"What are you smiling about?" Tyrone interrupted Thad's amorous musings. "I can smell that perfume all the way over here by Charlie. You're a lucky man, Thad Tucker."

Thad chuckled as he slipped the letter back into the scented envelope and inside his arctic jacket pocket. "I have a hunch you will be too, Tyrone." Thad had a question. "Say, Tyrone, do you know anything about something called Song of Solomon?"

Tyrone frowned at the odd question then shrugged. "Not much. It's a book in the Old Testament of the Bible. I've never read it." The fire needed more fuel, prompting Tyrone to move and pull chunks of chopped wood from a neatly stacked pile near the stove to keep it ablaze.

Thad contemplated Tyrone's words and reached for the Bible he had packed in with other supplies. Checking the table of contents, he found the book and turned to the given page number, preparing to read.

As the wind grew in ferocity, it seemed as though the walls of the shack would collapse on the sheltered trio. One gust of wind hit with a driving thud, startling both men. Again, another thud hit the shack with such intensity that Thad's and Tyrone's eyes grew large at the imminent collapse of the rickety structure. Thad replaced the Bible in his backpack and sat alert, listening. A third and then a fourth time the thud came, and it seemed that there was a kind of pulse to the thud. Could it be more than just gusts of wind? Tyrone and Thad looked at each other, then to the barricaded door. One word came to both their minds.

"*Bear!*" they both yelled, jumping up and reaching for rifles.

Thad moved cautiously to the crude door. Tyrone had pushed old rags against the bottom of the door to keep out some of the blowing snow and wind. What sounded like a muffled male voice filtered through the flimsy barricade. Releasing the bolt slowly, Thad both felt and heard another *thud* on the door. Slowly, he opened the door a few inches to see who or what might be out in the wild weather. A blast of snow pelted his face, making him blink and squint, unable to see anything beyond the doorpost until the wind sucked the snow away from the opening. The large form of a black bear loomed just off to the side of the door sending chills up and down Thad's spine like a dumbbell meter at a carnival game.

"*Charlie!*" the bear yelled, making Thad jump at the unexpected sound of a human voice instead of a bear's roar. Reason seemed to evade the startled hunting guide. Only Yogi Bear could talk.

Quickly, Thad pushed the door aside and reached out to grab hold of the fur. Yanking with all his might, Thad pulled on the bear causing the beast to stumble and fall halfway inside the doorway. Thad yelled as loud as he could against the howling wind as the sting of pelting sleet hit his body full force.

"Kroft!" He paused, closing his eyes to shield them from the vicious ice attack. "Is that you?" he shouted and realized his voice hadn't gone any further than his lips. He reached down as Tyrone came to help him, and together they dragged the fur inside. Struggling to get a foothold so that leg strength and arm muscles combined could pull the limp body to safety, Thad and Tyrone at last managed to drag the beast inside enough to close out the wind and weather.

"I don't know why we're bothering to close the door anyway. This shack is about to fly off to Never-Never Land," Tyrone commented loudly.

"It ain't goin' nowhere," a groggy Charlie moaned. "I anchored this place down with steel railroad signposts from the supply yard near Talkeetna. I just dug down a good bit, dropped four of the larger posts for corners, and built the shack walls around them. I used to have a snow machine years ago, but…" he drifted, then perked up, "I just added more posts for more strength. Look at the walls." Charlie directed. Sure enough, Thad and Tyrone saw several posts extending from the ground all the way up to the level of the tilted roof some eight-feet high at one end and some seven-feet high at the opposite wall. Tyrone shook his head in amazement as Thad whistled at the snug little fortress standing undaunted in the cyclonic winds repeatedly slamming the humble abode.

"Charlie, you're a wonder," Thad marveled.

"Hey guys," Charlie motioned weakly with his good arm. "That bear is moving."

# 12

## HEROES HAVE HEARTS

COLE GRANT COULDN'T HAVE BEEN MORE surprised or confused. Something wasn't adding up. The man behind the desk appeared to be in his late sixties. White-haired and so thin that the gray suit coat he wore seemed much too big for his frame, Dr. Garankof smiled pleasantly. Bright, violet eyes sparkled with expectancy though his voice resonated with quiet dignity. He nodded to Ed as though they shared a long-time friendship.

"Hello, Ed. Pastor Grant, it is a pleasure to meet you. When Ed called with your inquiry about my nephew, Andrei, I was both astounded and greatly relieved to know he is alive. For some time, we have tried to locate him." His English was precise though flavored with a Russian accent. "Please, won't you be seated?" He directed Ed and Cole to comfortable leather chairs facing the massive desk. Cole felt like they were approaching the judge's bench in a courtroom drama.

"Ed, how is Junia and the rest of the family?"

"Everyone is well and working. Donnie seems to have found gainful employment with FedEx as a package sorter at their hub. Denise has taken leave of her senses again and has run off to Alaska to visit Pastor Grant's engaged daughter, Leah." He chuckled and saw Dr. Garankof smile in understanding. Shakespeare's *The Taming of the Shrew* came to his mind when he thought of Denise Cox. Nevertheless, she always brightened his day with a visit full of chaos and bakery treats. Oh, how he loved the bakery treats.

"She took recruits with her." Cole jumped into the conversation. "Namely, my middle daughter, Sarah, and my granddaughter, Angie. Both have flown off to wild Alaska to conquer anything with two legs and a beard," Cole teased, trying some humor on the older gentleman. Dr. Garankof laughed outright, joined by a grinning Ed.

"If a man has to have a youngest daughter, Denise is the best there is. Praise God. I love her for all her crazy antics. I also pray more for her than all the others, hoping God will give her to a worthy man who will lovingly guide her energy in His service." Ed was reflective and no one spoke for a time.

"Alaska," Dr. Garankof repeated in a contemplative tone, turning to regard the pastor-father facing him. "Pastor Grant, you are probably wondering what is going on?"

"Yes, I am." Grant nodded. "Sarah told me that Andrei said he had no living relatives in the United States. I'm afraid I don't understand. Would you kindly fill me in please?"

"Yes, I'd be glad to tell you part of the story. Ed"—he directed—"will start us off."

"Sure, Dr. Garankof." Ed looked at Cole and began. Irina had entered the room and taken a seat on a couch near the threesome. A large ball of yarn released a strand of purple over and through her busy fingers as she crocheted quietly, listening to the familiar story once again.

"It's been about seven years since I was assigned to the Global Financial Investors case. The corporation came under the scrutiny of the FBI, and I was designated as the liaison for the Chicago Police Department as the chief detective. Your son-in-law, Andrei, had just started working for GFI. I honestly don't think he had any idea what he was walking into as far as the scope of the corruption worldwide. The FBI, in coordination with our department, had placed an agent in GFI. The FBI agent and Andrei were both working in the same executive's offices. From the information gathered by our departments, he knew Andrei had a background in Russian Intelligence. What he didn't know was whether Andrei was part of the corruption, or if he was pegged to be GFI's scapegoat since he was the 'new guy'," Ed emphasized with finger quotes. "The agent fed information about the company's illegal dealings to Andrei's computer as a test. The agent told me about it, and I advised that agent against this practice." Ed pursed his lips tightly together. "If you can't catch a crook honestly, then you're a crook yourself. As it turned out, the agent had his own little sweet deal going on with the CEO of this company." It still disgusted Ed. "Anyway, I submitted a complaint to my superior. McClosky's a good man in the department. He pushed the FBI to acknowledge the complaint, but nothing came of it. I talked to the agent about it and shortly thereafter was reassigned to a case in North Chicago. That's when I came across Andrei's dad and his uncle here, Dr. Garankof. I did some checking on Andrei's background, and when I found the brothers, Andrei's dad was dying of thyroid cancer. He had been trying to locate his son. But I'm getting ahead of myself." Ed nodded to Dr. Garankof to continue.

"I'm Andrei's Uncle Viktor." The white-haired man took over. "Andrei's father and I were paternal twins. That is to say, we were identical twins. Vladimir and I did everything alike except that Vladimir studied the sciences and chose to become a nuclear physicist. I, on the other hand, had no mind for science and chose to study philosophy in the United States. I spent several years at Harvard. It was the pursuit of the world's philosophies that nearly drove me to a drunkard's grave," Dr. Garankof testified with a chuckle. Pastor Grant smiled assent. "However, God in His marvelous grace reached down and literally pushed me into the Pacific Garden Mission some eight years ago. Before that, I had lived an," he paused, "urbane lifestyle you would not even want to imagine. My brother, Vladimir, who was himself very ill, found me at the mission—drying out yet again. Together, we rented a cheap apartment and lived quietly while he tried various treatments. We studied the Bible from cover to cover, exploring our new faith in Christ. It was a marvelous time of fellowship. We drank in the truths of God with such thirst and grateful hearts that Vladimir seemed to rally in physical strength. God was merciful to us." Viktor Garankof's voice caught as his eyes welled. Taking a deep breath and exhaling slowly, he continued, regaining control of the emotions that stirred at the memory of their spiritual brotherhood.

"Vladimir knew he was going to die soon. He was very concerned for his son, Andrei. Any information he had of Andrei was gathered from his wife's sister, Irina, whom he'd contacted after hearing of his wife's death. They kept in contact through letters sent to a post office box here in the city. Irina's last letter to Vladimir before he died said that Andrei was on his way to Chicago to work for Global Financial Investors. Now I will hand the story back to my detective friend, Ed."

Ed shrugged and grinned. "When Andrei's name came up in connection with the investigation and before I'd found his father and uncle, I did some digging into their family's history, finding the association with the Chernobyl disaster. It sent red flags off in my head. I decided to see what his connections to GFI might be, if any. Previously, Dr. Garankof had been a resident of Chicago's southside, but he had been evicted from his apartment months earlier."

Grant looked over to Dr. Garankof who simply shrugged. "Those were my before-Christ days."

Ed resumed. "I began to check the hospitals, homeless shelters, and missions for any clue to Dr. Garankof's whereabouts. This search took place about the same time as Andrei was ending his first week of work at GFI. I didn't know your daughter, Sarah, was in the city, Cole, or I'd have kept an eye out for her. Actually, I think it was before Leah and Denise had met at college." He saw Cole nod in agreement. "By this time, your brother, Vladimir had died and had been buried at the Cook County Cemetery."

Sadness pulled the gentle lines of the older man's face down in regret. Viktor had since been able to honor his twin brother's life and memory with a monument engraved with John 3 verse 16 written as a testimony to conquering faith.

"I am only a half a man without my brother." His lips trembled. Irina stood suddenly and moved to place a comforting arm around the remaining brother. Both could have been grandparents had their lives and love for each other connected years earlier. Yet, even in an imperfect world, perfect love could come at any time and at any age.

"Forgive me, Dr. Garankof..."

"No, it's all right. I'm fine. Thank our precious Lord there is hope!" He smiled and reached a hand to pat Irina's dainty one. "I'm fine now, my dear."

Grant caught the affectionate reference and frowned in confusion. To this point, he was totally amazed at how pieces of the puzzle were falling neatly together, yet this mind-boggling story seemed to have endless pieces. Where was the pattern? He reckoned how little his world was when others had journeyed from the ends of the earth to fit perfectly together in the bigger puzzle of God's plan of redemption. The church had faithfully and sacrificially supported missionaries in distant part of the world with his pastoral leadership, but he realized God was broadening his vision through the lives of his daughters.

"Pastor Grant." Dr. Garankof was once again cheerful. "May I introduce you to Andrei's Aunt Irina, my lovely wife of only three years. Though we are gray-haired and wrinkled, we are newlyweds still. After Vladimir died, we continued to write letters back and forth until I decided to bring my pen pal over to America so I didn't have to wait for days for answers to my questions about the Bible. You see, Irina was a member of Russia's underground church before glasnost. She could write books and books on her experiences. But we must get back to our story." Irina kissed her husband on the forehead and walked gracefully back to the couch to take up the crochet hook once again and resume her project.

"I'm honored, Dr. Garankof, Mrs. Garankof." Grant was genuinely amazed. He'd have a lot to tell Doris tonight.

"On with the facts," Dr. Garankof admonished, grinning. "I want to know where my nephew is and I would…we," he corrected when Irina's eyes met his, "would very much like to know about his wife, your Sarah, and our young grandniece. We are eager to belong to a big family." Dr. Garankof sat forward expectantly.

Ed continued, "I was able to locate Dr. Garankof through the mission on Canal Street. Mr. Samuels sent me to the tenement housing address. Andrei, however, had already visited his Uncle Viktor and left. Apparently, he had been searching for his father for several years too."

"I didn't know where Andrei had gone, but I suspected he'd go to his father's grave," Dr. Garankof interjected.

"That's where I headed next." Ed confirmed. "The grave was still soft, and as I examined the footprints around the edges, I noticed a small area where the dirt had been slightly disturbed near the small grave marker. I called my partner, Stan Evans, to bring a forensic team out to the site from our police department. We found a steel box with numerous computer disks carefully wrapped in a protective plastic case inside. There were no fingerprints on any of the evidence, except one set that belonged to the FBI agent. Andrei is either lucky or he is very clever. I'm inclined to think your nephew is adept in intelligence matters, but that's not all. Several of GFI's employees were listed on these disks. They were wanted in various countries for fraud, amongst other things. There were rewards for information and for the apprehension of these personages. Everything was on those disks."

"The rewards are where I come in," Dr. Garankof contributed. "Since I told Ed where Andrei might be and the disks were found at that site, I received the rewards, and the crooks went to prison. Andrei just needs to come and tell his side of the story."

"We believe he's innocent, though burying the disks wasn't the best way to handle the evidence. However, given the circumstances, his actions are understandable," Ed stated professionally.

"The hundreds of thousands of dollars in rewards, I have used to create Trans World E-Conomists," Dr. Garankof further disclosed. "When GFI folded, hundreds of charity organizations and thousands of hardworking people lost their investments. Andrei was part of this by association. His father deeply regretted the pain and loss caused to millions of people from the Chernobyl disaster, and he tried to find solutions until his dying breath. I simply wanted to try to make things right somehow. I accepted the reward and entrusted the monies to a reputable investment group known as The Sparrow Group. Ed and I are charter members of this all-volunteer executive group. Where there has been corruption, our challenge as an organization and investment group is to return good for evil. It was our desire to do this without accepting the federal bailout that was offered. There were biblical reasons for this choice, which I will not go into. Suffice it to say that righteousness exalts a nation, but sin is a reproach to any people, Proverbs 14:34."

"Do not be overcome by evil, but overcome evil with good. Romans chapter 12, verse 21," Grant recited aloud and saw both Ed Cox and Viktor Garankof nod their heads in agreement. All three quietly contemplated this divine charge.

"Why is it called The Sparrow Group?" the inquisitive pastor asked.

The professor's eyes lit up. "Irina and I live in a north side neighborhood of small row houses. They are so close together that only a narrow sidewalk separates the century-old homes. There's not much by way of a front yard, but thankfully, our little home has a long rectangular backyard with lots of trees and bushes. It is like our secret garden, and we enjoy watching the birds play and listening to them sing merry songs to us. One Saturday afternoon, I was feeling a little restless and decided to go outside and sit on the deck for a little while. The sun was shining, and it was not too warm. The leaves were changing to autumn, and it was pleasant and quiet except for the songbirds and distant city sounds. I must have dozed off because I felt myself jerk awake suddenly.

"The peaceful tweets of the birds had become insistent tweets of agitation. My eyes opened to see a red bird hopping after a little sparrow. Every so often, the big red bird would get close enough to peck the sparrow. No matter how the sparrow tried to dodge the attack, the bigger red bird moved faster and would peck at the sparrow again and again. I looked around willing the little brown sparrow to get away from its adversary. That's when I noticed a second red bird following the bigger red bird a little distance behind. However, it hesitated, then turned and hopped in the opposite direction. I wondered why. Then I saw something astounding. Across the yard came a large group of sparrows hopping toward the little sparrow that was being attacked. I had never seen anything like it in all my life.

"When the big red bird saw the amassing sparrows advancing toward it like an army dressed in brown camouflage, the beautiful red bird turned and hopped quickly into the bushes after the other red bird. The army of sparrows surrounded the wounded sparrow and stood in place for several minutes as it straightened and smoothed its feathers. I waited for them to fly away, but they didn't. Irina called me in to eat supper at that moment. I hated to leave this iconic setting, but, alas, I was hungry." Dr. Garankof chuckled. "Afterward, I stepped back out on the deck to see if any sparrows remained. I doubted they would still be there, but to my surprise, several sparrows hopped around the yard. I looked up into the branches of some maple trees, and the branches were full of sparrows. It made such an impression on me. I began to think about a passage I'd read in Luke chapter 12 verses 4–8, where Jesus reassured the disciples that no matter what happened to them, God had the power to care for those who were committed to Him.

"Little sparrows might appear to be cheap and insignificant in a world of flashy red birds, but not one of those little sparrows is forgotten by God. Jesus said that each one of us is of more value than many sparrows. God ultimately cares for His creation. We can learn how to care for one another even by watching the lowly sparrows care for their own. The sparrows in my backyard hurried to the aid of that one lonely sparrow under attack. They surrounded him until he was able to pull himself together, then they hung around supporting that sparrow and each other for an indefinite period of time. From this backyard tale of sparrows and red birds came the idea for The Sparrow Group," he concluded, his face shining with joy.

"God has blessed our efforts to promote righteousness where truth has fallen to the streets. Not only are we repaying those who have suffered loss, we have added thousands of investors who are looking for a trustworthy company in which to invest their hard-earned treasure. Trans World E-Conomists are stewards seeking biblical ways to fund aid to neighbors suffering hardships." Dr. Garankof waved a hand around the enormous office. "This is an impressive office space, but it's just space. The real wealth is in the hearts of honest people doing the right thing with their time, talents, and treasures. Irina and I live simply. We work in this office, five days a week reading reports, writing letters, signing documents, giving occasional lectures, and enjoying brown bag lunches together with our company's few employees. Other than that, The Sparrow Group manages the operation."

"It sounds very much like the structure of a church fellowship." Grant surmised. "Who are in this Sparrow Group?" Dr. Garankof smiled broadly, nodded agreement, and pointed to Ed.

"They are ordinary people pledged to do the extraordinary for their neighbors, both here at home and abroad. The board of directors consists of thirty men and women who specialize in legal and business matters related to overseeing charitable and personal investments. A designated fund supported by our investors pays their modest salaries. Trans World E-Conomists is the exact opposite of Global Financial

Investors. New name, new game. Instead of corruption, we strive for virtue in all financial dealings. And, yes, most of the directors are members in good standing in churches and missions around the Chicago area." Ed finished, checking his wrist watch. "We need to get back to the hotel. Cole, what information can you convey to Dr. Garankof about his nephew?"

"How would you and your wife like to see a picture of Sarah and Angie?" Grant asked, reaching in his jacket pocket for a leather billfold. Irina was by his side in an instant as he opened it and pulled out a photo of *Sugar-n-Spice* for viewing. He handed it to Irina who smiled with delight and moved around the large desk to show the photo to her attentive husband. Dr. Garankof's eyes widened and glistened with moisture.

"The little girl looks just like Andrei!" he exclaimed as Irina cooed over the beauty of mother and daughter.

"You may keep the picture, Dr. and Mrs. Garankof. My wife has more back at the hotel. I can send pictures to you if you would like," Cole offered.

"Thank you. We'd love to have any pictures you can spare," Irina assured. "What treasures they are, Pastor Grant."

"They are treasures, and I'm happy to be on my way to see them."

"Where are they?" Dr. Garankof leaned forward in anticipation.

"Sarah and Angie are in Palmer, Alaska. As for Andrei, the last I had heard, he was somewhere in the Alaskan wilderness heading to a remote cabin. Thad, Leah's fiancé, and his business partner, Tyrone, were heading into that same wilderness to find Andrei and bring him back to Palmer where he can contact the FBI—"

"It would be better if he contacted me, Cole," Ed interrupted. "Can you get a message to Thad to have Andrei call me?"

"I can do better than that. I can give you Thad's cell number. He mentioned that a Pastor Paytor was checking with a state trooper named Clovis Pine, for advice. The only reason I remember the name is because Clovis Pine is so unusual."

"Clovis Pine," Ed repeated, pulling a notepad and pen from his jacket and writing the name down. "I'm ready for the number. What was the name and number of the pastor in Palmer?"

Grant recited names and numbers. When Ed finished writing, he stood and extended a hand to Dr. Garankof, smiling.

"You've waited a long time, Brother. Let's hope God gives a happy resolution to all this. If you will excuse us, Dr. Garankof, Pastor Grant and I should leave and get back to our wives. I'll keep you informed as things progress."

"Fine, Ed. Thank you. Irina and I appreciate this so much."

"God is working in a mighty way," Ed proclaimed.

"Yes, He is, after all these years." The old man stood slowly and stretched out a hand to shake Ed's offered one. Turning to Grant, he offered again and shook hands with a new family member.

"It looks like your daughter and my nephew have made us family. I am honored and relieved to know you are also a brother in Christ."

"So am I, Dr. Garankof and Mrs. Garankof. I look forward to bringing our families all together under one roof soon as God makes it possible," Cole said sincerely.

"With God, nothing shall be impossible," Viktor quoted and smiled.

"Amen." Grant gave Viktor a gospel tract with his home phone number. "We'll be at the hotel overnight. Ed has the hotel name and room extension if you should want to talk."

Irina handed their business card to Cole.

"Thank you. We would like that very much," Dr. Garankof said in closing.

Ed and Cole quickly left the executive office. After the door shut, Viktor and Irina gave thanks to God for answers to their prayers for one missing nephew. They prayed for his safe return and for his wife and little Angie.

Out of tragedy, abundant blessing could come. The older couple left the modern skyscraper hand in hand, rejoicing at how God works all things together in the love story of salvation.

❧

Four anxious ladies sat in comfortable chairs and couches in the great room of a large, modern lodge near Palmer, Alaska. A fire crackled in the stone hearth, adding warmth to the group as each quietly contemplated their plight just two days before the marriage of Thad Tucker to his mail-order bride-to-be, Leah Grant.

No word had come since Thad and Tyrone left yesterday at noon to hike into the Alaskan wilderness to find and return a fugitive who was a brand-new Christian. Alma had signed to Leah that it might be some time before either man would be able to contact the lodge with any news of finding Sarah's husband.

Wedding plans continued which included a trip into Anchorage and an appointment at David's Bridal to find and purchase a dress that same day. Breakfast being ended, the ladies and little Angie had shuffled into the living room to make lists for their shopping spree. A small wedding cake had been ordered from a local Palmer bakery. Flowers for the bride and her maid-of-honor, the flower girls—Angie and Michelle—the groom and best man, the pastor and his wife, Alma, the wedding coordinator, Sarah, the pianist, and an arrangement to be sent to the groom's mother because she could not attend the ceremony, had been ordered and were being assembled.

There would be thirteen guests or more for the reception after the ceremony. The reception would be held in the den area of the lodge at ground level where there was a small kitchenette for convenience. Alma and Leah had already moved tables into place to be covered and set with dinner china by a catering service from Eagle River. Alma had given Denise several phone numbers of caterers to contact for availability, but the local catering services in Palmer and Wasilla were already booked solid with State Fair events and private parties. Denise became their heroine when she found and secured the caterer on such short notice. Of course, she'd worked a deal with the proprietor for a complimentary three-day hunting excursion with two of Alaska's finest hunting guides with Leah's enthusiastic support. Denise hoped and prayed they returned. Or maybe not, come to think of it since she'd toyed with their business assets in a trade for services without their knowledge or approval. Anyway, she'd hide behind Leah when Thad and Tyrone found out.

Leah stood up from where she'd been sitting on the couch and walked over to the large wall of windows. Looking out over the vast Matanuska Valley to the Talkeetna Mountain Range, she wished for the man of her dreams to come walking out of the wilderness and take her in his arms. The wish to know he was safe and real and here moved her eyes back and forth across the rugged land in search of some tangible evidence that everything would work out okay. Thick dark clouds had dropped over the mountain peaks until the only farm fields visible were below the tree line. Whatever was going on in those clouded highlands was invisible to her lowland eyes.

"The angel of the Lord encamps all around those who fear Him, and delivers them. Psalm 34 verse 7," Sarah quoted and put her arms around Leah. "I'm scared too. It's so hard to be brave, isn't it?"

"Yes, it is, especially when love is so precious, so idyllic." Leah tried to explain the kind of *love* she was experiencing for Thad, and even *idyllic* didn't seem exactly right either.

"Idyllic," Sarah mused, "maybe for a while when romance first blooms, it is idyllic. If love succeeds at all, it becomes more precious. If one is fortunate, there will be a few moments of the idyllic now and then."

"You're sounding very Jane Austen." Leah smiled wryly, giving Sarah a playful nudge.

"We should rent the *Pride and Prejudice* VCR tapes from a video store." Sarah suggested with a smile. "Mom and I watched part of the BBC series on the PBS channel last year while you were in Chicago. Personally, I'd like to watch all six hours. When we get back from shopping tonight, it would give us girls something to occupy our minds."

"Sure, although my mind is already totally occupied with Thad and the wedding."

Across the room, the phone rang on the desk. Three of the women jumped up and dashed for the little éclair-shaped handset, startling Alma from the long to-do list she was checking off with growing relief. She leaned back into the chair as Leah flew past her to grab the phone after its second ring. The red signal stopped blinking when she lifted the receiver. It was Thad, she just knew it.

"Hello, Thad? Where are you?"

"Hi, Leah." A male voice laughed. "Sorry, Honey, I'm not Thad. It's only your poor old dad." He laughed harder, humored by the ad hoc rhyme.

"Oh, Dad, you're hilarious," Leah joined in, laughing. "We've all been waiting to hear from the guys, wondering if they've found Andrei yet. I thought it might be Thad. I am glad you called, Dad. Have you heard anything on your end?"

"Yes. Will you hand the phone to Sarah, please?"

"Sure." With that, the phone was passed to Sarah.

"Yes, Dad? Go ahead."

"There's lots to tell you, Sarah, but for time's sake, I'll give you a message to get to Thad as soon as possible. Tell him that Andrei doesn't need to run anymore. Tell Thad he should contact Ed Cox first. Got it?"

"Okay." Sarah was puzzled, but compliant. "I got it."

"There's another thing, Sarah. Your mom and I are on our way to Anchorage. Our flight leaves in thirty minutes. The plane is boarding now, so I have to go. Please do all you can to get my message to Thad and Andrei. It's very important. I love you, Sarah. Give Angie hugs from her grandma and me. Tell Leah the cavalry is coming." He laughed happily. "Love you-uns." Dad Grant's receiver clicked off. Sarah heard the dial tone resume on hers before she put the phone back in its cradle.

"Mommy?" Angie's eyes were large with wonder, "What did Grandpa say?" Three other sets of eyes looked at Sarah eagerly.

"Grandpa and Grandma send their love and hugs to you, Angie. They have a big surprise for us. They are on their way to Alaska to see us," Sarah finished reaching for the squealing Angie and swinging her around in circles of delight.

"Oh," Leah said quietly with a nod. Old memories stirred chords of dismay. Leah was in a new place where she was not only accepted and loved, but valued. There was grace here. There was a home filled with peace and harmony. She didn't want what she now had to be spoiled by anyone's censure of her new life in Alaska. Alma noticed the anxiety in the bride's face. Denise didn't miss Leah's non-plussed reaction either and stepped over beside her best friend.

"You're not the same Leah I knew from Pennsylvania anymore. You're a believer in Christ and you're Thad's fiancée. 'Therefore, if anyone is in Christ, he is a new creation; old things have passed away; behold, all things have become new.' Second Corinthians chapter 5 verse 17," she quoted and saw a smile form across Leah's lips.

"Thanks, Denise. I needed that reminder."

"I'm actually surprised I remembered that verse. I learned it in Vacation Bible School as a kid. The Holy Spirit really is a Comforter, isn't He?" Denise was thoughtful.

"Ya know something, Denise? Alaska's been good for you too."

Denise chuckled and nodded. "Alaska and one Tyrone Johnson."

"I hope we hear from our guys soon. I don't like the looks of those clouds over the mountains." Leah shot a glance out the windows. "Let's get everyone together and pray."

A few minutes later, Leah, Alma, Denise, Sarah, and Angie had formed a circle, and each prayed whatever came to mind and heart. It was Alma who concluded this prayer vigil, signing with her hands prayer words interpreted by Leah's clear voice. The others joined in.

"Our Father in Heaven, hallowed be Your name. Your kingdom come. Your will be done on earth as it is in heaven. Give us this day our daily bread. And forgive us our debts as we forgive our debtors. And do not lead us into temptation, but deliver us from the evil one. For Yours is the kingdom, and the power, and the glory, forever. Amen."

When the prayer group broke away to resume wedding planning, Sarah found Taima and relayed her dad's message for Thad to give to Andrei.

"I'll do all I can to reach Thad, but it may be difficult to find a signal where they're headed, Sarah." Taima wanted to encourage her, but knew she would respect an honest answer.

"I understand, Taima. Thank you." Sarah's calm reply and smile was great relief to Taima who felt like he had experienced a lifetime of drama in less than a week's time.

# 13

## LOOK WHO THE BEAR DRAGGED IN

THERE WAS MOVEMENT UNDER THE MATTED fur for the first time since Thad and Tyrone had pulled the bulky form inside the crowded mining shack. A muffled groan floated out from beneath the lumpy form, and Tyrone stooped to pull the bearskin away. Though indistinguishable, there was a man folded inside the carcass. When violet eyes blinked open, Thad exclaimed in amazement, "Kroft, it's you!"

"Thad?" he mumbled groggily, "What are you doing here?" Covered in the bearskin, Andrei looked anything but human. Gingerly, he touched a large bump on the side of his head. Thad bent to examine the goose egg that all but guaranteed the Russian bear slayer a purple-blackened eye to match his violet ones.

"Did the bear give you this knot on your head?"

"No," Andrei grumbled. "Someone yanked the bear fur so hard I lost my balance and fell. I remember hitting my head." He blinked his eyes to clear blurred vision.

"Sorry about that, Kroft, it was me. Although, I must say, when I saw that big black furry beast standing in the doorway, it scared the life out of me!" Thad exclaimed. "Are you hurt anywhere else?"

"Just cuts and bruises from falling on the slate yesterday afternoon. That is all," he answered, agitated with himself. "That crazy bear kept stalking me no matter which direction I walked even up the side of a cliff. It was a nightmare!" He shuddered, pushing the bearskin away. "I got tired of being the hunted and decided to stand my ground."

"It sounds like you had a David-and-Goliath experience," Tyrone pointed out, shoving a bucket of water over to Andrei. Thad helped Andrei up to a log stool and began helping him out of his parka. "I guess you get my clean clothes, Kroft. Thad already gave his to Charlie." So saying, Tyrone began unzipping a large pocket on his pack to pull out a thermal crew-necked shirt, jeans, and socks. From another pocket, he pulled a bar of soap he'd often used as a tool rather than for hygiene. Andrei accepted it with gratefulness and began the grooming process.

"Charlie, are you doing all right?" Andrei inquired, glad to see the grizzled mountain man alive and able to talk.

"I'm not dead yet," was his bristly reply.

"He was here in the cabin when we found him," Tyrone informed.

"I brought him inside. I thought I could go for help before the storm hit this area, but," Andrei shrugged, "I could not seem to get away from the bear."

"What happened?" Thad asked as he checked Charlie's bandaged shoulder. Charlie would need further medical attention, to be sure, but contact with any rescuers wouldn't happen until the storm subsided. Thad knew Taima would contact Clovis Pine at six o'clock the next morning if Thad hadn't contacted him by then. Clovis and Thad's acquaintance went back to an experience with the Alaska National Guard several years earlier. Taima's map of a hunter's bonanza of wildlife had gotten both Thad and Tyrone miserably lost. Unknown to them, they had wandered into an area the weekend warriors used as a training site. Army colonel, Clovis Wainwright Pine, was first alerted to the intruders' location when a distress flare was spotted in the direction of a pack of howling wolves. Thad's own call of the wild stopped short when a pair of army boots blocked the small cave's opening. It had earned him the nickname Wolfe Tucker. Though no hunter's bonanza was found that day, a friendship resulted. Since then, Clovis had retired from the National Guard and was a semiretired Alaska State trooper. Thad valued his wisdom in civil matters. Clovis was also one of his hunting and fishing clients. Thad covered Charlie's shoulders to keep the wounded man warm.

"After I saw Sarah and Angelina, I determined to try and make things right. Sarah was right, I needed to stop running and face whatever consequences there were to face with GFI. You mentioned about going to the FBI, and I knew I couldn't do that because I'd found out the agent planted in GFI was funneling company information to me, disclosing its illegal global activities. Why he was sending this information to me instead of his people baffled me until I stopped by the payroll office to sign a waiver for tax exemption because I was on a work visa from Russia. The payroll clerk had printed out a dot-matrix copy of that week's employee bonuses. While she went to a file cabinet to retrieve the tax form, I scanned the list just because it was in front of me. I've read all kinds of stuff like that in my intelligence background. I just notice things." He looked at Thad. "You have a letter from your girlfriend in your shirt pocket. I can smell the rose scent. Tyrone, your girlfriend slipped a love note to you in your backpack. There's a pink tip of an envelope protruding from the pocket where the bar of soap used to be."

Andrei pointed as a surprised Tyrone turned to find the pink paper tucked inside. He teased, "You don't seem like the kind of guy who writes hunting tips on pink stationery." A ripple of laughter brightened the lowly hovel. Andrei looked over at Charlie who had dozed off again and was snoring lightly. In a lower voice, he advised the other two men, "I think Charlie has a spinal injury. He's going to need to be airlifted out of here as soon as the weather clears."

"Aren't we all?" Thad reckoned. "It seems like the winds are subsiding. Hopefully, we'll be able to contact help soon." Turning the conversation back to Andrei, Thad asked, "You're good at noticing details. What did you find out when you saw the payroll sheets?"

"The FBI agent's name was among the list of employees receiving bonuses from several undesignated accounts. His bonus alone was substantial enough to purchase a luxury car with cash or make a down payment on a nice home in the suburbs, maybe a condominium in a warmer climate. That's when it dawned on me that I might be stuck in the middle of something very bad. By then, Sarah and I were just newly married. My life wasn't my own anymore. I had someone who meant the world to me, depending on me for a home and a life together. I didn't know God at the time, except that Sarah knew Him and tried to tell me about the Bible. I listened politely because I loved her, but I never gave much thought to what she said." Andrei was thoughtful.

"You were in a predicament," Thad acknowledged. All was finally quiet outside the cabin. Night had followed receding gray storm clouds to reveal a star-studded sky. The aurora borealis played and danced over the mountain peaks in ribbons of lime green and white.

"Yes. There was a small first aid station on each floor of the building. Grabbing a pair of plastic gloves, I went back to my office and downloaded all the information the agent had sent to me onto floppy disks. I also retrieved the payroll files and downloaded that information, and then deleted everything on the hard drive. The next detail was to get the agent's fingerprints on the evidence. It wasn't hard. I called him and asked him if he had an extra disk box I could use in my office. Less than ten minutes later, he dropped the small plastic container on the chair by my office door on his way to a meeting with the CEO. I knew I didn't have much time. With the gloves on, I slipped the disks into the plastic container, snapped the lid shut, and put it in my brown lunch bag. A few minutes later, I took the elevator to the lobby and left the building through the main doors. I took a taxi to a department store and purchased a small metal cashbox with a lock and another pair of gloves.

"On my way to our apartment, I noticed a police cruiser parked outside the front door. I panicked and decided to go to my Uncle Viktor's place until I could think what to do. I'd visited him a week earlier hoping to find my father staying with him; however, my father had died before I could find him. Sarah was at the mission working in the kitchen, and I wanted to talk to her, but when I got to my Uncle Viktor's, he told me a police detective had called asking about me. I couldn't believe how fast everything was unraveling around me. If I told Sarah what was happening, I'd put her in jeopardy too, by association. So I left my uncle's place and took a bus to the cemetery. There I found my father's grave and buried the metal box with the disks next to the small stone marker.

"From Chicago I hitchhiked my way to the Canadian border. My visa got me into Canada for a while, and then I crossed into Alaska where I've been ever since. The plan was to return to Russia, but every time I thought of Sarah, I just couldn't seem to leave the continent. Now that I've found Sarah, and now that I am a father, a Christian, I thought if I could get to Charlie's place and collect my profits from our mining company, I could support my family and hire a lawyer to help me clear my name. I'd like to obtain US citizenship too, but here I am in Charlie's mining shack. I couldn't get away from that crazy bear. It almost felt like the beast was trying to corral me and keep me here."

Thad smiled. "Tyrone and I prayed and asked God to bring you right here to the doorstep. I believe He answered our prayer."

"You came looking for me?" Andrei was mystified. "Why?"

"This may sound strange to you, Kroft, but we want to help you get this mess of yours figured out. You are a brother in Christ, and if we can manage to call up a rescue squad, we'll be brothers-in-law as well," Thad predicted with a hopeful heart. "Leah and I are to be married in two days. Personally, I'd kinda' like to be there."

"So would I," Tyrone piped up. Denise's pink note made him more eager than ever for courtship. Andrei smiled as he looked at the pink paper Tyrone opened to read.

"You were right about my having a rose-scented letter in my jacket pocket from my fiancée, but what you didn't know was that I had two rose-scented letters in that pocket. The second one is for you, Kroft, even though the name written on the envelope is to someone called Andrei Garankof. Are you Lance Kroft or Andrei Garankof?"

"Andrei Garankof is my name. Please call me Andrei. Lance Kroft was swallowed by a bear," he affirmed. Thad pulled the fragrant letter from his jacket pocked.

"Then I believe this love note is for you, Andrei, my friend." Thad stretched the thick-packed business envelope out to Andrei's eager hand.

"Thank you, Thad." He swallowed with difficulty as this treasure was laid in his hand. That there should be any kindness directed toward him from someone who actually cared for him was deeply confounding. He didn't deserve her love, but it made all the difference.

"While you gentlemen read your love notes, I'm going to get some rest." Thad detached a sleeping bag from his gear and rolled it out on the dirt floor. "There's an insulated tarp with the gear if you'd like to curl up for a while, Andrei."

"I appreciate it, Thad," Andrei acknowledged as he opened the stuffed envelope and pulled out coloring book pages from his daughter, Angelina. Tears trickled down his cheeks at the love and acceptance readily shown to him as though they had never been estranged. There were Bible verses at the bottom of each coloring page. Apparently, David and Goliath was one of her favorite Bible stories. She had carefully colored David's hair in black crayon with tight little circles. Goliath's hair was colored in orange with brown spikes. Andrei relished her creative talent as only a proud father would.

Thad checked on Charlie's sleeping form before he scooted down inside the thermal sleeping bag. He turned away from Andrei to allow the opportunity for privacy in the crowded shack. "Tyrone, could you check and see if we have a signal yet?"

"There's none. I just checked."

"Wake me up in four hours."

"Will do. I'll keep an eye on Charlie."

"Thanks." Thad closed his eyes and prayed, giving thanks to his Father in heaven for bringing Andrei to them. He prayed for Charlie's wounds and for their need to get help for his transport to medical facilities. He saved his greatest request for last so he could fall asleep thinking of his sweet Leah and their wedding day.

Andrei brushed his hand over Sarah's neat handwriting, relishing the evidence of her presence in his life once again. The contents of the letter made his vision cloud with tears of relief in its offer of forgiveness and welcome to her family. He had not experienced joy in such a long time that this feeling of inner warmth seemed to ignite new life within his entire person. He had felt dead inside though his situation had propelled him to survive any way he could. The one brief glimpse of happiness in his life had been the bliss he had shared dating and marrying Sarah. These memories had both sustained him and haunted him over the near decade of wilderness wanderings, and then God's Spirit had wooed him to salvation because of the faithful prayers of his wife. For a while, his head remained bowed until his soul was cleansed of all the anguish of the past. Earlier that afternoon, he'd read the book of First John while sitting on a boulder by a stream just a few miles down the trail where he'd stopped to eat some trail mix Taima had supplied. His father had marked this particular passage of scripture in several places, making Andrei curious as to its importance. The word *love* had been circled some forty-seven times in those five chapters. It was as if his father wanted him to know that the love of the Heavenly Father could reach a son as well as a father. Vladimir Garankof's legacy was no longer shadowed by shame, but imparted in love and faith in the living God.

"I take it the letter was good news?" Tyrone offered friendship as he moved another chunk of wood nearer to the fire glow of the stove. Past dealings with Charlie and Andrei flitted briefly through his mind; nevertheless, he was the husband of Thad's future sister-in-law, Sarah, and father of Angie. As fantastic as this fact seemed, Tyrone was beginning to see there was more to this man than the surly outward appearance showed.

"Yes, it is." Andrei looked over at Tyrone. Gone was the snarly, defensive tone. "It's all good news," his voice caught, then he smiled. "There is hope of good things to come."

"Mine too." Tyrone grinned sheepishly. "We gotta get out of here first." For the first time, Andrei chuckled.

"Now that I don't have a pesky bear chasing me anymore, maybe we can leave this shack and try to get help." Andrei carefully put the letter from Sarah on the rickety table and resumed the task of cleaning the bear gunk from his hair.

"I'd like to hear how you came to be inside that bearskin." Tyrone was curious. Andrei nodded.

Some minutes later, he was cleaned up as best as a bucket of cold water could do for a large man with a thick head of hair, now combed back neatly. Clean clothes and a warm vest gave him a civilized appearance rather than that of a slime creature fit for a child's worst nightmares. Just then, the cracking sound of wood breaking and falling to a crashing thud startled all four men to attention. Charlie awoke with a string of ugly oaths.

"What was that?" Thad blinked wide awake.

"It sounds like that old mining hut on the side of the mountain finally came down," Charlie rasped dully. "It only took a hundred years and a thousand storms to bring that death trap down." A rattling sound in his chest erupted into a belly laugh that lasted only until a sharp pain from his shoulder make him wince and breathe hard. "Anybody got some painkiller?" he squeaked out. Laughter in the shelter halted with the injured man's request.

"I'll get you some from the first aid kit, Charlie." Thad rousted out of the sleeping bag to fetch the ibuprofen packet and a water bottle.

"How about some food, too?" the edgy miner grumbled from his sickbed.

"As you wish, Charlie." Tyrone moved to retrieve the food packs. "Everybody hungry? Alma put sandwiches and cookies together for us. I'll melt snow for some coffee."

"Absolutely," Andrei agreed. "Thad, you better give me a pill for this bump on the head. I got a headache."

"No thanks to me," Thad said lightheartedly as he administered the tiny tablets to the patients.

When the sandwiches were consumed and the cookies were washed down with cold water before the coffee was finished brewing, the accounting of the bearskin was given by an amiable Andrei.

"I first saw the bear tracks after I crossed the same mountain pass you did. It took me some time to cross the slate." He held up his palms showing the cuts from the experience. Tyrone pulled out a small can of orange salve and some gauze. He cleaned the cuts on Andrei's hands and applied salve and bandages while the story continued. "The bear seemed to be heading in the direction of this old mining cabin. I heard a shot fired in the distance and wondered if it was a hunter, so I moved more cautiously trying to stay hidden. I didn't recognize the report of the rifle. That's when I noticed blood in the bear tracks, so I kept following the tracks. Whoever fired that shot only wounded the bear. I found boot tracks leading away from the paw prints. That person was probably running scared."

"We found the same tracks made by the injured bear. It makes me wonder who else is wandering around this area." Thad frowned. "It could be a poacher."

"I hope whoever it was didn't get stuck in this snowstorm," Tyrone ventured.

"By then I was worried. It looked like the bear was headed for this place, and I knew if Charlie was still here, he might be in real danger. If he was drunk, he would not have the slightest chance of survival."

"Who's drunk?" Charlie piped up defensively. Three heads turned in his direction. Their frowns resembled those of clergymen gathered for a 1890s temperance rally. "I never get drunk, I just relax." So saying, Charlie closed his eyes and slept.

"The dead man speaks," Tyrone mumbled, urging Andrei to continue.

"There was another shot, and I knew this one was from Charlie's gun. I heard the roar of the bear and then Charlie's scream," Kroft stopped, recalling the terrible sounds locked into his memory banks. "I hurried as fast as I could to the top of the ridge to see where Charlie and the bear were. I saw the bear heading away from the back of the shack where Charlie lay on the ground in a twisted heap. When I made it down to him, he was unconscious. I checked for broken limbs, but there were none I could see. There was a wound over his shoulder. I carried him into the shack, here, and laid him on the old cot.

"I needed water for Charlie, so I went to the stream and filled the pail. Before I got back to the shack, the bear returned." Andrei shuddered, remembering the snort and growl of the beast. "I searched for Charlie's gun, but it was gone. Apparently, when the bear's claw pummeled him, the rifle was knocked out of his hand." Andrei shook his head as he spoke, "All I had on me was my Bowie knife, a little thirteen-inch knife against a wounded bear." His eyes were large with the telling of the nightmare. "I headed toward him screaming and throwing rocks at him. He stopped then turned and limped, growling into a thicket of birch trees and brush. I hated the idea of following him into the brush, but I didn't want to spend the night wondering if every bump against the shack or grunt outside the shack was his return for revenge on Charlie and me. I've lived that scenario for many years and I'm not living that way anymore. I was done with being the one hunted. I needed to get help for Charlie, too. I followed the bear for almost two miles. It was beginning to grow dark. One thing I was glad about, though," he reflected, "the bear was slowing down. I could no longer hear him growling even though I could hear him breathing hard and crashing through the underbrush ahead. I continued on until I reached an enclosed canyon. I hadn't realized where he was headed until it dawned on me that I could be trapped if the bear somehow circled around behind me." Andrei remembered all too clearly.

"I stood perfectly still, realizing it was almost too dark to see more than a few feet in front of my eyes." He closed his eyes and took a deep breath to relax grated nerves. "I heard the low growl behind me, and I knew what I'd feared the most had happened. The bear had flanked my right side and blocked any exit." He paused. Thad and Tyrone simply waited quietly. "I still had the Bowie knife in my hand. A poor man's feeble defense against a bruin's claws. I turned to face that devil and was shocked to see that the bear stood only fifteen feet from my position. I could not think of anything to do but stand there perfectly still." Andrei lowered his head. When his head came up, there was peace as he spoke sincerely, "All I could think of was the mission sign with the words, JESUS SAVES on it. Courage and strength seemed to pour into my soul. I charged the bear, shouting 'Jesus Saves' as loud as I could. It seemed to echo in the canyon of rock. I drove forward and charged the bear. His paws came around me, but they did not tighten or tear at my body. I felt the bear lean toward me and then roll off into a heap on the ground, dead."

All was quiet inside the shack while outside, the storm whimpered. Only Charlie's gentle snores labored through the post-battle recounting. "I just stood there in the middle of the storm feeling like a free man. It was so peaceful," Andrei said as his countenance grew lighter with peace and joy. "I am no longer afraid to live or to die. God is with me."

"Even here in this place," Thad confirmed, smiling, "at the top of the earth."

"It was at the end of the earth where I found the beginning," Andrei quipped, smiling broadly.

"Amen," Tyrone agreed. Clearing his throat, he began to sing. His rich baritone voice filled the rustic storm-haven with invitation.

Just as I am, without one plea,
But that Thy blood was shed for me,
And that Thou bid'st me come to Thee,
O Lamb of God, I come! I come!

Tyrone stopped after the first verse, and Thad commented, "I've heard that song somewhere."

"Did your mom ever watch the Billy Graham crusades on TV?" Tyrone asked. Thad frowned in thought.

"Yah, I think so. My mom liked to listen to the music and the preaching."

"My family and I participated in the city-wide evangelistic crusades years ago. Billy Graham came to Anchorage in 1984, some thirteen years ago. I had just finished my freshman year at the University of Alaska in Anchorage. Mom wanted all of us to participate in the huge choir at the Sullivan Arena. Our church choir practiced several songs to sing with the other church choirs from all over the state of Alaska. This invitation song, *Just As I Am,* we had to memorize all five verses. To this day, if I hear that hymn sung anywhere in the world, all the words pop right back into my head." Tyrone said, grinning.

"Well, Tyrone, would you sing the rest of the song for us?" Thad urged. Tyrone obliged, and once again his strong deep voice pierced the storm's weakening blast.

Just as I am, and waiting not
To rid my soul of one dark blot,
To Thee whose blood can cleanse each spot,
O Lamb of God, I come! I come!
Just as I am, tho' tossed about
With many a conflict, many a doubt.
Fightings and fears within, without,
O Lamb of God, I come! I come!
Just as I am, poor, wretched, blind,
Sight, riches, healing of the mind,
Yea, all I need, in Thee to find,
O Lamb of God, I come! I come!
Just as I am, Thou wilt receive,
Wilt welcome, pardon, cleanse, relieve;
Because Thy promise I believe,
O Lamb of God, I come! I come!

When Tyrone finished the last note of the song, a holy quietness permeated the humble shelter. Each man reflected on his relationship to the Almighty.

As if lulled by the Christian call to come and bow at the sinners' bench, the winds calmed as drifting snow settled down to blanket the rugged land. Winter had chased autumn away. Pardon's white snow covered the dark land in sparkling triumph. Andrei Garankof continued almost lightheartedly.

"It was getting much colder, and the wind had picked up, so I decided I needed the bear's fur more than he did. It was almost dark. I pulled the bearskin around my body for warmth and started back toward the shack, hoping Charlie was still alive. By the time I reached this place it was sleeting, and the wind was almost blowing me and the bearskin away. It really confused me that the door was bolted. I knew I hadn't locked it or even shut the door when I went for the bucket of water. The only thing to do was try to break the door down. Then someone grabbed me, and I felt myself being pulled forward. I lost my balance and I remember falling sideways until my head hit something." He gently rubbed the sore bump on the side of his head. Thad tried another sincere apology and received a smile of pardon. "Now, I'm here holding a love letter in my hands from my Saraianna."

Thad pulled his note out and announced, "Leah."

Tyrone grinned as he also displayed his pink envelope, "Denise."

Hearty laughter echoed throughout the mining shack. Poor Charlie snored on in bachelor's bliss.

# 14

## PICTURES IN FRAMES OF GOLD

TAIMA PACED THE FRONT HALLWAY, WHICH was something he never did! It was four o'clock in the afternoon, and he hadn't heard one word from Thad or Tyrone since they'd left just after noon the day before. He hadn't worried too much until the storm had settled in with a vengeance over the Matanuska Valley.

The radio station in Palmer and the TV station in Anchorage were both reporting high winds and downpours of rain over the south-central region. It had produced hail in their area earlier that day. When the skies had cleared enough to see the mountain peaks, Taima saw white-capped mountains for miles and miles along the horizon. He called Clovis Pine informing him of Thad's and Tyrone's trek in the Hatcher Pass area near Willow. The troops had been summoned; the rescue operation would be coordinated. He informed the ladies about the phone calls he'd made after a discussion with Alma about the possibility of altering the wedding plans.

At various times, he saw each lady walk to the front windows to gaze out in hopes of seeing the return of their men-folk. He knew they were as concerned as he was. Thankfully, plans for the wedding kept them occupied. Taima worried about hysterical women, but noted that they weren't pacing the floor like he was. Halting, he turned and took the staircase down to the den and into the garage then back to the den to gaze out the window to the main road a quarter of a mile below the lodge.

Alma came into the den and touched Taima's arm gently to pull his attention from the view to the mountains. His deep frown greeted her smile. "Taima," she signed, "we are all very worried about our men, but we've been praying and asking God to return them safely."

"Let's hope your prayers are answered." Taima was skeptical.

"They will be, Brother," Alma assured. She had not called him *Brother* in many years.

He looked at her curiously. "What if the answer He gives causes pain?" Taima directed with a mild bark.

"Then we'll trust His grace to help us through any pain that comes."

"That's easy for you to say, Alma." Taima muttered, and spoke again before he thought the better of his words. "How can you so easily excuse God for the losses we've endured throughout our childhood and as adults?"

Alma could not mask the deep hurt that rose in her heart, but chose to answer Taima for what he had endured. "You lost a lifetime with a wife and son. Both of us have lost parents due to the choices of others as well as our own choices. I found God's grace and forgiveness to help me find peace and hope for a better future. I don't know how any of this is going to turn out, I just know God cares even when I feel like there isn't much left to hope for."

The phone rang, and Taima reached for the receiver hanging on the wall near the small kitchenette.

"Hello," he answered, anticipation sounding in his voice.

"Taima, Clovis Pine here. Talkeetna Rescue just confirmed a helicopter pick-up of four civilians in Denali Borough. One has received life-threatening injuries from a bear. All four are being transported to Providence Medical Center in Anchorage for medical evaluations and treatment. The descriptions fit those of Thad, Tyrone, one Charlie Bachman, and a man the Alaska State Troopers know as Lance Kroft. I'm meeting with three of the four men at Providence. It may take some time to sort things out and make reports. Wait for a call from either Thad or Tyrone." Clovis took a breath. "Taima, sit tight and keep the phone line open," he directed. "We'll be in touch."

"Sure thing, Clovis, thanks." Taima hung up and turned to find the four females eagerly awaiting the details of the phone message.

"The men have been picked up by helicopter and are being flown into Anchorage. I'm to wait for a call from Thad or Tyrone. We'll need to keep the line open for their call. Official reports have to be made to sort things out, so it may be a while before we hear from the guys. Sarah, your husband is with them. We're to sit tight here and wait for more news." Taima chose not to mention that one of the men had been mauled by a bear. Clovis hadn't said which man had been injured anyway, and until he knew more, he was not about to add to the anxiety of those in his care. With measured relief, the ladies headed up to the kitchen to make some sandwiches, Taima pulled Alma aside and told her about the bear mauling.

"I'm figuring that Thad and Tyrone are okay since Clovis said one of them would call with more information. I just don't know if it was Charlie or Kroft—I mean Andrei who was mauled."

"Time will tell," Alma signed quickly. "Thanks for letting me know. You're right, we should wait until we hear from Thad or Tyrone." Just then the chimes at the front door sounded, and Alma headed for the steps up to the entrance. Joe Dorrance and little Michelle stood smiling at a surprised Alma who greeted and welcomed them inside.

"I apologize for not calling you ahead of time, but I needed to talk to Taima right away, so I loaded Michelle up and came over." He paused to chuckle. "She was so excited to see Angie again she almost got here before I did." Joe's friendly smile warmed Alma's face and heart completely. Nodding with a smile, she directed Joe down the stairs to the den where Taima had taken a seat to read the *Anchorage Daily News*. The skies had cleared and the sun was shining as if there had been no storm at all in the farm valley.

"Hi, Taima," Joe greeted his friend.

"Hey, Joe. What's happening?"

"I heard the distress call from Thad to the troopers over my Ham radio about an hour ago. The helicopter was circling the prospectors' mine site looking for a place to land but couldn't because of deep snow, so they were hovering and planning to try a basket lift. Thad told Rescue 1 that Charlie Bachman had been mauled by a bear, and he suspected spinal injuries." Joe shrugged. "I lost the signal for a few minutes. When it returned, Thad was saying to Rescue 1 that there was another bear roaming around the mine area and it was heading straight for the basket in front of the mining shack. Rescue 1 answered back, affirming they had the bear in rifle sights. I heard two sharp cracks from a rifle and a bunch of guys yelling, "Got it! Bear Down! Clear! Up Basket!" Joe recited, himself a volunteer member of Palmer's Forest Fire Rescue squad. "After that, the radio signal broke up. Thad must have been the last one up."

"Man! Those guys have all the fun," Taima teased, relieved to hear about the rescue except for Thad's close call with another pesky bear that hadn't found a place to hibernate before the early snowfall. Taima said more seriously, "So it was Charlie who wasn't so lucky this time?"

"Apparently so. As tough and belligerent as he is, Charlie should survive his wounds and maybe even civilization in general. It's hard to think he was ever a young boy," Joe commented. "He's always been tough as nails."

"Alma and I have known Charlie since we were kids," Taima confided thoughtfully. "Our families came from St. Paul in the Pribilof Islands. During World War II, there were over eight hundred Alaskan natives evacuated from nine villages in the Pribilof and Aleutian islands to places called Duration Villages. These internment camps were in Southeast Alaska along the panhandle. Our people were removed from our homes and transported by ship to abandoned canneries and rotting gold mining camps that had no plumbing, electricity, or toilets. For two years, our Unangax people endured the cold without warm clothing or supplies. The camp food was poor and often inadequate. The water was tainted. Many of our people became sick with pneumonia and tuberculosis as well as other sicknesses.

"Seventy-four of our young ones and our elders died in those internment camps. Alma got the sickness with the fever. She was just a small baby. It destroyed her hearing and her voice box. Our mother later died of pneumonia. My father was never the same, though he took care of us the best he could. We were returned to St. Paul two years later, in 1945, after the Japanese threat had been vanquished. All our homes and our churches had been burnt to the ground as a precaution should the Japanese invade, but our people did not despair. We rebuilt our villages, and we remained patriotic to our country. Twenty-five of our Unangax men joined the United States Armed Forces, and all twenty-five were awarded the Bronze Star. Charlie was one of the twenty-five men awarded a Bronze Star. Both his parents died at the Funter Bay Camp while he was off fighting in the war. My family was at the Funter Bay Camp too. Charlie's father had been our village elder and one of the few elders who remembered the native languages and customs. Of course, Charlie took it real hard. He is a few years older than I am, but I remember him as being restless and eager for a fight. I mostly stayed out of his way. His last name isn't Bachman, either. I don't know when he changed it." Taima shrugged.

"I had no idea, Taima." Joe was amazed. "I'm beginning to understand some things about Charlie and about Alma and you."

"About Alma," Taima said pointedly, "she wasn't raised in church like the women you know. She's lived a hard life and suffered for it more than anyone has any right to know about. In fact, she probably will not meet your standards of womanly virtue should you come to know her history. As her older brother, I don't want her taken advantage of and then thrown aside when she doesn't fit your high Christian ideals. Do you understand what I'm saying?" He saw Joe's eyebrow lift slightly.

"I understand, Taima, and I promise you I will endeavor to honor your sister, Alma, in every way. God is my witness." Joe pledged.

Just then, Sarah came down the steps and into the den. Concern showed on her gentle face. "Taima, I need to get a message from my dad to Thad. Is there some way I could talk to Thad? It's very important."

"Yes. We should be able to call his cell number by now. I wasn't able to get your message to Thad earlier." Taima pulled Thad's recharged cell phone from the inside pocket of his vest and pushed a number sequence on the keypad. After a couple of ring tones, Thad's loud voice was heard from Taima's phone. Taima greeted him and told him Sarah had an important message for him. He handed the phone to Sarah, and she relayed the important communication. Minutes later, Thad was talking to Detective Ed Cox in Chicago.

Laundry was neatly folded and put away while the spacious lodge was tidied by several eager hands. Taima and Joe had moved up to the great room to build a fire in the fireplace and offer what assistance the ladies might request. The ladies moved to their rooms to freshen up, their steady chatter bounced back and forth from room to room like ping-pong balls.

In all the flurry of activity, Leah paused to look at Thad's bachelor photo. Only six months ago, on a snowy Valentine's Day, she had sat in a booth at a date-matching agency quietly studying several bios of Alaskan bachelors looking for a "meaningful relationship." Thad's request had been for someone to sew on his popped buttons. It was this same photo she held in her hand that had captured her further interest and her response. Subsequent letters of amity followed steadily to and from the pen pals. If all went well, tomorrow she, Leah Grant would be married to her chosen Alaskan bachelor, Thad Tucker. The realization made imaginary butterflies take flight in her stomach as the minutes ticked away toward the moment when her vows to love, honor, and obey would be pledged--forever. Doubts? There were none where loving Thad or his loving her was concerned. Her only doubt was in her ability to manage his home and a family when their family included children. Being a teacher had taught her to schedule, plan, organize, follow through, and evaluate the needs of her classroom from day-to-day. Would marriage be similar? Planning meals three times a day every day for 365 days a year for years and years to come seemed overwhelming at the moment. How had her mother done it and managed ministry commitments too? Perhaps some of the tension in their home had resulted from juggling all the duties her mother had shouldered in being a helpmate to Leah's dad. She had never thought of her mother as being anything other than an authoritarian figure she had to obey without question. Yet her mother had been a young bride at one time too. Had she been apprehensive about being a wife? Leah wished for an opportunity where she and her mother could sit and talk openly about these things without the authoritarian side of her mother's vast experiences making her feel incompetent and immature. *Lord*, she prayed silently, *help us to find common ground where we can meet as allies instead of adversaries. I just want her acceptance and friendship.*

Leah blinked back the gathering tears, wondering if she had prayed for the impossible. A gentle whisper passed into her subconscious spirit: *If you want acceptance and friendship, you must give it too. A man who has friends must himself be friendly, but there is a friend who sticks closer than a brother.*

An old Sunday school Bible verse Leah had memorized as a child came back in a flash. She stood motionless as the Holy Spirit's admonition urged a change in her mind and heart toward her mother. The guidance of the Holy Spirit was the friend who would stick closer than a brother in her life as a believer, a daughter, a sister, and a wife. *Be anxious for nothing, but in everything by prayer and supplication, with thanksgiving, let your requests be made known to God; and the peace of God, which surpasses all understanding, will guard your hearts and minds through Christ Jesus.* Yet another Bible verse memorized when her heart was soft and pliable to God's Word came to mind. Leah was amazed by the faith God had placed in her heart before resentment and rebellion had squelched it. The butterfly feeling accompanying her bride-to-be jitters passed with the promise that she would have the help and blessing of God's Spirit as she recited her marriage vows to Thad. Her tender gaze moved from Thad's photo to the bathroom door where her bridal dress hung in waiting. Joy and confidence filled every part of her being.

A while later, Leah and Denise sat in the great room while Sarah corralled two little girls who were hosting a bridal show with fashion dolls. Angie and Michelle were intent on their stage production of the make-believe wedding. Michelle had brought her Barbie Doll fashion case filled with every fashion and accessory the grand wedding of the two girls dreams could desire. Thad Tucker's hunting lodge had become a wedding wonderland.

It was Denise's turn to walk over to the front window and watch for the first sight of the men coming up the drive. Taima and Alma had driven to Hatcher Pass to pick up the Chevy Suburban and bring it back to the lodge right after lunch and had returned with news that the three men would be leaving Anchorage after their reports were recorded with the State Troopers. Alma and Joe had just entered the large living room to get orders for ice cream sodas when Denise announced that a truck was coming up the drive.

Alma smiled at the diverse expressions on the faces of her three new lady friends. Sarah stood up and froze in place. Leah was already bolting for the front door while Denise seemed undecided about what to do and tried to remain poised and calm but looked like she was about to explode. Angie and Michelle ran to the window and looked out as four men exited the four-door pickup.

"It's Thad and Tyrone! They're back!" Angie exclaimed with excitement.

"It's Mr. Pine. I know him. He's my daddy's boss when there is a mountain fire," Michelle informed wide-eyed and very importantly.

"Hey!" Angie snorted when she saw the man who was her dad get out of the truck. "He's here too." Annoyance was evident in her voice. At first, she had been overjoyed to think she had a dad, but he had gone away--again. Why did he keep going away? It made Mommy sad, and Angie saw the worry lines return on her mother's tired face. Angie didn't think it was a nice way to treat her mommy. Resentment toward her long-lost dad was growing steadily. Grandpa Grant had always been there for her until they had come to see Aunt Leah here. Now Taima and Thad were there for her too. Even Michelle's dad was there for her, but her dad was a stranger, and she didn't like strangers at all! Her mind was made up. If he wasn't going to be there for her and Mommy, she wouldn't be there for him. Angie turned from the window.

"Come on, Michelle. Let's play Barbie Bride Day."

"Angelina," her mother called from the doorway. "Come and greet your dad."

Angie looked over at her mom knowing that she was expected to obey. Rarely had the little girl disobeyed; she was a mostly compliant, cheerful child. In this instance, however, she hesitated as defiance raised an ugly head in her will. Sarah repeated the directive with parental urging. Angie stood to her feet but didn't move toward her mom.

"Angelina Joy, come and greet your dad."

"Why is *he* here, Mommy? He's a stranger," she finger-pointed.

Sarah's heart sank as she took note of her daughter's uncharacteristic disobedience and challenge to her authority. A moment later, anger flared up in Sarah's heart toward her daughter's response, and she walked across the length of the great room considering her options for discipline. Peeved as Sarah was, she addressed her daughter in a quiet tone. Joe saw the confrontation and called Michelle to come into the kitchen for her ice cream soda before they would leave to go home. Michelle could tell this was not a good time to play with Barbies and walked quickly to the kitchen. She and her dad had had a few times like this about her not wanting to go to kindergarten next week.

"Angie, I want you to think about something I've had to remember about people." Sarah motioned Angie over to sit on the couch beside her. Angie moved and took a seat beside her mom. Sarah took a deep breath to quell the anger Angie's rebellion provoked. "We all need God in different ways. Some people need healing for sickness. Some people need forgiveness. All of us people need Jesus as Savior. Even after we ask Jesus to be our Savior, we have problems in life that only God can work out. That man you're calling a stranger needs God's help right now. He needs our kindness and our forgiveness too. You didn't know you had a dad, and he didn't know he had a daughter. Both of you are strangers to each other. Your being mad at your dad is hurting all of us more than it will help us find our happiness together. He's not a good dad yet because he'll have to learn how to be a good dad. You have learned how to be a wonderful daughter, Angie. You are the best daughter in the whole world. Your dad is so blessed to have you, and he knows that too. Can you give him a chance? Even if all you can do is just say 'Hi, Dad.'" Long dark lashes fell and rose again in quiet contemplation as mother and daughter adjusted attitudes toward one man who longed for their acceptance and love, knowing he didn't deserve it.

"If Jesus can forgive my dad, I can try to be nice to him." Angie wasn't ready to forgive, yet. Another question popped into her childish mind. "Mommy, do you think he likes little girls like me at all? He seemed so mad at me at the trading post that other day, and when we saw him at that old place, he seemed like he didn't know what to do about me."

Sarah smiled. "I'm sure your dad was surprised to see you both times. Like I said, it may take him a while to get used to having a beautiful daughter like you in his life, but I'm sure he's looking forward to the experience. Give him a chance to show you he loves you, Angie."

"Okay, Mommy." Her violet eyes promised readily. The tension in their mother-daughter space evaporated as peace settled in its place.

"Are you ready, Angie?"

"Yes, Mommy." Angie smiled and spoke with childish earnest, "Thanks for not spanking me. I'm just learning too." Sarah smiled and reached to hug her daughter, glad she had not reacted in anger.

Sarah realized they would need breathing room for adjustments in the days ahead. Rather than punishment, patience would have to be the rule until all of them found their places in this fractured family. *Train up a child in the way he should go, and when he is old, he will not depart from it.* Sarah thought about the training she and her two sisters had received. Rachel, the oldest, was very self-righteous and judgmental. She was a good judge of people, and that was the point—she judged others without compassion. Leah, on the other hand, had resisted anything religious, only going through the motions dutifully. She went along with the crowd but did her own thing anyway. Sarah thought about her own walk with God. It had been difficult to understand grace or truth, period.

For a long time after Angie was born, Sarah had a difficult time trusting God. She felt God was angry with her and disappointed in her as others were. It had taken great courage to continue to be faithful to attend church services. She struggled to find favor with God and people by working hard to prove her worth in Christian service. It wasn't until Angie was about three years old that Sarah began to understand the love and acceptance of her Savior, Jesus Christ. It was during one of her dad's Sunday morning sermons that God's Holy Spirit opened the eyes of her understanding with a passage of scripture from Ephesians chapter 1 verse 6. Sarah only remembered a phrase from the verse, "by which He made us accepted in the Beloved." Her dad had preached that it was God the Father's sacrificial love that made each believer accepted in the royal courts of His Beloved Son. Each believer lived within the eternal realm of God's love and His glorious grace. It was not an exclusive club as the world might interpret it to be; it was a literal place of inheritance where one completely belonged and was sealed by the indwelling of the Holy Spirit. Sarah had found peace and joy in this truth, and it changed her personal walk with God. His love and grace restored her trust and gave her strength to live what was true with courage.

Mother and daughter moved toward the double door as it opened. All eyes focused on Taima who entered and grinned slyly at the anxious ladies. "They're all down in the garage— if you want to see them." He was being facetious. Of course the girls wanted to see their guys; but the guys were in the garage for a reason.

The footfalls of several feminine feet thumped down the steps in rapid succession and continued around the corner to the garage. Taima heard the door hinges to that area squeak as the door was opened. He made a mental note to spray some WD-40 on the complaining hardware. Happy greetings started but stopped abruptly. Leah was the first to encounter the three supposedly human beings of the mankind. She stopped at the sight in front of her, and in domino effect, the three ladies behind her all bumped to a sudden stop. A rancid odor prevented Leah from making any advance toward Thad. Denise, Sarah, and Angie zigzagged around Leah and halted as the smell assaulted their noses. They had expected to greet the same fine-looking, clean-smelling men they'd uttered Godspeed to over thirty-six hours ago, but what moved in front of them gave them reason to believe that Charlie's overnight accommodations had indeed been primitive. All three men looked as if they had just walked out of a monster movie set. Sarah was the first to greet them and move toward Andrei. He smiled a welcome as muddy boots came off and hit the floor with a heavy thud. There was still grime in his hair from the bear innards, though clean bandages covered scrapes and cuts on his forehead and hands. Cautiously, Sarah moved closer.

"Andrei, I've never seen you this way," She gulped and squinted, waving her hand like a fan to move the strong fetid, animal scent away, but it only seemed to stir up more stink. "Whew!" She looked up at him. Her honey-brown eyes stirred his being. Winking, he opened his arms and leaned toward her for a hug and saw her pinch her nose and raise a pointer finger of warning. He laughed out loud. Sarah pushed him back and laughed with her husband. The others watched the married couple with interest. Affection had not diminished, though the lengthy estrangement time had tested their love.

"I got your note," he said simply. "I had to get right back, you know. So I came as I was," he teased blandly noticing Sarah's lips form a smirk. "Actually, I'm a lot cleaner than I was, thanks to Tyrone." He motioned over to Tyrone who was being scrutinized by Denise. She stood off to his side waiting for him to step out of his boots. When Andrei headed for the bathroom in the den, Sarah followed with a garbage bag for the cast-off clothes.

Leah whistled slowly, making Thad laugh heartily.

"Was that a wolf whistle?"

"No. It was a warning whistle," she replied, putting a hand over her nose in efforts to block out some of the smell. "You guys look like something the cat dragged in."

"We were almost something the bear dragged in." Tyrone explained to the two women and laughed at Denise's astonished expression. He took a step toward Denise. She took a step backward, giving him a guarded look that stopped his nonsense.

"Why do you guys smell so bad?" she asked. In addition to the animal stench, there was also the acrid smell of liquor that hung in the air like a bad dream. Denise knew this smell from Jack's occasional drinking binges. It was another disgusting reason why Denise had finally reconciled herself to spinsterhood. She sniffed the air with a wrinkled nose. "I smell liquor, too." Leah shot a startled look at Denise then back at Thad. Like a flash across her mind's eye, the question about Thad's perspective on alcohol use in their marriage and home sent yellow flags all over the playing field. They hadn't talked about alcohol yet. Dread filled Leah, and she considered Thad anew.

Thad and Tyrone looked at each other and hollered at the same time, "Charlie!"

"Sorry, ladies," Thad offered. "Apparently, Charlie had been drinking pretty heavily before the bear attack. When we found him in the mining shack, the place smelled like a distillery from his recent binge."

Denise asked the question before Leah could, "Do you guys drink alcohol?"

"Does it matter?" Tyrone asked, suddenly sensing a change in direction.

"Yes," Leah answered for her best friend too. Seeing the serious look on Leah's face, Thad stopped moving hiking gear away from the truck and stood looking at his bride-to-be directly. He was brief and to the point.

"On occasion, I will purchase a six-pack of my favorite beer and drink a bottle or two of it at leisure. Sometimes I will share a small flute of wine with my clients when we eat out at a restaurant. Other than that, I don't drink much at all." Thad saw the shine in Leah's eyes fade. Her eyes dropped from his. When her eyes met his dark-brown ones a moment later, he saw resolve in them.

"I'm a teetotaler. No alcohol whatsoever." Leah explained, and Thad took a deep breath before answering. Tyrone and Denise felt like statues in a park observing lovers making destiny-altering decisions. The best man and maid-of-honor seemed unable to do anything about it but strike a granite pose.

"Is this going to change our plans?" Thad's heart constricted.

Leah started to cry. An awkward silence held the foursome captive.

"Now don't you two do anything hasty," Tyrone advised, finally breaking free of the statue's vow of silence. "Maybe you guys just need some time to figure this out."

"I think that's a great idea," Denise said quickly, eyes wide and head bobbing. "The Lord will help you figure this out if you pray together about it. The wedding can wait a couple of days. No big deal."

At Denise's mention of praying and asking for guidance, Thad realized that as a new Christian, he hadn't had time to consider some of his old habits and how they might affect his faith. He thought about his reading in Matthew's gospel of Jesus leadership of the disciples. Would they have drunk a six-pack? Honestly, he doubted it. Of course, Jesus drank wine at a marriage celebration, didn't He? Thad wasn't exactly sure what this might mean. Leah's background pretty much ensured her resolve against any liquor at all. They were at an impasse until he could figure out what to do. Though his own heart was breaking, he could see the intense pain on Leah's tear-stained face. He walked over to her and was about to put his arms around her when he realized his grungy state. Instead, Thad reached for Leah's hand.

"I can see this is very important to you, Leah. Honestly, I never even gave it a thought because an occasional few beers is not a big deal to me.

I need some time to figure this out, and you need some time to deal with any doubts you might have about me. If you can't trust me, then this isn't going to work. I love you, Leah, so much that it hurts, but if we need to wait, I am willing and happy to wait for you. Will you wait for me?"

"Yes." Leah managed a smile up at Thad. "This is important, Thad."

"Do we need to postpone our wedding?"

The question hung in the air. Cancelling the caterers, the cake, the church, and Pastor Paytor seemed a little overboard to Leah. *Would the wedding take place?* She wondered, and in that moment had peace that it somehow would take place. Was her taking a stand against liquor in their home really that important? *Yes! Lord, I believe it is.* Leah's lips formed a gentle smile.

"Yes, Thad, we will need to postpone our wedding. I honestly never gave beer or wine a thought when we started writing to each other because it was never even a consideration in my home. My dad's sermons never condoned alcohol of any kind. I'm sorry, Thad." All of a sudden Leah's eyes popped wide open. "*My dad!*"

Thad's eyebrows rose. "What about your dad?"

"My mom and dad are on their way to Anchorage!"

"What? More guests?" Thad teased. "I'd better get cleaned up then," He smiled broadly.

"You knew all the time!"

"I did. I got Sarah's message and called Denise's dad. He told me your parents were on their way. In fact, their plane should be taxiing to the gate right about now." So saying, Thad winked at Leah and headed for the steps up to his room to clean up. Tyrone decided it was a good time to make an exit for the bathroom near the den. The ladies headed up to the main level to help Alma fix tacos while Taima made ice cream sodas for the crowd.

"So--the wedding is still on, but it's off," Denise surmised. Leah's eyes rolled to the ceiling in disbelief at this latest pre-wedding knot. "Oh, girlfriend, relax. I support you wholeheartedly. This is important for both you and Thad to figure out. God spared me from a serious mistake, Leah. I never told you this, but Jack drank like a fish, and his breath stank. One of the main reasons he stuck with me for as long as he did was that I was his designated driver. To this day, I can hardly even go into a restaurant where they serve alcoholic beverages. I have to leave because I can't stand the stuff." Denise put an arm around Leah's shoulder. "It's all going to work out. Maybe sooner than you think with your dad on his way. Thad can talk this out with him."

"Thanks, Denise. I wonder what Tyrone thinks of the stuff?"

"He was awfully quiet, wasn't he?" Denise frowned. She'd broach the subject with Tyrone later. "Let's head upstairs and find out what the latest news is."

"I hate to mention our postponing the wedding to Alma and Taima," Leah said soberly.

"Wait until Thad is beside you for support." Denise advised. "Both Alma and Taima will want what's best for both of you. You are very blessed, Leah."

"I know I am." Leah sighed then pondered, "Will I ever—"

"—settle down and think before jumping in to things?" Denise finished correctly, making Leah laugh. "Probably not until you're eighty years old, and too slow to jump."

# 15

## PILGRIMS

COLE AND DORIS GRANT HAD RENTED a car at the Anchorage International Airport and were headed to Palmer, where the travel agency had reserved a room at the Valley Hotel for their brief stay. Thad had received a call from his future father-in-law informing him of hotel accommodations and had issued an invitation to them to come over to the lodge to meet friends and future in-laws. The invitation had been accepted.

Thad found Leah sitting quietly in the den by the patio doors gazing at the stone terrace where he'd proposed only a week before. He told her of the evening's plans as he sat down close to her. Leah was more nervous about the new hitch in wedding plans than Thad was about meeting her parents. Leah fidgeted, twirling her diamond engagement ring around and around her finger until Thad took her hand and kissed her ring finger. She leaned into the circle of his arms, grateful for this quiet time together. She had been pondering their present decision to postpone their wedding over the alcohol issue. Her feelings were divided by her love for Thad and her inborn training against the use of alcohol. More than that, there was the statement Thad had directed to her, *If you can't trust me, then this isn't going to work*. It made her stomach knot and her heart ache.

"You're very quiet. I think I can almost guess what you're thinking about. Could it be," Thad tried some humor, "horses?" She was amazed by Thad's calm demeanor and un-rattled nerves.

"Not so, my dear." Leah laughed at that random idea. "I wish my only thoughts could be about horses. We would simply ride off into the sunset together."

"I like that idea," Thad agreed, thinking about Sunrise and Sunset; the two horses corralled a short distance from the lodge. His hired help, a teenaged neighbor, had been doing a great job grooming and exercising them for the past two weeks. Never had he expected life to become as complicated as it had in the past few weeks. But here it was, and he was thankful for the friends who surrounded him and helped keep everything running fairly smoothly.

"I was thinking that I really don't want to postpone our wedding. Alma was very understanding when you told her we might need to wait. It was smart for her to have a contingency plan in place in case you guys weren't able to get back in time, but I was the one who threw a wrench into the works, as we say. I'm so grateful for her kindness and your patience, Thad."

"Well, before you feel any worse, I want to tell you about a phone call I had with Pastor Paytor a few minutes ago," he said as Leah turned to face him, a glimmer of hope making her eyes shine. "I got to thinking about a chapter I'd read in the book of John, and I figured Pastor Paytor might be able to help me understand what Jesus would do. When I mentioned about our postponing the wedding because of our differences about alcohol, he was very understanding, which surprised me. I had expected he would condemn me, but he didn't. I asked him about Jesus turning water into wine at a wedding his mother attended, and he gave me a perspective that helped me to make a decision about drinking beer and wine."

"Thad," Pastor Paytor asked, "are you willing to be completely honest with God and with yourself about the matter of alcohol? I ask for this reason. Until a man is willing to open the hidden places of his heart for Holy God to sanctify, he'll ultimately close himself off to the power and blessing of God on his life. This is why so many men drift through their Christian life with little influence for Christ in their homes."

Thad thought about this challenge. Already he sensed the presence of God at work in his heart as he read the Bible with eagerness to know and understand about his Heavenly Father. His soul was thirsty for the Father's love because he had not known an earthly father. Finding God more and more to be a perfect Father, Thad wanted to please Him out of devotion and growing love. God wasn't a genie in a lamp to grant one's selfish wishes, nor was God an idol made in the minds of man to appease or curse at whim.

"I'm willing to be honest, Pastor Paytor," Thad pledged. "Go ahead, I'm listening."

"There are a lot of views, both pro and con, regarding drinking fermented substances such as beer and wine as we know it in our society today. I've studied this passage of scripture in John chapter 2, and I've come to one simple conclusion: Jesus took the water and turned it into the finest, richest grape juice there ever was, period. This is based on the character of Christ and the Greek word for wine used in this passage. The Greek word used here is *oinos*, meaning wine that is pressed. There is the distinct possibility that this wine may not have aged yet. Even the Hebrew word *tiyrosh* refers to the kind of wine that is fresh grape juice just squeezed and not yet fermented. If Jesus had turned the water into fermented wine, the Greek word *gleukos* for wine would have been used, meaning that this wine would have been sweet, highly inebriating fermented wine. But it wasn't. It was *oinos* or fresh-squeezed grape juice. Interestingly, there is a metaphorical meaning attached to *oinos* here because it refers to the winepress of God's wrath.

"The miracle at the wedding feast in Cana could very well have been a symbolic picture of what Christ would do in shedding His blood on Calvary for us. Christ's blood wasn't tainted by fermentation or by sin. He was the perfect Son of God and able to deliver us from the winepress of God's wrath. For this reason, I personally have chosen not to drink beer or wine. I know that occasional drinking may seem harmless, but I belong to Jesus Christ, and His Holy Spirit lives within me. My body is His dwelling place. I don't want to grieve the Holy Spirit, and I don't want to cause confusion or distress to those I love."

Pastor Paytor finished. "For me as a follower of Jesus Christ, I can't touch the stuff. As a minister of the Gospel, I don't condone the use of alcohol at all." There was silence for a brief time as Thad contemplated Pastor Paytor's explanation. For the most part, Thad could do without the occasional six-pack and the celebratory glass of wine with a client. The only bit of information his mother had told him about his dad was that they had fought over his dad's drinking binges. For the love of liquor, his dad had left his wife and son to fend for themselves. Thad had a choice to make.

"Thank you, Pastor Paytor. I have to talk to Leah. I'll be in touch."

"All right, Thad. We'll talk to you later then."

"Have you made a decision, Thad?" For once in her life, Leah sat quietly and waited.

"Yes." Thad nodded, taking her hands in his as if to make a vow. "My mother often reminded me that people are way more important than things. Liquor is a thing. You are a person. I value you, Sweet Leah, far more than any can of beer or glass of wine. I also value my faith in God, and I want to honor Him. So there will not be any beer in our refrigerator, and we will not be celebrating with wine. Instead, we'll drink apple cider or sip grape juice as we ride off on Sunrise and Sunset." Leah was so excited and so relieved that she missed Thad's reference to the two fine horses awaiting the couple's wedding-day ride. Thad grinned with the keeping of his secret.

"Let's go tell Alma there's going to be a wedding tomorrow afternoon!" Leah jumped up and pulled Thad up. He drew her into his arms and looked into her eyes.

"Can you trust me, Leah?" he probed. "Can we trust each other to find our way through problems that test the areas of our faith I don't understand yet? I'm willing to learn and make changes as God shows me what I need to do and what I need to be. My fear is that I'll fail you somehow, and you'll lose your love and respect for me. It only took a six-pack of beer, however wrong we both now agree it may be, to stop our wedding ceremony. What would it take to divide our home?"

Leah nodded slowly as she considered Thad's questions. "I was thinking about the same thing before you told me your decision. So far, life for me has been fairly carefree. Oh, I've had some struggles with parents and heartbreaks here and there, but I've pretty much breezed through troubles or done my best to evade them and leave others to figure them out for me. I've never trusted enough to see an unchangeable situation through where I'm stuck for good. Honestly, I've thought of marriage as the happiness of the wedding day lasting forever. But after the issue of alcohol came up, I realized that the wedding day is the party, but the marriage is a partnership. United we stand, divided we fall," Leah quipped meditatively. "You mentioned having a fear of losing my love and respect. I have the exact same fear as you do, Thad. Will we ever get to the point that we feel stuck with each other and treat each other with contempt? I've seen this so much in married people. It makes me want to run, except that my love for you is so much stronger than this terrible fear. I don't want this wonderful love we have for each other to wither, ever. I want it to grow stronger."

"So do I," Thad confirmed. "I have no doubt whatsoever that we are to be together, Leah. You are my miracle, and the one God sent to capture my heart through faith in Christ. I will always love and treasure you, Leah. We belong to Jesus Christ, and it was His love that drew us together from opposite ends of the country. I'm going to trust Him to keep our love alive for each other as we seek His ways together. I make this commitment to you here and now before God even before we recite our vows in front of family and friends, Sweet Leah."

His confidence in God's divine purpose for their faith and love gave her a sense of enduring security and peace about the vows they would make and keep. Leah smiled as peace and joy filled her soul.

"I also make my commitment to you, Thad, before God without fear or doubt, knowing God is able to keep what we've committed to Him in faith and obedience."

"How about a hug?" Thad winked and smiled. "We'll save the kiss for our wedding day."

Leah giggled happily and reached to give Thad a hug, so very grateful to have the love of a man whose heart was filled with genuine faith. If Thad treated her like Christ treated His bride, the church, she would never have to worry about abuse or neglect. Her prayer was that she would be of more help to him than chaos.

Upstairs, by the entrance of the modern lodge, the chimes of a doorbell announced the arrival of guests. Cole and Doris Grant waited expectantly, marveling at the bright evening sun. In Pennsylvania, it was dusk by seven-thirty in the evening. Here in Alaska, at seven-thirty, August sunshine still gave warmth and light to the long arctic autumn days until ten o'clock. No dark storm clouds blocked the sunshine with foreboding casts of gloom. It was as though heaven's eternal day was lent to the wedding couple.

Taking two steps at a time, Thad pulled a quick-stepping Leah up to the double doors.

"We'll get the door," he called. Leah saw Taima slow to a stop and nod with a smile of compliance. Thad stopped in front of the door to let Leah catch up. After taking a deep breath and noticing how anxious Leah looked, he winked at her.

"Are we ready?"

"Never," Leah deadpanned then smiled and emphasized, "I'm *behind* you all the way."

Thad laughed as he opened the door to greet his future in-laws. "Pastor Grant, Mrs. Grant, please come in," Thad said warmly, stepping back to allow room for them to enter.

"Thank you. I assume you're Thad Tucker, and we're at the right mansion." Leah's dad smiled in greeting.

"I am." Thad nodded and turned to greet Doris Grant, not missing the reference to the impressive lodge as a mansion. It was simply *home*.

"Leah!" Dad Grant reached for his daughter. "It's good to see you, Lady Leah. Your mother and I have missed you and your sister greatly, though I understand you've been forming a new friendship. I'm happy for you."

Mrs. Grant greeted Thad pleasantly. "Hello, Thad. I'm truly happy to meet you. I hope we can be friends," she offered kindly.

"Me, too, Mrs. Grant. Please let me know how I can make your stay more comfortable."

"Thank you, Thad. Alaska is a very different place," Doris Grant said honestly, and glanced quickly over at Leah, noting the shine of happiness in her daughter's eyes. "I can see Leah has found a place for her restless heart." Looking directly into Thad's discerning eyes, Mrs. Grant confessed, "All I've ever wanted for Leah is a genuine faith, and a place for her abilities to thrive." Doris Grant leaned toward Thad, smiling stiffly. "We've been on opposing sides most of the time, but I love her dearly and want the best for her." She retreated, eyeing him with measured satisfaction. "Somehow, I think you might just end up being the last best choice for her after all, Thad Tucker." Doris was trying her best to show acceptance, but she felt as if it had all come out wrong anyway and there wasn't a thing she could do about it. Positive first impressions of other people did not come naturally for her. She was out of practice.

Thad swallowed, grateful Mom Grant had imparted her favor, though he wasn't exactly sure how to read it. She reminded him of his own mother, and he wondered if that generation of women all was of a kind that could make a prospective son-in-law's spine tingle. He found himself uttering something like, "I will endeavor to be the best I can be for Leah." It came out sounding like an army pledge. Thankfully, the awkward moment ended with the voice of a child.

"Grandpa! Grandma!" Angie squealed, hearing their familiar voices. She ran to meet them, bounding with happiness. Sarah and Andrei followed slowly behind to give some time for hugs between grandparents and granddaughter. A few more awkward moments followed before introductions were made around the group. Thad invited everyone into the great room to sit and renew family ties then excused himself to tell Alma that the wedding was back *on*. She just grinned and nodded with a confident smile before heading up to the great room to check on the comfort of their guests. Next, he called Pastor Paytor and confirmed the rehearsal time at the church to be in a half hour. He figured activity would keep things rolling until everybody in the group found common ground.

When there was a break in the conversation, Thad announced, "We'll be leaving for the rehearsal at the church in about twenty minutes. We need to load some decorations for the church into the Suburban. If you men would like to help, you can follow me down to the garage." Taima, Tyrone, Andrei, and Pastor Grant stood and left the great room with Thad. After they left, Doris was the first to speak. Angie had been sitting beside her grandma holding her hand and snuggling against her until Grandpa Grant stood. He winked like the Pied Piper of Hamlin, and Angie followed skipping after him. The air was pensive as Leah, Sarah, and Denise contemplated what the older woman might say. Only Alma was relaxed as she stitched a hook and eye onto the back of the formal dress she had purchased to wear for Leah's wedding.

"Well, girls," Doris confessed, "I am completely out of my element here. Alaska is a big place." It was a startling statement coming from one who seemed never to have been out of control in any circumstance. Since Leah and Sarah had lived within the realms of parental control, the wide open spaces presented limitless possibilities. Denise, however, understood.

"I know exactly how you feel, Mrs. Grant. Alaska is a whole lot bigger than I am able to comprehend. It's a beautiful place, to be sure, but the distances between cities and conveniences are disturbing for me--especially the distance from my family in Chicago. I like being able to drive quickly from one place to another on regular roads and highways."

"Then you are still planning to teach at the school in September, Denise?" Mrs. Grant asked. It was a dangerous topic to broach since Leah had chosen not to renew her teaching contract in order to follow her heart to Alaska.

"Yes, I'm still planning to teach at the academy in two weeks, Mrs. Grant."

"Good." Doris nodded, feeling resentment toward Leah creep into her thoughts. Acting on those resentments would alienate the two of them even more, and it surely would add discord to the occasion. She could get over it and be part of the happy group if she wanted. It would mean that she would have to give up control; that she would have to behave as a guest; that she would have to swallow her pride. Doris knew the right thing to do. Cole had talked to her about their support of both daughters in matters beyond their understanding. He had said, "We trained them up in the nurture and admonition of the Lord the best we knew how, Doris. We have to trust the Lord with the rest of their spiritual growth. They are adults reaching out into the future in faith with the hope that they will experience success in their marriages and in their vocations. We can't treat them like children anymore when their aspirations are the same as ours were on the day we married. We're now their support team, not their drill sergeants." To her daughters, Doris Grant spoke cheerfully, though it was a struggle for her to make the change and she felt awkward. She knew her next words could be a new beginning in their relationship.

"I am truly happy for both of you girls. Sarah, you've kept right on being faithful to God when even I didn't..." she faltered, "believe or support you as I should have. I'm sorry. I hope you will forgive me. I look forward to getting to know your husband, Andrei, and welcoming him into our family." Sarah seemed frozen in place, disbelieving what she was hearing until her mother's confession broke through the walls of hurt separating mother and daughter. Tears gathered and fell from her eyes as she moved to her mother. Alma stood and signed to Denise that they would check on the guys' progress at loading the decorations.

After some tender moments, Sarah and her mother moved apart. Leah didn't know what to do. There had never been any closeness between her mother and herself. It had always been a head-to-head competition between them. Fear and anger had volleyed back and forth without a net to block spikes. Dad Grant had refereed their matches until Leah's last game play when she left to meet Thad in Alaska. Church discipline had resulted after these matches, and she had been benched! She watched as her mother and Sarah made relational amends. Something inside her choked at the thought of reconciling their differences.

"I've got to pull some things together for the rehearsal," she announced abruptly with a tight-lipped smile. "I'll meet you down at the garage." If ever there was a need for an escape artist, Leah Grant was your woman. The truth was that Leah needed to pull herself together. Leaving the hallowed scene in haste, Leah took the steps up to the next level two at a time and speed walked to her room. The flight had left her breathing hard. Standing in the middle of the bedroom, where only two weeks ago she'd had EMTs working to save her life from a serious allergy to Taima's infamous Road Kill Stew, Leah's thoughts flashed back to her prayer for salvation. Sweet peace had flooded her heart, and newness of life had made the old life and its haunts disappear. The appearance of her mother brought the old stuff back by association. Apparently, her mother was trying to make things right. Why? Why would she even try, especially the night before her wedding when these should be her happiest moments? What could she possibly say that would erase years of tension and berating? If her mother asked for forgiveness, Leah wasn't sure she could give it.

"Leah? Are you all right?" Sarah approached her sister who stood with hands over her face.

"No. I'm not all right, Sarah. I expected Mom to be Mom. I was just going to grin and bear her disparaging remarks and disapproving frowns until after the wedding. She and Dad would go back to Pennsylvania. Thad and I would live happily ever after."

"Until the grandchildren start coming," Sarah put in, "and then you're back to square one." Sarah cleared her throat, trying not to laugh. Leah looked over at her sister and they both laughed. "I think you better deal with this now, Leah. Besides, just maybe you're the one who needs to ask for forgiveness. Answer this question, Sister. Who was the one doing all the rebelling?"

Leah blinked at that revelation.

"It's all in how Jesus looks at it, isn't it?" Sarah gave Leah a hug. "I love you, little sister. You've made things right with God, now go make things right with Mom. Then you can live happily ever after--even after the grandkids come," she promised. "What do you want to do, Leah?"

"Give me a minute, Sarah. I'll be down." Leah promised. After Sarah left the room, Leah bowed her head. "Lord Jesus, I understand now. Thank you for forgiving me." She exited the room with a lighter heart. All the resentment she had held toward her mother had fallen away as she realized the contribution she had made to all the years of conflict. It had been right to ask the Lord's forgiveness; it would be honest to ask her mother's forgiveness.

Doris Grant stood gazing at the majestic view of the Talkeetna Mountains. It was the first time in her life she had seen anything so rugged and grand. She couldn't put a finger on it, but there was something about this great land that reminded her of the young woman she used to be, the one who had been driven to succeed. Doris had hit walls of resistance aplenty, but had either prayed through them or decorated them. Though she and Leah had clashed a good bit, Doris had been more protective of her youngest daughter then of Rachel and Sarah. Leah had been born a month prematurely with complications requiring her to remain in the neonatal unit until her heart was stronger. Two months later, they returned their infant daughter to ICU with pneumonia. Both she and Cole had tag-teamed keeping a watch over tiny Leah. As each shallow breath seemed to grow weaker, her parents had agonized in prayer for God to spare her. Why God took her precious baby girl to the brink of death, Doris didn't know at the time, but it changed her preacher husband's walk with God for the better. Leah gradually recovered from the pneumonia. For the first three years of Leah's life, however, she was slower in development, tired easily, and caught whatever sickness was going around the church family. Years later, an x-ray was taken when she had an outbreak of bronchitis. Though the x-ray showed the bronchitis, the picture of her lungs showed no scar tissue whatsoever from the pneumonia.

Naturally, Leah's independent nature had yearned for more leniency. When it had been denied, defiance reared its ugly head. Right or wrong, Doris confronted it head-on as was her custom. Cole supported her, but he had a softer spot in his heart for all three daughters. Now, here she was, staring into the distance and keenly feeling that distance growing tangible between herself and a deeply beloved daughter. She wanted to wish her all the joy and happiness in the world while hoping and praying fervently that the man she had chosen to be her husband would treat her with care. Would he be clumsy and selfish, thoughtless and rough with her? Doris would move heaven and earth to spare any of her daughters from such men. Indeed, it had taken every ounce of grace and a Holy Spirit-directed memory of Wolfgang Brandt for her to greet Andrei Garankof with acceptance after all the pain Sarah and Angie had endured.

By the looks of things, Thad could provide for Leah. Doris prayed he was a genuine Christian man who would escort his family to church regularly and lead his home with wisdom and devotion to God. Her eyes noted the beautiful cathedral ceilings and rich wood beams running toward the huge stone fireplace. Modern, name brand furnishings looked as though an interior decorator had been hired to tastefully design the living space for a women's magazine. The wedding ceremony could easily take place right here. A church wedding was a good indication of both Thad and Leah's desire to make a sacred commitment instead of a civil one.

Doris was thankful that Leah's humiliating church discipline hadn't completely alienated all desire for God. The whole business had gotten blown out of proportion and Doris regretted her part in the whole mess. This thought caused her brown eyes to drop from the window view of the Creator's rocky handiwork as if she had been found guilty of casting stones at her own daughter. *Forgive me, Lord. I expected things from Leah that drove her away from You. I'm sorry. Your ways for her were not my ways. I was wrong. You know what's best for her. I yield my expectations and my pride to Your will for her life and Thad's. Please give us back our closeness.* Doris brushed tears away quickly. Footfalls approached behind her.

"Mom?" Leah began nervously, but was resolute. "It's a beautiful view, isn't it?"

Doris turned and smiled agreement. For once they agreed on something. "Yes. I've never seen anything so magnificent in all my life. Just looking at it seems to change one's perspective."

Leah stepped beside her mother to study the depth and scope of the Divine Artist's fresco. "The first time I saw these mountains in full daylight, I remember thinking that I couldn't fool God anymore. I had to be honest with myself and with God." Turning to face her mother, Leah opened her heart. "I want to be honest with you too, Mom. My rebellion against you and Dad caused a lot of strife in our family. I used to think you and Dad were the problem and needed to make amends to me, but now I realize I'm the one needing your forgiveness. I'm so sorry for being contrary and obstinate and sneaking around behind your backs to do as I pleased. Can you ever forgive me?"

Doris swallowed with difficulty as her eyes stung with tears. Deep wells of suppressed longing for a right-hearted relationship with her youngest daughter broke free and rushed ointment and warmth to the wounded areas where Leah's rebellion and rejection had whispered painful failings as a mother. Her tough exterior softened as she reached for her daughter and they both cried, not only in the relief of this moment, but for the years of missed joy.

"I forgive you, Leah," her mother said gently. Releasing Leah from her embrace, Doris requested sincerely, "please forgive me for responding in anger and with harshness. It only provoked your resistance more and grieved the Holy Spirit in our home."

"Mom, I forgive you even though I deserved most of the discipline you and Dad administered." Leah admitted with a smile, sniffing back a runny nose from the emotional cleansing. "I'm so glad God made forgiveness a big part of life, or there would never be a second chance for any of us."

Doris laughed in happy agreement as she hugged her daughter again. It was awesome to be able to hug each other and enjoy one another's company and mutual faith. She thought of the story, *The Pilgrim's Progress* by John Bunyan and of Christian's journey to the celestial city. His heavy burden of sin had fallen off when he approached the Cross for forgiveness. Strange how some things come to mind at random moments of importance.

"We're ready to leave for the church, Leah," Thad beckoned and invited, "Mrs. Grant."

Both turned to acknowledge him with happy smiles, and Thad offered a silent prayer of thanksgiving. Mother and daughter didn't seem to be on opposing sides any longer.

# 16

## MOM TUCKER

TWO HOURS LATER, THE WEDDING REHEARSAL was over, the flower arrangements were in place decorating the modest sanctuary for celebration with bursts of late-summer color in purple, yellow, and white. Silver candelabras were in place with long white tapers ready for lighting with two long matchsticks. The white aisle runner had been tacked to the bottom step and was ready for Andrei to unroll to the foyer where the wedding party would wait for the bridal march to be played by Sarah. It was ten o'clock in the evening, and the skies were still light enough for Alaskan children to play outside.

Several pizzas were ordered for the rehearsal dinner afterward. The atmosphere was lighthearted and everyone joined in with funny stories or anecdotes. Pastor Paytor and Pastor Grant kept the party roaring with funny ministry experiences. It was the best party Thad had ever hosted. He grinned at Leah, happy to become part of her family with the exchange of their vows tomorrow.

In the midst of the fun, a stack of pizzas were delivered to the grand lodge. Shortly after that delivery was made, a yellow taxi cab rolled to a stop by the front steps. An elegant woman gracefully exited the vehicle with a flourish of her arms while laughing merrily. Taima had seen the approach of the yellow cab from the windows in the great room and frowned like a grumpy, old man. *Now who was arriving?* "It can't be," he muttered when he saw who it was. "Thad!" he called above the chatter of the group, and silence ensued. He nodded in the direction of the window as Thad approached, puzzled by Taima's uncharacteristic outburst. A glance out the window turned into a wide-eyed stare of disbelief. Every head turned in his direction.

"Uh-oh," was all Thad could manage as if he had been sucker punched. Two words fought for preeminence in his thoughts. One was *nightmare*. The other word was *frenzy*. Swallowing to unfreeze himself from surprise or shock or both, Thad turned from the window and moved quickly to Leah's side. In the few seconds it had taken him to cross the room, he had processed the unexpected arrival of his mother and was resolved to make her feel welcome. All eyes were upon him. Practiced good manners made him smile politely and announce, "My mother has just arrived. Please excuse us while we welcome her." Taking Leah's hand in his confident one, Thad moved them both to the entrance and out the door. The cab driver was lifting several suitcases out of the trunk all the while his matronly rider talked nonstop. She halted midsentence at seeing Thad descend the steps to the sidewalk. A pretty little thing bobbed down the steps behind him.

Leah's first impression of her future mother-in-law would best be described with the naming of a person. "Elizabeth Taylor," Leah whispered, standing as tall as her five foot four inches would allow. Thad's mother was at least a head taller than Leah. Louise Tucker made one do a double take to check if she was indeed the famous actress. Black, teased hair was perfectly styled to frame the bronze-tanned Arizona skin. Gold chandelier drop earrings hung parallel to a long slender neck without touching the collar of the duster length coat. Blue-gray eyes sparkled with merriment. Each eyelid was brushed in blue shadow and the lash line was traced in fine black pencil above ebony-coated lashes which were long enough to curl and capture attention. Each lip was tinted in frosted pink, which tastefully contrasted with the evenly tanned skin. Long slim fingers whose manicured nails were painted in dark mauve were bedecked with rings-holding every shape and size of gemstone. Like miniature hula-hoops gone wild, bracelets chimed in a chaotic racket around the wrist. A cream-colored suit was embroidered with her monogram "LET" in gold on the lapel of the jacket. The tailored cut showed off a slim figure accessorized with a pair of two-inch beige, snake print wedges. The same dark mauve polish coated the peeping toes. Arizona looked very good on Louise Tucker. Where were the paparazzi?

Leah swallowed uneasily. Decorating the den for the wedding reception this morning meant casual clothes had seemed the wiser choice—until now. She was attired in a loose fitting pink gingham shirt, denim jeans, and sneakers with bright fuchsia socks that Angie had chosen for all the ladies to wear—just for fun. She looked like a throwback to adolescence. If only she could turn the clock back just ten minutes for a quick wardrobe change. It was too late now. Leah half-expected to see paparazzi appear to snap pictures of the actress's look-alike and couldn't believe she was actually thinking such a thing as this.

Mom Tucker turned to greet them after sending the taxi driver off with a generous gratuity. She rushed upon her son with a boisterous greeting and that's where her resemblance to Elizabeth Taylor ended. "Thaddeus, my boy! Come give your feeble mother a big hug!" She fell upon him, gave him a smacking kiss on the cheek, and firmly patted his back as if burping a baby. Leah reckoned there was nothing feeble about Louise Estelle Tucker. "Oh, son! I'm so glad to see you! God bless you." She held him at arm's length to study the man he had become. "You look good, son," she stated with genuine approval. After that, she focused on Leah who felt awkward but tried to remain calm, hoping to say something appropriate that would show she was worthy of this mother's son. Blue-gray eyes pierced Leah's soul for something every mother desires for her sons' happiness—that his chosen bride will do him good.

"Ah. What a lovely, sweet girl she is, Thad, and such beautiful skin." Thad's mom reached up and gently stroked Leah's soft cheek with her bejeweled hand. "Honey, you're an answer to my prayers for Thad." She pulled the baffled Leah toward her for a hug then released her to make a promise. "Leah, I know we're going to get along just fine, sweetie. I want you both to know that I'm not going to interfere at all in your married life. I promised myself that I'd never be an interfering mother-in-law, and I want you to know that you don't have to take any advice I might offer." She smiled in satisfaction at having delivered "the good mother-in-law speech".

"Oh, Thad! She's so cute!" Louise gushed. Thad frowned. There was that word *cute* again. Leah was beautiful, and that's what his heart registered every time he got the chance to look at her and draw her gaze to his. *'Cute' was for kittens.*

"Mrs. Tucker, I—"

"Oh, don't call me Mrs. Tucker," she stressed. "Just call me Mom, or Louise if you wish." Leah hated choices like this. She felt uncomfortable calling Louise Tucker, *Mom*. It seemed a betrayal of her own mother for some strange reason yet this was Thad's mom, so she decided to try a compromise.

"Mom Louise?" Leah ventured and saw Thad's mother nod in approval.

"Sounds good to me." She declared the matter settled.

Thad grabbed the matching luggage and directed his mom up into the lodge to meet the others at the rehearsal party. Mom Louise was introduced to the group and at once entered into the festivities. She was an active woman who enjoyed people in general and talking in particular. With a flair for animated conversation and laughter, her personality brightened the party. When the evening's activities ended, everyone had enjoyed themselves and awkward new acquaintances turned into budding friendships. Mom Louise made people feel accepted, even though she had some pretty strong opinions that raised her son's eyebrows in warning to her every so often.

One of those opinions surfaced on the morning of their wedding, and Leah found herself right in the middle of a muddle between her mother and Thad's mother. It had all started so innocently, or so she had thought. Both women were highly opinionated when it came to marriage advice. The future living arrangements of the wedding couple began to take on a very different slant. Leah tried to steer the subject matter in another direction, but age dominated youth two to one. She looked for an escape route, but the mothers had come to her room to view her wedding dress. After their positive appraisal, recounting of their wedding woes had ensued. At first Leah had been hopeful of encouraging words or tidbits about Thad's father, but those hopes were quickly dashed.

"I remember my first year as a married woman. It was a difficult one," Louise Tucker started. "I was sixteen years old and expecting Thad. We had been married by a justice of the peace and had nowhere to go, so we decided to head for Canada. I didn't know at the time that Wayne was dodging the military draft. He never mentioned it. We were flower children living in a Volkswagen bus. I painted the flowers on the bus." She giggled. "They washed off in the first rainstorm." Both mothers laughed. Leah was sure this wasn't something to laugh about. "Because I was not feeling well at all, we returned to Arizona and moved in with his parents since mine had disowned me. He hated the idea of getting a job, but at the insistence of his parents, he found one. He became a crew member on a merchant ship and was gone for three months the first time. When he returned, the sight of me being seven months pregnant was a shock to his system. He had also developed a taste for beer in the process of sailing the seven seas," she divulged with a sigh.

"The pressure of responsibilities to me and our coming child cramped his ideals of living carefree and easy. I have to give him some credit, though. He did try to make it work, but we fought about everything. He found a local job as a construction worker and stayed on the job as a maintenance worker until two weeks after Thad was born. We got into an argument about something I can't even remember now, and he left. The last I heard of him, he went back to the merchant ship. He ran like Jonah. I haven't seen him since, but I did receive court-ordered support for Thad until he left for college." Thad's mother lamented, "Oh, how I cried over that man. I cried until I got tired of crying. Thad was an infant and I had to pull myself together for both of us." She went on. "Wayne's parents didn't appreciate their son's ties to me and blamed me for his unhappiness and for his leaving home. His mother was the kind of woman who personified 'when mama ain't happy, ain't nobody happy'." Her head bobbed up and down. "And nobody was ever very happy in that home. I eventually left with Thad and returned home here, near Palmer, to live." She paused with a furrowed brow. "In my opinion, newlyweds should have a place all to themselves. It might have made a difference with Wayne and me."

Doris nodded and began her own woeful account of her first year of marriage. Leah wondered what positive advice could be gathered from all this.

"Cole and I lived with his spinster Aunt Maybelle, for the first six months of our marriage. Cole was working on his seminarian degree at a Christian university nearby, and his aunt graciously opened her large home to us from July to January while we waited for married housing to come available on campus. Aunt Maybelle had a schedule and a routine, which she kept religiously." Doris chuckled at some of the old lady's idiosyncrasies. "All outside doors were closed and locked promptly at nine o'clock at night. All lights were to be out by nine-fifteen. No toilets were to be flushed during the night. No snacking between meals. No TV, no radio, *no noise* after nine-fifteen, period. Meals were at 7:00 a.m., precisely at noon, and at 5:30 p.m. If you were late, Aunt Maybelle lectured on promptness. If Cole missed a meal due to studies at the college library, he didn't eat, I used to smuggle food in my sweater pockets to feed him." Doris and Louise laughed together. Leah smiled warily. She never knew any of this had happened to her parents.

"Aunt Maybelle heard every creak. Cole and I had to be so careful when we were alone...if you know what I mean, Louise." She winked to her *comrade-in-alarms*, and there was a mutual understanding that Leah missed. When these intimate details registered, Leah felt her face heat and her stomach knot in protest. This was not the advice she had expected to glean from her mother's marriage experiences. The nightmare continued.

"One morning as we ate our dutiful bowls of gooey oatmeal, Aunt Maybelle made a comment that nearly choked us both to death." Doris mimicked Aunt Maybelle's southern drawl, "'You young'uns are awful restless. I just can't figure it. Maybe you two ought to take separate rooms so we can all sleep more peacefully,'" Doris finished as Louise roared with laughter. Leah could only wish this would end, but it didn't.

"If I said it once, I'll say it again. It is my firm belief that every young married couple should have a place of their own entirely by themselves for the first year of their marriage," Louise Tucker declared with conviction. Warning sirens went off in Leah's mind.

"Two women in one house is a bad idea, period," Doris added from her past experience without thought to Leah's present situation. Old habits just carried her along in the flow of the conversation.

"Especially the first year," Louise restated, smiling as if trying to make a point for Leah's sake. Leah wondered if this sanguine woman could be artfully stirring up trouble. Leah quickly attempted to change the subject.

"It's going to be another beautiful day. The sun is so warm and bright for a wedding day. What was your wedding day like?" The moment she asked the question, she regretted it.

"It rained!" they said in unison, looked at each other, and the bonding process between mothers-in-law was completed. Leah might as well have been standing knee-deep in alligators for all their notice of her. Mom Louise took off with another wild story. Excusing herself politely to check on wedding preparations in the den, Leah slipped out of her bedroom and took the steps down to the den to see if Alma could use some help somewhere, *anywhere!* Tables had been set up and decorated for the simple reception after the ceremony at the church.

A three-tier wedding cake from the local bakery towered elegantly in the center of a round, white, linen covered table. Purple and yellow silk tea roses garnished each layer of the white cake from bottom to top. A silver heart with a romantic wedding couple posed in an embrace in its center, graced the top of the towering confection. Several arrangements of purple and yellow silk roses with white tea roses and daisies added for contrast were placed on tables and stands giving the hunters' den a bride's touch of charm. Scanning the room with a smile of pleasure and anticipation, Leah was amazed this was her wedding day. She was standing in the middle of her dream-come-true, lingering in happy wonder until thoughts of Thad shooed her dawdling heart forward toward the hour of their matrimonial vows.

When she didn't find Alma in the den or garage, she checked the patio, but Alma wasn't there either. She was about to turn around and re-enter the den when she heard muffled voices in the direction of the arbor where Thad had proposed to her almost one week ago. Curiosity moved her up the stone walkway to a terrace overflowing with late summer flowers. These hearty blooms still thrived even though recent storms in the mountains caused temperatures to drop near freezing in the farm valley below. A row of young Douglas fir trees about six feet in height had been planted just beyond the flowers to form a wind break for the log dwelling and the patio area. Beyond them, white birch trees formed a sentinel guard at the base of the mountain behind the lodge. Towering above the birch, aspen swayed and bowed as they danced the north wind's timberline waltz in praise to the Creator.

There in the pristine setting under the arbor she saw Alma, Thad, and Taima talking together in earnest. When she approached, human voices ceased while bird chirps continued their merry exchange. Had Leah been a lowly sparrow landing on a branch full of territorial red birds, she couldn't have felt more like an intruder than she did at that moment. Alma was clearly troubled about something, and Taima's deep frown aimed directly at her made her soaring heart plunge in a free fall. Thad greeted her with only a bland smile. Words seemed to fail him in this suddenly strained atmosphere.

*What now?* Leah wondered silently as she stopped and looked up into her beloved's guarded eyes. It absolutely crushed her that there was discord between them.

"Honey, is something wrong?" Every fiber of her being knew there was. His voice was kind enough, but as cool as the first hint of a killing frost.

"I guess we never talked about some of the living arrangements that will transpire after we are married, Leah." She missed the endearing *love* he'd been whispering in her ear.

"Living arrangements?" She was puzzled.

"Yes." Thad confirmed with a nod. Alma saw the confused look on Leah's face and began to sign.

"Taima accidently overheard a conversation about newly married couples needing to have their own place for the first year of marriage."

Leah exhaled, nodding in understanding but not agreement. Thad studied her reaction carefully. This place was their home as well as his.

"Alma, those comments Taima overheard were from our"—Leah pointed to Thad and herself—*visiting mothers*. Unfortunately, their experiences as new brides were unhappy. From those experiences, they formed opinions that I don't agree with, and if I could have gotten a word in edgewise, I would have politely told them so," Leah said, her ire raised.

Pushing aside the annoyance she felt at the moment for the concern she had for Alma and Taima, she spoke from her heart. "You've graciously welcomed me into your home, and in a few hours," she paused, pursing her lips together to quell the emotion causing tears to blur her vision, "if we all manage to make it through the ceremony, I'll become part of this home and family right here." Her face turned red as she swiped a tear from her cheek. The corners of her lips bent down. Anger danced dangerously below the surface of her countenance. Though her eyes flashed fire, Thad figured it was righteous indignation. "I'll take care of this right now." She was resolved and started to turn from the group when Thad reached for her shoulders to stop her warrior charge and turn her to face him. He knew for a fact that righteous indignation aimed at visiting mothers wasn't going to be good for Leah or either of the visiting mothers.

"Love," he addressed calmly, though the fire in her eyes made him consider his words carefully, "we understand how you feel, now, and no matter what anyone thinks or says, we together know how it's going to be." He took her hands and pulled her close. "I'll take care of it," he promised. The tension vanished from her face as her mood brightened from storm clouds to sunshine.

"Let's go for a walk. We've got time." Thad smiled cheerfully just as Alma reached out and touched Leah's arm to gain her attention.

"Taima and I understand these things too. We were just caught off guard by it all. I'm very sorry about this, Leah." Remorse showed on Alma's expressive face.

"So am I," Taima added sincerely.

"There's nothing for anybody in this group to be sorry for," Leah assured. Smiling, she teased, "When Thad's out with clients on hunting and fishing trips, somebody's going to have to look after me, ya know."

"Heaven help us!" Taima blurted, then laughed with the others. Thad was eager for a walk on his wedding day.

"We'll be back shortly," he stated stepping onto a path wide enough for the couple to walk side by side, hand in hand.

Taima and Alma remained in the arbor a little longer talking about plans of their own to make the living quarters more comfortable for the newlyweds. Alma's plan was to move Taima's living space down to ground level near the den and bathroom. The kitchenette was already there for his personal use with access to the patio on one end and the garage on the other. His room off the den would have a view of the mountain directly behind the cabin. It would give Thad and Leah the entire main floor for their living space. Alma knew how to design the layout, and Taima knew how to make it happen. It would be a surprise for Thad and Leah when they returned from their honeymoon trip to The River View Lodge in Gakona, Alaska. The project would give them something to look forward to after the mayhem of the wedding as they made adjustments and changes from a threesome to a foursome.

Meanwhile, Thad and Leah made their way over the beaten track Thad had so often climbed to view the lodge and horse barn when they were both being built. It was the place he'd reined his horse, Sunset, to a stop in order to contemplate the "miracle" letter from Leah. This was their wedding day in Alaska, and both wanted to enjoy it at their leisure. The longer they walked, the more they relaxed. One hour later, Thad led Leah from a densely wooded area onto a broad rock ledge overlooking the Mat-Su Valley above the lodge. In the distance, snowcapped Pioneer Peak seemed to stand directly level with their position.

"You know? I'd like to camp up here sometime," she remarked, scouting the horizon from her left shoulder to her right shoulder then facing forward again before closing her eyes to feel the warm breezes blow her curly hair straight back like the mane of a galloping horse.

"How about when we get back from Gakona?" Thad was already listing what they would need for the adventure—including horses. "I used to bring a canvas tent up here and stay a few days at a time just after I bought this property." He was thoughtful before speaking again. "When I read your letters about your teaching experiences in the Christian academy, I began to consider religious ideas again. I did go to church a few times when my uncle Peter was the speaker. He always treated me like there was some goodness and value in me. I respected what he had to say even if it went in one ear and out the other. Oh, he made mistakes like we all do, but he always owned up to them, taking responsibility and making things right.

"My uncle was and still is an honest man, and I followed his lead even though I was obstinate." Thad recalled with candidness. "If I could meet Jesus in person now that I know Him as Savior, He would remind me of my uncle Peter, or maybe it's better to say that Uncle Peter reminds me of Jesus." Leah smiled up at Thad with a heart grateful for a man whose faith was genuine and growing stronger and clearer daily. "We'll plan a visit to see Uncle Peter and Aunt Anna. Now that my mom has surprised us all by showing up for the wedding," he glanced at his watch, "Oh, Leah!" His eyes popped open as his mind registered the passage of time like the falling sands in an hourglass. "We have to be at the church in an hour and a half!"

"What?" Leah exclaimed in panic. "They'll be frantic!" Then she giggled with delight, "Won't our mothers just fly! They'll call out the rescue squad, again." She laughed merrily.

"Ha-ha," Thad said dryly. "Three times in two weeks isn't good for the family business. Clovis Pine would never let me live that one down," Thad remarked, taking Leah's hand back in his. He moved ahead of her setting a pace that allowed for a safe descent but with a hiker's push to get to a destination. They stopped to drink from a glacial stream just minutes from the lodge.

"By the time we get back home, we'll barely have time to clean up and dress, say nothing about getting to the church on time." She giggled, thinking about the musical score from *My Fair Lady*.

"You can take as much time as you need, Love. Pastor Paytor isn't booked for any other weddings this afternoon," he assured, hoping to take any stress away from Leah that would threaten the joy of her day. They continued their descent over the rugged terrain. Thad noticed Leah's agility and the fact that she anticipated her next steps and didn't have to be told what to do every step of the way. She neither complained about the situation nor seemed irritated by the time crunch. He smiled, thinking she was gradually becoming more acclimated to life in Alaska with each passing day. At least the mishaps were less frequent—minus their present one—and this was great relief to him personally.

The lodge was now in view, and Thad breathed a sigh of relief; until the sound of a helicopter directly above them turned their eyes to the sky. It circled the lodge. Thad frowned in irritation.

"I wonder what they're looking for," Leah was completely baffled.

"Us," Thad said flatly. "They're looking for us, Leah. I should have brought the cell phone," he observed blandly. Though Thad was peeved, Leah found the whole thing very funny and couldn't help laughing as she had when she first saw Thad's amazing abode. She had expected a shack with snow packed around it like an igloo. Her ability to laugh at things he didn't find humorous often mystified him, but helped Thad choose the lighter side of life. Suddenly he had to get her to the church on time. Thad signaled the pilot that they were okay, then watched the mechanical dragonfly tip slightly to the left and turn away from them and the spectators watching from the patio. Before Thad headed for the patio, he turned to Leah and spoke briefly.

"Love, I have a few things to say to some acquaintances of ours. Take Alma and Taima inside with you and take whatever time you need to get ready. I'll see you at the church." He winked and kissed her forehead as they walked to the patio where their parents anxiously waited. Dad Grant looked both relieved and apologetic. The moms looked, well, at least Mom Grant looked uncertain and guilty. However, his mother looked justified, like she expected an explanation after all her *frenzy* and concern. Before his boots hit the stone patio and before his mother had a chance to say a word, Thad was already talking. Leah headed straight for Taima, took his arm and gestured for him to follow with a nod of her head. He looked absolutely miserable. She waved for Alma to follow from the kitchenette in the den, and the three of them headed up the two flights of stairs to Leah's room without a backward glance. Leah paused at Denise's door to check whether or not her best friend had left for the church and found that room empty. The plan was working. Denise and Tyrone were to make sure everything was ready for the ceremony at the church. Denise would meet Leah there with the rings and bouquets. Sarah, Andrei, and Angie had left for the church right after breakfast so Sarah could practice wedding selections on the piano prior to the ceremony.

"Taima," Leah directed, "nobody gets in this room until I'm dressed or until I say so. If my mom comes, just let me know. I'll need her to help with the final touches so that Alma can get ready too." Taima grinned proudly and took his position as bodyguard just outside her bedroom door; his shoulders back with arms crossed over his chest like an Indian Chief.

"Alma, *help me!*" she mouthed and made a panic face then smiled with excitement. Alma winked and smiled her delight as both moved into action giving and taking from one another throughout the transformation from an old maid schoolteacher to a bride.

Outside, stratus clouds slowly floated below snowcapped peaks in solemn matrimonial procession. The wispy white clouds took the shape of a bridal veil drifting slowly east as if making ready for the trumpet call from Heaven. Inside, the bride, dressed in white, studied her reflection in a floor-length mirror and whispered a prayer. "Thank you, Lord, for helping me be the answer to someone's beckon."

# 17

## THAD TUCKER SPEAKS

WHEN THAD STEPPED ONTO THE STONE patio, no one would have suspected he was even mildly annoyed. He greeted them with a tight-lipped smile, but did not offer any explanation as to his and Leah's whereabouts for over two and a half hours. Instead, he chose to speak about his main concern—Leah's wedding day. *Their wedding day.*

"I have a few words to say to all of you," he addressed them as though preparing clients for a fishing trip. There was enough authority in his voice and in his demeanor to cause a smile of respect to appear on Dad Grant's face. It caused both moms to reconsider their present positions in his home as guests.

"In thirty minutes *or more*, if Leah needs more time," Thad emphasized pointedly, "our wedding will take place in a little church not big enough for a lot of…" he paused and watched a few eyebrows raise in anticipation of his next word, "commotion." He let the word slowly roll off his tongue. Louise Tucker started to open her mouth in defense, but Thad's hand went up as if he were halting the cavalry and she backed off. "Upstairs, there is a very excited but nervous young woman who is about to become my bride. She needs your encouragement in positive ways, not your opinions of how you think things should be or how different it was on your own wedding day." He directed this last statement toward his mother, a no-nonsense look on his face urging her to consider the words of her grown son and alter her present course. Doris Grant regarded him with marked interest. Perhaps she was considering her youngest daughter in a new light where Thad's respect and protection of Leah's best interests meant no one could control her daughter emotionally anymore.

"I've seen tears in Leah's eyes twice today, and I wasn't the cause of those tears." The edge in Thad's voice did not mask the irritation he felt on her behalf. Both Louise Tucker and Doris Grant averted their eyes from Thad's probing ones. He waited until their eyes rose to meet his again. Both women looked at least contrite and mostly apologetic. Before either could utter an apology, Thad grinned and his voice took on an amiable quality. "If you'll excuse me, I'm going to get cleaned up, dressed, and ready to leave for the church before the bride and her parents leave. Mom Grant, Leah will need your help upstairs. Dad Grant, I'll need some help with my tie. I have no idea how to make the knot. Can you help me please?"

Dad Grant smiled broadly and nodded assent to his future son-in-law. Thank the Lord, Leah would be treasured and cared for by this man. "I'd be glad to help you tie the knot, Thad." Chuckles could be heard as everyone turned to their duties.

Thad smiled genuinely and finished his *few words* cheerfully: "See you at the church, folks." He was already headed for the patio door into the den, which had been transformed into a wedding bower.

"Mom." Thad took his mother's arm. "I'd appreciate your help pressing my suit and shirt." He spoke kindly and saw a smile of pleasure cross her face as she nodded quietly. To Dad Grant he said, "Could you meet me by the front door in fifteen minutes?" and received an affirming wink. Several footfalls could be heard heading into the den where the sweet smell of cake icing was a reminder of the special occasion meant to celebrate the happiness of two grown children.

Mom Tucker followed Thad up the steps to one of two master suites on the main floor. Each suite had two large rooms with a full bath. The bedroom in Thad's suite adjoined a large private living room that led out onto the north deck over the patio area where everyone had awaited the return of the missing couple just a few minutes ago. Cream colored walls gave warmth to the rooms while varying shades of green and navy blue added contrast to objects and fabric. Rich, dark-stained mahogany furniture gave the appearance of masculinity and security. Thad showed his mother where the ironing board and iron were stored before pulling out a new black suit, vest, and white shirt from the walk-in closet and handing it to her for pressing. She went to work on the pants and then ironed the white shirt and finally the suit jacket as Thad moved quickly through a shave and shower. The pants and shirt were rehung and slipped discreetly onto hooks on the bathroom door. When she finished the suit jacket, Louise took a few moments to study Thad's sanctuary.

On a desk in the comfortable sitting area, her bejeweled fingers lightly touched the picture frame, which held a recent picture of her. She turned from it and saw Leah's picture on the mantel above a stone fireplace. A smile made the corners of her pink-frosted lips turn upward as she examined the pretty face smiling benignly down at her. She understood why Thad had spoken earlier down on the patio. She was proud of her son and knew Leah was a lucky girl. At one time, Louise had longed for a man who would care for her and for her son in such a way as Thad was demonstrating toward his Leah. Time had passed with the business of living and caring for others until the prospects of love seemed remote and unattainable. She crossed her arms and turned to look out the glass door past the deck and on to the vertical horizon of rugged mountains.

Perhaps it was her son's wedding day or perhaps it was the comfortable surroundings that prompted thoughts along melancholy lines. The majesty before her eyes caused flashes of memory about her estranged husband. She wondered where he was, what he was doing, and if he was even alive. As she gracefully worked the gold herringbone necklace around two of her long fingers, Louise's eyes clouded with tears as she silently asked God to redeem her husband just as He had redeemed her son. Though her eyes traveled the length of the smooth white peaks in the distance, her mind's eye traced the last memory of her husband's face. Perhaps new love was remote and unattainable because she still felt tied to her first love.

Minutes later, Thad walked into the sitting area and over to the window where his mother stood in trancelike stillness. Dressed, except for his tie and suit jacket, he saw her quickly blink away extra moisture in her eyes when she turned to regard her handsome son who fiddled with gold monogrammed cuff links.

"I used to know how these things worked." He lamented as his mother reached to take over the task with ease.

"There now," she took charge of the cuff links, "you're almost ready except for your tie, which Pastor Grant can take care of for you. When you were small, I always bought the clip-on ties because I never knew how to make the knots either. Your dad called them neck-nooses and vowed never to wear one." There was no bitterness in her voice as she smiled up at Thad. "Tie or not, I think your dad would be proud of you. I know I am," Louise said sincerely, hugging Thad.

"Thanks, Mom." Thad didn't need any affirmation from an absent father now that he had affirmation from his Heavenly Father; but he did appreciate his mother's support and her effort to help him think a little better of his father when her old resentments had forged a disparaging view of fatherhood.

"That's why I like living up here so much, Mom. There's not much need for a tie except for going to church with Leah." Picking up his suit jacket, Thad walked over to the door and waited for his mother to cross the room.

"I hope you'll make church a priority, Thad." She was not trying to be pushy, only sincere. "Church provides stability when the world seems to spin out of control." She chuckled. "It's one of the few places you're forced to sit beside each other when you're both upset with each other after trying to get the kids dressed for church." There was the subtle hint about grandchildren Thad noticed as she winked and pulled him forward for a brief hug and kiss on the cheek. Her eyes were filled with tears as she quickly rubbed the red smooch mark from his cheek with a thumb lick before gliding out into the hallway.

"Mom, are you getting all sentimental on me?" he teased with a lopsided grin.

She laughed it off, then related sincerely, "I was just remembering my wedding day. It was a very happy day for me despite the circumstances. It was happy for two reasons. I loved your father, and I was carrying you, son. Of course, it was before I knew the Lord Jesus as my Savior, and it was before I cared about doing what was right in God's eyes. You have been my joy even though we've not always agreed about spiritual matters. I'm so grateful that you and Leah can begin your married life as Christians. Your home will be blessed even through the inevitable hard times that will come. Always remember the blessing of this day. It's your day, Thad, and someone wonderful waits for you," she finished supportively. For all her fanciful ways, Thad knew a mother's love and care.

"Mom, thanks for praying for me all these years. I didn't always appreciate..." Louise cocked her head to the side pretending astonishment. Thad laughed and corrected himself, "I really hated your sermons."

"Yes, you did. However, God chose to direct your salvation through someone who would become the love of your life--and it wasn't your mother," she conceded amiably. "All you needed was a pair of big brown eyes."

Thad agreed, smiling, as he fidgeted with the unfamiliar tie draped around his neck.

"Let's put that tie into the capable hands of Pastor Grant." Mom Tucker directed, and they walked out where Dad Grant waited to assist the groom. There was a curious grin on his face.

"This is the first time I've ever fixed a tie for another man, Thad. What with three daughters and never having a son, I only had to knot my own ties, so here goes." Practiced hands quickly lifted the white shirt collar and slipped the long tie around the back of Thad's neck. Dad Grant adjusted the lengths of the draping tie tips. Sensing Thad's nervousness, he started to hum the *Bridal March* and saw his future son-in-law smile and relax. The purple and silver striped tie flipped and flopped, circled and dived until a precise knot formed and was slid smoothly into place perfectly centered over the top button of Thad's snow-white collar. The wings of the collar were flipped down and smoothed. Unused to ties, Thad turned his head from side to side testing for confinement but found freedom of movement. "A preacher can't preach if he's choked to death by his tie," Dad Grant commented with a voice of experience, and Thad found his transparency both humorous and endearing. He understood the connection between this father and his daughter because they both had caring spirits and could help people smile away troubles--even if they were the ones who had created the trouble in the first place.

"This tie feels just right, thanks," Thad said with gratitude.

"I have something for you, Thad," Dad Grant reached into his jacket pocket and pulled out a small jewelry box. Opening it, he presented the paternal gift to the groom. "I thought you could use this today." It was a silver tie bar with a black onyx set in an oval cameo frame on the end. In the middle of the shiny, smooth, black stone, a cross was etched with precision. The flash of an inset diamond at the intersection of the cross caught Thad's eye as it passed from Dad Grant's hand to Thad's right hand marking the transfer of protection from the father of the bride to her knight in shining armor. Surprise showed on Thad's face.

"Thank you, Dad Grant," Thad said solemnly as emotion worked its way up into his eyes. He blinked it away as he clamped the keepsake into place over the tie. A much stronger bond formed between the two men who were both respected in their fields of service to others. Thad's heart was especially touched by the kindness of his bride's father who would soon be *his* father by marriage. God seemed to be answering his boyhood prayers for a dad in an unusual way, even after all these years. For the first time in his life, Thad Tucker felt a father's acceptance, and he felt valued; not for what he had made of himself, but for what God had given to him, though he had not deserved such love and grace.

"I appreciate this more than you know." He swallowed and blinked as Dad Grant gave him a bear hug and a firm pat on the back. Just then, happy voices could be heard as the bride and her mother approached the stairs leading down to the entryway. Both men glanced up, and Thad started for the door.

Louise Tucker had been standing quietly off to the side allowing her son and the bride's father to have some bonding time. She dabbed tears from the corners of her eyes when she heard the voices at the top of the steps. With a sweep of her hand, she waved her son out the door and followed him.

"Go," she urged with a smile of excitement, "and don't look back." Thad pulled on the dark suit jacket just as it caught a gust of wind and flapped around his torso. Pulling the tailored jacket close, he headed down the steps then turned to offer his mother his arm. He glanced to the top of the steps wanting just one glimpse of Leah even though he knew the first glimpse of his bride should be witnessed by their mutual friends and family gathered to hear the making of their vows. The transformation of a woman from jeans and plaid to satin and lace would spark another defining moment in Thad Tucker's life. Mom Tucker understood Thad's pause as she gently moved them forward.

"You'll see your lovely Leah all in good time, Thaddeus Wayne Tucker." She enjoyed this prenuptial duty with parental satisfaction even if Thad was thirty-four years old.

When the moment comes for words that ought to be remembered, there are precious few who have the gift of touching hearts with well-chosen ones. Others struggle to say what needs to be said in love. The rest of us stumble all over ourselves in sincerity. Sometimes sincerity is all there is when words have been hurtful and misunderstandings have divided houses.

As a pastor leading saints in their worship of God and in their walk with God, Cole Grant was the one whose words should always have reflected the wisdom of God. At least as a pastor, he'd prayed they would be wise and helpful. Instead, his greatest ministry challenge had been keeping the peace in his own home.

Standing at the base of the steps, he looked up into the shining faces of the bride and her mother. They smiled and chatted amiably with one another, finally united in their effort to enjoy this special day to the fullest. Grant marveled at the change between them and, for a moment, wondered if these two women were the same two who had created years of underlying tension and conflict in his home. He loved them both dearly, although at times their tugging and pulling on his heartstrings had tested his patience as a husband and father. He thought Leah's leaving home for Alaska would bring some measure of serenity after all the uproar, but the underlying tension had remained until a third daughter and granddaughter had been driven northward as well. And that's when he realized the crux of the matter.

A house divided by competition, fault-finding, and pride often rotted the family tree from inside out while the winds of resentment and un-forgiveness threatened to push it to the ground. Yet here they were, descending the steps arm in arm, like best friends at a pajama party. *It just wasn't logical,* Dad Grant thought with a wary frown. The idea of coming to Alaska for Leah's wedding had seemed to tempt fate where Doris was concerned. Flashes of potentially ugly confrontations surrounded by steel domes of silence or negative remarks and threats of lifelong estrangement between mother and daughter had halted any suggestion of a trip to attend his Lady Leah's wedding. Better to stay home.

Then Doris had walked into his study, sat down, and crossed her legs as if she expected to have a long conversation with him. Truly, Doris did most of her conversing standing. The only time she sat and talked was while eating or giving instructions she expected others to follow to the letter of the law.

An old college professor had admonished seminary students to pray when they didn't know what else to do. So Cole had led in prayer, and miraculously, God had pierced the heart of his wife with the sword of His Spirit. Doris herself had suggested the trip north to Alaska. Since that moment, the tension he sensed in his home had vanished like a demon bound and cast into the bottomless pit in the name of Jesus. Doris had changed, but so had Leah. He could see the transforming power of Christ radiated in her peaceful face and in her attitude toward her mother. Dad Grant quoted a Bible verse aloud as mother and daughter stepped down onto the stone-tiled floor of the lodge's entry.

"I, therefore, the prisoner of the Lord, beseech you to walk worthy of the calling with which you were called, with all lowliness and gentleness, with long-suffering, bearing with one another in love, endeavoring to keep the unity of the Spirit in the bond of peace. Ephesians chapter 4, verses 1 through 3."

"Thank you, Dad, for faithfully speaking the Word over me even when I resented it. More of it stuck than I ever realized." The holy words nourished her soul, and she reached to hug her dad. When Dad Grant's eyes met his wife's shining ones, she nodded in understanding and smiled back. Tears clouded Cole Grant's eyes. Doris, his own beautiful, sweet bride, had broken free from years of grace-less piety.

# 18

## HITCHED

ANDREI COULD HEAR SARAH PRACTICING WEDDING selections on the piano, and it brought to mind sweet memories of their courtship. Certain sensations of joy and agony that seemed to be from another time and world filtered back to him. His thoughts flashed from the chaotic past to the present filled with change all around him. Andrei had no idea how to make sense out of it in order to make a place in this world for those he loved dearly. There was no place to live, no income to supply the needs of his family, and seemingly no way to make anything right that had been all wrong for a very long time. He tried to concentrate on what he had. Faith in Jesus Christ, though his was the size of a mustard seed, was shared with Sarah. She was strong in faith, and it supported him as a man, husband, and father right now. He prayed that God would teach him to be worthy of her love and respect in the days and years ahead.

Andrei looked down at the buttons on the sleeve of his borrowed black suit and caught sight of the tips of the borrowed black dress shoes he wore. Until running from happiness six years ago, he'd never borrowed anything from anyone—except trouble. This thought, though somewhat disconcerting, actually made Andrei smile at its irony until he was startled by a masculine voice behind him. *When would he ever stop jumping at every random sound?* Angelina Joy loved playing "Boo! I see you!" at every opportunity. He was still working on his lighthearted daddy response.

"Andrei, there's a call for you in my study," Pastor Paytor beckoned from the door with a smile of encouragement. Andrei nodded acknowledgment and walked toward the summons. "Thank you."

"It's your uncle, Viktor, calling from Chicago. I'll leave you." Pastor Paytor started out the door, but Andrei raised a hand to stop him.

"Please wait. I'd like to talk with you after the call, if possible." He saw the pastor nod assent and step aside to let him pass. Andrei picked up the receiver lying on the desk as the pastor returned to his chair.

"Uncle Viktor?" Andrei heard the thick Russian accent of his father's brother reach out in happy greeting. Andrei's heart constricted at hearing the welcome from a distant place. For several minutes the conversation passed back and forth between questions and answers. When the call ended, Andrei returned the receiver to its cradle and took a seat across from Pastor Paytor. His face expressed amazement.

"Only a few minutes ago I was wondering how to make all the wrongs I've done in my life and in Sarah's and Angie's, right. It seemed impossible, but…" he faltered as tears stung his eyes.

"With God, all things are possible, aren't they?" Pastor Paytor offered sincerely with a confident voice. "God made a preacher out of an alcoholic." Andrei blinked in surprise. "God is the justifier of all who come to him in repentance. What the devil means for destruction, God's love and mercy makes into a treasure. You, my young brother, are a great treasure."

Never in his life had Andrei thought of himself as a treasure. From childhood, he had been taught that his purpose in life was to contribute his intellect and backbone to the masses and then fade away silently. It was staggering to think God could treasure such a man enough to redeem him. He wept at this revelation, and in so doing his heart became pliable for the restoring work of God's Spirit. He was filled with peace and a new kind of confidence that gave him courage and vision for the future.

Pastor Paytor saw Andrei's countenance lighten as the redeeming work of Christ continued to transform a vagabond into a man of godly worth. "If your vision for the future is greater than your memory of the past, you can go forward," the pastor quoted. "Someone wrote that in a card of encouragement to me years ago, and it helped me to respond favorably to God's call into the ministry. I'll write it down for you." The quick strokes of his pen against paper made the words Andrei heard a mind imprint in ink. The pastor handed the notepaper across the desk.

"Do you have a vision for the future, Andrei?"

"Yes. I believe I do. It seems my uncle is long overdue for retirement. He has asked me to come to Chicago and prepare to oversee his company. He's offered me a position in the Sparrow Group until I am ready to fill his responsibilities."

"How soon?" the clergyman asked.

"As soon as I talk to Sarah and give him our decision. We could potentially leave as soon as this evening." Andrei began to stand, as did Pastor Paytor.

"Could I pray for you before you speak to Sarah?" he asked.

"Yes. I would appreciate your praying for us." Both men bowed their heads respectfully.

"Father, God," he addressed reverently, "in the name of Jesus our Savior, I ask for Your blessing and guidance on the life of Andrei and on the lives of his wife and daughter, Sarah and Angie. Please go before them and prepare a place of safety where they can serve in a way that will honor You and fulfill Your will for their lives. I pray the power of Christ over you, my brother, for the sake of the Gospel. May the Lord be worshiped as a result of your testimony of His grace in your life and work." Raising his hand in benediction over Andrei's head, Pastor Paytor added the blessing from Numbers chapter 6:

> The Lord bless you and keep you;
> The Lord make His face to shine upon you,
> And be gracious to you;
> The Lord lift up His countenance upon you,
> And give you peace.

In the name of the Father, Son, and Holy Ghost, amen."

Later that afternoon, Andrei would make and confirm reservations for the three of them to depart after midnight on a flight out of Anchorage to Chicago. The Grants flight from Anchorage was scheduled to leave at nine o'clock that evening. They had a layover in Chicago's O'Hare airport and decided to postpone the flight to Pittsburgh a few days in order to accept an invitation to stay with Viktor and Irina Garankof while Andrei and Sarah searched for housing. This reunion would continue. However, a wedding was about to take place in Palmer, Alaska.

When Alma pulled up to the church with the bride and her parents, there were several cars parked around the front. Denise suddenly appeared in the open door of the church looking eager to attend to Leah's every need as a best friend and maid of honor. She wore a dark-purple suit with a shawl collar on the jacket. A single button closure included a white lace modesty inset. The straight mid-calf skirt had a kick pleat in the back for free movement. Yellow tea roses with white baby's breath and greenery were fashioned into a corsage and pinned to the side of Denise's collar. On the counter in the vestibule, a large bouquet of purple, yellow, and white roses was bundled together with white satin ribbon awaiting Leah's first touch of the fragrant nosegay.

Dad Grant helped his wife from the Suburban before assisting Leah as she stepped down onto the sidewalk leading to the front steps of the church. Joe Dorrance parked the vehicle for Alma then escorted her inside. Denise took over as the Grants nodded and gave the bride and maid of honor a little time to enjoy some pre-ceremony jitters.

"Oh, Leah, you look so beautiful, girlfriend! Can you believe it, you're getting married today!" Denise exclaimed, and they squealed like girl scouts winning a sack race.

"Is everything okay out here?" Tyrone's deep voice broke their revelry. Both quickly straightened, regaining demur composures.

"Yes, Tyrone, we'll be in shortly," Leah assured, smoothing the full skirt of her street-length bridal dress. The door closed, leaving the duo in huddled conspiracy.

"Have you met Tyrone's family yet?" Leah lowered her voice for Denise's sake.

"Just his parents and sister came, and they are very nice people,

Leah. The more I get to know Tyrone, the more I like him, but I'm still not ready to commit to Alaska anytime soon, though." Her eyes caught a glimmer of red just behind Leah, and her voice dropped off suddenly then rose in astonishment.

"Wow!" She leaned aside, gazing around Leah and gave a long wolf whistle of admiration. "Look at that red Corvette! What I wouldn't give to drive that set of wheels!" Leah turned to check out the new distraction and giggled at her friend's fickle ways.

With a glance each way, Denise stepped out of the doorway, down the steps, across the sidewalk and onto the gravel parking lot for a closer look at the dream car.

"Denise, where are you going? Don't mess with that car! We're already late for my wedding. You're supposed to be imparting some last-minute wisdom to me as my maid of honor." Leah called after Denise as she lifted layers of white satin and crinoline to hop after her best friend--in white satin high heels, no less. Leah couldn't help laughing at Denise. It was so like her sanguine best friend to chase the moment wherever it flew. It used to be fun to follow Denise's whim, but since Leah had followed her heart to Thad, she had found his stability and steadiness to be a great relief.

"Oh, I can't resist a Corvette. This baby is fine!" Denise cried giddily as she walked around it, admiring every detail of the shiny sports car. Leah sighed and rolled her eyes.

When the bride and the maid of honor didn't appear after several minutes, questioning glances were aimed toward Tyrone who shrugged and headed toward the door. Meanwhile, out beside the red Corvette, Leah was trying to scoot Denise toward the church.

"Denise, you're crazy, you know. Whoever owns this Corvette is inside that church. If you want to drive it, you'll have to find out who owns it *after the wedding*," Leah emphasized laughing good-naturedly. Denise acknowledged the logic with a nod and smiled.

"I'm sorry, Leah, yours is the voice of reason. I should have listened to you a lot more than I have. Let's go, girlfriend." Denise linked arms with Leah and started toward the church, but she couldn't resist a last glance at the red Corvette. Her hand reached to touch the glossy finish.

"No, Denise!" Leah warned. "Don't touch it! It probably has an alarm…" Sirens blared and lights flashed as if a jail break had occurred. "…system." Leah finished softly, hands over her ears.

Inside the church, heads turned in the direction of the blaring noise. Thad looked at Pastor Paytor, excused himself, and taking long strides up the aisle, passed through the vestibule acknowledging Dad Grant with a nod and tight lipped smile before exiting out the door behind Tyrone. Cole waited patiently with a huge smile on his face. Though he would think fondly upon their misadventures together over Leah's growing-up years, now it was Thad's turn to handle sweet Leah's goofy shenanigans.

The sight of Leah in bridal white with her veil stirring gently in the valley breeze made time stop for Thad exactly like the first time he'd seen her walking toward him in Taima's trading post. Now as then, the fullness of his heart confirmed the presence of her companion heart. Magnetized by love, their eyes met and held as Thad walked straight to Leah. He smiled admiration at her rosy skin, soft red lips, and luminous brown eyes shining their love and gratitude for his present act of chivalry.

"They're waiting for us," he said simply, and taking her hand, he escorted her back into the church where he handed her safely to Dad Grant who winked assurance that the bride would make her march to the altar.

Tyrone's eyes flashed irritation, though he paused long enough to consider the attractive purple-suited goddess dancing around his Corvette and thought the better of the rebuke righteously teetering on the tip of his tongue. The fact that she cared more about his Corvette than their mutual best friends' wedding irked him significantly. He wondered if he would ever stop being both irked and hopelessly drawn to one Denise Cox. Tomorrow she would be flying back to Chicago where she belonged, and then he'd simply forget all about her, or *try* to forget her. Taking the key fob out of his pocket, he pushed the button that silenced the car alarm. The wind took up the whispered sounds of nature once again as Tyrone's footsteps crunched across the gravel to Denise's side. The surprise on *her* face surprised Tyrone.

"This is your Corvette?" she asked with hero-like wonder. Tyrone blinked at her disarming inquiry. In that moment, something significant changed their opinions of each other forever. At least there was one thing they both liked enormously—red Corvettes.

All Tyrone could answer was "Yes."

Denise put her hand through his arm, smiled genuinely and said, "We should be inside helping Thad and Leah celebrate their day."

Tyrone smiled down at Denise, and they walked inside, took their places, and gave full attention to the bride and groom.

"Are we ready yet?" Pastor Paytor spoke just above a whisper in Thad's direction as Tyrone stepped into place on the platform in the front of the sanctuary. Sarah had already played several wedding arrangements as the guests waited for the processional to begin. She looked up at Pastor Paytor for his signal to start playing *Canon in D*, and then the *Bridal March*.

Thad leaned over to Tyrone. "Ready?"

"Yes." Tyrone looked over at Thad. "I'm glad you got your miracle, Thad." He saw Thad nod and smiled broadly back.

"Thanks, Tyrone. The same goes for you."

To Pastor Paytor, Thad affirmed, "We're ready if the bride is ready."

Pastor Paytor looked at Denise who turned to see Leah's eager nod and then give him a thumbs-up. A nod in Sarah's watchful direction changed the movement of her fingers as she transposed from C minor to D major in a smooth chord progression. Denise made eye contact with Sarah as she started the first measure of music on the piano. Rehearsing this part of the processional earlier, she had moved forward precisely on the first beat of the second measure. Thus, the first step signaled the start of the ceremony. Conversations halted as heads turned and followed the maid of honor's measured foot cadence to the front. The music stopped momentarily. A nod from Dad Grant to Sarah signaled the start of the *Bridal March*.

Leah didn't notice the nods passing between the wedding attendants signaling the start of her march down the aisle because a tall, confident Alaskan prince awaited her approach with a smile that radiated joy from his heart. It matched hers along with the joyous peace that they both had waited and chosen wisely. Had she given in to the pressure of other's choices for her, she might well have marched toward Rusty Glick for the sake of a *Mrs.* title, thinking she was strong enough to make *regret* work for the rest of her life. Tears of gratitude for God's grace and mercy moistened her eyes behind the white fingertip veil symbolizing chastity. Her heart felt the squeeze of divine love surging through every vein of her being for a man whose own heart had been touched by the redemptive handprint of God. Leah blinked away the tears to clear her vision of Thad. A giggle slipped from her lips making Dad Grant turn his head to check his daughter's welfare.

"Are you okay, Lady Leah?" he asked with mild concern. She giggled again and nodded.

"I'm fine, Dad. Thad doesn't look nervous at all, does he?"

"You mean there's no executioner-style foreboding marked in stress lines across his sweaty brow?" Dad Grant pretended alarm, causing Leah to laugh outright. Curious smiles stirred on the faces of guests as father and daughter stepped left foot, right foot, pause, left foot, right foot, pause...

"Uh, oh," Dad Grant cautioned, his voice low. "Your mother just gave me *the look*. We better nix the cornball and concentrate on getting you down the aisle before anything else happens." He heard Leah's half-giggle then heard her words of sincerity.

"Dad, I love you so much. Thanks for being here by my side today. Thanks for praying for me, Dad. God answered Mom's and your prayers." His heart squeezed at the thought of giving her away in marriage. The two consolations he was counting on were Thad's genuine love for Leah and God's promise to care for them both as long as they put God first over their own wills.

"I love you too, daughter. I'll miss all the trouble you caused us and all the times I wanted to yell at you but ended up forgiving you when the consequences of your own mistakes made you cry." He stumbled, and Leah patted his arm affectionately.

"You are the best dad in the world." She smiled at her dad and winked. "I'm marrying someone who's a lot like you." Dad Grant beamed and straightened his shoulders. His chin came up, and his eyes focused on the front of the church where Thad stood. Both men were resolute.

Layers of crinoline gave fullness to the satin skirt of Leah's wedding dress and made a soft swishing sound as she made the ceremonial journey to the altar. Leah felt the sway of the retro-style dress with its simple lines. This particular dress she had chosen from the bridal boutique in Anchorage. The movie *Funny Face* was one of her favorite movies. Audrey Hepburn's fitted-lace bodice with boat-shaped neckline and a thick satin waistband connecting a gathered skirt of pink satin had been Leah's dream dress since adolescence. Sabrina, the bridal consultant at the boutique, had known exactly what Leah envisioned. Two similar tea-length dresses of white satin and lace had been brought out for Leah's consideration. One was too small while the other was too big. Naturally, there was no time for alterations at the boutique; however, Alma, Denise, Leah, and Sarah all took turns making the needed alterations to the oversized dress until it fit Leah's figure perfectly.

While nimble feminine fingers pinned and stitched, Thad and Tyrone had trekked the Alaskan wilderness in search of Sarah's husband, Andrei. Taima had fielded numerous calls from business clients inquiring after the welfare of their favorite hunting and fishing guides. Leah had overheard Taima commenting that both men had survived their ordeal although Thad was facing the toughest day of his life, namely his wedding. She had snuck up behind Taima and waited for him to turn around and see her standing there, arms crossed over her chest and giving him a dubious look with one eyebrow raised in mock annoyance. It had been a priceless moment for Leah while the cheeky Taima had nearly jumped out of his skin.

"Gotcha!" She had smiled and danced away like a leprechaun.

Strange the things that go through one's mind at the most important moments of one's life. Leah shot a glance at Taima and saw a crooked smile lift one side of his cheek as he gave a nod of approval her direction. She returned a smile of thanks then turned her eyes upon Thad and felt her heart swell with total joy as the musical notes of the bridal march brought her close enough to feel his presence without touching him.

"Who gives this woman to be married to this man?" Pastor Paytor's noble voice broke into the fading melody. The answer was delivered without hesitation.

"Her mother and I do." Dad Grant lifted Leah's hand from his arm and placed it in Thad's extended hand then, laying his hand over top of both of theirs, he prayed. "Father, You gave Leah to her mother and me for safekeeping until such a time as You determined that another could safe-keep her. We have cherished her as best as we knew how and together, her mother and I present her to Thad as our living treasure and as a testament of our love for each other. The LORD bless you and keep you; the LORD make His face to shine upon you, and be gracious to you; the LORD lift up His countenance upon you, and give you peace. Amen."

Dad Grant smiled happily as he sat down beside his wife and held her hand. It was the one thing he missed the most as a preacher because he rarely got to sit beside his wife in church. When she pushed up against him and squeezed his hand, he realized she'd missed sitting beside her husband in church too. The guests were seated and stirred into comfortable positions as Thad led Leah a few steps forward onto the platform to stand in front of Pastor Paytor. Their eyes focused on the pastor as the marriage ceremony of Leah Annette Grant to Thaddeus Wayne Tucker began.

"And the Lord God said, it is not good that a man should be alone; I will make him a helpmeet for him. And the rib, which the Lord God had taken from man, made He a woman and brought her unto the man. And Adam said, 'This is now bone of my bones, and flesh of my flesh, she shall be called Woman, because she was taken out of Man.' Therefore shall a man leave his father and his mother and shall cleave unto his wife, and they shall be one flesh.

"This first marriage took place in the Garden of Eden and is recorded in Genesis chapter 2, verses 18 to 24. After Creation, God looked over the magnificence of His handiwork and peered into the heart of Adam. God had made man in His own image and breathed life into his nostrils. Adam had intelligence, strength, ability, and life that could be eternal in those early days before sin altered a perfect creation. He also had fellowship with God in the garden. What more could a man want?" There were a few chuckles in the pews. Thad looked down at Leah and winked at her when she looked up at him. He was very glad his bachelor days were behind him.

"God and Adam talked about naming the animals and tending them, gardening tips, and guy things. As they worked in the garden together, God noticed Adam's puzzlement. The animal population was growing. The birds made their nests in pairs and raised their young together. They sang sweet songs to each other that Adam couldn't fully comprehend. God knew that someone was missing. Did Adam know? Creation wouldn't be complete without a helper made especially for Adam. Eve was the last and best of Creation.

"God put Adam to sleep, took a rib from his side, and formed woman. Here Thad and Leah stand, thousands of years later, seeking God's way of complimenting and completing each other as one man and one woman in marriage. They are leaving their families to form their own home, raise some children, if God so determines, and fellowship with God wherever their garden is planted here on this earth." Pastor Paytor paused to turn a page of notes he had placed in his Bible.

"When a man and a woman honor the commandment of their Creator, the Lord God, by caring for one another in love, faithfulness, and honesty, they can have a marriage made in heaven." Pastor Paytor looked directly from Thad to Leah and back at Thad then spoke frankly, "Marriage is not an easy task. There will be trials, numerous misunderstandings, maybe even hidden sins that cause conflict between the two of you until confession is made to each other. There may be tragedies that threaten to destroy your marriage. You will have to honestly address each of those threats and submit together to obey God's Word if you want to have a victorious marriage and love each other for a lifetime. A week from now, after you return from the honeymoon, your married life will gradually begin to take on a daily routine. I challenge you as a newly married couple to make time for Bible reading and prayer together." A smile crossed the pastor's face. "A man who fears the Lord can't hold anger in his heart for very long when he has to kneel beside his praying wife. There is something very humbling about prayer when addressing Almighty God."

He addressed the couple with kindness, "Thad and Leah, your hearts are filled with love for each other at this wondrous moment. My heart's desire for you as your pastor and brother in Christ is that ten years from now, you both will look at each other with even more love and regard than you demonstrate here in this sanctuary today." Pastor Paytor looked beyond the bride and groom to the witnesses.

"Does anyone here know of any reason why this marriage should not take place? Speak now in the hearing of these witnesses or remain silent." There was breathless silence.

"So be it."

Curiously, there were sighs of relief all over the sanctuary. Leah and Thad both shrugged at the same time. Pastor Paytor stifled a chuckle and motioned them to turn and face each other to repeat their vows.

"Thaddeus Wayne Tucker, will you take Leah Annette Grant to be your lawfully wedded wife, to love her, honor her, cherish, protect, and provide for her in sickness and in health, in plenty and in want, giving yourself only to her until death separates you both?"

"I will." Thad smiled broadly, his eyes shining the love and devotion from his heart to hers.

"Leah Annette Grant, will you take Thaddeus Wayne Tucker to be your lawfully wedded husband, to love him, honor him, obey and complete him? Will you aid him in sickness and in health, encourage him in plenty and in want? Will you give yourself only to him until death separates you both?"

"I will." Leah pledged, realizing with this voiced promise, she was leaving her world of decision-making behind to embrace Thad's world where he would make a majority of the decisions for their home. No longer a teacher overseeing the education of students and facilitating their physical challenges, Leah was now embarking on an unknown path of duty. For a brief few seconds, the weight of her pledge seemed absolutely terrifying, and her eyes dropped from Thad's. The confidence she had known when marching down the aisle disappeared, giving way to the fear that she was losing her identity to Thad's expectations of a wife. Her hands started to shake, and Thad squeezed them.

"Let's pray." Pastor Paytor suddenly bowed his head and began praying. Every head bowed except Dad Grant's because he had noticed his daughter's hands shaking. While Pastor Paytor prayed, Thad drew Leah's eyes up to his searching ones. His heart caught in his chest when she looked up at him with abject fear in her eyes. She was trembling all over, and he pulled her into his arms to whisper in her ear. "Are you all right, Sweet Leah?"

"I'm so scared, Thad." She barely breathed.

"So am I. I can hardly swallow," he confessed, "but I love you scared. Do you love me scared?" he asked with a tremor in his voice in which Leah found a measure of comfort. This brave man was as scared as she was. Maybe he needed her share of courage to bolster his own as well.

"Yes. I love you scared. I'm okay now. Are you okay?" She dared a feathery kiss on his cheek. Pastor Paytor was still praying--with one eye open! The trembling had stopped, and they parted, resuming their ceremonial bridge. Leah saw Thad relax and swallow. She winked and smiled at him, knowing they'd helped each other over the first hurdle of marriage—fear itself.

"Amen!" Pastor Paytor said and moved quickly into the ring ceremony.

"Thad, please take the wedding band you have for Leah and place it on the fourth finger of Leah's left hand then repeat after me. With this ring, I thee wed."

"With this ring, I thee wed."

"In the name of the Father, the Son, and the Holy Spirit. Amen."

"In the name of the Father, the Son, and the Holy Spirit. Amen." Thad repeated clearly and reverently.

"Leah, please take the wedding band you have for Thad and place it on the fourth finger of Thad's left hand then repeat after me. With this ring, I thee wed."

"With this ring, I thee wed." Leah's feminine voice was sure and steady.

"In the name of the Father, the Son, and the Holy Spirit. Amen." Pastor Paytor led.

"In the name of the Father, the Son, and the Holy Spirit. Amen." Leah finished with conviction.

"In as much as you, Thaddeus Wayne Tucker and you, Leah Annette Grant, have consented together in the repeating of vows and the exchange of rings in matrimony, I testify by your vows now recorded in the annals of heaven and in conjunction with the great state of Alaska and this congregation that you are man and wife. You may kiss your bride."

Applause and whistles sounded all around them, but their first kiss as husband and wife lasted only until the alarm on Tyrone's Corvette went off--again. He shot a look at Denise who instantly raised both flower bouquets in the air and shook her head from side to side.

"I didn't touch anything!" she declared and everyone laughed.

Tyrone frowned in puzzlement as he reached into a pocket to retrieve the key fob and pressed the alarm button to silence the antitheft device. During the moments when words form binding ties and families become in-laws, one uninvited guest came in late to observe the wedding ceremony and view the guests. He slipped out almost undetected and left in a chauffeured black limousine. Only Louise Tucker noticed him and frowned. What was *he* doing here and how did he know it was his son's wedding day? Louise Tucker was determined to find out, but not until she had a chance to search things out, first, before mentioning anything to Thad. She wouldn't allow dark clouds on his wedding day.

"It is my pleasure to introduce you to Mr. and Mrs. Thad Tucker!" Pastor Paytor announced with enthusiasm. Leah reached for her bridal bouquet and lifted it up in victory as Thad wrapped her arm in his and they strolled down the aisle as everyone clapped congratulations. Thad's smile shone with happiness. Leah sure had cheered up this Alaskan bachelor.

Sarah immediately started playing the processional from *A Midsummer Night's Dream* and went on to play a medley of hymns as the guests dismissed themselves to greet the newlyweds.

A short while later, pictures were taken of the wedding party. The sanctuary was quickly put in order, and everyone headed back to the lodge for the reception. Tyrone obliged Denise's fancy for a ride in his Corvette and surprisingly, it was Denise who sat in the driver's seat. What was even more amazing was that Denise didn't drive like the Chicago maniac she was. Indeed, no car had ever been driven as carefully as this one was being driven. So slowly was she navigating the red sports car out of the church parking lot that Thad and Leah led a line of cars, all honking their horns, around Tyrone and Denise. Denise was jubilant and squealed with delight behind the steering wheel while Tyrone's faces of mock panic made everyone laugh at the best man and maid of honor's vaudeville clown act.

"See you in a month or so," Tyrone yelled after the others as Denise pulled slowly and cautiously out onto the highway. When Denise looked over at Tyrone, he winked, settled back comfortably into the leather bucket seat, and propped his arm on the smooth ledge of the open window. The warm autumn breeze blew the tension all away, and he enjoyed the ride with a beautiful lady in the driver's seat beside him— which is exactly what he had hoped for.

Thad and Leah's wedding was definitely stirring Tyrone's thoughts toward finer things.

# 19

## Phantom's Oats

Thad had made arrangements with the wedding photographer to have pictures taken at a secret location a short distance from the lodge. Alma and Taima would transport the rest of the wedding guests to the lodge while Thad and Leah drove to a beautiful valley spot for wedding pictures. He hadn't told Leah where they were going; only that the pictures of them in wedding attire against the backdrop of nature would look great in their photo album. Leah was touched by his thoughtfulness.

The line of honking vehicles disconnected from Thad and Leah's to make a left turn onto the driveway lined with tall evergreens that led up to the charming mountain lodge. Austin, the photographer, had been the caboose trailing the train of cars but now followed Thad's Chevy Suburban. A few minutes later, they stopped at an overlook for pictures with the Matanuska River and the Talkeetna Mountains as a backdrop. Austin finished the wedding poses and left after offering congratulations to the newlyweds. Thad was eager to leave the scenic overlook for one other stop before heading to their wedding reception.

Alone for the first time as husband and wife, the couple's first conversation as they traveled back toward the lodge was a topic both knew well and loved. It was about horses. It was Thad who initiated the topic to the puzzlement of Leah, though she added her experiences and knowledge to his enthusiasm. One would have thought the conversation would have naturally leaned toward honeymoon plans, but Thad's mind focused entirely, and only, on horses.

A right turn off the main road onto a dirt path, indented by the parallel lines of tire tracks arching to the left, led the newlyweds into a thick stand of white birch. Bright-yellow leaves had begun to drop from spindly branches to cover green fern, thick moss, and tiny yellow wildflowers nestled in the underbrush of the tree canopies. Here and there, bunches of tall fireweed showed magenta-colored teardrops already unfolding at the tip-top of their summer blooms. The higher the color climbed, the sooner the warmer weather would give way to cooler temperatures, signaling the end of the Alaskan summer. It was the Creator's sign that harvest time was ending, and winter's blast was soon to begin in the farming valley. By now, the ants and squirrels would be packing the last of their gathered seeds and nuts into underground caverns or rotted holes in tree trunks.

Leah noted the density of the woodland just beyond her window and wondered how many bear and moose had tramped zigzagged trails where the Suburban was leaving tire indentations. When she turned her sight forward to check the view over the hood of the Suburban, she blinked in surprise. The dense brush ended as they drove toward an open hayfield lately cut and rolled into huge bales. Pressing a button on the armrest, Leah made her window hum down about two inches. The sweet earthy smell of hay filled her senses with pleasure and remembrance. Beyond the hayfield was a small barn-shaped building. It looked like a new build-because it was yet unpainted and still had the local lumber yard's logo stamped on the plywood that was solidly nailed to the frame. The structure was bolted securely to a six-inch thick cement slab reinforced with rebar. The smooth, gray surface extended some ten feet beyond the barn's length. A roof extension covered the area like all the other horse barns Leah had ever seen. Suddenly, her curiosity was piqued.

"We're stopping at a barn?" She was baffled and saw Thad's familiar grin slide her direction with a handsome look of mystery in his hazel eyes. Desire rushed warmth into her face. Thad noticed and winked.

"I have a surprise for my blushing bride." The Suburban came to a stop in front of the cement. Thad shifted into park, shut off the engine, and opened the door. "I'll be around to open your door and help you down, Love."

Leah could only wonder what Thad's surprise might be. What animals were kept in this barn? Who owned this barn, and what connection did Thad have with the owner? Thad said he had a surprise for her. It couldn't be horses since he was a hunting and fishing guide, not a rancher. What if the surprise was a milk cow or two? After all, Thad had worked on some general farms in the valley, but surely that wasn't right because Thad seemed to be talking more enthusiastically about horses than livestock. Of course she'd just die if his surprise included nanny goats. Memories of being bit on the bum by a nanny goat while on a field trip to a petting farm with sixteen deaf students had definitely curbed any cuddly feelings for that *rude* animal. Thankfully, her hearing-impaired students hadn't heard her cry out in pain, nor had they heard her blasting remarks condemning that nanny goat to everlasting Hades! Now that she thought of it, God had surely been merciful to her, a sinner. For all of Thad's positive qualities, Leah hoped with all her heart his surprise didn't include certain farm animals or her knight in shining armor might well be slipping off his steed. The door was pulled open, and Thad extended his hand to help her step down. Leah saw the shiny wedding band on his finger and placed her hand over it, relishing their matrimonial bond.

"Please, just close your eyes and trust me, Leah." Thad gently urged. "I think you'll like the surprise."

"Okay, Thad." She closed her eyes and allowed Thad to lead her forward until her sense of smell began to register a few things. Clean hay covered the smell of horse manure, and Leah knew the difference between animal manures and smells by their food sources. There were stories about that, too. The smell of a leather saddle made her stop in her tracks as distant memories collided with the present sensations nearly taking her breath away.

"Open your eyes, my love," Thad said gently at the same time his horse, Sunset, snorted recognition and stomped for attention. A second chestnut-colored Arabian horse whinnied and turned its head to study the stranger wrapped in a cloud of white. Sunrise swished her black tail from one side of her flank to the other as if eager for an introduction.

Leah's eyes popped open when she heard the ever familiar sounds of horses. Her mouth opened in wonder at the sight of the twin horses each occupying its own stall. They were beautiful, and the sight of them made her heart glad and sad at the same time.

"Oh, Thad, this is a wonderful surprise. You know how much I..." she faltered, "loved my horse. They're beautiful," she managed, struck with awe as she observed their height and markings. "They're yearlings."

"They are." Still holding her hand, Thad coaxed her forward. "I'd like to introduce you to Sunset. He's a good buddy of mine, aren't you boy." Sunset stepped forward, eager for the affectionate strokes of his master while communicating this delight with nickers and snorts.

"You two know each other?" Leah was intrigued as she reached to stroke his forehead. The horse in the stall beside them neighed loudly, and Thad chuckled.

"Okay, girl, we're coming." Thad smiled at Leah as he moved them to the second stall. "Yes, Leah, we're good pals. You see, these two horses are miracles. Their mother was bred to my old horse, Phantom. The mother's name is Bonnie Bright. She and Phantom are both in Texas, where the weather is warmer, and the two horses can roam the plains freely. I had hoped for just one healthy horse to take Phantom's place, but God gave me two horses. They are brother and sister. Though I had no time for God at the time of their birth, He gave me people who promised to pray that I would come to know God through a particular answer to prayer. Sunset is my horse, but his sister, Sunrise, needed someone to ride her. About a year ago, this unbelieving Alaska bachelor asked God for the miracle of a wife to ride the second horse." Tears gathered in Thad's eyes. "You, my lovely Leah Tucker, are my miracle. I knew it the moment I read your first letter, and God confirmed it when you arrived at Taima's trading post two weeks ago." Thad paused to give Leah some time to process his love offering. Her eyes shone with joy. "I love you, and my wedding gift to you is Sunset's sister, Sunrise, named for the song from the movie *Fiddler on the Roof*. I remembered that the horse you lost was named Sunrise, too. I hope this is okay." He was concerned. Leah nodded and smiled assent, deeply touched by his thoughtfulness, though the memory was still painful.

"These are your horses?" Leah was trying to grasp this latest revelation along with Thad's calling her his miracle. She felt the same about him.

"These are our horses, Love, to ride the trails together, to groom, and to feed," he went on. Leah smiled as she reached for her wedding present, Sunrise, and felt the friendly horse yield instantly to her touch. Indeed, this yearling, turning into a mare, so reminded Leah of her beloved old equine friend that it was like her horse had returned in a younger, stronger form. The heartbreak she had suffered on that bitter cold winter night rose like swirling floodwaters sweeping buried grief to the surface. Tears rolled down her cheeks as her arms enfolded the neck of the horse. Her shoulders shook with the intensity of spent emotion as sobs escaped freely. Thad stepped behind her, arms encircling his bride while tears fell from his own eyes to see her sorrow. He let her cry it out and sensed the bond of love and trust growing stronger through shared pain. When Leah took a deep cleansing breath and exhaled quietly, he handed her white cloth handkerchief his mother had handed to him when she cleaned her lipstick off his cheek right before the wedding ceremony. Leah blotted her eyes and cheeks then blew her nose and took a deep breath. When Sunrise shuddered, Leah quickly turned and patted the horse confidently.

"Easy girl, I'm okay now. Thanks for lending a shoulder." Leah soothed and took charge of her young horse confidently. Sunrise sputtered and tossed her head in response.

"What am I, chopped liver?" Thad teased, blinking away his own tears and sniffling as Leah turned and gave him a bear hug with a giggle.

"Thanks for making this the best day of my life."

"Same goes here, Leah." The lovers lingered, swept away in currents of long tender kisses until their horses' jealous neighing broke ardor's fervent hold. Leah giggled as Thad shook his head in mild annoyance then laughed heartily. They both patted the snorting horses into contentment.

"They're just going to have to get used to us showing affection for each other because I'm not stopping on their account," Thad promised good-naturedly and winked at Leah.

"I'm sure they'll settle down or give up eventually." Leah chuckled happily.

"We better head up to the reception or our guests will call out the rescue squad again." Thad had no idea what time it might be but figured guests would be getting nervous by this time.

"Thad, could we come back later and take Sunrise and Sunset for a ride?"

"Sure." Thad smiled, pleased with her suggestion. "We could ride up to the clearing above the lodge where we walked this morning if you want to."

"I'd like that very much, Thad." Leah's smile of gratefulness warmed his heart completely.

"I have a cache of camping supplies nearby if you want to camp out overnight up there. If not, we'll stick with the plan to spend our first night in the lodge. We'll leave for Gakona later tomorrow. There's no rush."

"I'll have to think about camping out, Thad." Leah hesitated as she gave Sunrise a last hug and took Thad's hand to leave the horse barn.

"We can always try it another time, Love." He walked them over to a wall phone and made a quick call.

"Brad. We're leaving the stable, but we'll return about six o'clock to take the horses for some exercise. I'll let you know what plans are for the evening at that time. Thanks."

"Let's go so we can get back." Leah said with excitement. The full skirt of her wedding dress swished as they walked to the Suburban making her very thankful she hadn't chosen a long gown. She was right where she belonged.

# 20

## Northern Lights Over Palmer

"Welcome home, Mrs. Tucker," Thad grinned lovingly at his bride as they entered the lodge's lower den. Mounted heads of moose, Dall sheep, and caribou dotted the walls of the man-space making little kids wonder if the rest of the big, scary animals were on the other side of the wall. These trophies stared blankly above the decorations of the wedding reception. Large vases of flowers, tapered white candles, and starched white tablecloths with elegant Victorian dinnerware had been tastefully placed on four round tables for the wedding party and guests. The contrast of huntsman and schoolmarm in this modern lodge expressed the coming together of strength and beauty.

Cheers of congratulations erupted when Tyrone introduced Mr. and Mrs. Thad Tucker as they breezed through the doorway into the celebration. The newlyweds greeted their guests with smiles and laughed at the teases about being late to their own party. Thad winked at a blushing Leah.

Tyrone and Denise had arrived just a few minutes before the wedding couple. They grinned at each other but said nothing about their developing plans that would take the spotlight from their best friends' special day. The brief ride in Tyrone's Corvette had included a drive around the city limits of Palmer with a view of the golf course. The ride had changed their views of each other. When Thad and Leah drove up to the lodge, Tyrone and Denise stood ready to meet them with smiles of welcome. The best man and maid of honor gave their full attention to the wedded couple's every desire. For once, Denise was not the life of the party, but deferred to Leah's happiness with a servant's dedication to making everything perfect. Tyrone noticed the change and rewarded the love of his life with lingering looks of admiration. It made Denise's heart quicken. Tyrone was her man. Thad noticed his friend's frequent glances at Denise and smiled to himself. It was a comfort to see his own happiness rubbing off on his old college buddy. Speaking of long-time acquaintances, Thad saw two familiar faces enter the room. He seated Leah at a round table beside Denise then excused himself to meet the guys he had personally invited to his wedding reception.

"You go ahead and eat. I'll be right back," Thad encouraged as food was served to the guests.

"How did you like driving Tyrone's Corvette?" Leah asked Denise when they had a few moments to talk at the table. Plates of poached salmon, piped potato rosettes, and grilled asparagus spears sprinkled with parmesan were placed in front of them, causing both to smile their appreciation to the caterer. Both picked up forks and began eating. Leah had only been able to eat a few teaspoons of oatmeal for breakfast due to nervous excitement.

"I'm a changed woman," Denise sighed solemnly between bites. Leah was caught off guard by Denise's uncharacteristic response. She studied the serious expression on Denise's face to check if she was kidding, half expecting Denise's joker's laugh to erupt, but when it didn't, Leah had to stifle a giggle of amazement.

"What happened?" Leah lowered her voice, eager to know some details.

Denise's lips curved up on one side as she shrugged. The gesture was pure surrender. "Tyrone told me I was the only other person he'd ever let drive his Corvette. He told me as far as he was concerned I would be the *only* woman who ever sat in the driver's seat. Oh, Leah, I could tell he meant what he said." She nodded and smiled with confidence. "I told Tyrone his Corvette would be the only one I'd ever drive. We made a pact." Best friends looked at each other and started to laugh and hug.

"Well, Denise, I'd say you finally met your match. And to think you didn't even have to go to a dating service to pick out your Alaskan bachelor."

"God has been good to you, girlfriend, and He's been very merciful to me," Denise stated sincerely as they both started to eat again. After a few more bites, Denise stopped eating abruptly. Two vaguely familiar guys walked into her view. When Denise's eyes grew large with astonishment, Leah turned to follow the line of her view and gasped.

"Oh, good grief! I don't believe it. Those are the two guys we met when we went to the George Endicott Show in Chicago last November."

Both women exchanged uneasy looks, their forks still hanging in the air. JC North and Andrew Vanderhoof had just greeted Thad and Tyrone and were being welcomed with hearty handshakes by the groom and best man.

"It's a small world, Leah," Denise said slowly, letting her fork descend and land gently on the almost empty plate. Foreboding was in her voice. "What are they doing here?"

"For some reason I don't think they're hunting or fishing clients because Thad and Tyrone are treating them like good friends." Leah put her fork down then nervously brushed a curly strand of hair around the back of her ear.

"Good friends?" Denise was skeptical. "I'd like to know how."

"Well, I'm sure we'll know shortly." Leah saw Thad motion the two guests in their direction.

"One can only wonder if…" Denise couldn't finish.

"Yah…" Leah drifted off as her brown eyes fastened on Thad's merry gray ones. *They could be old friends just here to congratulate Thad,* she thought. *Surely Thad hasn't seen that show. Oh Lord, please don't let anything about that stupid show come up in conversation. Andrew has probably forgotten all about that show anyway.* "I never thought in my wildest dreams we'd ever see *them* again." She wished to be invisible. Eye contact broke when Taima greeted the four men and halted them for some conversation. A quiet feminine voice behind Leah and Denise pulled their attention away from the men.

"Alaska is a big place," Tyrone's younger sister, Terry, acknowledged timidly. She had approached Leah and Denise hoping to befriend Tyrone's new girlfriend and greet Thad's bride. Perhaps in her mid-twenties,

Terry Johnson was painfully shy, plainly dressed, and wore black-framed glasses with coke-bottle lenses that made her eyes bulge like a fish. "Hi, I'm Terry, Tyrone's younger sister. I've known JC and Andrew since we were all kids. JC and Tyrone played high school basketball together. We all lived on Roselle Drive in Anchorage. Those three guys hung out together until my brother left for college, then JC didn't come around anymore." Terry's soft-spoken response held obvious heartbreak. Leah and Denise looked at the sad faced Terry with interest as the four men approached.

"Oh, no." Terry was distressed and started to back away, but Denise put out a hand to stop her.

"You're one of us now, sweetie." Denise glanced quickly at Terry and winked. If three was a crowd, Terry was a welcome addition. There was safety in numbers.

"Oh my goodness!" Leah felt the heat rise to her face. She'd sat on Andrew's knee.

"Oh, brother!" Denise was exasperated. She still had JC North's business card in her Bible. "I gotta' get rid of that business card. Its judgment day."

"Well, Denise, Terry, we're going to get through this together." Leah said as if rallying the troops for battle. As Thad moved to Leah's side, both she and Denise stood as if ready to face the firing squad. The tiniest of groans sounded from Terry, which brought Denise's steady arm around the waist of the twitter-pated maiden.

"Leah, Denise, I'd like to introduce you to some friends of Tyrone and mine whom Terry already knows," he acknowledged kindly with a nod to Terry who dropped her eyes. "This is JC North and Andrew Vanderhoof."

Leah figured it was no use to try to appear as if she didn't know Andrew or JC, so she greeted them with recognition.

"Hello, JC. Hello, Andrew. You're the fisherman, right?" Andrew nodded and grinned while Thad frowned at her. *He doesn't know,* Leah thought.

"That's right," Andrew assented. "You were the cute one I told Thad about."

"Oh?" Thad's left eyebrow rose. Leah started to fidget, twisting her napkin.

"Yes, you remember the video of the *George Endicott Show* I lent to you to watch, Thad. This is the girl—"

"That you met at the show," Leah interjected as anxiety swirled in the pit of her stomach and spiraled upward. She swallowed to force it down.

"Here, Thad." JC handed a small package the size of a VCR tape to Thad. It was wrapped in white tissue paper with a bright-pink bow stuck in the middle of the rectangular gift. "This is the recording of that show. I thought you and Leah might like to have it for posterity's sake." Faster than a streak of lightning, Leah snatched the gift from JC.

"Thank you, JC and Andrew for the thoughtful wedding gift. I'm sure Thad and I will find this amusing after we've been married ten years or so." *Never!* Leah promised silently.

"I'd like to see it now, wouldn't you, Leah?" Thad said matter-of-fact, and gently pulled the gift from Leah's hands. The den had grown suddenly quiet. Heads turned in curiosity.

"Uh, well, that's not necessary." Denise decided the time to rescue Leah had come. "You see, it was *all* my fault. I goaded Leah into going to that show to see the Alaskan bachelors. She didn't want to go, but I dragged her through the door. We were going to sit in the last row and just observe. We were never supposed to…" Her eyes grew large. Leah figured the cat was out of the bag anyway and continued.

"The audience was packed, and the only seats available were down in the front row, smack dab in the middle. There was no hiding from the TV cameras or from the Alaska bachelors for that matter."

"I saw your Leah sitting there looking as scared and uncomfortable as a ground squirrel in the middle of a pack of wolves." Andrew smiled and nodded at Thad. "She looked like a nice, decent lady, and I figured I'd rather choose her to come up and sit on my knee than some silly woman like that red-headed one. Sheesh!"

"I think she might have been part of the staging for the show," JC speculated.

"I saw her, too." Dad Grant piped up and got an elbow in the ribs from Mom Grant. Everyone started laughing, including Thad who could no longer keep a straight face. He pulled a chair out and, reaching for Leah, pulled her onto his lap and kissed her soundly.

"You knew," Leah charged and laughed along with Thad.

"Yep, I took a boat motor to Andrew's boat shop for repairs just after I got your first letter. I showed Andrew your picture, and he recognized you right off. The second time I watched the video of the show, I watched it all the way through to the end and saw you sitting on Andrew's lap. I didn't know who Denise was though, but when she arrived in Alaska to rescue you, I recognized her as being the one who sat on JC's lap." He looked over at Denise and grinned. Denise raised both hands in the air.

"I give up." She looked directly at Tyrone. He crossed his arms and shook his head.

"Not to worry, Tyrone. She never writes, she never calls." JC sighed. "If I were you, I wouldn't let her get away, though."

"On the contrary, JC, I have no intention of letting Tyrone get away." Denise moved over beside Tyrone and slipped her hand through his arm. "He's the greatest catch of my life," she said sincerely and received a wink of promise from Tyrone.

"You're a lucky man, Tyrone," JC conceded then looked at Andrew. "So are you. You're wearing a wedding band on your left hand too."

"What's this?" Leah and Denise gawked at Andrew who smiled broadly.

"It's true." He flashed the wedding band for all to see. "I married Jennifer Endicott, George Endicott's daughter."

"Oh, wow! There is some justice in this world after all," Denise exclaimed.

"Ah-h. I'm so glad for you and her. She must be a wonderful person to have captured your heart, Andrew," Leah said genuinely.

"She is the best person I know, and she's also a Christian. When I'm not commercial fishing, we go to church, and she does Bible studies for the ladies in our neighborhood."

"That's great, Andrew. I'd like to meet her."

"We'll have to get together soon," Thad invited. "I've been doing some Bible study with Pastor Paytor."

"Did I just hear my name?" Pastor Paytor called from the table next to the bridal party. Conversation started around the room once again as guests returned to their plates of food.

JC noticed he and Terry were the only ones without partners at the moment. "Hey there, Terry. I haven't seen you in a long time. You were just going into ninth grade when Tyrone left for college in Fairbanks. What are you doing these days?" JC North considered the changes ten years of time had made on Tyrone's little sister. She was taller, period. The bulky gray sweater she wore over the ankle length, dark-navy skirt gave no hint whatsoever of a feminine shape. She still wore the same style eyeglasses as in her youth. Even then, he'd teased her and called her "fish eyes" not realizing how devastated she'd been by his thoughtless remark. Yet, for the love of JC North, Terry's heart refused to know any other man as her Prince Charming. Until Denise had stepped to Tyrone's side, JC hadn't noticed Terry was standing with the ladies. Ten years had matured him to the point that he wouldn't tease Terry by calling her "fish eyes," at least not out loud. Then she spoke, and he knew she'd grown up.

"I'm a librarian at the University of Alaska, Anchorage." Terry gathered courage from a job she dearly loved and one that corralled her inner confidence. "I work in the research department gathering information and writing reports for native corporations in regard to mineral rights projects. I also help write grants for nonprofit groups needing funding for building projects in rural Alaska." It was more than she needed to say and much more than she even thought she could say, but she had grown so accustomed to working with academia and explaining how she could assist professors and professionals in their research that it was second nature. It had also been a long time since Terry Johnson had looked into the eyes of JC North. She didn't want to stop looking at him or him to stop looking at her, so she made her job description longer. She wanted to memorize every inch of his dark masculine face just in case he was in her dreams tonight.

JC noted the quiet depth of her professional response and the interest she conveyed in her work. She was tall and plain, but she wasn't silly and empty-headed, and that fact registered clearly in his mind. She deserved his respect. He would never call her "fish eyes" again.

"You turned out real good, Terry. In fact, I might have a research project for you if you would be interested. My construction company is bidding on an off-shore oil drilling project. I need some more information in order to put in the best bid possible."

"I'd be glad to research your project for you, JC." Terry couldn't believe her ears. Was JC really asking her for help? Thank God.

"Give me your e-mail address and phone number, and I'll call you for a time to meet and discuss the project." JC was all business as he pulled a notepad and pen from his jacket pocket and wrote down her information.

After the reception, Terry found Denise packing her suitcase in one of the guest rooms. Determined to get some fashion advice from Denise so that her next meeting with JC North might gain his further notice and maybe even a date, Terry knocked and was invited into Denise's confidence. One hour later, Terry emerged as a remarkably different-looking librarian with a list of new ideas. On the list was a visit to an optometrist.

When the last guests departed for overnight accommodations or plane flights from Alaska, the newlyweds headed to the stable for a ride in the evening light. The sun had circled the arctic sky until it had slipped behind the mountain range to the west. At almost the same time, the moon made its appearance over harvested potato fields around Palmer. The Matanuska River's swift current rushed along the bank, making course changes that would form new paths of silt in the riverbed during low tide.

Thankfully, the wind was calm at the moment, preventing the blizzard of river silt that often caused a thick blanket of grainy sediment to coat the city. The sound of the river's flight back to the ocean muffled the hoof beats of the horses as Thad and Leah trotted along a trail by the river before moving Sunset and Sunrise in the direction of the lodge. Calls of birds in the trees or in flight above them announced their passage through the golden wilderness to the lodge, nestled against the backdrop of tall spruce rising up the side of the mountain. Where one had ridden this scenic trail alone, now two rode together. Yet, there was a third Who watched them from above--forever the Gracious One who had worked all things together for good in the lives of Thad and Leah as they were learning to love Him.

Later that evening when the light in the sky had faded to dark gray, Thad and Leah walked hand in hand from the master suite out onto the east facing deck to see if stargazing might be a possibility on their wedding night. Warm coats had been pulled on before the couple stepped out into the frosty air. Sure enough, they found the North Star overhead and looked for other constellations not yet hidden by high-drifting clouds. The evening sky was still too light to see pastel waves of northern lights ribbon-dance over Pioneer Peak. Thad drew Leah into his arms, and she snuggled closely to him, peace and contentment filling her with happiness. Cherishing her partnership, Thad chuckled at the memory of Leah's arrival in Alaska and her first night sleeping on the couch.

"I couldn't take my eyes off you when I saw you sleeping so peacefully on the couch. You're all I could think about the whole time I was supposed to be guiding Ishioti and O'Brien to the best fishing spots on the Copper River up near Gakona," Thad said sheepishly and felt Leah's giggle against his chest where her head rested. "I was so mesmerized by my sleeping princess that Taima snuck up behind and scared the life out of me."

"I must have been sleeping soundly because I had no idea I had a captive audience."

"Well, you certainly made a lasting impression because I was a miserable guide that whole crazy trip. I couldn't think straight, and I talked nonsense." He laughed now as he thought of the confused expressions on Ishioti's and O'Brien's faces when they asked about the presence of bears in the area and he replied, "All ya gotta do is cast a line and reel those big boys in!"

"Ishioti and O'Brien wanted to stay up in Gakona a few days longer, so I decided to leave two hours earlier to get back sooner. I was just past Sutton when I remembered I had agreed with the Copper River Lodge to bring three of their clients back with me to catch an Anchorage flight to Washington state." He shook his head. "I had to pay for rescheduled flights as well as overnight accommodations and meals in order to redeem the family business," Thad bemoaned. Leah leaned away from Thad to look wide-eyed into his face. This was yet another revelation of her husband's own natural inclination for skew-ups. So far, they had been able to laugh about it, either forgiving or accepting these human traits in each other. Leah hoped it would never become a source of contention between them.

"No wonder you were a bit moody and..." she paused to think of the right word but tried a different approach, "not your normal, cheerful self." Thad laughed outright.

"I was in a mood all right," he confessed, his eyes soft with love for Leah. "After you reminded me that I was to behave like a gentleman, I watched you walk away and I knew I might well have blown any chance of ever having your love and companionship. It was the most devastating moment of my life because I knew, without you, the rest of my life would be joyless, my love. I realized what a fool I would be to let my own bad mood drive you away."

As strong and good as a man could be, the love for a woman molded a man for good or bad depending on whether the woman was wise or foolish. Thad thought about the influences of his mother and of Alma. His mother had chosen to raise him without a man to support and protect them. She remained a loyal mother, working hard to make the best of her situation for both of them.

Now that Thad thought about it, he had never been fatherless because his mother's faith and prayers had beckoned the throne of his Heavenly Father day and night. The comfort she had found in prayer then had been answered in the comfort he now found in faith and in the wife whom he held in his arms as his own sweet miracle. The love of his mother had done him good. Then there was Alma's gentle, quiet spirit giving him a blueprint of a graceful, creative woman diligent in the building of a material home. She had made him proud to bring Leah to his Alaskan home, lately a lodge for both clients and family. Leah had brought beauty, virtue, and fun into his life, showing him how much he could care about the needs of someone else over his own wants and ways. He wasn't an only son and an only child anymore. His family ties to Leah now included brothers-and sisters-in-law as well as a mother-and father-in-law.

Strange as it may seem, he already looked to Leah's dad as his dad too. In the short time since their first phone conversation after Leah's allergic reaction to Taima's Road Kill Stew, Thad and Dad Grant had gotten to know one another better. There was mutual respect and a mentoring faith that bonded them together. Leah's mother reminded him of a University of Alaska Fairbanks college professor named Marge Barber. She was smart, perceptive, and practical to the point of being rather austere where the social graces were concerned. She could perceive the inner workings of people and could detect disingenuous people and call them on it. Thad had experienced her sensory powers as a student in a business and ethics class she taught. As a result of her influence, he and Tyrone ran an honest business. Her very last words to each class were, "Some of you I will read about in the newspapers because you will be indicted for dishonest business practices, and you will do time in jail. Of course, you will not hold me responsible for your lack of integrity since I've taught you otherwise. Some of you I will read about in magazines because you will have worked hard to build your little business into an empire. That's fine as long as you remember that people are way more important than empire building. The rest of you I will never read about in business magazines or newspapers, but I will hear of your good reputation from satisfied customers you have made to feel valued and necessary to your business and your life. Again and finally, I hope you all will remember that people are way more important than money, power, or things."

Leah's mother expected people to look her in the eye and tell the truth. There was no pretense about Doris Grant and Thad admired her and hoped she understood he was a man of integrity who would always treat her daughter as a precious gift.

"What are you thinking about?" Leah sensed Thad was deep in thought as he stared into the gray, cloud-covered sky. A few drops of rain fell with splats on their upturned faces making both blink quickly and look down.

"I was just thinking about all the wonderful ladies God has put in my life. I always used to think of how bad it was that I didn't have a dad like the other kids. I never realized how good I've had it over the years because God put several good women in my life who helped me grow into a decent man. I had the best. My Aunt Anna always made sure I had soft sugar cookies and something cold to drink after school.

She loved to hear about my day at school and sent me a box of baked goods every month I was away at college. When my mom worked long hours at the hospital, she would sit at the table when I was doing my homework and quietly crochet. She never scolded me when I lost interest in doing my assignments, either. She would look over the top of her glasses at me and say, 'You're a very smart boy, Thaddeus Wayne Tucker. Smart boys always finish their homework,'" he chuckled, "and I did, every time."

"Oh, the power of a compliment," Leah quipped and huddled closer to Thad as the few drops of rain became a steady drizzle.

"Let's go inside, love. Pastor and Mrs. Paytor gave us a special wedding gift. They requested we open it when we have a quiet moment." Leah shivered her agreement as Thad pulled the sliding glass door to the side, and they walked into the warm sitting area of the master suite. An orange fire crackled and snapped in the fireplace where a carefully laid bundle of logs had been arranged for the newlyweds' comfort. A tray with two mugs of hot chocolate, a plate of sandwiches, some savory snacks and sweet temptations was placed on a large, round, leather ottoman in front of a light-brown sofa.

Thad helped Leah out of her coat and hung it with his in the closet and sat into the sofa beside her. He handed the gift to Leah and watched as she began to pull the decorative ribbon and paper away to disclose the gift. A beautiful wood carved picture frame some twenty-four inches square made both Leah's and Thad's eyes widen in awe. A poem written by Pastor and Mrs. Paytor was perfectly penned in calligraphy on textured parchment. At the bottom of the poem, Thad and Leah's married name was engraved on a small, gold plate with their wedding date along with the name of the church, the city, and the state. A personal note and a Bible verse were written on the back. "God bless your home. And if it seem evil unto you to serve the Lord, choose you this day whom you will serve…but as for me and my house, we will serve the Lord" (Joshua 24:15). Our love and congratulations, Pastor and Mrs. Paytor.

Thad leaned closer to Leah to follow the words as she read them aloud.

### TODAY

Today we met at the altar to marry,
We chose each other's joys and sorrows to carry;
We spoke of our love, so true,
You promised me, I promised you.
Today we pledged aloud, "I do!"
God made one from two.
Today we sealed our love with a marriage kiss,
We'll know Eden's marital bliss.
Today our family and friends are witnesses,
We joined the ranks of Mr. and Mrs.
Today we shared our Wedding Cake,
A "Home, Sweet Home" we promised to make.
Today our Wedding Dreams come true,
God's Way brought us through.
Today, O Lord, we humbly pray,
Your guidance and grace we'll seek together day by day.

Thad and Leah sat quietly together thinking about the words of the poem given to them from a pastor who had become their spiritual mentor. They talked about the poem and its meaning to them as a married couple, then they talked about things privy only to heaven's ears; things sacred and beautiful between a husband and a wife, which shall remain their own.

At the peaceful lodge near Palmer, one solitary figure stood out on the deck viewing the distant fireworks display marking the last evening of the Alaska State Fair at the end of August. It was almost midnight and dark enough to see the umbrella-shaped trails made from the exploding rockets. Flashes of bright lights in Ferris-wheel patterns dotted the sky high above the grandstand where spectators watched the techno show in awe and clapped their approval. But Taima didn't hear the cheers of the crowds or catch a whiff of buttery popcorn, pepperoni pizza, or fried peppers, onions, and sausage that mixed with the sweet smells of cotton candy and fudge. He heard only the distant cracks and booms of the annual carnival and reckoned he preferred the ethereal sounds of the Northern Lights to the ear-splitting blasts. It reminded him of a distant war when a bus ride to army boot camp had transported him from boyhood to manhood in one day.

Taima gazed at the North Star and wondered what the Creator thought of him. The love and peace he saw in Alma's eyes seemed to draw him toward God in a way that nothing and no one had been able to do. He would never have admitted that he was a sinful man to any preacher, but something about reckoning with the Holy God made him acknowledge the sinful man he was. Pastor Paytor had quietly handed a Gospel of John to him as he was leaving the church following the wedding. Normally, he wouldn't have accepted it, but curiosity had prompted him to take the scripture booklet, and he had slipped it inside the pocket of his suit jacket. After the reception had been cleaned up and he had time to reflect on the day's celebration, he had pulled the booklet out and read the first three chapters of John's Gospel. Shortly thereafter, he had fallen asleep thinking about the conversation Jesus had with an old man named Nicodemus.

He could identify with Nicodemus since he was feeling older these days because of the changes happening around him. His routine was all messed up. Not that he minded it in view of the happiness he saw in Thad and Leah's union. It just made him uncertain about his old beliefs and interested in finding the truth, whatever it might be. A barrage of fireworks exploded over Palmer causing the sky to reverberate with the multitude of booms, whistles, and pops. Taima turned to catch the grand finale and watched until the last cascade of sparks faded into the smoky haze before drifting away, pushed by northern winds. He looked heavenward where the North Star shone night after night, always pointing a true direction for those who navigated sailing vessels along the vast Alaskan coastline. Thanks to Thad's search for a bride, Taima could gaze up at the heavens and, instead of wondering what spirit was in charge, found that he was beginning to understand why the house that Thad built was filled with peace and joy. He turned and walked back inside. He wanted to finish reading the Gospel of John.

Much later that evening; to the far northern coasts beyond the Brooks Range, the Northern Lights danced in wavy white stripes above the arctic horizon, moving like the fingers of God writing to His beloved. Their celestial aura made native stargazers listen closely for snapping sounds made by the electrically charged dust particles. God rejoiced to hear the awe in their voices, but longed to see faith in their hearts. Had they missed the meaning of His heavenly display of majesty because of ancient fables or superstitions? No matter, He would keep writing His love across the heavens even if it took several millennia for men, women, and children to recognize Him as the Source of the radiant winter lights.

*"And we know that all things work together for good to those who love God, to those who are the called according to His purpose."*
Romans 8:28

The End

Printed in the United States
By Bookmasters